Sacrifices

EMBRACED BY DARKNESS

BOOK ONE

Sacrifices

Written by:
Tarah L. Wolff

Edited by Sharon Harris
Cover art purchased at iStockPhoto.com

All Rights Reserved
ISBN-10: 0985022809
ISBN-13: 978-0-9850228-0-8
First Paperback Edition

www.tarahlynn.com
www.embracedbydarkness.com

dedicated to my incredible mom
who taught me the meaning of strength

PROLOGUE

Osondrous' head was back and the fall sun was on her face. She had been training soldiers at Rayakdool since the Keltch wars and it showed down through the very bones of her. She dressed as a man, leather vest and leggings. The vest was cut out in the back and criss-crossed with long strips of leather, black with sweat, pressed across her hot skin. He knew the old leather was the softest thing about her.

Telenay was following her with three of her Centaur Seconds between them. He was gnawing his bottom lip because they were walking so casually. And she was just sitting there with her horse, Tamarack, between her legs instead of him. She was propped back, practically dozing. They could have been to Rayakdool by now but she was leading, making pace, seeming to enjoy the last of the warm weather, as though she had not been out in it for years.

He felt her in the back of his mind, tantalizing and laughing at him.

Not fast enough for you?

It will be winter before we get there.

He growled as her laughter echoed around his head. He could block the other Wards out but not her. From the day that willowy little girl showed up at the castle, he had never been able to keep her out. His only satisfaction was that it was mutual.

Peeking out of the back of her leggings was the brown hilt of the only dagger she carried. Her chosen long sword, Mlore, jutted out from where she had sheathed it to her saddle. He adjusted his sword, crossed across his back; he had not worn it, or even needed it, in a long time.

You have been locked in that castle for too many years, Telenay. Enjoy the ride.

Osondrous was smiling at all those naughty things that Telenay had at the back of his head. She was smiling because all she had to worry about was Telenay's impatience.

Her horse heard the arrow first. His head snapped up.

She gasped.

The arrow clipped over Tamarack's ears. A long black shaft, aimed right at her heart. She dove out of the way. Too late. The arrow hit and threw her back.

Telenay saw the hunters up the lane, just kneeling shadows, great bows bent back. With his will he saw them in detail, average men, peasants really, up and running for their lives.

Osondrous' voice cut into all of their minds in a scream: *Get them!*

The Centaurs were gone, sprinting up the lane, pulling out their short swords.

Telenay reached her and grabbed the Warlord around the arms, heaving her onto his saddle. She fought him, squirming and roaring, infuriated.

Osondrous grabbed the arrow and yanked it out.

"Damn it, Osondrous!"

"Let me go!"

"You are going to bleed to death!"

Her eyes burned violently. "Those bastards will be mine!"

But already blood had stained the front of her tunic and he unlaced her vest enough to show the round sweetness of her left breast. The arrow had been released with a hunter's long bow, meant to penetrate the thick skin of a boar or deer. With her will, she had slowed it down or the long shaft would have gone completely through her. He gauged the depth of the breach through her breastbone with his will, felt how the arrowhead had clipped her throbbing heart.

Osondrous paled considerably. "Telenay, you have to run."

Rayue and Tamarack heard her. The two horses turned as one and bolted up the lane, back the way they had come. Back to the Castle of the Wards where the only Healers in the land could save her. Rayakdool pounded away behind them; they had been within an hour of reaching their destination.

The last thing she said out loud was, "You can blame me."

The night before, Osondrous had said with her face against his chest, "Tomorrow."

"I know."

"Telenay, tomorrow we are going to be out in it together again."

"I know."

They needed him to run the castle, to keep the guard in order, because Shankan, their King, was just was not capable. Telenay was a Ward, a ruler of the land; this is what he had sworn to do. And yet, so often now, he had been thinking, *All I was ever meant to be was a Warlord.*

Last night Osondrous had curled against him, his fingers spanning her back and breasts. He had felt her heart beat. The feminine little flutter that was entirely Human, entirely woman, entirely unlike everything that Osondrous was.

She looked at him with her narrow blue eyes. "You are finally coming back with me."

"It has been too long."

4

"How do you survive being locked up here?"

"I do not."

She had kissed him then. "I want you to leave but I cannot let you." She had not been talking about their ride together for a few days to Rayakdool then. The field was calling him and she knew it because the field called the Warlords in the same voice. She always told him what he was hearing before he heard it because she always heard it first.

The Healing Ward Karalay had said that morning, "You both together, alone? You must take a Darkhalk or a Healer with you! I will go."

Telenay could see Karalay's dark eyes, plain as the path flying beneath him now. Could hear her words mingled with the horses' sucking breaths.

He had snapped at her, "As a Healer you should know this is a time of peace."

Karalay had set her mouth. "It is not safe. You are targets for darkness. I should go with you."

Karalay had been standing beside Osondrous and Osondrous had been smiling arrogantly, waiting for Telenay to end the charade. Karalay in all of her silk and lace gowns in a dozen different green hues and Osondrous, dressed in the color of mud. The Healer smelling like lavender with clean hair sweeping around her fair features. The Warlord with her hair tied back in a strangle, her skin smelling like she had been burned and her hands heavy with calluses.

And they both knew that Karalay was beaten. She had put her head down and the sweep of her shining waves had covered her face. They had gone and Telenay had not said goodbye, so eager had he been to get out of there. Osondrous had swung onto her horse with a grin shot at Karalay, as if she had won something. As if she could not always get what she wanted of him.

He did remember the look on Karalay's face, the reply to Osondrous' smugness. Her eyes had been hollow and very sad. He had hurried away from that far, lonely look and now he was so desperate for her. For a Healer.

Telenay pushed out his will, his own arrow, as far as his strength would dictate, screaming for help. His will would reach the castle long before the horse. The castle and the Darkhalks would bring Karalay.

Nine times. Osondrous' voice was a soft little echo in the back of his thoughts.

Nine times what?

I have died nine times now.

5

You will be revived nine times, too.

It is a long way.

Save your strength.

I was so looking forward to tonight. You and me out in it again. Like it was supposed to be. Eikian is going to have words for you.

This is your fault; you let your guard down.

It was only because of Osondrous' order that Eikian had stayed behind so Telenay could leave the castle. If Eikian had been a Human, he would have been the warm body in Osondrous' bed every night and Telenay would have been the old man she never needed. But there were laws against Humans and Centaurs lying together and it kept Osondrous coming back to his room, month after month, leaving Eikian behind. Oh, yes. Eikian would have words for him.

Her breasts and vest were running with blood now. Osondrous' stallion fell back behind them. Tamarack had been her only mount since the beginning. He was an old horse now with his head down, shielding his face from the sand flying from the hooves of the horse before him. If he could have spoken, he would have demanded Telenay let him bear Osondrous, that they would have moved faster, if one of the horses were not bearing the weight of two. Tamarack was beginning to feel the strain. He was bigger than Telenay's horse, Rayue, but he had often been outrun by much smaller horses and always Osondrous had told him that she wanted steadiness, not speed. But not today. Today both he and Rayue were big-bodied, thick-necked creatures that took after more of their northern ancestors than their flighty southern fathers. They were not fast runners.

Telenay knew this, sensed the beginning desperation in the way the horses were running. He could hear the frenzied panting of Tamarack and the loud, roaring grunts from Rayue.

The sun passed over the tree tops as they pounded on into blue shadow. Rayue's red hide was dark with sweat and in the shadows, it became black. Telenay clutched her with one hand around her back. Osondrous stopped breathing.

PART ONE

Eikian had once been asked how it was possible that a Centaur could serve a woman. The Centaurs did not allow their females to fight in war. He had responded with "Osondrous is not a woman; she is a Warlord." And that really was the end of every conversation that included Osondrous as a topic in Eikian's presence.

His hooves were so loud as he clopped along the parapet that he did not hear her come up behind him.

"It has been a while since I saw you here."

He jumped in surprise.

The Healer Karalay stood under the stone archway, a shawl pulled around her bare shoulders, her dark hair a wide sweep down her narrow back. The castle was an iron whore around her softness. It was four stories above ground, eight stories below with numerous levels beneath that. It was the biggest single stone structure ever built in the last five hundred years, since the Humans had risen in power and the Wards had freed them. Telenay had made it bigger, surrounded it in walls and added twelve towers, one at every corner of the castle and one at every corner of the inner parapet.

Karalay was smiling, her dark eyes intense.

"A while." He scratched his stubbled cheek, suddenly self-conscious of his dirtiness. He had been in the fields of Rayakdool with Osondrous and had not been in what they referred to as "civilization" in months. Warpaint still stained his chestnut coat in black swatches and his hooves were caked in cracked mud.

She went to him and held his arm, lacing her fingers with his.

He felt her warm will against him immediately and it felt good.

She asked, "How are your back and your legs?"

He looked away. "I do not have much."

Her eyes narrowed. "If I had gotten to it sooner. . ."

"No. I am very grateful." He tugged at her arm.

Five years earlier, the stone streets of Kamamine had been glazed in ice. He was part of a guard sent out to help a shipment of mead from Diggamara get to the castle. Two horses had fallen and the weather was deteriorating into piss. He and his Second had lashed themselves to the front of that towering wagon and they had pulled it up the last hill.

There really was never any hesitation. They shifted a little, drew in together, put the brakes on the wagon and started down. He did not remember much except one last image of the wagon going over, his Second being pulled beneath it. What Eikian did remember was waking up knowing his back was broken, knowing that one of his soldiers was dead. Knowing he was freezing and soaked and he could not feel his back legs.

Then he had felt her hands and when they had moved to his ribs and his back, Eikian knew he would live. She had saved him and he would never tell her that often in the night he would be awakened by such pain that sometimes he wished she had let him die.

She knew anyway, of course. She was a Ward; there was no lie that could possibly fool her.

He changed the subject. "Tea?"

"I would love some tea!" She looked relieved.

They walked together to the dining hall. Her guardian, a Darkhalk, followed them. The Darkhalks wore two weapons, a Cape and a Sword, that gave them tremendous Ward-like powers of will and ability. They did not eat or sleep and were so old that no one knew exactly how the Darkhalks came to be. The servants and peasants told stories of how the Darkhalks had descended from the Creator's very hands. Looking at them though, it seemed more likely that they had climbed up from real darkness.

Karalay's Darkhalk was a mere shadow following them, and no one looked or took any notice. You never saw a Ward or Healing Ward without one. The Warlords did not allow the Darkhalks to guard them in a time of peace. Of course, now Telenay regretted that more than ever. A Darkhalk could have used the power of the Cape to heal Osondrous. As Karalay and Eikian sat down before tea and brandy, Telenay was screaming at the castle with all of his will and his horse was beginning to stagger.

Karalay held her hot cup between her fingers and leaned her head on her palm. "They should never have gone without a Healer or a Darkhalk. Not those two. Not alone."

Eikian grunted.

She smiled. "Were you trying not to think of it?"

"If you are really worried, I could take you out there . . . "

She said, "No, I am just not happy about them leaving alone. The most likelihood is, Eikian, they have reached Rayakdool and are fucking in bliss."

Eikian hooted. He filled his cup again. "How has your work been?"

Her face flushed in pleasure. "You remember what I have been working on?"

"Of course I do."

"Oh," she said. "I had not meant to offend. No one cares what I am doing in the library."

Eikian frowned at her. "All of the greatest knowledge ever brought to Humans was by scholars in libraries."

She shook her head at him but the compliment reached her. "I am getting nowhere."

"The great Lionel?"

She nodded. "The greatest mystery of all Humankind. What happened to the father of Wards? What happened to the greatest Ward? What happened to the man that saved us all from slavery?"

"You must not give up."

She looked at him closely. "At some point, I ran out of texts to read. Took me fifteen years but I did it. There is nothing left here. No knowledge that I have not searched through. The mystery of Lionel cannot be solved here."

"Perhaps you need to find it somewhere else?"

She laughed. "Where?"

Eikian finished his brandy and filled his cup again.

He frowned. "I heard that Shankan still has not been found?"

Karalay's dark eyes twitched uncomfortably. "Telenay has not gone to find him."

"No one was dispatched to find the King?" Eikian gaped at her.

She said, "Of course. The lead Centaurs were placed in charge. But they have not been able to find him."

"Prush was in charge?"

She shrugged. "I believe so. Telenay said he would go to find him when he returned from Rayakdool. . ." She reached over and took a sip of Eikian's brandy.

He said, "How long has he been gone?"

She whispered, "Quite a few days."

He stared at her.

She cried, her voice low and urgent so no one else would hear. "I am aware! It is insane that Telenay has not gone to find him yet!"

"But, why has he not gone in search?"

Karalay shook her head, rubbed her face. "It is a time of peace, I suppose, and Telenay hates Shankan."

In that moment, Telenay's will reached them as a whisper, not yet on a level strong enough for Karalay's will to hear but all of the Darkhalks in the castle heard him.

Her Darkhalk, Brach, was at her side and had her in his arms in a blink.

Eikian gasped, "What the hell?"

Karalay said, "Someone needs me!" Her voice jerked as the Darkhalk ran her from the room. Eikian galloped after to watch her Darkhalk leap off the inner parapet, jump over the height of the ten-foot outer parapet and evaporate into the evening.

2

Karalay squeezed her eyes shut and clamped down on her stomach. The Darkhalk's Cape lifted and snapped in the air like a bat sail as its power worked, increasing his strength and speed. He had leaped the castle walls in seconds and was running around behind it, leaving her pale and gasping. His feet hit white sand and she knew something had happened to their Warlords.

Karalay threw her will up the path, pushed with her heart and met Telenay's outstretched will. They laced their wills like the lacing of the fingers of held hands.

Telenay!

Run!

What happened?

Osondrous got hit by an arrow.

I told you!

I am fully aware of that! Now hurry.

He cannot run any faster . . . Is she dead?

She stopped breathing.

Wake her up! Scream at her, Telenay. Make her use her will!

She opened her eyes and could see the darkness of horses up the shadowed lane. A fall breeze had picked up from the north and chills raced toward them.

Telenay reined his horse in and pulled Osondrous off its back.

Karalay reached out and pushed her will into Osondrous' body before she reached them. The Warlord had slipped into the blackness of her death and Karalay searched for the last remnants of her spirit. When Karalay reached her, she cradled the Warlord's face between her hands. Deep in Osondrous' being Karalay found her floating, eyes focused on something far away. She embraced the Warlord and pulled back.

Karalay healed over Osondrous' wounds and started her heart again. It stuttered and coughed.

She ordered, "Blood! Telenay, cut your wrist."

He produced a dagger, cut it across where his palm met his arm and then sliced open the inside of Osondrous' elbow. He pressed the open gashes tight and, with his will, he pushed his blood out into her wound and Karalay pulled his blood into the Warlord's heart. Osondrous was not yet aware of anything; Karalay was the one who first felt Telenay's blood reach the Warlord's starving heart. It gasped and drank and began to pound again.

Osondrous became aware, not yet beyond the inner reaches of her darkness but she knew there was an intruder in her heart. She knew there was the will of another Ward, a Healer at that, inside her mind. Osondrous reacted viciously and Karalay's head snapped around as though she had been slapped, though Osondrous never moved off the ground.

"Bitch!" Karalay rubbed her cheek.

Telenay dropped Osondrous' arm, holding out his cut wrist. She grabbed his hand and healed him. They got to their feet. Karalay dusted off her bottom.

He said, "Thank you, Healer."

She looked into his amber eyes and nodded. The eyes stood out starkly against his dark skin and black hair, the toss of which fell across his forehead in a wild way. He was looking at her closely and her sad eyes did not meet his.

Karalay walked up the lane, nursing the growing bruise on her cheek, annoyed to the core as she always was by the defensiveness of Warlords. She would have healed her own bruise but she was feeling the strain of having to pull someone back from the brink. She wanted to be certain to check on Rayue and Tamarack before she wasted any energy healing herself.

Rayue was down, pawing frantically at the path. She laid her hands beneath his rolling eyes and healed him. She helped him up and calmed him with words. Tamarack nosed forward for her attention, holding a hind hoof in the air. She healed him as well.

The horses touched her with appreciation.

Telenay came up behind her and smoothed her hair off of her back. He kissed her bare collarbone. She shivered away from his hot lips.

He said again, "Thank you."

She said, "We need to get back."

He rolled his eyes.

"We need to get her somewhere better than the road." She pointed back at Osondrous lying in the middle of the lane, her face in the sand. "She is going to be out for a while; she did not let me do much."

"She has been through worse."

"Can I ride Tamarack?"

"Probably."

She held out her hand to her Darkhalk and her guardian lifted her up. She spread her legs around the horse and her skirt slipped up to mid thigh. Telenay glanced obviously down her bare leg before mounting Rayue. The Darkhalk handed Osondrous up to him.

Karalay called, "Ride behind me, Darkhalk. No need for you to walk."

Telenay sneered, "Are you serious?"

Karalay put her nose in the air as the Darkhalk slipped up behind her. She urged Tamarack on and the big horse eagerly took the lead. Telenay's presence was in the back of her mind.

You know they do not get tired. Why do you insist on treating them like . . .

Like what, Telenay? Like they are living creatures? Like they were Human once with a mother and a father?

Like you love one of them.

Her eyes flashed in rage. Karalay put Telenay out of her mind, as only a Healer could, and did not allow the Warlord back. She clenched her teeth and rode on. Karalay did not want Telenay to see her cry.

Without explanation, her true guardian, Jaridd, had left a month ago and she had been waiting for him. She touched Brach's hand in longing, wishing desperately that it was Jaridd. But it was not; he was only a stand-in. Every moment she was becoming more certain that Jaridd would not come back to her and the dawning of it was a knife deeper than she ever could have imagined or admitted to. How lonely and pitiful could she be if she needed an emotionless soldier so badly?

3
Telenay

Telenay laid Osondrous down in her chamber and helped Karalay strip the Warlord naked. There were three servants, the eldest Healing Ward, Olisize, and Eikian standing by watching. They made no effort to be discreet; everyone in the room had seen Osondrous naked. They looked over her wound.

Osondrous' chamber was so long unused that the bed had to be remade. Everything in the room was basic and unadorned. It was the chamber of someone who never lived in it.

Olisize stood beside Karalay. The old man said, "You did well today, Karalay."

She smiled. "Thank you, Olisize."

In the corner, by the crackling fire that he had just made, Eikian stood with his eyes down and black. Karalay glanced at him as she took Olisize's hand and led the old Healer out, but Eikian had eyes for only Telenay. The big creature's jaw was locked, showing his muscles and his sharp leanness.

The servants followed the Healers out, giving both Eikian and Telenay wary glances.

The door closed. Eikian growled, "How could you let this happen?"

Telenay could still see Karalay glancing into the trees as they had ridden back around the great castle. He could still feel Osondrous' weight in his arms and Karalay's eyes had been so sad.

Eikian roared at him, "What happened?"

Telenay blinked. "Easy, Horsey."

Eikian paced, his big hooves reverberating through the stone floor. The fire lashed as he strode by it.

"We let our guard down."

Eikian roared, "Obviously!"

Telenay stared evenly back at the Centaur.

"If I had your will, this would never have happened!"

"You were not there. And Osondrous was leading."

"She is only twenty-five-years-old! She is just a girl! What is your excuse?"

Telenay laughed at him. "I will be sure to tell her you said that. She will be out awhile. Keep an eye on her."

The Centaur turned on him until he was chest to chest with Telenay and looking down on the Warlord as if he were tiny. "I do not take orders from you."

The heat of rage came off the Centaur in waves of brandy stink and horseflesh.

Telenay shrugged. "All right, abandon her then." He headed for the door.

Eikian pointed at him. "You are the eldest Warlord. You should have protected her."

Telenay ignored him and was very relieved when he stepped into the hall and shut the door behind him.

Karalay was waiting for him. She was standing beneath a torch with hair and shadow covering her face. She had forgotten to heal the bruise on the side of her cheek and now it was a dark stain in her creamy complexion.

He stepped across the hall and looked down into those deep eyes.

He hated scholars. Karalay was the worst, filled so with endless, useless information. Telenay turned away from her, looked down the dark hall. He could see the stars already clear and shining tonight. He would take enough food and weaponry. It would be like it should have been for him: Warlord, horse and field, nothing else.

With one little gasp of breath, Karalay composed herself.

"Tea," she said, looking on him and not seeing him as anything but company.

They walked together through the castle, toward the dining room. The evening was winding down and his soldiers had already eaten. The servants were doing evening chores and the first of the night guard were standing along the parapets and in the towers. They were all glad to be in the service to the Wards, to the land. Most of them had been orphans, whores, real servants left to starve somewhere else when they came here. They were all saved and free and safe behind the castle's walls. They were all glad for the work, the bed, the food, the care. Telenay had only dark looks for all of them.

The dining hall was quiet. They went into the kitchen and Karalay lit a lonely fire in one of the many stone fireplaces. He poured a cup of brandy, drank it and refilled it.

They sat side by side so they did not have to look at each other.

She sighed. "I miss Jezaline."

Telenay nodded but did not agree at all. Jezaline was the sixth Ward and had left a week earlier, to his relief.

Karalay made herself a cup of tea.

His black, curly hair was in his eyes, straggling down his cheeks, toward his brandy. His dark skin was a shade of obsidian in the dim light. When he lifted his amber eyes, they reflected the light and caught fire.

He slipped into her mind and searched for the night they had spent together. Karalay shut him out.

"What do you want to know, Telenay? I would rather you just asked me."

16

His fingers flexed into fists, not used to being denied anything. "You have been thinking about us."

"Us?" Karalay sipped her tea.

She thought: *You actually believe that it is you I have been thinking about?* She did not let him hear it.

He glared at her. She could feel the look and gave it the same disregard she would pay an arrogant fifteen-year-old boy. She went to the fire and pushed the logs around. Her slim gown showed the crease between her legs, the long curve of her slender waist and back. He could smell her sweet lavender across the room. He moved quickly, almost soundlessly; she knew he was coming and pretended not to.

He grabbed her around the waist and forced her backside against him.

He said in her ear, "You have been thinking about us."

Karalay closed her eyes and fought a quiver. She had never forgotten the night he was talking about, never forgotten the bruises she had come away with. Telenay was a Warlord; he was extremely strong and his hands on her now were as forgiving as rocks. His cheek against her neck was as rough as a rasp; she could smell the sweat and Osondrous' blood drying in his leathers.

Telenay's mouth opened there on her neck, tongue slipping hotly over her skin. It felt good and he knew enough to know that she would have given herself to him. If he had asked. His hands wandered and she could feel him hardening against the back of her. He wanted her to throw herself to him and simply beg him to stay.

Later she would realize her mistake, realize that this had been her chance to stop him from leaving. She would have stripped down entirely, spread herself out on one of the tables. But she could only see Jaridd and how much she wanted her Darkhalk.

Her teeth snapped shut and she wrenched herself from Telenay's hands. "I will not be your Osondrous stand-in. Have a servant if you want, but you will not treat me like a whore."

He thought that he could stay for her if she would just let him between her beautiful legs, but he watched her go without a word. He stood for a time in the dining hall. It would not feel long to him but the night would settle and the second guard would relieve the first before he stopped grinding his teeth. He drank the last of his sixth brandy.

He could not stay here any more.

He would abandon his post as a soldier, as a Warlord to this castle and, most importantly, as a Ward to the people. Twenty-eight years echoed around his head with each step that took him out. The oath of the Wards said that he gave his life to the people, that he would never forsake them, that he had been chosen by the Creator to have the power of will and that he would be a Ward until he died.

Rayue snorted with excitement when he entered the stable and it took barely a moment to brush the horse down. His hands flew and the packing he did took very little time. He was hurrying now to stay ahead of the only thing that could stop him: Osondrous.

Telenay stepped out into the blueness of dawn.

The night was gone. Rayue's breath was a wet cloud that hung in the windless air.

He froze. The long slippery tendrils of darkness in his mind sent chills down his back.

He turned. *Darkhalk?*

I need to speak with you.

He searched the shadows and found him. Telenay gaped. In all of his years as a Warlord, he had seen the faces of only four Darkhalks. They had been killed and he himself had peeled their masks off and looked into the faces of men young and old where no Human age ever touched. But they had been dead; standing before him now was Karalay's missing Darkhalk guardian.

Jaridd's face was pale and thin. There was no emotion there, though Telenay sensed that this man was no longer controlled by the Cape and the Sword.

"What happened to you?"

Jaridd barely moved when he said, "I passed through Addilade on my return."

"What happened?"

Jaridd said, "Addilade is dead."

"You need to go to the King with this."

Jaridd ignored him. "You need to do something."

Telenay snorted. "What would you have me do, Jaridd?"

Jaridd's blue eyes glanced at Rayue and the horse shifted his weight uncomfortably. "When were you leaving?"

Telenay glared. "This is the King's concern, not mine."

"You are abandoning the Wards." There was no malice in Jaridd's voice, but hearing it out loud stung.

Telenay looked at his horse to avoid Jaridd's eyes. They were a shade that could be called blue. They were the color of a frozen lake. The color of death.

Jaridd said, "Have you not tried to seek out the King?"

He looked at Jaridd. "Do you know where Shankan is?"

"I know he is deep." Jaridd slipped away and the shadows embraced him and his black leathers as though he were one of them.

Telenay turned to Rayue and the horse sighed as if to say, *Well, we almost got out.* Telenay slowly led him back to the stable. Took off Rayue's bridle, loosened his girth and gave him a little hay. He mulled over his options for a while, listening to the stable and the servants cleaning stalls, horses breathing. It came to him in a heartbeat and he ran for the Ward chambers.

Everyone was sleeping; he used his will now and woke Karalay and Olisize as he raced up the staircase. When his feet landed in the hall, Karalay's door was opening and she was holding her dress closed with her hands, her eyes dancing in panic. Her hair was mussed from sleeping. He hurried by her, sweeping his arm around her waist, into Olisize's chamber where the old man was pulling a blanket around his narrow shoulders.

Telenay fixed them with his darkest glare. "Something has happened."

"Well, what?" Olisize's hand rose and grasped at his wild gray hair.

"Something killed Addilade."

A time passed while Olisize and Karalay took in the news.

Olisize spoke first. "How do you know?"

"Jaridd told me."

Neither of them noticed the effect the name of Jaridd spoken out loud had on Karalay. Her face flushed and she gasped.

They began to argue about the risks and possibilities.

Eventually Olisize said what Telenay was waiting for. "What could possibly have been powerful enough to destroy all of Addilade? The Elves there are stronger than any of our Human armies have been in history."

Telenay grew grave. "We need to send a Warlord to the forest; that is too close to Diggamara."

And both of the other Wards saw that he was leaving then and they gasped the same word at the same time, both out loud and in his mind with their wills, *"No!"*

He continued on, grim and serious. "We have no choice. If Jaridd thinks we needed this information, then he thinks we need to do something about it."

"No, this is for the Elves to deal with." Karalay shook her head.

Telenay said, "Addilade is dead. The Elves can do nothing. We need to do something."

Olisize nodded. "You are right, but it can wait until Osondrous wakes and she can go. You are too important here, Telenay. Two days will change nothing."

Telenay shook his fists and the Healers stepped back. "Did you not hear me? There is a force out there powerful enough to destroy Addilade! We cannot wait. Jaridd said that something must be done immediately. This is only a few steps off the back door of one of our capitals!"

And it finally affected Karalay too deeply, this last mention that Jaridd was alive, that Jaridd had returned, that Jaridd was in the castle. Her heart beat so erratically with excitement that both of the other Wards heard it.

Olisize stared at her. "Did you know he had returned?"

Karalay gasped and for a glimpse of a second, her walls fell, her gates fell, her locks fell and all of the secrets she had been holding tight and guarded were in plain daylight. And both Telenay and Olisize saw her heart. They saw the times she had touched Jaridd. All the times she had tried to get a male rise out of the Darkhalk. They saw the many nights she had pressed her will into Jaridd and sat in his heart, beside him, like a lover.

Olisize spoke first, voice full of shock and repugnance. "Karalay, you know better! You know what the Cape and Sword could have done to you. They could have destroyed your heart, you could have become addicted to their power, just as the Darkhalks are. How could you be so stupid?" And the last word came out like a knife across her cheek.

Olisize would have continued, but Telenay's rage took over the room.

He attacked her, grabbed her by the back of her delicate neck and screamed in her face, "You could have gotten yourself killed!"

Karalay recoiled and screamed back, "You both treat me like I am a child! Jaridd never hurt me." But her voice broke like that of a child and tears spilled out of her eyes and she turned in shame.

Telenay pushed her away and she fell to her knees.

He spoke to Olisize. "We do not have time for such abhorrent behavior. Someone must go now."

Olisize sighed, "Go then."

Telenay kept himself from running by only a slight margin. Too many days letting this place harness him like a broken pony. Too many days doing the King's work. He had no second thoughts and saw no one and no part of the castle on his way out.

Rayue was waiting for him; so were fifteen Centaurs of his elite guard.

Olisize must have known the moment he was awakened that Telenay was leaving. The old Healer had awakened the Centaurs with his will and commanded them to wait in the courtyard and be packed for travel. Telenay was impressed but not surprised.

He said, "Let us go then."

They were on their way out, in fact no more than a few more paces and the gate would have been behind them. But as Telenay lifted his foot to mount Rayue, six words popped into his head: *I will not let you leave.* He panicked, momentarily stricken, when he thought it was Osondrous.

But it was not his fellow Warlord.

Karalay ran out of the castle, skirt held up between her fingers, jaw set in fury.

"Stop!" she commanded; the elite Centaur guard froze. Telenay stepped slowly around his stallion.

He said, "Someone has to go."

Her mouth sneered and she said in front of all of the castle in the very loudest, steadiest voice that she had, "Coward!"

He laughed shakily. "What is wrong with you?"

She said in his mind, *I have seen your heart now. You cannot hide from me. You are leaving for the wrong reasons and I will not allow it.*

His anger darkened his voice. "You cannot stop me."

She actually laughed. "You cannot hurt me, Telenay. I will stop you."

He rolled his eyes, headed back to his horse when Karalay threw out her hand and, across ten feet of sand and grass, grabbed him with her will. He was overtaken by white light, the ringing of bells deafened him and her brilliant Healer will cast him to the ground.

It stung with fierceness.

Karalay was technically right about one thing: in a battle of wills she would win. He could not hurt a Healer with his will, could not touch her at all, actually, but Karalay underestimated his fury. Had grown a little too soft in the idea that maybe Telenay liked her.

He reached her in three strides.

Karalay's eyes widened in shock. "You would not dare touch me!"

He reared back and smacked her hard across the face.

Karalay flew through the air, a fine line of red bloody beads leaving her lip. Over a thousand soldiers in the parapets and towers had heard her call Telenay a coward and now their breaths caught as they watched her fly. And the Centaurs behind Telenay stood stock still, mouths gaping. Her hair was a blanket of feathers, flying, flying, flying. She connected. The

21

beauty in her flight evaporated as her body slammed into the dirt.

She lay small and still.

Telenay ordered, "Cray, take her back to her room."

Cray, the Second in the Centaur guard with them, left the line. He rushed to her, his hands out. He lifted her up and carefully dusted the dirt off her face. He took her inside with her head against his chest, paying Telenay one hard look back.

Telenay mounted Rayue with a grim smile and the rest of the Centaurs followed him out in silence.

They passed beneath the gates at a walk but, when the streets went to dirt and Telenay turned off the path into the empty fields to the east, Rayue ran into the gray grasses. The wind blew in Telenay's face and even the presence of the Centaur guard behind him could not diminish the moment.

It would be easy to shake these Centaurs in Addilade. He would slip away among the dead trees, surely taken by the same unknown horror that destroyed the Elves. And just maybe, if he were lucky, he would be declared dead.

4
Karalay

Cray carefully lowered Karalay to her bed. He curled his hooves beneath him, laid down beside the bed and held her hand.

It only occurred to him then, in the still warmth of her bedroom: Why had Karalay's guardian not protected her? He looked around and there was no Darkhalk in Karalay's room; there was no Darkhalk protecting her at all.

Cray's chest was tight with anger. He called on the only one who was above him in rank and whom he trusted completely. He scrambled to his feet. Outside Karalay's room, Osondrous' door was only fifteen paces. Before he knocked, her door opened. Eikian looked out expectantly.

"I must show you something."

Eikian followed Cray without question.

When he saw her, Eikian gasped. "Who hit her?"

He tenderly touched Karalay's bruised cheek.

While rubbing the back of his head, Cray explained what he had seen happen.

Eikian said, "What the hell?"

The two Centaurs stood in silence for a few minutes, Eikian's arms crossed over his chest. They watched her breathe.

Cray asked, "What is happening?"

"I do not know." Eikian rubbed the back of his head in a similar fashion.

"Have they found the King yet?" Cray looked at him.

Eikian's lack of response was answer enough. Shankan had technically been missing for eight days now. There was no way the King had left the castle without being seen. The other Wards had left it up to the Centaurs to find him and they had simply not been able to.

When Karalay opened her eyes, the last thing she had seen was Telenay's fist and the last thing she had thought was that he was probably going to kill her. Now when she saw two Centaurs gazing down at her, their braids and wild hair framing their strong faces, her heart literally sobbed in relief and she gasped.

Eikian said, "It is all right. Telenay will not touch you again. You are safe."

But Karalay shook her head. "Go, both of you. Let me rest, I . . . I need time." She dried her eyes, held their hands tightly and then shooed them away.

Eikian and Cray left and stood in the hall glaring at their hooves.

Cray whispered, "You do not think he would have actually killed her, do you?"

"I have no idea."

"We would not have been able to stop him! None of us were even close. Where was her Darkhalk?"

"Cray, I have no idea! Of course, Telenay would not have killed her. Why would he?"

"Maybe he is just a Human male like the rest of them."

Eikian put his hand on Cray's shoulder and told him, "Go back to your regular duty. If things get too dark, I will order you to Karalay as a guard, all right?"

Cray looked up. "You would?"

"Of course. Now go."

5

Karalay stood and looked out the window, arms crossed over her breasts and her mind on Jaridd. She had listened to the Centaurs talking outside with her will. Cray and Eikian were right; where was her Darkhalk guardian? If Jaridd was here, why had he not come to her? If for no other reason than that he was sworn as her guardian until death. She reached out with her will and found them with no effort. A Darkhalk could find a Ward but not as easily as a Ward could find a Darkhalk. The Darkhalk's will was a bright, screaming beacon that never rested nor slept.

She found all of them gathered together in one of the empty wings of the castle. What were they doing? But she did not dare press; just finding them was enough. If she pressed to read them, any of them, they would know she was looking.

Karalay slipped out of her room and worked her way downstairs, shielding herself. If any one of those Darkhalks really wanted to find her, even when she was trying not to be found, they still could, but only if they were looking. As it was now, she could walk right up to the door and they would not know it until they turned to see.

And she did. Deep in the storage chambers of the basement, Karalay crept up to the solid oak door and listened. The Darkhalks were having a meeting. She could feel that well enough, but they were communicating by will; she could not listen without being noticed. She bit her lip in frustration.

The storage rooms were not kept lit except by a single torch at the side of each door. She had taken on the duty of blessing the torches and their oil; they would burn for a month before needing to be replaced. In a few weeks she would have had grain for the winter to hide behind but, as it was now, she had only the pitch black and thirteen immortal guards who could see in the dark.

Reason told her it was ridiculous to think that she was in any danger. Why would the Darkhalks care if she knew they were here? None the less, her hands were shaking and she pressed to the wall as far from the light as she could.

It did not take long. The Darkhalks began to file out. If Jaridd's replacement, Brach, had decided to return to her as her guardian, he would have found her then but he did not. She wondered if that meant that Jaridd was still her guardian.

Twelve Darkhalks left the room and her heartbeat doubled. If Jaridd had been one of them, she would have recognized him even though they were entirely masked in leather. They left and she was alone with knowing he was on the other side of the wall. She crept toward the door. She wanted to leave, wanted to get the hell out of this windowless black room, but she could not.

Karalay opened the door.

In the blackness, down the wall, he was leaning just inside of the light. He looked up, expecting anyone but her. He stared. His jaw muscles worked; his blue eyes flickered uncertainly. She had never seen his eyes but had somehow known that they were that shade of ice blue.

The door fell shut behind her.

When she breathed it came out as, "Jaridd?" She shook her head. "Where did you go?"

He shrugged and the emotion was so strange on him. She had never seen him use emotion. He looked of an age that could only be lived in darkness. She found herself pulled to touch him, like she had been caught by a hook, her hand out. She needed to touch his face, to be certain it was real.

Her hand slipped up his cheek. The trepidation on his face was growing more and more severe. His skin was smooth. She felt his very Human warmth. He tipped his head and her fingers fell down the side of his jaw and she could not stop herself from going forward, slipping those fingers around behind his neck. His face turned down to hers and her face up to his.

Jaridd looked into her brown eyes and saw a thousand moments from what now seemed like a dream for him. A dream that had been years and years standing beside this beautiful creature as her guardian. It came at him with the look of her, with the smell of her, with the feel of her. She realized his hands were bare and one encircled her wrist and pulled her hand from his neck. His fingers were hot.

Their movements were slow and deliberate, as though they were both dealing with a wild animal.

She slipped her will into his mind and his spirit felt the same, but this time there was life around her, slipping, moving, smelling and tasting, a real spirit that touched her spirit back.

He froze; she froze.

I missed you.

Karalay. Do not touch me again.

I missed you so much.

I am not Human.

But Jaridd saw her naked in the years he had been her guardian. Jaridd saw her stripping, laying out, easing her fingers into her heat before him.

Ordering him to lay down on the bed so she could touch him. And all of those times he had been unaffected, untouched.

When she pulled her hand out of his grasp, and pushed it around his neck again, he was not capable of stopping her.

Karalay's heart hammered. *How long have you been here? Why have you not come to me?*

We cannot do this. I am still a Darkhalk. You do not want this.

Do you not remember me? In their minds, her voice broke even there. She blinked back tears. Her face was desperate for him to at least remember. At least to like her. Someone, anyone, to want her, but especially him. It had always been him beside her.

Of course I do!

Do you remember? Her face flushed and she glanced down and he stared along her cheek and neck and shoulder.

"Yes." He found his voice and it surprised them both. It was scratchy and deep, like someone suffering from years of yelling at the top of their lungs. Like cold rain when it passed over her, chills raced down her back.

He said, "I remember everything."

He saw her shiver and his chest began to ache. He had been scared of this; she saw it and understood it. Her heart was a hammering roar in her ears. Her body was in the throes of such complete and total excitement that physically she was incapable of expression. She could not have known that that was where his desperate place was, but Karalay put her hand flat out on his hard chest.

Jaridd gasped and she turned her face into his mouth. She stepped in one more time and they were as close as they could be without pressing. He knew soon she would feel his twitching hardness no matter how he pulled it away.

He wanted her to feel it.

He tried to stop, tried to step back and only managed a slight lean and that was when she connected. Her mouth opened on his lips and her lips were sweet softness.

He grabbed her.

He pushed her against the wall. His tongue met her tongue. His fingers pulled up her skirt, pushed between her wet legs. Karalay's voice was raw as she gasped.

He was unlacing her dress. Throwing it to the floor. She was taking off his armor. Pulling it off of him. Kissing his body, his stomach. Kissing his chest. He was. Kissing. Between her legs. On the smooth stone. She was hot as lava. And the burn. Best thing he had ever tasted. She opened her mouth. Then he penetrated. Finally broke her open. She gasped. Reached for his heart.

You are perfect.

6

She said to him, "If you are leaving, you must take me with you."

She had read it with her will, in his mind, that he was departing.

He said, "Anything you want."

Karalay was sitting cross-legged beneath the torch, hands on her bent knees, back straight. Her hair was in her eyes and trailing down to her dark, pink nipples. He was getting dressed reluctantly. He wanted something, could not remember what. Did he smoke tobacco when he had been Human? When had he last been Human? That question was too scary, not going to approach that now.

Karalay whispered, "How long?"

She was reading him so easily it was disturbing.

"What?"

"How long, Jaridd."

"Four hundred and ninety eight years, three months, two days."

She smiled a little.

He said, "What?"

Naked before her, his body had been like a spear. Long, hard, sharp to a point, and deadly in its perfection. With her will, she had felt his holding back in almost every way. She had heard it in every call of his spirit; he had been afraid of hurting her. She was humbled before his raw power.

She said, "I love you."

He knelt down beside her like he was cowering. He pressed the side of his face to her hip and her smooth, hot side. "I love you, too."

Her face went into his neck, her lips went to his cheek, her tender nakedness went against his black armor.

He said, "I will never be Human again. I am a Darkhalk. The Cape and the Sword are here, waiting for me. Can you feel them?"

She closed her eyes. "Yes. You are a Darkhalk." She closed her eyes because she could see the Cape and the Sword. And though they had no faces, the powerful things beckoned. Always beckoned. Even to her.

"When are we leaving?"

"Right now."

"Should I pack something?"

"No."

"How many days?"

"Five."

"Can you put me to darkness?"

"We can."

"Are you all leaving?"

"All but one."

"Who?"

"Teek."

"Why?"

"He thinks he needs to stay."

She pulled on her dress.

"Is that the dress that you want to go in?"

She looked down at it and it was nothing but a slip of simple cotton.

She shrugged. "As good as any."

"Then can we go now?"

She nodded, albeit slowly. Jaridd picked her up.

As he moved through the castle, his brethren appeared from the dark places and followed. They vaulted both parapets and slipped away. There were only two guards that noticed and as they passed, she had assured them.

The castle faded away behind their speed, the wind slipped by them and soon there were no farms, no windmills, only the wild gray in the east. She was alone with the Darkhalks who moved as though they were never Human, but creatures taken directly out of night and shadow.

They were not given real speed until the wild horses answered their call.

The Barbakas were a breed of equine, more like a deer that an actual horse, with cloven hooves and bodies bent and iron-like. When the Darkhalks climbed onto their mounts, Jaridd looked her in the face and said, "I will see you in a few days."

They could not be slowed by a Human's need to eat or sleep. She felt the tang of the Cape on her tongue as one of the Darkhalks cast her away. She felt a moment of pure panic as her will was suffocated. Then everything went black for Karalay.

Osondrous' throat was a grainy fire. With great effort, she picked her head up. Her thin hair fell down her cheeks in wet tentacles. She turned her legs over the edge of the bed and pressed her bare feet to the cold floor. She touched the arrow wound on her chest: a red, five pointed star. It was closed, healed more than a week by Karalay. It ached fiercely. Cold sweat dripped down her sides and slipped into the deep grooves between her ribs. On the table was a covered plate of breakfast. Beside it was a pitcher of water. She licked her lips, stared at the six or so steps of space between herself and the water.

The skin around her eyes was dark and her face was white from blood loss. She stood and darkness closed around her vision. First one knee and then the other took on her weight and trembled. Teeth gritted, she forced the darkness away and focused. She worked her way to the foot board and rested at the bedpost.

Only two steps to the table.

Osondrous reached out and tentatively closed the distance. She eased down into the smooth wooden chair. She closed her fists around the fat, cold base of the pitcher.

Made of clay and kiln-fired, the pitcher was heavy even without water. She clutched it with both hands, tipped it over the closest cup. Water poured out. The cup jerkily filled. Her shaking became violent. She dropped the pitcher with a smack. Water sloshed over the rim.

She lifted the cup and drank it down. She looked at the pitcher again, closed her fists around the fat base of it, tried to lift it again and failed. Her head fell in defeat.

The door opened and Eikian entered. "You up?"

His mass trembled the floor. He stood with his hands at his sides, his chest a broad expanse of muscle. He wore several thick leathers across his chest. Two swords crossed his back. He did not look at her. He rubbed his chin and glared at the floor.

Osondrous saw his face and shook her head tiredly. "I will not deal with that look right now."

He grimaced. "Have you talked to Aerick yet?"

She glared at him. "Why would I talk to Aerick?"

"Well, if he was not a little bitch, he would have reported to you of what happened while you were enjoying your nap."

He stepped closer to her, his hooves clopping on the stone. His hide was clean and smooth, the color of chestnuts. His tail was braided tightly and with care. The grime of Rayakdool was gone from him. He smelled clean.

Her nose wrinkled. "All right, what is it?"

He muttered, "The bad or the terrible?"

Her eyes were knives and they lashed at him for hesitating.

He said, "Telenay is gone."

Osondrous threw out her will. She swept the castle as far as she could reach.

No Telenay.

She slammed her fist and screamed, "Spineless bastard! Where did he claim he was going? Or did he just abandon his post?" The wound in her chest throbbed.

"Addilade."

"Why?"

Eikian explained as best he could, then said, "You need to speak to Olisize."

"Was that the terrible?"

"Yeah."

"All right, what is the bad?"

"Karalay is gone, too."

"What? Where is she?"

"You need to talk to Olisize and you need to be healed."

Eikian stepped to her dresser and grabbed a fresh pair of leggings and a clean shirt. He handed them to her and watched as she carefully balanced to get herself dressed. His eyes followed the smooth doeskin as she pulled it up her thighs, covering her womanhood, and the shirt as it paused at her breasts, then fell to her hips. The fabric covered the lines of her deep tan and the pearly skin of her Stonedowner blood. He remembered the little girl that used to burn red all summer long, sloughing it off and burning again. Osondrous did not burn anymore.

"Why is he in here? Did you call him?" Osondrous motioned across the room.

A Darkhalk stood beside her door, hands clasped behind him.

Eikian looked at him with surprise, having not noticed the Darkhalk at all. "How long has he been here?"

"You did not command him here?"

"No."

Osondrous frowned. "Teek, I commanded you away from me years ago. This is a time of peace. You are not my guardian."

Teek said, "I will be your guardian until you or I die."

Eikian and Osondrous glanced at each other.

The Centaur said, "All right, let us go speak to Olisize."

They entered Olisize's chamber without knocking.

The room was stacked with books and rolled parchments. The fire was low and everything was swept up in the gloom. The Healer was pacing by the fire; his head snapped up when they burst in. Where years ago he had once been tall and strong, Olisize was now crumpled down with his hands held close to him. His knuckles and eyes were big and wide.

Osondrous stood offensively. "Where is Karalay?"

Olisize's heart rate was up with anger; she could hear it across the room.

His hands balled into fists. "Karalay left with the Darkhalks."

Osondrous said, "The Darkhalks left?" She pointed at the Darkhalk that had followed her. "How so?"

"All but Teek."

She looked at Teek. "Why did you stay?"

The Darkhalk said, "Bad things are coming."

"Oh. Thank you. That is very informative. All right, why did they go, Teek?"

"To protect the last Crystal shard in Diggamara."

She turned her dark eyes on Olisize and snarled, "How could you let Telenay go!"

Olisize raised his cane in a fist. "If I had known that we would have been without Karalay, I never would have allowed it!"

She saw the feelings of betrayal in the old man's eyes. He simply could not believe that Karalay would leave so rashly. No, not his incredible, perfect Karalay. Osondrous growled and swatted at the empty air.

Olisize gasped, "Osondrous, you must find Shankan!"

She crossed her arms. "Why would I do that?"

He stared, appalled. "This is not a game! We need our King. The Ring needs the King."

She said, "You do not think I am capable of this? I am a Ward!"

"You are a little girl. You have never been here. You have never been a Ward! You will never compare to Karalay."

Osondrous closed the distance between them in two strides and hit the old man across the mouth. Olisize hit the floor. He curled around his heart;

his hands spanned his chest and he gasped for air.

She stood over him. "Can you not heal your heart?"

His voice was muffled. "My heart is old. You will be alone here very soon and when that day comes, our people are doomed." He stared up at her rebelliously, challenging her to hit him again.

Osondrous laughed. "I have never needed any of you and I never will."

She left and paced in the hall to dispense her anger.

Eikian stood, powerful arms crossed, looking at her with a troubled face.

"You should not—"

She lunged at him. Eikian towered over her; he turned down his dark face so he could meet her squarely.

She screamed at him, "I should not what?"

Osondrous waited for no reply; she headed for the dungeons. In Eikian's mind she had seen the only good news of the day: they had captured the hunters that had tried to kill her. Eikian followed. Osondrous passed through the castle without seeing it. The place was full of constant activity. As she went, the crowds parted for her.

She went down until there was no more sunlight or servants and the stone halls were dark and low and damp.

The guards stepped back.

She said, "Unlock the cell door."

The door swung in and she with it.

The torch outside flickered into the dark cell. It was barely wider than a coffin. Sitting in the farthest corner was the one hunter whose arrow had killed her. His hands were lined with dirt and calluses. His clothes were peasant's and soaked through with sweat.

The room stank of fear.

His head slowly came up and it dipped and trembled with exhaustion.

His eyes filled with the image of her and he went still. "Please, no!"

She grabbed him by the sides of the face and dove into his heart. The man squirmed and quivered but she did not allow him to scream. Osondrous swept through his memories, his entire past and life. When she was done, Osondrous' eyes cleared and she stared at the stone wall, thinking, mulling. The man shook in her grasp; his piss hit the floor.

"Please . . ." he begged.

She braced her feet. Her fingers slipped in the sweaty gruff of his cheeks. She jerked. His neck snapped and Osondrous dropped him.

She stepped outside. "Kill the other two as well. Get rid of the bodies."

Eikian followed her out into the light of day and into what the locals called the hall of silence. It ran down the entire front of the castle, spanned with pillars so large no one could wrap their arms around them.

She leaned on a pillar, arms crossed, breathing and thinking. Above her the carvings of their history seemed a fraud. Lionel, their great first Ward, arms spread, casting the rivers and granting the Humans freedom. And signed in every Human language and the written word, were the carvings of "peace" and "freedom" and "sanctuary" because always the Castle of the Wards had been a sanctuary to all. There was no Human alive who had not been raised in the certainty that without those two rivers, they would either die or be shackled by another species again.

Eikian grunted, "Well, whose brother did you kill that they were getting revenge for?"

"No one."

"Then what?" He looked at her.

She looked down. "They were not lying. They had no intentions of killing me, not their intentions anyway. They were driven mad by . . . something red."

"By what?"

She whispered, "Red man . . ."

"What?"

"I do not know."

"How is that possible?"

She just shook her head.

Aerick walked across the span of the courtyard; when he saw her, he hurried. Her glare darkened when she saw him coming. Telenay had risen Aerick to the rank of Second years before any other Human in history. He was very young and his attitude always seemed a little too casual for her. He had been at Telenay's arm constantly over the past two years.

He bowed to her. "The Ring."

She grunted, "Aerick, is that what Telenay was using you for? I am sure your speed in battle was desperately needed in the Ring."

He smiled crookedly. "Constantly."

"So, what do you have for me?"

"Nothing was done yesterday."

"How many then?"

"Forty-eight."

Eikian began walking away.

She said, "Where are you going?"

"Someone has to handle the guard with Telenay gone."

She growled, "What if I commanded you to handle the Ring?"

Eikian laughed. "I would like to see you try." His hazel eyes sparked over his big shoulder.

She glared at his tail.

The Ring of Wards was a large round chamber. It encompassed the majority of the first floor of the castle. With the ending of the Five Hundred Year War, by the creation of the rivers, the Wards had risen in power over the middle realm and those creatures left to survive in it. The Ring was carved with the writings of dozens of different Wards: testaments, promises, that Humans would never live enslaved again. The Ring had been the beacon. Osondrous had read that for generations after the building of it, Humans had come just to see the promises and to believe.

Above her head, in the written tongue of the Humans, were six words: LET FREEDOM NOT BE TO DIE.

The Ring had been built to deal with the numerous quarrels regarding leadership between the large cities. After the governors were chosen and a voting system set into place, the noble purpose of the Ring had deteriorated quickly.

As Osondrous entered, her ears were filled with the murmurings of all types of peoples of the land. They were all Human and most of them were very poor. They scraped together enough supplies to travel, sometimes for weeks, to reach the Castle of the Wards to have a final decision on whatever conflict needed to be solved. This was long after these people had taken their problems to their local governments and, either the governors were unable to solve the problem and sent the people to the Ring, or (in most cases) the people were simply not happy with the resolution they were presented with.

Before Osondrous, the majority of the people were tired and angry. When they saw her, she was not met with relief. They had expected the King or perhaps Telenay, certainly not her.

She took her place at the head of the Ring with Aerick at her side.

She said, "Let us start." Then into Aerick's mind: *Bring me brandy.*

Before her stepped a man carrying a goat and, beside him, a starved servant boy.

"Well," she said, "proceed."

The man said, "This was my servant for several years."

34

"The goat or the boy?"

"The boy! This is my prize female goat!"

"Is this about the boy or the goat?"

"He will not leave my goat alone!"

"Is he your servant?"

"He was! I banished him from my property!"

"Why?"

"I found him with my prize goat. Out in the back paddock one night. He says he loves her and now he will not leave her alone. He keeps sneaking into the paddock. He was with her!"

"Excuse me?"

"He was *with* her!"

Osondrous' jaw fell open.

8

Forty-seven problems later, Osondrous was finishing off her second pitcher of brandy and had developed a noticeable twitch. Her blond hair had tangled loose and she was consistently smoothing it back so hard that her eyebrows raised.

A woman stepped forward. She was wearing a cotton dress that was of good quality, dyed green. Her eyes were blue and intelligent; her hair was tied back in a long braid. She was carrying a baby goat.

Osondrous sat up. "No! Not another goat."

"Oh!" the woman said. "No, no. I just could not leave him outside. He is an orphan and I am the only one he will take milk from." She put the goat down. The baby pressed fearfully to her legs, bleating.

"What is your name?"

"My name is Gladys. I am from Stonedowner."

"And what is your problem?"

The woman pointed behind her. Sitting on opposite ends of the Ring were two men relishing their own pools of discontent.

Gladys said, "I am sworn to the man on your left. His name is Garil. The man on your right is the man that I love. He is the man I will be with for the rest of my life. His name is Zary."

"And Garil disagrees?"

"No. Garil can live with my leaving him. Garil's problem is that I want our land."

35

"Why?"

"Because it is rightfully mine. Eighteen years ago, my parents died and heired it to me. Garil is threatening to kill Zary if I do not give up my birthright."

Garil grunted from the back and nodded. Osondrous glowered at him.

Gladys continued, "It is the farm I was raised on. It is worth a lot. It is mine and I will not step down."

"What did your governor say?"

"Our governor is Garil's father," Gladys spat.

"Both of you come here!" Osondrous motioned.

The two men were stark contrasts. Garil was pudgy and wearing expensive leathers. The sword on his hip gleamed. Zary was tall, angular and looked like a man who had worked as a servant. A large scar traveled across his right cheek and ear. The sheath that held his sword was frayed and showed that his blade was not shiny but black with use.

"Will either of you stand down?"

Garil said, "I have worked that land until I bled for the last decade. Just because she is a whore does not mean it is right that I lose everything!"

Gladys held back her retort. She picked up her goat and held it tightly.

Zary reached for his sword. "You have no right to call my love a whore!"

Osondrous held up her hands. "You do not want me to stop you, so do not. Garil, you poor, poor man. I am sure you would be left on the street with no land or income. I am certain you have felt no luxuries in the face of your father being governor. Certainly you could not find work or lands."

They stared at her sarcasm with mouths gaping.

Gladys said, "So?"

Osondrous glared at them, then finished off the last bit of brandy in her cup.

She said, "Zary. Would you die for Gladys' honor?"

"Of course."

"Garil, you will not let this go?"

"Never!"

Osondrous' dark eyes leveled on Garil. "All right, you arrogant bastard. Let us at least know why you want to draw your sword. It has nothing to do with the land. You are embarrassed and you believe that at least saving the land will save you some shred of your dignity and manhood." Osondrous stood. "Garil, nothing will ever save your dignity. You have none."

Osondrous motioned for them to follow her and they did so. Outside the sun was waning and Osondrous walked stiffly. In the middle of the courtyard sand, she stopped. The courtyard cleared around her. Servants and soldiers moved out at her presence.

Osondrous motioned and Zary and Garil inched forward.

She said, "Draw your swords. Prove it to me. A fight to the death. Garil dies and Gladys has no more problems. Zary dies and Gladys gets her land and Garil saves what he thinks is a shred of dignity. Do it."

Garil drew his sword and parried. Zary stared in shock.

Gladys rushed to her. "No! Please no! Zary cannot be killed."

Osondrous glared. "Confident in your man, I see."

Gladys gasped. Zary drew his sword.

The two men attacked. Osondrous looked pleased. A crowd of soldiers and servants, fists raised, cheering, circled them.

Gladys began to cry.

Eikian joined Osondrous. "Interesting way you are handling this one."

Osondrous smiled. At the steps to the Ring, Olisize limped into sight. He stepped aside as the men tripped into each other, the sand exhausting them. Sweat sheened across their faces.

These were no fighters. The men were waning, both bleeding, lunging desperately at each other. Osondrous drew a fine dagger from beneath her vest and fit it into Gladys' hand.

Gladys stared at it like she had never seen a dagger before.

Zary tripped backwards. He struggled to regain his footing and caught his heel in deep sand. His hands went back to catch himself and his sword hit the ground. Garil dove and sank his blade into Zary's stomach. Gladys screamed; she rushed forward, raised Osondrous' dagger above her head and stabbed Garil in the back. Garil fell.

The two men lay side by side, bleeding massively.

Gladys poured herself over Zary. "No! No! No! He cannot die. Please." She looked at Osondrous. "Please. I do not care anymore. I would give my land for his life. I would rather die."

Osondrous stepped forward and leaned over Gladys. "You would rather die? I could have that arranged, too."

Gladys nodded as the tears flooded down her cheeks.

Osondrous sighed, watching them bleed, watching Zary's eyes begin to float.

She shrugged. "Olisize, heal him."

The Healer hurried through the grounds and laid his hands on Zary.

Gladys was stunned. She held her man silently and with all of her strength.

Osondrous knelt over Garil. Blood ran out of his mouth. She grabbed his head and tipped it up so she could see his eyes. "I cannot believe a dark thing like you would have the salt to show yourself to a Ward. You so thought that you were right and that justice would be done. Do you see that?" She tipped his head at the weeping couple as they held each other. "Justice, Garil. Can you even stand to live in a land where this is justice?"

His face contorted.

"Now, you die right now and I swear to it that your name will be remembered with dignity."

He shook his head.

"No? You live and you give up the land and go crawling back to your father. Or you could always stay here . . . Work as a servant or join my army. Though I do not think you would survive either. Still want to live?"

He nodded, coughed, "Live."

She said, "Olisize, heal him, too."

Osondrous went to Gladys. "I will send a few soldiers back with you. To make certain that this man's father knows all of his thoughts."

Gladys stared up at her with awe. "Thank you."

Healed, Garil got to his feet and heard the last of Osondrous' words.

His eyes widened in panic. "No! That is not right. A Ward cannot read our minds without proper agreement."

Osondrous laughed at him. "I am a Warlord."

Her eyes settled on him and Garil stepped back and hurried away, head down, face pale.

9

Osondrous slept fitfully all night. She reached out for Telenay with her will and could not find him.

She dressed quickly, tightening the laces down the sides of her leggings and the front of her tan shirt. She walked down the hall, surrounded by fifteen empty Ward chambers. Karalay, Jezaline, Telenay: all gone. She was left with Shankan and Olisize. It had been prophesied by the very first Ward, Lionel, that nine Wards would always rise to rule. There had not been nine Wards in a hundred years. There had always been young ones, Wards in training. In Osondrous' opinion, she had been the last young one to come to the castle. There was Constance, a fifteen-year-old girl from Stonedowner. But in Osondrous' opinion, Constance had never proven she was Ward material.

She hurried away from the empty floor.

The courtyard was filled with wagons with a dozen more waiting at the gate. Eikian stood at a pillar, arms crossed. She stepped up beside him.

He smiled. "The Implins finally got here."

Servants gathered to help and the Implins blinked their huge eyes in the morning sunlight. They grasped the female servants and many were carried into the castle.

Bred by the Willower, the Implins were small green-skinned animals. They were not far from Humans in that they could speak and understand. They had been found and cherished because of their innate will to serve and be cared for. Everyone was happy to see them. They were smaller than children and stood hunched over with enormous hands and gigantic bare feet.

Eikian's hide was gold ash in the sunlight. She ran her hand down his horse back, starting where his animal met his Human, ending with a stroke down his haunch.

He said, "Sorry I was not there when you got up."

She frowned at him. "When did you start thinking I needed you to be there when I woke up?"

He smiled at her, than looked back out at the Implins. "Look at how happy they are to be here."

She laughed. "They only just got here."

He said, "Come have breakfast with me."

"No." She turned into the Ring and he frowned after her.

There were only twenty-two problems waiting for her today. She moved through them quickly.

When it was over, she was suffering a throbbing headache and the wound on her chest screamed. Despite the pain, she had avoided Olisize and would continue to do so. There was a certainty about pain that she could understand. A quality that left her able to believe that everyone was given what they deserved. When her chest throbbed, she could not forget.

Eikian was waiting for her in the same place she had left him, as if he had not moved in half a day.

He rubbed her from behind, his fingers trailing up her waist and spine. "Let us get you something to eat. I am hungry."

She rolled her eyes. "You are constantly hungry."

"I have more to feed than you. Come on."

Eikian sat her at a table near the back of the dining hall. Moving a chair out of his way, he laid his awkward frame down and rested his arms on the table. It was built low so Centaurs could do just that.

She laid her aching head by his arms. "How many do you think will be in the Ring tomorrow?"

He said, "I am taking bets on when you will break."

"You say that as if it would surprise me."

He pounded the table and yelled, "Come on, some food here! This is your Warlord starving in your dining room!"

Across the room, Constance stood with long blond curls trailing her slender back. Almost sixteen, her blossoming was beginning to show in every curve of her body. The few soldiers on break watched her every move as they ate. When Eikian called, she grabbed a tray and hurried over to them.

Constance served them each a cup of brandy and water.

Eikian said, "You are doing good here."

Constance blushed. "I will bring you something fresh."

As the girl hurried off, Osondrous said, "Do not encourage her."

"She needs it." Eikian touched her arm. "She reminds me of you."

Osondrous drank her brandy. Constance did remind her of herself, if she had ever had innocence, naivety or chastity.

Constance brought a tray of food and with it a perky bounce.

Osondrous pushed the plate away.

Eikian pushed it back to her. "What now, like two days without food? I did not see you eat yesterday. You want to get your strength back, so eat!"

"You do not follow me around."

"Should I ask Aerick?"

Osondrous pulled the plate back to her and started to eat. The food tasted good and her stomach felt better the minute she started. The potatoes were mashed with goat butter. The meat was deer and cooked until it fell apart with onions and red peppercorns.

Eikian gobbled several portions, watching her closely.

He said, "You are very pale." His hazel eyes took on a sunrise quality when he was pitying.

She stood up. "Leave me be, Eikian. I do not need this."

She hurried out and left the dining room behind. She walked with the great castle beside her, four stories high, and the vastness of the gray east on her other side. She stepped beneath the arch of one of the four main watchtowers of the castle. She leaned back into the corner, stealing herself from the wind.

Osondrous' mind was on the darkness behind the hearts of the three hunters. She had had one glimpse of a gliding darkness, all wings and teeth. She did not understand what had happened to them and that left her agonizingly suspicious. It was not the darkness that haunted her but the one glimpse of a man of red that left her heart still.

Her adrenaline raced for Shankan. If those things could drive three good peasants to try to kill their Ward and Warlord, what if they went after a King? Shankan was no warrior. Why had his Darkhalk just left with the others and her own Darkhalk stayed?

Unless Shankan was already lost.

The sound of a Centaur's gait raised her eyes. She recognized the distinct beat from an injury that left him with a limp.

Eikian stepped into the shadow. Osondrous grabbed the leather belts around his belly, slipped her fingers between them and touched the ridge of a gray scar that they hid. The only one of his scars that had not faded with time. The only scar that was gray. He pushed her into the depth of the corner so no guard could see them, pulled out her shirt from her leggings and slipped his fingers up and over her bare belly and her scar. The thick gray thing that had not faded either, that cut her navel in half. Their faces were close.

She said, "The nightmares are getting worse."

He growled, "Not necessarily."

"We need to do something. We cannot live like this forever."

He looked away. "We cannot find Shankan."

"Do not change the subject."

He tried to pull away but her hand gripped him.

She said, "We are going back to Cobblestone. We are going."

She felt the fine steel before she saw the dagger in Eikian's hand.

He pressed it to her throat. "Let go."

She smirked, eyeballing him. Letting him go, she slammed her fist into his hand and the sound of his dagger clanked on the stone. He had let her disarm him, that they both knew. Eikian walked away and she stood still for a long time before leaning down and tucking his dagger into her belt.

10

After the Ring the next day, Osondrous stood silently by herself on the parapet. A storm was closing in; it would be the first of the many cold, soaking rains of fall. The dark clouds were moving in a tight front, casting back the blue skies of summer days.

She walked the entire distance of the courtyard and passed it as the outer parapet reached farther out than the inner. She walked out to where the parapet arched above the first gate. The parapets were twelve feet of thick stone, a precious thing, having been hauled from miles around. She remembered the last stones being laid in place, Telenay's work as the Keltch began to gain their footholds across the Human lands. The walls had protected the Wards, twenty thousand servants and soldiers. But their capital cities had no walls. She remembered the day very well.

The Ring had been packed to the breaking point. Governors and mayors from a hundred leagues around had come to demand retribution for their raped wives, their eaten children, their slaughtered livestock. She had watched in awe as Telenay stood before that horde and calmly listened to each and every Human who needed to have their say. His black hair had been held smoothly back and his dark skin had made him stand out, a Diggamaran surrounded by Stonedowners and Willower. In the end, in the same casual ease and with eyes sparking viciously he had said, "We go to war."

He had sworn that they would not just push them back but wash over the Keltch until there was not another left in their land. He swore they would even cross the rivers. They would hunt and they would burn every last one of them. She had been fourteen at the time and had stood as still as she could, trying to be like Telenay, even as the rages of excitement and glee claimed her. That excitement had perished quickly. War was hunger, it was cold nights and endless rides. War was thirst and blisters. Her hands had grown hard, her body had grown rigid and she became like Telenay long after she had stopped trying.

Osondrous closed her eyes before the end of those seven years could come back to her. She saw it enough in her nights. She looked up at the black clouds, now overhead.

Eikian was standing at the other end of the parapet. He saw that she was looking and turned away. He had not come to her chamber last night either. She broke into a run as he left the stones of the castle and slipped down into the grass and black dirt between the parapets.

She sulked after him, hands at her sides. "Eikian, what is it?"

The grinding of his teeth rolled the muscles down his jaw. He drew the sword at his hip, his chosen weapon. She drew her own, a slow steady movement. Khayue and Mlore, the legendary Keltch killers. Her fingers fell into the grooves formed there, against countless enemies. It had been a long time since Osondrous had gripped Mlore. It felt sensationally good.

She lifted her blade and stepped forward. Eikian defended himself and the clash reverberated down their strong arms. The torch flames flickered as it began to rain. He pushed her back and she retaliated.

She threw his sword from her again and again. Sweat and rain ran in their eyes. Her stamina was non-existent, her heart beat madly against the cold ache in her chest. The Centaur's power overthrew her. She staggered back, catching herself and throwing a desperate swipe. A fine cut opened up his side. Blood dripped down his flat stomach. She took the advance, sliced her blade across his bicep. He threw her back, blade nicking her cheek.

"What do you want, Eikian?" Their swords met and their faces were close.

Their breath mingled as she gasped for air. His grimace was a fine, sharp line.

She flipped around, throwing him off of her. He stumbled, slipped in the wet grass and went down to his fore knees. She dove on him, sword tip landing as his came up, swiping, missing her stomach as her blade fell on his neck.

They froze.

Eikian's breathing halted; he gritted his teeth.

Osondrous stared down into his eyes. "This is over."

The Warlord planted her boot on the Centaur's chest, kicking him down, kicking him away. She sheathed her chosen weapon and sneered at the bitter taste of dissatisfaction that was on her tongue.

Eikian stood. "Do not dare walk away from me. Draw your sword."

Osondrous whipped around and went at him with her teeth bared like an animal. "You shut your mouth. You think you can order me to do anything?"

"Then walk away like you always do."

"I walk away because I do not want to kill you."

Eikian picked up his sword so fast she did not see it. As she ran toward him, he brought the hilt up. Her momentum threw her against him. The hilt slammed into her mouth and Osondrous hit the ground.

Eikian snorted. "Kill me, huh?"

He left her lying in the mud.

11

A half hour later, Aerick heard a rumor that someone saw Osondrous lying between the parapets. He tended to take everything seriously and checked it out himself. Her Darkhalk stood silently nearby as she lay on the ground shivering .

Aerick asked Teek, "Why did you not take her in?"

The Darkhalk replied behind his thick mask, "She brought this upon herself."

The Second carried her to her chamber and laid her down. Aerick took her wet, cold hands and cupped them between his own, blew on them.

She woke and jerked upright. Aerick jumped out of her way.

"Where is he?" she gasped.

He shrugged.

Osondrous skulked out of her chamber, blond hair a mess of mud and rain. She entered the next floor of the castle and hurried down the hallway. Doors flew by her until she reached Eikian's chamber door. She paused, staring at it.

In a grunt, she tossed it in. The door cracked against the wall.

"Talk to me now, Centaur."

Eikian lifted his eyes from bandaging his shoulder wound.

"Eikian!" Her yell was heard throughout the floor. "Talk to me!"

The Centaur took a breath and slowly walked around his low, broad bed.

"Osondrous." He spoke slowly. "We have already killed each other once. How could you want to feel that again? Do you want another matching gray scar to hide?"

She said, "What did you say?"

"You want so badly to go back there. You want to live that again?" He roared, "Then step closer and I shall kill you another time!"

The stony taste of her grinding teeth spilled on her tongue. "So you like the dreams then, Eikian? You like seeing their faces every night? You like hearing those screams? Well, I cannot live with them! We made a promise. I cannot live knowing that the corpses of my men were left in shallow graves to be eaten by the grasses of Barbaka! You do not think they deserve better than that?"

He clutched the post of his bed. "I cannot go back there."

She stared at him.

He shook his head. "How could you?"

Her mouth set. "I have no choice."

"You cannot ask me to follow you back to Cobblestone, Osondrous."

"You would go against me?"

"I will not go back there."

"Then you would go against my command?" Her voice was deadly.

"Then cut off my head." He stood against her will.

Osondrous stared in disbelief. "You would forsake me to allow your fear to rule you?"

"Do you not remember what happened there? What we became?"

Her chin went up. "I am ashamed of nothing."

"We were nothing."

She screamed, "I know!"

"Do you remember what we did to each other? Do you not see the scar that opened you, Osondrous, and the scar on me?"

Very deep in his eyes, there was hurt there.

"Do not plead with me, Eikian," she said. "How can you let them lie there? Your own soldiers?"

"They are dead."

"You know they are still there!"

"Why can you not let them lie? It is your will that holds them here; it is your will that brings our dreams!"

Osondrous was still as she stared at him.

She shook her head defiantly. "Then so be it, Eikian. You submit to your fear, you submit and damn your own soldiers."

The Warlord turned for the door. An indecipherable motion and his dagger appeared in her hand; whipping around, she pitched it at him. It stuck with a thud through the bedpost beside him and quivered. He stared at the dagger until it grew still and her steps had faded and the slamming of his door stopped echoing off the walls. He took his hand off the bedpost and revealed the bloody tip of the dagger, having gone completely through the hard wood and into his palm.

12

It was another goat that finally broke Osondrous. After half a day in the Ring and the last problem settled, Osondrous had had enough. She took her Darkhalk with her and told no one.

She went to find Shankan.

No light save her torch lit her Darkhalk's back. They were in the lowest level of her dungeons. Endless bars reflected the light where imprisoned fingers had clutched them smooth. She recognized the smell of old decay. Bodies seeking the answer of complete silence brought on by becoming skeletons. Osondrous had left the traitors during the Keltch wars here. Her eyes were black as she walked, remembering, enjoying that these traitors had suffered long starving deaths.

They finally reached the last cell. It was at the head of a long hallway, flanked by nothing but solid stone walls. In the beginning the mines had been closed over by stone but previous Warlords, for no reason they had written down, had reopened the mines. She had never ventured into them and had no reason to believe that anyone else still living had either.

Osondrous peered into the dark. Smooth black stone changed instantly into knocked-out clay. At best, the mine tunnels beneath the castle were shoddy and crumbling, but still intact. They silently moved down the long stairway. Half the steps had collapsed to nothing. She followed the Darkhalk carefully.

The staircase ended in an aqueduct where several tunnels branched out. Old cart tracks led into the darkness of each of their choices.

"Any ideas?" she asked.

Teek shook his head. "I still cannot feel him; the walls are thick."

"Do you think he is still alive?"

"He was going mad. I know that but nothing else."

They stood silently. Others may have felt stranded with Teek; people who had not seen the Darkhalk in battle may have felt utterly alone here. Osondrous was confident as she could not be with anything but a Darkhalk.

She said, "Let us go down."

They moved together into the farthest left tunnel, their feet adjusting to the steep incline.

The floor was littered with stone and fallen rock and dirt from overhead. The tunnel was low and Teek ducked. The tunnel weaved and dipped, was crossed by other tunnels and always kept going down. Moisture began to blacken the walls and the smell of it was mold. Osondrous held her will out of her, sweeping, searching for Shankan's will.

Teek said, "I found him."

The will of the Darkhalk outdistanced her own. They jogged, taking care, but moving very quickly. They finally got close enough and she touched Shankan with her will.

She gasped, "He is hurting!"

Teek nodded. They began to sprint.

The dampness in the air seemed to swallow her torch. Down and down they ran.

Teek's black back stopped in front of her. She cautiously went around him, following her torch.

The Wards never knew what had been mined here or by what creatures. It was something the size of the Humans; they knew that from the size of the tunnels. But the mystery of this place had been absolute for centuries. Before them, the ceiling disappeared into darkness and the cart tracks went on. Her torchlight claimed little, only that the room was enormous and what little sound they made echoed out from them and on and on.

The cart tracks led them forward. Her torch gave them the first sight of something else. Homes. Hovels.

"This is a real village. Did you know this was here?"

Teek shook his head. "No."

The homes were broken down, many with roofs caved in, rafters rotted from moisture. But that was the only wood in this place that she could see. The hovels were tiny, one-roomed clay huts with small, black holes for windows. She did not stop to investigate. A small river trickled down through the heart of the town; they stepped over it. The feel of Shankan's will was very close and she hurried on.

At the end of the road, the cart tracks stopped at the largest home of the village. A matriarch looking out over its abandoned children with their caved-in roofs and gaping windows. Osondrous ran up the crumbling steps.

The doorway was short and she ducked in. The dark was close and wet. She worked her way cautiously across the large hall. She stepped up to the gloom of a far, small room and her torch shrank in the black, threatening to go out. The power of will was tight and suffocating.

Heavy breathing reached her ears as the arch of the door enclosed her. Shankan lay on his back, curled up like an animal having found a suitable place to crawl away to and die.

"Shankan!" She fell to her knees beside him and grabbed his face.

"Shankan, focus your will!" she roared. His will was silent.

She plunged into him, diving through the great fields of her King. She searched for Shankan and stared upon the valleys of his heart having fallen into green and rotten decay. Creatures flapped over the hills. Darknesses with teeth that were shiny black points. They screamed and turned for her. Osondrous raised her sword and growled.

She knew these things: Humans, warped and wicked, who had settled into the darker art of slipping their souls out of their bodies. They were attempting to take Shankan; they were known as Reapers.

She could smell the cool winter of the Darkhalk beside her. Teek raised his blade.

The Reapers came at them, claws out, sheening black eyes filled with hate. She swept her hand through the air and they shattered before her will. Osondrous pressed her boot into the body of one dying at her feet. As her boot crushed his chest, he grinned up at her and his teeth were red with blood.

Teek grabbed her and she stood beside him on the edge of a cliff. In the distance Shankan knelt, out of reach, hands bound with sharpened wire, face gazing up into the last light left in his autumn sky. Beside him was a red man, grinning. He was no Reaper and Osondrous' blood ran cold. The red man held a two-headed battle ax at his side. Blackness cut the light out and the red man lifted the ax.

Shankan never moved nor fought. His cries echoed across the valleys. It began to rain and it was his tears.

The ax came down. Her King was beheaded. The room collapsed.

She hit the stone floor with the cracking of her elbows on the stone. She scrambled back to Shankan's side. The room was dark and close and very cold.

The King Ward lay rolled up, like a child. His eyes opened, his mouth gaped and then fell open and still.

She grabbed his shoulder and roared into his dead face, "You stupid old man! I did not fail you! Why did you not ask for help when Telenay was here to aid you? You are wretched. I knew you were this weak. This is not my fault. This is your fault!"

Osondrous caught her breath.

She said to Teek, "You should have told me of this sooner."

"It would have made no difference."

"Perhaps I will not choose to believe you this time." She shook her head, got out of the little room and the crumbling building. She breathed deep the stale air now and silently moved back through the empty town. Torchlight appeared down the tunnel before her. Olisize rushed forward and their spheres of light met. She should not have been surprised that Olisize was watching her and had followed them.

The old man gasped, "The King Ward?"

"There is nothing you can do."

Olisize looked at her closely. "Your eyes have fought a great battle, Osondrous. You failed him?"

"He was not strong enough! He did not even try, did not even try to save himself."

Olisize's bottom jaw trembled. "Then our King Ward is dead?"

"Yes." Osondrous grabbed the side of his face and showed him with her will the battle she had fought. Though she did not show him the same red man that had driven the hunters mad. She held that back.

He covered his small, trembling chin. "The people will lose their faith if they find their King Ward's will was not strong enough."

"Then we do not tell them," she said. "Shankan died of a sickness."

"Then it is their Healer that failed. I am their Healer!"

"Would you rather it be the King and their Warlord, or you that failed, Olisize?" She rested her hand on his shoulder. "No, we do not think on this yet. Word of the King Ward's death must not go beyond our ears. The people not need know until we decide what to do."

Olisize's hand shook as he rubbed his face. "We are the only Wards here now. Six down to two." In the light of the torch the man looked ancient; the carvings of age down his cheeks were black crevices. He had shaved his beard three years ago and the spindly face that had been revealed was vile and spoke of death.

When he leaned for her, she stepped away.

He said, "Osondrous, you and I both sense that something is coming. And everyone who will not be returning."

She ignored his words. She said, "We leave Shankan where he is for now. No one will stumble upon him down here and the staleness will help preserve his body."

They both knew that she was blatantly lying about the staleness. The mold and wetness of this place would actually have Shankan falling to black and bloated rot very quickly. But Olisize needed time to think and relented with a sad nod. She led the old man forward. They reached her dungeons.

"I hate it in these depths." Olisize cursed under his breath.

"You surprise me, Olisize. Has it not been you who has healed the most gruesome wounds of soul and heart?"

"The souls you and Telenay have tormented here cannot be healed."

"As we had hoped."

The Healer followed in silence. Osondrous led him out of the dungeons, up into the warm light of the castle.

Olisize shook his head. "Your heart has hardened, Osondrous. You were never meant to feel the pain of others."

"And what makes you think that you were?" Her voice sharpened.

"Quiet your tongue, Girl. You know not the words you speak."

"I plan my words carefully, Healer. You had best tread lightly around me."

"I will treat you as I always have, Osondrous. Like a little girl with too much power and not enough experience to know how to use it." He leaned on his staff, impervious to her angry will.

"You have your secrets, Olisize. I see them in your eyes. They mark your soul."

"As do you, Warlord." He sighed. "You are much crueler than you used to be."

13

The cool air brushed her cheeks and Osondrous closed her eyes. She stepped across to one of the pillars of the hall of silence and leaned against the cold stone. She missed Telenay so badly she could barely breathe.

Shankan was dead, beaten by Reapers, darkness worshipers and, that thing, the red man. Their supposed strongest so easily quenched. Telenay should have been granted King Ward status long before Shankan. A warrior should have been the one chosen to lead them. Was the Reapers' plan to destroy all of the Wards? They were weak, only two supporting the foundation of the castle now. If they were killed, Eikian was the only one left to take command. It seemed the coming of the end of the Wards. She felt the darkness like a cape settling over the horizon.

She found Aerick and ordered, "I want the commanding Seconds in the Ring within an hour."

"It will be done." He turned and ran off.

Without Telenay, she found herself a naked branch trembling alone in the winter wind. She retreated back into the confines of her castle. Up the staircase to the second floor and the many empty Ward chambers. She sat before her mirror and stared at the pale face that looked back out at her.

Cheekbones pronounced her features, adding an extreme look to her down-turned eyes. She remembered being called pretty once. She was not pretty anymore. That word was reserved for Healers and women who wanted children. Reserved for those ladies like Karalay.

She went to the Ring after a time, walking with her head down, her eyes dark and with purpose. They were all waiting for her.

There were eighteen in the castle with the rank of Second. And of the eighteen there were ten in full command of each branch of the Wards' army. Three Humans: Aerick and Majeik, in full command of the Human guards and Crik, in full command of the Human archers. Beside them three Centaurs shared the Human guard command: Minre, Prush and Serkin. Then there were the Centaurs: Jeday, Dade, Cray and Eli who held command of the entire army of Centaurs and command of all posted guard duties.

The Centaurs were clean and brushed, their hooves shiny, black and well shod. Their hair was mostly cut short or held tightly back in braids, out of their eyes and faces. She hated to see them this way. Without their war paint, even their tattoos looked tame. And none of them looked at her as though this was where she belonged even as she looked at them in the exact same way. They all belonged in the field, at war, with blood beneath their fingernails and mud and paint hiding the fact that they were mortal. They had all fought together in the Keltch wars.

She spoke directly to Eli, the biggest of the Centaurs besides Eikian. She said, "We will not be training at the castle anymore. I want you to send word to Rayakdool and send any men still in training out there as well."

Eli nodded. "It is done. But why?"

She said, "Also, have them send me the ninth branch of men. Tell him they are trained enough and if he wants to keep one or two of them as Seconds, he can."

Aerick had already begun writing her commands on parchment.

Majeik spoke up, one of the only three Humans, a farmer's boy with lined skin and dark, furrowed brows. "Why will we no longer be training men here at all?"

Her eyes snapped at him. "Because I want the day watches doubled and the night tripled. The distraction of men in training is no longer something we can afford. Understood?"

None of them asked where Eikian was but she could see it in the flickering of the Centaurs' eyes.

Cray stepped forward. "Shall we take down the training courses then,

51

Osondrous?"

She nodded. "Might as well, for now."

They all nodded in agreement.

She said, "All right, that is it for now but hold your guard tighter. If you happen upon anything out of the ordinary, tell me."

Dade asked. "What of the King?"

She bit her tongue a little. "He is still not to be found but I have taken it upon myself. I will find him."

They nodded and began to clear out. When she reached the hall of silence, she noticed Eikian on the parapet, looking their way. She turned aside and headed for her chamber.

Osondrous removed Mlore from her hip. Its length was that from her shoulder to her finger tips and nearly twice the width of her arm. The blade was heavier than any other made, save for Telenay's blade and the sword that Eikian carried. She cleaned the sword, then rested it on the stones before the fire where she bowed to it by getting to her knees and putting her forehead on the floor.

"Thank you, Mlore. For fighting your brother sword and my brother in blood. I shall not forget your willingness at my side."

Khayue and Mlore had been beaten together out of the same metal. Osondrous had first been unable to lift it when she was thirteen. It had never left her side and she grew strong from holding it so close. Mlore was the living testament of her promise as a Warlord. If she broke her promise, it would behead her and when she was dead it would be buried with her. Though all that duty and honor now were little more than superstition.

Osondrous lay down in her bed and looked out her chamber window. In time, she stood and closed the shutters until her room was lit by nothing but fire. She lay back down and drew the blankets to her chin.

She was too young, even too young for being a Warlord, far too young for being a Ward; how ever could she be a queen? Yet, she was special, different. She was a survivor of Cobblestone. She was legendary. She pulled her knees to her chin, closing her eyes. She slept without comfort.

"Ward?" The call permeated her dreams.

"What?" She sat up, still half sleeping.

Aerick called through the door, "The Ambassador of Stonedowner has arrived. We cannot find Shankan and words must be had upon how much wheat we are willing to trade."

She struggled out of bed. "Come in here!"

The Second stepped into the room, eyes averted from her nakedness.

She glared at him, twisting her hair back. "Get me a bottle of brandy. Where is the ambassador?"

"He is waiting in the Ring."

She dressed. "What time is it?" She opened her door.

"Mid-morning."

"Where is Eikian?"

"I do not know."

The Second followed her. Osondrous made her way, scrubbing at her tired, watering eyes. Pausing outside the Ring, she adjusted her clothes until she felt decent and then entered.

"Ambassador?" She was calm. She looked across the room at the two men waiting. Garbed in traveling robes, the eldest of the men glared at her. They were from the old Stonedowner blood. Blond hair, blue eyes, narrow noses and very tall. Their fingers were long and bony.

"I have waited long, Warlord. Where is Shankan?" His voice was low and harsh. He was an elder among his people. The highest ranked of the Stonedowner. Back before, in a time she made no effort to remember, Osondrous had been born a Stonedowner. But no songs had been sung of her within her own people. Her family had been little more than poor farmers with none of the pure Stonedowner blood. There was no pride for her. Instead, Osondrous had been little else but scorned. If she had been a man, things would have been different.

She took a seat. "Do not exaggerate; your wait has not been long. Sit yourselves."

The men stepped up to the table and sat down. As were the traditions of the Stonedowner, the second, younger ambassador would not be speaking. An Implin hurried into the room, tray clutched between his hands, balancing a pitcher and two cups. Osondrous took the tray and poured them brandy.

"I do not desire any." The ambassador shook those long fingers at her. She noted with amusement that there was a resemblance between those long bony hands and the appendages of the Implin.

"Drink some brandy." Osondrous smacked the full cup down in front of him.

She stared at him until he picked it up and took a drink.

"Thank you," he said.

She sat down and took a long drink herself. "Now, Ambassador, how much wheat have we given you for your cheese and milk in earlier years?"

"Seventy thousand bushels . . . Yet, seeing it has been such a prosperous year for the castle in wheat . . . "

"The arrangements previously made will remain. Unless you can prove to me you need more, you will not be granted it."

"I am simply asking for another ten thousand. Our villages are growing."

"Then start eating your goats. You only need one male to keep a hundred females pregnant and milking," she said. "Or start cutting your babies from your women to stop the growth like the Willower are doing."

He winced. Stonedowners had always had as many children as possible, claiming that children were a sign of prosperity and a gift from the Creator. Her words were blasphemy to true Stonedowners and she enjoyed saying them and seeing the ambassadors struggle with their anger.

"We are already eating our male goats, Warlord. Please, we ask for but a bit more."

She gnawed her tongue. "What is your name, Ambassador?"

"I am Lortie, chief adviser to the mayor, Jordan."

"I will think on it. Stay the day and the night and rest yourselves. You are dismissed."

The ambassadors stood, bowing to her before turning away. As they left, his name finally reached her. Years ago, in a message sent by a rider from Stonedowner, a rider who was a servant to one of her many brothers. He had fallen before her in exhaustion and he had reeked of travel and sweat.

The message had been that her eldest brother, Karshack, had been sentenced to death for blasphemy by the chief adviser and chieftain to the mayor, Lortie. She could see that bony finger raise and point at her brother's face, casting the sentence surely in the name of the great God. She had argued for many long hours with Telenay.

Telenay had said, "You can do nothing."

"Nothing? Are you serious? I am going to send a raven tonight. I will not allow them to execute a man for preaching the truth!"

She had heard of Karshack's rantings, had known about his following by the whispers of rumors. She could hear him speak when she closed her eyes and remembered her broad-shouldered and brooding older brother. *"This God you worship is nothing more than the last shred of slavery given to us by the Draegoone!"*

Telenay had roared at her, "If you do that, you will be crucified. Do not be such a stupid woman!"

She had backhanded him them, with all of her rage and her will. She had sent his blood in a long shower across the wall. She had pointed her dagger at him and said, "Say it again, Telenay. Tell me how stupid a woman I am."

Osondrous had sent that raven and had saved her brother's life.

The ambassadors were gone from the Ring and she sat alone. She drank the rest of her brandy, grabbed the pitcher and left the Ring. Outside the door she reached back and rubbed the pounding spot at the back of her head. She leaned back against the wall and closed her eyes. She had expected to see Karshack. He had no reason to stay in Stonedowner. Or she had at least expected to get a message from him. She had saved his life and heard nothing.

"Warlord?"

She jerked awake.

Constance was standing up the hall from her, leaning away, looking very small and timid.

Constance said, "I am sorry to disturb you. I will . . . I will return to you at a later time."

"What do you want, Constance?"

Constance's blue eyes were wide. "Olisize said that you might be willing to help me in becoming a Ward."

"Did he?"

"Yes."

Osondrous locked eyes with her. "And why would I waste my time on a girl that has no power?"

Her will was a deadly force that slipped into the girl. Constance trembled.

The girl turned and hurried away. "I am sorry!"

Osondrous called, "Do you think Wards cry, Constance?"

The girl stopped.

Osondrous pushed herself from the wall. "We do not cry because we do not feel pain, we do not feel jealousy. We do not feel resentment. And why is that?"

Constance did not answer.

She yelled into the girl's delicate, perfect little ear, "Because we are greater than any other on this isle! Do you know why? Because we are the chosen. We are indifferent because we are the jury of fate."

Constance squeezed her eyes shut, leaning away.

Osondrous rolled her eyes. "Get out of my sight."

Constance rushed up the hall.

Tipping back the pitcher, Osondrous drank until it was empty and stumbled to her chamber. She fell into her bed and finally slept.

14
Constance

On the first lower level of the Castle of the Wards, old walls of firestone still lingered. It was always warm. Until the upper levels had been constructed, it had been the main living quarters of the entire castle. Now, it had been sectioned off into tiny servants' quarters. Many lived three to four in a room. Closets had been converted into tiny bed chambers and often, servants would share a bed, one sleeping while the other worked before taking their own turn.

Relhie was one of the eldest of the servants; she was considered a leader among them and had taken in countless young girls who had been orphaned to serve at the castle. She herself had come searching for peace when there had been no work to be found and the winter had seemed so long and food had been very hard to come by.

Relhie had only just fallen asleep when Constance burst through her chamber, ran to her own room with hand over her mouth, sobbing.

"Constance?" Relhie bolted to her feet.

Constance covered her face.

"Constance?" Relhie fell to her knees and put her arms around her. Constance pulled away.

"Oh, Constance, what happened?"

"No!" She scrambled to the wall, eyes red with pain. "I will not cry!"

Relhie stared at her. "You spoke with Osondrous?"

She nodded.

The woman sighed and sat down. "I told you to wait until the time was right. The Warlord's emotions are as varying as the weather and the rumors say she and Eikian have been very put out. You know what I told you: you should have waited until he was with her. Eikian might have helped you."

"I thought I was strong enough." Her voice was muffled by her hands.

"All things are destined, Constance. I believe that. If you are to be a Ward, you will rise on the right day. You cannot force it now."

"Why would anyone want to be a Warlord?" Constance asked.

"It is a knowing that destruction is what you are meant for. So do not

56

hate Osondrous for being particularly cruel; she will know no happiness in her life. Unless it is in giving death and pain. And you know," the woman sighed, "it has been seven years of peace in this land."

Constance squeezed her eyes shut. "How can they live like that?"

Relhie said, "I do not know."

"I want to be happy, Relhie."

"And I want you to be happy."

"I will be welcomed into that ceremony next month . . . Will it hurt, Relhie?"

The woman sighed. "I see now. If you were to rise as a Ward, you would at least avoid that. You will be sixteen next month."

At sixteen, the servant girls were up for pickings to all of the Human Seconds and those captains ranked under them.

Constance said, "Does it ever feel good?"

Relhie said, "Of course."

"I am scared."

"Ahh, but what about Aerick? You do not think he will call on you first?"

Constance blushed fiercely. "I do not know." But at the mere mention of his name, her heart fluttered and her mood improved. If there was any chance that he would be the one to call on her first, then no one outranked him.

Relhie smiled. They were silent for a time.

"When was Osondrous named Ward?" Constance asked.

"The Keltch campaigns began four years after her arrival when they burned the wheat fields. War began and it was four years of war that made her a Ward. Osondrous left a girl and returned a Warlord. She was eighteen."

"Who spoke those words? I have heard them quoted before."

"It is a verse of a song, sung of Osondrous when she returned. I do not know what the wars were like. I only know the rumors. Eikian and Osondrous barely left each other's sides after they returned."

"But, I thought it was treachery for a Human and a Centaur to—"

"Warlords do what they want." Relhie's eyes hardened.

Constance held herself.

Relhie forced the girl's hand into her own and pulled her to her feet. "Come on. We must serve tonight."

Constance did not argue. Serving was the one absolute in her life. She was given food and a warm bed in return for her service. Technically no one at the castle was a true servant. Everyone who served the Wards, including Relhie, came and did it willingly. It was the law that all Wards in training, regardless of power, must work as servants until being named Wards.

They entered the kitchen already filled with cooks and choppers. It was a mass of open fireplaces, set up high and filled with foods. Constance breathed deep the hot, delicious smells. They wrapped on their aprons.

"Has the second guard come yet?" Relhie asked the head cook.

"Yes! And they are hungry!"

Constance was already wiping sweat from her eyes. She had no blood brothers or sisters and when she had worked with her parents to survive, it had meant few-and-far-between meals and endless work that left them stumbling, day after day, in exhaustion. Those were days she tried hard to forget; they did, however, make this work seem good to her.

She grabbed the nearest full tray and hurried out the swinging doors into the murmur of soldiers. Her wintry eyes scanned the tables; finding the fifth bare, she hurried to it and set the tray down to grins and cheers. She hurried back to the kitchen and fetched another until her fingers ached and every table was filled and no soldier called for anything more.

In the corner she saw, where no torches burned, Eikian brooding into a tall cup of brandy. She tiptoed out and wound her way around the tables, avoiding the grabs and strokes offered her way from sly soldiers. She had gotten used to the constant attention her age was bringing her way. Most of the time, the soldiers were harmless. Her eyes remained on the Centaur who never looked up and who sat alone.

"Excuse me?" Her voice was very small.

His hard eyes lifted. "What do you want?"

"I . . . I had . . . had hoped to ask if you might be willing to ask Osondrous to help . . . help me become a Ward."

His deep frown made her cringe. "Have you spoken with Osondrous?"

"Yes."

"And what did she say?" He drank his brandy.

"She said no."

"That is my answer." His cup of brandy smacked the table with a bang; his tail swished.

She hurried away, face flushed. The hands of a soldier met her. One hand slid up between her legs. It was Marcus. His eyes were black and slitted under a hooded brow. His breath stank and his fingers were hard, jabbing points. This was not the first time he had done this.

"Let me go!" She struggled in his arms and he grinned into her face.

The soldiers around them pointed and laughed. His tongue entered her ear, a slippery eel drilling deeper and deeper.

"Marcus!" The boom echoed from wall to wall and silenced the dining room.

Marcus stopped, frozen.

Eikian growled, "She told you to let her go."

She snatched herself away and rushed to the kitchen. Marcus returned to his table, laughing it off. His comrades smacked him on the back.

Into his brandy, Marcus said, "She tasted damn good."

15

Relhie grabbed her and gave her a hard hug. "Easy now. Think about Aerick; maybe he will be the one next month. Maybe he will command it that you never be a servant again!"

Constance laughed, her eyes red and wet. Relhie kissed her cheek but had to return to the crockery.

Constance slid down the wall. None noticed her small, hunched frame. The mention of Aerick banished Marcus from her thoughts. The last time she had spoken to Aerick, he had smiled at her in a way that no soldier had ever looked at her. His eyes had been shining and sweet. He was masculine and lean. Of the line of highest ranked people at the castle, right now, Aerick was in the top twenty. Shankan was first, then the other Wards, then Eikian, then the Warlords' eighteen Seconds. Aerick was one of those and one of only three Human Seconds.

He had said to her, "May be I will see you soon?"

And it had been a question, not a command, and her heart had quivered and skipped.

She had barely been able to say, "Of course."

And he had asked, "Would you like that?"

She had been left dumbfounded, staring at him with her mouth open. "I would really like that."

And then he had given her that smile.

That had been two days ago and she had not seen him since, except in her mind. She had replayed the scene over and over again. The fact of her turning sixteen had been the one most prevalent thing that occupied her every waking moment. *Today I am another day closer to being laid out naked for any Second that wants me.* She half-hoped one of the Centaurs would take pity on her and call her first. But she knew better. Karalay had appealed to Centaurs when she had turned sixteen; no one had questioned her nights spent with Centaurs until she had become a Ward.

Constance had not been so lucky.

The Centaurs were more careful than ever and the mature Seconds would not put themselves in a position to be accused of having a servant girl. Thank the skies that the barbarians like Marcus had never been ranked higher than foot soldiers.

Thinking of Aerick made her hands tremble and she blushed fiercely into her palms. There was a large part of her that chastised herself. Tried to convince herself that Aerick had only been fooling with a naive little girl. But her heart fluttered with hope, unable to quell her thinking of his gorgeous eyes.

A tap came to the outside of the kitchen door; she did not move. The tap continued and finally she lifted her head and turned.

"Constance?" Aerick stepped into the kitchen.

She gaped at him, then scrambled to her feet, her hands over her cheeks to clear the lines of tears. She twitched to right her dress and fix her hair. The Second cocked his head at her, eyes narrowing as they walked slowly up and down her body. She blushed violently.

"I heard what you asked Eikian."

She shook her head.

"Today was not a good day to approach either of them." He stood with his muscle-laden forearms crossed.

She squeaked, "Well, that is obvious now."

He moved in closer and her heartbeat leaped into her throat.

He whispered in her ear, "Meet me somewhere tonight?"

She gaped at him.

He laughed and his white smile spread. "Graveyard at dark?"

She held it together long enough to nod.

He left.

She leaned back on the wall and grinned.

Relhie smoothed by. "Told you."

The giggles flooded out of her throat.

"Boys still need to be fed!" Relhie called.

Constance got herself back to work but she barely felt her feet touch the ground.

Osondrous tossed and turned in her bed, hot as hell with a room that she had let go very cold. The nightmares had awakened her. She sat up and looked into the blackness, the only light from the last red embers of her little fire. She took a deep breath and rubbed her head.

It was all bloody gray grasses as far as she could see. It was Cobblestone.

She ran from her chamber as if it were killing her. Osondrous went down the silent halls and the stairs to the next floor, the floor of the Seconds. Eikian's was the first door and she slipped into it like water returning to a river. The door shut behind her and he sat up in the light of his fire.

Osondrous pulled off her shift so she could be as naked as he was. So she could be like him. Be as close alike to a Centaur as possible.

She spoke in his Centaur language, "How mad could I be?"

"I wondered this time." He spoke in his language, too, and it sounded right to them both.

His hands were spread out on the blanket that covered half of him. She crossed the distance slowly, filling up the empty expanse of stone before leaving it bare and cold again. She held her cold chest, wet with sweat and chilled now to the blood. She shrugged when she reached the bed and nudged his hind hoof that had slipped off the straw mattress. It was clean and black and very hard. He nudged her smooth bare thigh right back, leaving a white imprint of the bottom of his hoof.

"So, come here."

She shook her head. "I hate bed."

He sat up, ran his hand back through her hair and it fell against her shoulders and neck in a damp, curly sweep.

"I can make you."

She rolled her eyes.

He smiled a little but, like all of his smiles, it never reached his eyes; it was just habit. Habit from days living with Centaurs, with happy things and a good life. A life lived before this one, before he was reborn in Cobblestone, right beside her. The rings were deep under his hazel eyes and she knew the nightmares were getting worse for him, too.

Osondrous sighed herself down on the edge of the bed. He grabbed her and pulled her back. He lay down and she smoothed over him, across his animal and his Human half. The blanket stayed between them.

"Forgive me?" He spoke right into her ear and the warmth of his breath felt safe and good.

She said, "What is to forgive?"

17
Jezaline

Jezaline was racing over the cracked earth in cotton sandals. Tears were threatening her and closing her lungs. The brilliant blue sky was marked only by the boiling sun. She had lived in Willower her entire life and always on the farthest edges of civilization, where the sand dunes drew closer every year. The desert sun whipped her dress against her ankles. She ran until there was no home behind her, she ran until the sand surrounded her and her eyes were filled with the red, red, red heat of everything she had ever known.

Jezaline was sixteen and this was the day that dictated her future in its entirety. This was the day that made all other days in her life become pale and distant. Holidays, horses, playing and living and working on her family's ranch. Evaporated. Their importance diminished in comparison to this one moment.

Her father had said, "You have been promised to the son of the Berchess family. We are lucky. It is an honor for them to want you."

And she had stared in incomprehension. *What? What are you talking about, Daddy? You can not mean to send me away? What have I done? What? What? What?*

She was an excellent horsewoman; this she had thought would be her future. Breeding and training the stunning black-skinned horses that her family had raised for six generations. This is why they had migrated to such a harsh place, right on the edges of civilization where the wild horse lands bordered the Human.

He said, "It is an honor for them to want you." As if she were not desirable in any way and they were lucky anyone could ever want her.

She stood beneath the arid desert sun, face turned up to its fire, arms out, hands turned up as though to catch it. She had never been aware of her gender so deeply. Her throat closed and she began to sob. Every hour, moment and second she had spent of her life in that barn, learning to be the greatest horsewoman of all time. None of it mattered. There were only horsemen. She was a woman. A girl built and good for only one thing.

She had managed to speak only a little to her father before he had left. "But Grandpa said. . ."

"What your grandfather said is irrelevant!" And his face had turned red in fury. "You will honor this family!"

Her grandfather had said that she was one of the greatest trainers of all time, far beyond any of the men of their family. Her grandfather had adored her. His death last year was still working its waves down, affecting her life still. She knew Grandpa would not have let this happen to her. She knew he would have called this a waste.

She had said all of these things to her mother, hands out. "Mom! I belong with the horses, not married to some city man. How . . . How can he—"

"You shut your mouth, Girl. You are a woman, this is your duty to this family. You should be happy."

And Jezaline had run, feeling as though she were dreaming. Dropped off the land in the night and awakening to find everyone she thought she had known were strangers in her own home. And it was not her home anymore either. It was her father's home.

But he could not take the desert from her and she looked into the murky horizon and thought that she would walk into that and vanish. That would be a better end than to lose her life to childbirth or in servitude of a man. She had run and run and run.

The sun burned the back of her neck despite how her skin was dark already from hours a day outside in it. It was at the height of the day and the boiling reflection of the sun off the sand began to make her dizzy. She stumbled back to her feet and went west, knowing of the river running through the dunes of their ranch.

It was there, marked by palms and rugged desert cacti. She hurried to the clean water and crystal cold shade that waited for her. All of her life was set aside for desperate physical needs. Water. Shade. Coolness.

He picked his head up though she did not see him, her eyes so filled with the river.

When she reached the first palm and the second, her exhausted feet stumbled and she slowed. She blinked rapidly. He waited for her on the other side, water dripping down his chin, up to his knees in the rushing water.

She stopped still and stared.

There were still wild southern horses living in the desert. She had caught glimpses of them in her life, while with her own horses. Wild mares would visit the outskirts of their property and touch noses with their captive sisters.

She had never seen a wild stallion before, though.

If the desert was the color of fire, then this horse was the color of embers. He was a shade deeper red than she had ever seen on a horse. His color, in the light of the sun, was dazzling. They stood for a long time staring at each other. His delicate ears pricked, his nostrils quivered wide, nose in the air, catching her scent. He took a step toward her.

She took a step toward the river, toward him and all thoughts of cool water and shade slipped from her mind until there was nothing there but him.

He was on her side of the river and she did not see him take all of the steps. He was before her, brilliant red stallion of the desert, reaching for her. She was incapable of being cautious, of wondering that this was very strange behavior for a wild animal, any wild animal. His delicate muzzle was extended and she could feel his nicker on her eardrums, so deep. She was overcome with want to touch his brilliant red coat.

His muzzle pressed into her shoulder, her fingers slipped up beneath his mane. His coat was unblemished and smooth and she looked into his black eyes as he breathed. She could not look away. Jezaline's legs were paralyzed. She pulled back and did not move. She heard his nicker and it changed, no longer the sound of a horse.

Something else made that sound.

It could have been the throaty laugh of a man much older than she was.

She gasped in panic.

The muzzle felt like a hand; it circled over her shoulder and then slipped up to surround her neck. Jezaline opened her mouth to scream and she could not. The eye of the horse grew until all she could see was vast shiny blackness. She felt herself lowered and knew she was laid out on the ground. The smell of the stallion evaporated; her nose filled with the smell of burning. It grew so hot she could taste it in the back of her throat.

Her eyes cleared and, laying between her legs, supported with his hands on her arms, was a man. His skin was the color of the stallion's coat. The definition of red. He was bare naked, hairless and his eyes were essentially black. He looked into Jezaline's face and spoke something she never heard. She felt the rock between her legs. He shifted and she felt it against the fabric of the dress. Thin summer cotton, the only thing stopping him from penetrating her and breaking her open.

She was a virgin. She was finally able to scream.

Her stricken sound carried out from the shade of the palms and echoed across the dunes where it vanished in the heat without ever being heard by any living thing.

He attacked her, covered her scream with his wide open mouth. Her mouth filled with fire and her eyes opened wide in the realization that losing her chastity in a rape may not be the worst thing that could happen to her. She held her breath, pushing back, coughing, heaving into his mouth.

Nothing stopped the fire.

It poured down her throat.

She held her breath to stop it. But she had to breathe, had to scream; her body convulsed for air.

She gasped.

The fire filled her nose, coursed into her lungs. The boiling thing reached her heart and detonated. He uncovered her scream and it raised louder than any noise or terror she had ever made before in her life. She screamed and screamed the death howl that became no longer the noise from a Human but that of an animal making its last noise of life. When it escaped and finally dwindled and her throat was a highway of pain, her arms were around him and her hands spread out over his solid shoulders. His face was turned into her neck and his body was as still as it was stiff.

Jezaline gasped and the thing between her legs was as hard as rock still and it was all she knew, it was all she understood.

"Hurry!" Her voice had changed; now warped by pain, it was the deeper tone of a real woman. She pawed at him with the fierceness not of a child, but the passion of someone much older.

She said, "Finish it! Do it!" She moaned for him, clawed at her dress, pulling it up, revealing the body still of a sixteen-year-old girl. That part of her was pink, delicate, the place between her legs veiled still by the fine hair of a child.

Nothing could stop them now.

She demanded it. Her head snapped back against the sand as he pulled her apart with his fingers. Her farm hands dug into his shoulders and left long, jagged scratches across his back. His shaft of dark red forced into her and splashed into the solid wet cave of Jezaline.

He went slow, but she did not know it. Her mouth opened and she breathed the fire. Her eyes closed and she drank the fire. When he was all the way in and adjusted and comfortable and she was holding him as tight as she could, she became the fire. The fire opened her up all the way, spread her apart, filleted her like a fish.

Jezaline began to cry and he held her as she worked him with her hips. Incapable of anything now, she was pure instinct; her body trembled and she shook against his chest. When it happened, she was a girl for one last instant and she saw the blue sky. As she watched, as the fire reached the tips of her fingers and the tips of her toes and the delicate pinkness that had been her body had become redder and darker than him with blood, the sky changed. It blurred with her tears and then it warped completely and she screamed into his shoulder, then bit down as her climax hit its height. Her mouth filled with his blood and it tasted cooked, burned over an open fire for days.

Her scream became a moan and changed as the sky changed, as her world changed. She was fire and when she had thought it would be too hot to bear, when the wave worked the scream from her throat, she found she could take the pleasure and not be burned alive. She found she wanted more.

18

Jezaline had ridden on through the last village, not remembering or caring about its name or any of the people in it. It was special only because it was the last one, the last chance of a real meal on a real plate, on a real table, the last chance to sleep in a real bed.

They had followed the protected road for a week, stopping at every other village along the way. Telenay had been the creator of the protected roads that split their land and connected the Humans. Each village helped staff the towers built by the Wards along the way. The towers chased off the scrub wolves and numerous other predators.

She had not expected to be gone from the villages and the protected roads for more than two days; the prophet's house was not far. But looking at the houses and the faces, feeling the road beneath Carmin's hooves, it felt as though it was going to be much longer than two days. She had been called by the prophet, Tarrick, to come to him for he had a premonition he needed to tell her in person. Not stupid enough (or smart enough depending on how things turned out) to ignore it, she left with four Centaurs in tow as her guardians.

She was looking out over the black river with her horse beneath her and she was glad to be away from the other Wards. This was the first time she had thought of the castle since she left.

It was not surprising that the river inspired these thoughts.

She looked out on the darkness of it and felt a shiver down her spine. The river was an atrocity on the landscape, a straight cut of blackness that rolled and moved as though it were thick and gurgling. It was not natural and it was one of two that split their island into thirds. The Humans were in the center, the other creatures taking their places apart. This was the power of the rivers, the shocking truth that they killed any creature that tried to pass, except for Humans and Centaurs.

Its eastern brother sat right beside the Human capital, Diggamara. Seeing the river at the western border of their Human lands, she felt very far west. As far west as possible, actually, without crossing. The rivers were a product of war. The rivers were cast by the very first Ward, Lionel, and they had ended the war. Humans then were just servants, willing to work in all manner of horrors to survive. The Fai were an offshoot of Humans, winged beasts that had slowly gained momentum and power across their land to the east. In the west, the Draegoone were descendants of the dragon and had learned that Humans made excellent workers and, in a pinch, were not bad eating.

The two powers worked their way to the center of their land, taking the Human villages as prisoners. Jezaline had been told stories of the evilness of the Draegoone and the Fai. How no one believed that there had been any Humanity in any of it. The Humans were on the brink of either complete extinction or slavery.

At first one city did keep its independence. Diggamara. So close to the Elves of the forest of Addilade that even the Draegoone and the Fai hesitated. But it was the Draegoone that longed for the riches in the mines beneath Diggamara. They sent an army to its gates under the insignia of treaties and talking of peace. The army sent had not been Draegoone but yet another cousin to the Human, the Vamepire.

What happened in the fair city of Diggamara after the army was allowed to enter was what began the war. Whether it had been a cross word, or the Vamepire had been impossible to negotiate with—it just never mattered how it started. But the slaughtering of Diggamara was heard across the land. The Draegoone had tried to reconcile, tried to claim that the Vamepire had not followed their orders, that the slaughtering had not been intentional.

None of it mattered. The Fai King with his many generals sat salivating for war, wanting what the Draegoone claimed was theirs. And it had begun, not in a small squabble, but in an all-out uprising, Fai against Draegoone, with Humans dying between them.

The very first Ward, Lionel, had been watching the blood of his Human people run down every single street. Jezaline did not know the depth of the history here now. This was the mystery of the starting of the Wards. Lionel had been tremendously gifted as a Ward. He was able to get his hands on a Fai Crystal of power. With it and his will, he ended the war by conjuring the rivers of poison, exempting all but Draegoone, Fai and Vamepire. She knew Karalay had devoted many years of her life to what happened next, as many scholars had done before her. Lionel just disappeared. The Castle of the Wards had stood deserted for many months.

The river before her should have made her glad, should have been the monument to the beginning of Wards. The monument to five hundred years of Humans living free. But she still frowned for, it seemed to her, it was not so unlike running blood.

As she watched, a large green butterfly crossed over the water and fluttered casually in the breeze. But the butterfly quickly left and there were no insects to hear near this thing, no singing insects, no cicadas or crickets. As she realized the silence, her horse took an uneasy step back and Jezaline's casualness faltered into true unease. She turned Carmin around and they moved quickly back into the town.

His hooves hit the rock-paved street. Ahead a group of men erupted in laughter. Barefoot kids ran by, emerging from their little shacks, scrubbed and clean after dinner. The town was made up of an inn, a blacksmith, stable and one tavern.

Servants waited for her behind the inn, five boys wearing rags the color of mud.

"We will see to your stallion."

She never looked at them. "None of you could ever be clean enough to see to this horse."

She rode him into the largest empty stall in the straw-roofed barn. Like most of the buildings in this part of the country, everything but the roof was stone. Trees were hard to come by around here.

She unsaddled and unbridled her stallion and he shook himself contentedly. She brought him grain and hay, then picked up a brush and began rubbing him down.

His skin was black and thin, his mane and tail wispy and waving. In his age, he was fading from black to the color of a storm. After a bite, he turned his attention to her hands as she brushed, then to her cheek when she smiled at him.

He stepped his chest against her chest and put his head down her back. This they did every night and Jezaline patted his smooth skin and smelled his wonderful, hot smell. She lingered for a time. The servants peeked in, in awe at her large breasts as they pressed against the horse. Their faces were stark with envy of the horse.

The inn's main room was dark and damp with wet stone walls. At the bar, her four Centaurs were leaning. Sethian was the captain and he stepped to her side immediately. He was the color of slate. As he tried to move delicately around the close-set tables and chairs, he looked like he was dancing. She stifled a chuckle.

"How is the drink?"

He shrugged. "Same thing in every town. Some kind of corn alcohol."

"Good enough."

He followed her to the bar.

A man was wiping down the beer-splattered counter. When he saw her, he froze.

She said, "Do you have food?"

His eyes filled with the sight of her. Ward of high power with breasts hiked tightly above a corset of lace and a skirt of velvet. Her hair was a black sweep of night sky, framing her cool skin. Her eyes glowed as only pure-blooded Willower women's eyes could; they were shocking emeralds.

The bartender's wide face turned burgundy; he opened his mouth and stuttered unintelligibly.

Sethian translated, "They have rabbit stew and flat bread."

She shrugged. "Bring some for everyone and I want a cup of anything."

The bartender hurried away.

She turned to her other three Centaur guardians: Quadick, Derkay and Ajax. They raised their glasses at her and grinned. Their gleefulness was contagious and, though this was her first time with Centaurs, she was beginning to understand why Human men hated them so.

The bar door opened and they squinted. Shepherds herded in, eyes weary and lined beneath wide-brimmed hats. Staffs of wood were black against their rough palms. They were local and stopped instantly at the sight of Centaurs. One man's lips moved. *Savages.*

Her Centaurs raised their mugs and cheered.

Jezaline's eyes narrowed blackly. She saw the shepherds' minds turning to the malice of prejudice. She took a step forward and Sethian stopped her.

"Does not matter," he said.

She could see those men brought to their knees beneath her will, apologizing for ever considering such thoughts. This was the first time she had been out of the castle since she had become a Ward. She had had no idea how hard this was going to be. Two days ago she had almost killed a peasant when she, without his permission, had seen in his mind hateful things toward her Centaurs. Sethian had only just stopped her then, too.

Sethian patted her back and they silently watched the shepherds rush out of the bar. The three Centaurs behind her swigged their drinks.

She looked at Sethian and spoke in his mind, *I hate them.*

He said, "They are ignorant. Not their fault."

She snapped, "It is still their choice."

Servants brought trays of food and there was quiet for a time while the Centaurs ate. She was on her third drink before they cleaned their plates for the last time. Full and weary, they were quieter tonight than they had been, or maybe it was because of the river running not far away. She doubted they would stay too close to it tomorrow; she hoped they would keep it out of sight.

The stable boys' hands had not been clean enough to touch her horse but Jezaline took them to bed with her later. It was midnight when she cleaned up and washed.

She had a last drink and was feeling irreversibly tipsy when Sethian stumbled into the room. Earlier in the day, while Jezaline had dallied by the river, the Centaurs had had the Human bed removed from the room and replaced it with a bed big and low enough for a Human and a Centaur. Now Sethian fell down beside her. The bed hopped and bucked before settling with the smell of straw.

Jezaline was slipping into a lucid place she rarely found while drunk. Even as her vision swirled and moved, she felt very focused, very awake.

"You are a bit late," she slurred.

"Sorry." With great effort he raised his head and smiled at her.

She said, "Get up here."

He clawed and shifted his mass forward, until his head was on the pillow at her hip and she was looking down at him.

Sethian napped for a time, then woke up with a start.

"Are you all right?" he asked, spilling out a wave of tangy alcohol breath.

She turned his face away. "Yes."

He smiled again and his hand found hers. He held it to his mouth.

There had not been a night in the past years of her life that Jezaline had slept alone. The older she got, the worse the night terrors had been stalking her. Sleep was not a luxury for Jezaline but she had found that the presence of another, and a candle left burning, helped greatly. Sethian had been her bed companion on this trip. She took no moral ground when it came to who she felt like sleeping with. A man's hot body comforted her to such an extent that, as the years passed, she had lost any semblance of guilt for her ways.

She took his hand and spread it out over her flat stomach, tracing the fingers and rough surfaces of his big knuckles. They both watched, mesmerized as their awareness drifted in and out, and the blurs and the doubling of his hand made everything seem unreal. His fingers brushed the underside of Jezaline's ample left breast. She released the tie on her silk robe and pulled it open. Every luxurious pink curve of her revealed, Sethian gawked.

He said, "Is there something you want of me, Ward?"

Jezaline could have commanded anything and Sethian would have done it but Jezaline wanted something he could not give. Why she had revealed her bareness to him, she did not know but would feel no shame or embarrassment later for this or for anything else she ever did. There was something left inside of her. An empty ache that she spent the vast majority of her days ignoring. It was men that she had desperately taken to try and fill it, but no man ever could for long. A Centaur could do little but keep her company.

"I just want you to stay with me tonight." She rolled onto her side, into him, held his hand tightly and found herself crying.

Sethian's eyes widened. "Why are you crying?" He held her just like any Centaur would hold a crying woman.

When she got control of herself and she had returned to her back, they lay in silence. Jezaline was drifting on liquor, Sethian watching her beautiful breasts rise and fall.

She said, "Have you ever wanted me?"

"I want you right now."

Sethian would not remember any of this. She knew she was looking at the blank eyes of a Centaur who had passed out a long time ago.

"How do you want me? With all of you?"

"With every part of me that is a man, I want you. It ends at the waist."
His voice was sad, even annoyed. "I wish I could be a man for a night. For
you." She laughed because she knew it was not true and he grimaced.
"Lying to a Ward is stupid."

She said, "You would rather die than be a man. Even for a night."

"You are right."

"I have seen the servants touch you."

His eyes widened. "No."

"Yes, they do. The girls like you, Sethian, because you are big and
handsome and a captain. The Seconds just ignore them . . . But not the
captains . . . Not you."

He did not say anything.

She said, "Do you like it?"

They were both watching his hand again, resting now between her bare
breasts, clutched in both of Jezaline's hands.

"It feels kind of . . . bad. Like I shouldn't let them, even if they seem to
like it. I wish they would just let me touch them. That is all I want."

She was silent for a long time, staring at the ceiling as the night passed
too quickly. She wondered if she would remember any of this. If she were
dreaming all of this.

"Would you like to touch me?"

He was quiet so long she thought he was sleeping but when she looked
over at him she found he was chewing his lip, looking down to avoid the
sight of her breasts.

He said, "You are the most beautiful woman I have ever seen."

She covered her breasts and the rest of her body. "I am sorry."

He looked sad, looked into her face and sighed. "I apologize, Ward, for
speaking out of my rank."

"You call me Jezaline." She rolled into him. The fire had gone down and
a breeze pushed through the window; she shivered. He covered her with a
blanket and held her like he had held Jezaline every night.

"Tell me you want me," she whispered.

He said, "I want you."

"How do you want me?"

"With every Human part that I have. I want you."

"Say it again."

"I want you." He rubbed her back.

Feeling loved, Jezaline could sleep.

They woke with no recollection of what was said or done the night before. They both feared the worst, though neither would admit to it. Jezaline was beginning to wonder if maybe she needed to stop sleeping with Centaurs. Sethian wondered how the hell he managed to get to her chamber in the first place because his memories stopped somewhere between the bar and the hallway. They had no idea that they had had a similar conversation every night they had slept together for the last week.

Sethian got up first. He went out back and laid his head on a tree, stretched out and peed for so long he fell asleep. The racket of the servants and horses on the street woke him. He rubbed his face and head. When he returned, he heard her moan. He gazed down at the wonderful warm place beside her. She and the bed both still held his shape. His head ached blindingly.

She said, "Come back."

"It is late."

"Come back now."

"Well, if you order it, I cannot deny your orders." He sank down into that place and she wrapped her arms around his waist. Her body was cold and wet with sweat. He had never told her how her screams had often woken him since the beginning of their journey.

This part he did remember and Jezaline's morning ritual, no matter how much she drank the night before, was always the same. Once she was awake she could not return to sleep and she was awake now, whether she was aware of it or not. While he waited for her, Sethian napped with one hind leg and his tail hanging off the bed, trying to keep cool as the morning sun began to heat the room. Inevitably he started to smell like a horse.

Jezaline smiled. "Smells like a barn."

He woke up. "Uhnn?"

"Need to get up."

"Yuh . . . "

She stretched and her smooth hard length beside him woke him up totally. His head felt marginally better. Cautiously she approached a sitting position, one hand out before her as though her head were a giant ball of glass.

"I really do not want to lose my supper." She talked to herself.

Her robe had fallen open and from his position he could see the side of her left breast. For some reason the sight did not seem remarkable to him, though it was certainly the first time he had had a peek, or so he thought.

He said, "I can see your breast."

She snatched her robe closed and snarled, "You are a bastard!" There was a cup of water beside the bed; she slowly got herself over to it and drank it down. "Go get them up. We need to get out of here."

He did as he was told.

It always impressed the Centaurs how capable Jezaline was, both drunk and hungover. She had herself packed, dressed and Carmin brushed and tacked up and was waiting at the gate before any of them were finished rubbing the sleep from their eyes. They stumbled up to her and she raised an eyebrow at them.

"You are all too slow for my taste."

Sethian bowed to her. "We will make better haste from now on, Jezaline." He was smirking.

She kneed Carmin into the street.

Behind them, Jezaline heard the servants and bar men talking. "They are nothing but savage dogs!"

She looked at Sethian to see if he had heard. He grinned at her.

"Does it not bother you what they say?"

The other Centaurs were close enough that they listened to her.

Sethian said, "Every one of those men would give up every child, every woman in their lives to be in my position with you, right now." He took her hand and kissed it. All of the Centaurs whooped and grinned back at the men standing in the street, watching. The men glared and hurried out of sight.

She was powerless to stop her smile.

19

Jezaline had stumbled from the desert, her skin parched and desperate for water. Her lips were cracked and red. But her thirst was fully quenched and she was smiling. She reached the ranch yard and the horses smelled something that scared them. They snorted, whinnied and shifted in their pens and the horses in the barn began to kick their stalls with solid panicked thuds.

Her father came running from the house, her mother following. They carried torches and clubs and Jezaline stood still as their light reached her.

They saw their little girl smeared heavily in something that looked like blood and smelled like death. Her mouth was covered in it, her hands and dress were soaked. Between her legs was the wettest of all.

74

They stared with horror.

Her mother gasped. "What happened?"

Jezaline continued to grin and it was ghastly.

Her mother was frightened. "Jezaline?"

Her father said, "What happened to you?"

They approached together, cautiously clutching each other's arms. She saw the fear in their eyes and listened to their scared thoughts. She had never been able to hear thoughts before. Never had a will to press on other people before this moment. She used it and she saw the gold handed in great big bags to her father as he promised her hand in marriage. Jezaline threw her head back and laughed. Her parents recoiled and the horses' whinnies reached ear-shattering noise.

She put out her hand and yelled, "Enough!"

The horses grew still and silent.

Her parents' eyes grew large and they gasped. She walked around them and went into the house. In her room, her basin was still full from the night before. She slipped down into the cold water and closed her eyes and her mind was filled with him.

Jezaline answered no questions. Her parents probed with concern at first and then annoyance and then anger.

Her father had roared, "How dare you disrespect me!"

Jezaline had laughed long and hard at him. She lifted her fist and covered his mouth from across the room, cut off his air until his face turned red and he clawed at his throat.

She said, "I will not respect a man who would sell his own daughter."

His eyes widened in panic before she let him breathe again.

She stood over him. "I am a Ward, you stupid old man. You should feel honored."

Jezaline would have let him be and left.

He had pointed at her back from the floor and screamed, "You are never welcome here again! You are not my daughter. I have no children."

She turned and went at him to kill him. She pressed out her will and encircled his arrogant heart. She felt every little heartbeat, heard his wavering life slipping away and grinned.

"Stop!" Her mother dove between them, covered his body with her own and begged, "Just go, Jez. Please do not do this! You can do whatever you want now; you have the power, do not let it be this."

She let go and he drank the air in with long hard wails. Her mother cried and Jezaline shook her head at the tears that fell down the woman's cheeks.

"Duty then," Jezaline sneered. "A woman's duty, huh?"

She paced away and then back.

She fell to her knees before her mother, her hands up, shaking and begging. "Let me kill him, Mom! Let me! Duty is no way to live."

The woman with the same hair and eyes as Jezaline turned away from her daughter. "There is no other way."

20

Carmin walked lazily beneath her. She rubbed his neck and he glanced at her from the corners of his eyes.

The Centaurs had been holding up a constant commentary for the last day, even more than usual now that they were getting closer to the prophet. They were finally rounding the last turn of their journey. Jezaline was having a hard time holding back her anxiety. She was not scared but she was nervous. She had no idea what to expect. A small part of her wished they could continue out here in the middle of nothing forever.

"The prophet chooses his home practically under the eaves of the forest of Everdale, in the middle of nothing but grass and rock," Sethian said.

"What could he be living on?" Derkay asked.

Ajax approached a hill ahead of them and mounted it, his hooves taking him to the top. They bridged the hill and stopped beside him. For the first time since the last village, they could see the river again. The cabin was hacked into a hill; its roof boasted the grass and shrubs that grew there. The windows were lit with single candles. They caught the sight of movement and one of the candles was blown out, the other snatched from the sill.

Jezaline frowned. Carmin followed the Centaurs down toward the home.

The closer they stepped, the more the night was silenced by the river.

They stopped before the house.

The front door opened. The candle lit a woman's face that was very still and cold. She was slender and short. She stepped out and held a moth-eaten shawl close against the chill.

The woman said, "The Ward Jezaline has come."

Jezaline dropped from Carmin's back and dipped her head. "I am Jezaline, Ward of high power and these Centaurs are my guardians. I was

76

told to seek out the prophet that lives here."

Jezaline was probing with her will.

The woman spoke into her mind, *Wards used to respect privacy.* She blocked Jezaline out entirely.

Jezaline's blood ran cold. This creature had will, not as much as a Ward, but will nonetheless. She had no idea what this little female was and it disturbed her.

Seriousness marred all prettiness from the female's face. "I am Cousai. My home is large enough for you all and the stallion can be left out back."

Jezaline glanced at the Centaurs. Carmin glared at the woman before Quadik led him away.

They stepped inside after her and Cousai lit the kindling in the fireplace.

Cousai held out her thin hand. "Come. Please, warm yourself beside my fire."

Jezaline pushed her hood back and sat down on the wooden bench under the window.

Jezaline said, "Where is the prophet?"

Cousai frowned and something flickered in her eyes: fear, worry. Jezaline watched closely.

"I know not when Tarrick will return. His journey took him to the Krept."

"That cannot be."

"Yes, he left over a month ago. He was asked for."

"By whom?"

"I cannot say." Cousai stared at her, unblinking.

Jezaline pressed, annoyed. "You can say."

"He told me to say no more of it; as his love I will do as he asks."

She glared at the woman. "He sent word for me to meet him here."

"I am sorry. He did ask for your presence. He states that if you return to the Castle of the Wards, you will be killed and that your journey lies elsewhere."

"Elsewhere? Tell me, Cousai, where is this elsewhere that you so lightly speak? Would I, a Ward, be to walk across this island until you tell me to stop?"

The woman looked at her, eyes frowning down the bridge of her narrow nose. "There is nothing more I have to say to you. I do not have much extra food but downstairs will keep you warm and out of the wind."

The woman lifted a bucket of water and dumped it over the fire. The room sizzled; flames flickered to black. Jezaline went to Sethian. They followed the ring of light from Cousai's single candle. She led them down narrow steps.

The basement held nothing but shelves along all the walls, bare except for dust and a few clay pots. A fireplace was in one corner with old firewood left parched in its mouth.

Cousai immediately left them and Jezaline frowned after her.

Sethian untied the pack strapped to his body and dropped it to the ground with a grunt. The other three did the same and Ajax lit the fire. They stretched out their beds in the flickering light.

"We cannot go back to the castle." Sethian lay down beside her.

Jezaline said, "We know not if she is speaking the truth."

Ajax agreed. "She is far too strange to take as being honest."

"It is something else," Sethian said. "I cannot be the only one to have noticed her posture, the way she moved?"

Jezaline stared at the fire.

Sethian said, "There is a prophet, his name is Tarrick. I have heard too many rumors of him for him not to exist. All say he lives here. Perhaps he was called to the Krept and his love stayed behind for such a journey is wrought with danger. It would make sense that she would be left behind with condolences to Jezaline."

"Come, we are all tired. Let us rest awhile." She reached up and unclasped her cloak. The heavy fabric fell with a thud, joining the sounds of the Centaurs shifting their heavy frames to sleep. She slipped beneath the many blankets of her bed and closed her eyes but did not sleep. She lay in silence as the Centaurs settled. Jezaline would let the Centaurs talk because there was just no way to shut them up. She already knew more than they had guessed. The woman had not always kept her guard up perfectly and Jezaline had gathered that this was no Human, nor was she even a normal Fai. This was a royal Fai trying to disappear. How she came to be a lover of Tarrick the Prophet or to even be in the middle realm, Jezaline did not know.

21

Jezaline had tried to make a life for herself in the capital city of Willower. She was pure-blooded Willower and her family name was known. It was not hard to find work and a living. And with her will now,

Jezaline took full advantage of what she was capable of. She found herself able to influence how people thought of her, how much people wanted to give her and soon enough, she had everything she had ever wanted.

Except a life with the horses, of course.

She argued with herself that this at least was a life she had chosen. This at least was not bent over in servitude of a man. In fact, Jezaline now had two of her own servants. Both were men and every time she commanded them to do her bidding, she felt herself chanting, *Take that, Daddy. Take that.* And the village believed that she was a real Ward, born with the will. And every moment of every single day, she became more and more convinced that it was true.

Her father actually had awakened her will by infuriating her to a place she had never gone emotionally before. The memory of the red man and the fire was the hallucination of the desert that had claimed so many people. By the time months had passed, the red man was only in her nightmares and in the empty place he had left in her chest. A place she learned to live with, a place she learned was only a part of her and not something taken. She never once allowed herself to consider that maybe she was no longer whole. Maybe the red man had been real, maybe he had taken something and maybe he had given her this will of a Ward for a reason.

She allowed the red man to become her repeating nightmare, learned ways to sleep anyway and she coped and convinced herself entirely: she was born a Ward.

But none of it could eliminate her yearning to return to the horses. Until she had left, Jezaline had spent every waking moment on the horses, with the horses, talking to the horses.

She missed them.

Eventually the local constable of the city heard about her influence. She found out that a group of soldiers from the Castle of the Wards had been sent to investigate. The constable described her as a thief behind her back and Jezaline supposed it was not entirely inaccurate. She was able to slip away in time and she went in the only direction she knew. She went north into the desert. She ran home.

Jezaline found her father in the barn, hobbling on canes, heart damaged by her in their last meeting. When he saw her, there was no malice at first. For a split second, Jezaline was his daughter again. She remembered being here, in this same place, loving him, respecting him with her father loving her, respecting her and wanting her around him.

Once he had been proud of her.

Jezaline blinked and it was gone.

Her mother was cleaning stalls when she heard her husband gasp.

He pointed. "You are not welcome here!"

She felt her life evaporate as swiftly as smoke in the wind. She would never be his daughter again. She would never be sixteen again. She would never be a normal Human woman. Her mother appeared and saw it evaporate with her and her mother began to cry.

Jezaline would not cry. "You should be proud of me, you stupid old man!"

He sputtered, "Get out!"

Her mother gasped, "If you are a real Ward, then go to the castle, Jezaline!"

It had never occurred to her and she stared at her mother with her mouth open.

Her mother put her arms around her shaking husband and soothed, "She is going. Do not worry, she is going." She ushered him out the door.

Jezaline stood in the aisle that was her childhood, in the smell of horses that had been her entire life and felt something clench in her chest. She broke to her knees on the stone and could not stop it. She cried for everything that was. She cried for the little girl who had died.

When she got herself together, and found the momentum to leave for the last time, she knew the horse that would bear her away. Her father's pride and joy, the stallion that had been born into brilliance.

Carmin was glad to see her and she was glad to be in his presence again. She saddled and mounted him and she cried again, this time in relief, this time in the utter beauty of being on a horse again.

22
Constance

From the kitchen, Constance watched the sun finally start to go down.

Relhie said, "Are you ready to go start cleaning chambers yet?"

Constance had forgotten about that. She winced.

Relhie crossed her arms over her chest. "Oh, I see you have somewhere else to be tonight?"

Constance blushed fiercely.

"Oh, you cannot *wait* to go tonight?"

She nodded.

Relhie laughed. "All right. I will be upstairs with the rest of the servants. Be careful, Constance. Do not leave the castle alone–"

"Oh, no. I would never!"

"So is it that what Aerick wanted earlier?"

Constance's blush exceeded normal red. "Yes."

"All right." Relhie left, grinning.

Constance hurried down to the servants' quarters and brushed out her hair. She changed into her newest, cleanest dress. Then she waited as long as she could bear it before heading through the castle. She eased the back door open.

The back grounds of the castle were a royal burial ground and a war cemetery. The parapet reached out and embraced it in long dark lines. There was a time that she found it eerie, being totally surrounded by stone with only one way out. But the parapet was built and designed by Telenay. She had grown to feel not contained, but protected.

The cemetery's unmarked stones ran in rows, on and on. One to represent every hundred Human soldiers that had fallen in war. There were thousands of them.

She did not often come back here and she felt a chill.

"You came early."

She jumped, turned around. Aerick leaned against the castle wall, smoking. He was so easy compared to the rest of the soldiers.

He smiled at her and offered the smoke. She shook her head.

"Never tried it before?"

"Never."

"Tobacco is a wonderful thing the Centaurs taught us."

She took it and sucked awkwardly on the end. Constance coughed hard but Aerick did not laugh at her. She winced, her pale eyes watering.

He slipped off the wall. "Come on."

"Where are we going?"

"Some place more enlightening than this."

He took her down through the stables. Constance gazed at the horses on their way by.

"Do you like horses?"

She smiled. "Yes."

"I will take you for a ride then. Soon."

She followed him deeper into the castle. The halls were warm and the murmur of dogs was filling the air. This was where Osondrous bred her war dogs. Constance had always feared coming down here. Had always believed what the other servants said: that the dogs would rip out her throat if she got too close.

Everything was dim and quiet.

Aerick put his finger to his lips, smiled keenly and opened a door. She slipped in after him and gasped.

Eight puppies looked up from their cozy places and mumbled at them. The mother lay in the corner, content and sleeping. Aerick quietly shut the door and Constance knelt in the thick straw. The pups came to her, mixtures of black and brown balls of fluff. They fumbled over her knees and chewed on her fingers. She sat down and they swarmed into her lap, licking and yelping. The mother woke, eyed them, then went back to sleep.

She breathed. "Aerick, this is amazing."

Aerick looked pleased with himself. "I thought you might like it."

The pups tired themselves out, collapsing across every part of her that they could. Aerick sat down and leaned back against the wall, just close enough to be able to run his fingers down her back.

She barely contained her own noises of glee.

When they left she told him in the hall, "That was incredible."

"You did not have animals in Stonedowner?"

They headed outside where night had fallen.

She shook her head. "I was raised in the city. My parents baked bread."

"Did they do well?"

"Sometimes," she sighed. "It was hard, though."

"What made you come here?"

"They died."

He touched her back again and she was infinitely conscious of his strong fingers.

"What happened?"

"A fire one night. They were working late and I was home sleeping. My aunt woke me up to tell me what happened."

They stopped in the hall of silence. All of the castle was quiet. The second guard was halfway through their duty. The rest were sleeping. A chill was in the air and she held her arms to herself. Aerick reached for her and Constance froze as his arms slipped around her shoulders and back. He leaned down and his face was so close she could feel his breath on her cheek.

"What are you doing tomorrow?"

She closed her eyes. "Nothing."

He chuckled. "When?"

"After noon serving." She could barely breathe.

He nodded. "Will you meet me here?"

"Yes."

His lips parted, touched her cheek. "Go inside and warm up. I will see you then."

She turned away with her head down, her fiery cheeks hidden by her blond curls. Constance barely made it out of earshot before she squealed.

She burst down into her chambers and gasped at Relhie's sleeping form, "He wants to see me again!"

Relhie laughed. "That is good, Child!"

Constance went to her little room off of Relhie's chamber. It was a closet and on the floor in one corner, her mattress was surrounded by nothing but stone. She lay down and stared up at the stone ceiling as it flickered in the fire light. She could still feel his lips on her cheek.

Constance hardly slept at all.

In the morning she was called to the noon meal after having completed her various other chores. She was tired but not flagging. The doldrums of everyday servitude and everyday work were gleaming in her eyes. She barely kept herself from skipping from one job to the next.

Osondrous entered the dining hall, a cloud of doom. The blond Warlord sat down in the back alone.

Constance begged another servant, "Please do that table for me!"

The other servant rolled her eyes but nodded and took a pitcher of brandy to the Warlord.

Constance sighed with relief. She took a tray of food to a table of soldiers. They cheered her on.

"Do you need anything to drink?"

The soldiers checked their cups, shook their heads and waved her off.

The dining room filled and emptied and filled and emptied as noon dragged by. She wiped the sweat from her brow with her apron. Her back ached from standing and walking on stone for so long.

Relhie smiled tiredly. "Go."

"Are you certain?"

"Go."

"Thank you, Relhie!" Constance untied her apron and left it on the counter. She entered the dining room and spotted Aerick leaning against the door frame.

"Hey." He was smoking and offered it. She slipped out of sight, into the hall of silence, and took a drag. A warm wind blew by. It lifted her hair away from her face. She opened her mouth and breathed deep. The smoke gathered in the back of her throat. She took another drag and this time Constance swayed, had to put her hand on the wall to steady herself.

She giggled.

Aerick's hand slipped down her back and he leaned against the wall in front of her. Her body was hotly aware of his body so close. They went unnoticed to the soldiers entering and exiting the dining room.

Aerick said, "Come back to the graveyard with me."

He took her hand and led her into the castle. The torches slipped by until they reached the back door. He opened it and they stepped out into the autumn sunshine.

"I come back here a lot," he said.

"Why?"

"Peace."

He did not let go of her hand. They walked down between the graves.

In the breeze with the sun in his eyes, Aerick looked at her. She was certain he was the best-looking Human she had ever seen. She swallowed hard. In the sun it was hot and she picked her hair up to feel the breeze on her neck. He appreciated the view.

"When is your birthday?" His eyes gleamed.

She blushed. "Three weeks."

He smiled, lit another smoke and blew it into the breeze.

"Why did you come here after your parents died?"

She shrugged.

He prodded. "Why did your aunt not take you in?"

"My aunt was very poor. She was working as a servant for one of the sons of the governor and they did not need someone as young as me."

"She told you to come here?"

"Yes."

"Do you ever regret it?"

She looked at him. "I never have."

"What was Stonedowner like?"

She went into great detail, using her hands to describe the big mountain city. "Where do you come from, Aerick?"

"Diggamara, though I have no Diggamara blood. But my mother did not do well. I wanted to be a soldier from the day I can remember anything."

"Are you happy?"

He laughed. "That is an odd question. Are you?"

She shrugged. "I am always happy. This is a good, safe place."

His eyes grew troubled but he did not say anything.

Then his face lit up. "Come on."

"What?"

"I am going to take you for a ride."

She gasped, "Oh?"

"I make good on my promises."

He held her hand all the way to the stable and then introduced her to his horse. "Constance, meet Holjel. Holjel, meet Constance."

She held out her shaking fingers and the animal's big, soft nose pressed into them.

She said, "You are magnificent. It is good to meet you."

Holjel's nose quivered and his ears flickered as he listened to her.

Aerick smiled. "Flattery will get you everywhere with Holjel."

The big animal had many things in common with the other Warbreds in the stable. He was not young nor flighty. He was big and solid. Constance helped brush the horse down. She worked the few tangles out of his mane as Aerick saddled him. Holjel quivered in excitement.

"It has been a while since I have had the time to take him out."

Outside, Aerick slipped his fingers around her waist, pecked her on the cheek and lifted her up to the stallion's enormous back. She sat behind the saddle. She felt the immediate heat in her calves from the big horse's flanks. Holjel glanced back at her, shifting from one hoof to the next in anticipation. Aerick mounted and they flew away.

The castle's gates were a blur and they knifed out into the sunshine, out into the fields of Kamamine wheat.

She let the horse's gait move her hips as she clutched Aerick's back. They galloped south. She felt the big horse dig in and stretch out. Her hair was a mane of blowing gold. Aerick glanced back at her every gleeful gasp and laugh. He was smiling.

Eventually they slowed and stopped in the shade of a stand of aspens.

Aerick said, "The servants exercise the horses but they really just want the chance to run and feel free for a while."

"I know how they feel."

Aerick chuckled. "Me, too. Why not come up here?"

"What?"

He turned, slipped an arm around her and she squeaked as he pulled her around. She pressed into his side and then into his chest. The pommel pushed into her hottest tingling place, between her legs.

His arms encircled her and his fierce eyes probed hers. Nose to nose, she stared, quivering. Her hands caught around his shoulders.

Aerick pulled her off of the pommel and on to him and their lips met. Her legs slipped over his thighs. Constance quivered and felt the heat pass all the way through her. He opened his mouth and so did she.

Her heart roared in her ears.

When they parted, she gasped. "Aerick, will you . . ."

"What?"

She tried to compose herself. He had to be able to feel her rushing heartbeat.

He touched her cheek with his mouth. "What?"

She whimpered, "When I turn sixteen, will you call on me first?"

He smiled. "Do you want me to?"

She nodded. "I want it to be you!"

He kissed her neck. "Then I will."

Later in her bed, Constance stared at the stone ceiling and found she no longer wanted to be a Ward. She was glad to be a servant.

23
Osondrous

Osondrous told Eikian her plans for leaving the castle.

He shook his head adamantly. "No. I should go, not you."

"I must get out."

She did not tell him that Shankan was now in her dreams, buried beneath the castle in the tomb he had chosen for himself. Even Eikian had no idea that she had found the King. Osondrous was beginning to feel the weight of the stone closing in on her. She understood Telenay now, deeper than ever, to be willing to give up anything to get out. She had to get away. It was becoming a matter of her very sanity—her very survival.

Eikian saw something desperate in her eyes and it was enough.

He nodded. "All right."

An Implin entered her chamber, carrying a tray of food.

Osondrous raised her eyebrows at the Centaur. "My breakfast in my chamber? You are that happy with me?"

"Do not expect it to last."

Osondrous uncovered the tray. "Bring the wine from my cupboard, will you?"

Knowing her time here was short, Osondrous already felt better. The darkness on her heart was lightening and immediately she knew she had only one last thing before she could get away. Something she had to do or it would follow her.

Eikian brought the wine. He lay down beside her at the table and buttered a piece of bread.

Aerick stepped in and sat down across from her.

Aerick said, "All of your orders have been fulfilled, all new recruits are being sent directly to Rayakdool and our watches have both doubled and tripled according to your orders."

"Good. Having pleasure with Constance?"

Aerick ignored her and buttered his own piece of bread. She poured everyone a cup of wine and took a drink. Osondrous sat back and stared at the young Second.

Aerick cleared his throat.

"Speak," she said.

"Many of the men have asked of the King Ward's health. For he has not been seen for—"

"He died." She did not hesitate.

Eikian froze and stared at her.

Aerick said, "Wha— how? How did this happen?"

"He died from the bite of a Srist spider. He was deep in the mines beneath the castle, exploring for the good of the land. After we finally found him, Olisize did all he could but the poison had taken hold for a long time. It was too late. We shall be planning his funeral this afternoon and hold it at dawn tomorrow. You must send ravens immediately to the three capital cities, so that all may mourn."

Aerick emptied his cup and set it down closer to her. She refilled it.

The knock to her door was sudden and frantic.

She knew who it was and made no effort to hide the smug little smile that lifted the corners of her lips.

Olisize stepped into the room, gray eyes filled with angst. "You just decided this."

Osondrous sat back. "I am glad you always listen to conversations that you have no part of, Olisize." Her smile was cruel and absolutely triumphant. She laced her fingers behind her head.

Olisize said, "Eikian. Aerick. Leave us now."

Eikian followed Aerick out of the chamber, shutting the door with a glance at her. The old Healer gritted his teeth, making a visible effort to control himself.

"Olisize, now—" she started calmly.

"Is this how you make all of your decisions?" he spat. "Over a cup of wine when you feel like shaking things up a bit?" The old man's saliva sprayed toward her.

"We could not keep his death a secret for much longer. It is better this way; I can control it now. I said that he was bitten by a Srist spider and we simply found him too late. You will need to have him prepared by dawn tomorrow."

"Will you be queen? I will not allow it!"

Her eyes shone with malice. "Then you, old man, shall step up and take the power." *Something we both know you no longer have the strength for.*

The old Healer took her whispering in his head like an affront to his very soul. Olisize clutched his staff, staring into her eyes and then finally looking down. "I am not fit enough. The ceremony of connecting me to the rivers and the shards would probably kill me. It takes formidable strength."

She leaned forward, elbows on the table. "At one point, Olisize, you might have been. I am too young and you are too old. I am going to try to leave the kingship empty."

"That is impossible, Osondrous. You as the Warlord would have total rule. And you are already despised among the leaders of Stonedowner. How would you convince them to be led by you if your choice is only to stay a Warlord and not lead them as their queen?"

"We must give this some time; it will take time to spread the word. Now, you must think on how to make Shankan's body look as though it died this morning."

"That is impossible!"

"He must be seen or we will need explanations for things we do not have explanations for!"

The old man looked at her from under his thin eyebrows. "Then you shall help me bring life back to his body."

"Does this insanity strike you often, Olisize?"

"You will, Osondrous." His shrunken finger raised and pointed straight at her. "To pay your respects." The sound of victory in his voice was not lost on her.

"Where will we do it?"

"In his chamber. We need to get his body there without anyone noticing."

"I have my Darkhalk."

"You are fortunate Teek stayed."

Osondrous stood. "I will get his body."

She stepped toward the door and outside Eikian looked at her from across the hall. "Where is Shankan, Osondrous?"

"You will not move from that place unless I blatantly order it and make you suspicious of my intentions?"

She watched Olisize as he stepped by her and shook his head disapprovingly. She pretended she did not notice.

Eikian waited for the old man to leave, then leveled his gaze back on her and crossed his arms over his chest.

She sighed. "Follow me then. Teek, cloak the minds of any that wonder where we are going and our purpose. No one knows."

The Darkhalk's Cape swayed as it worked. Osondrous traced the path down to her dungeon, using a narrow way in the deepness of the back of the castle. Eikian's hooves were the only sound and they followed her, an echo that was her shadow. They passed the last torch as they stepped down the last stairway and she took it from its sconce and raised it before her.

The darkness was empty and she led them through it. In all the long way down, as the walls went damp and finally wet, they said nothing.

They stopped at the entrance to the vast chamber. She held up her torch. Eikian brushed her and they glanced at each other. They walked side by side through the empty village. The Centaur stared around with a tight face, his eyes flickering uneasily.

They climbed the steps of the matriarch, its mouth black and toothless.

Osondrous held out her torch and they went to the back room.

The King's white skin flickered in the firelight. His body was bloated and purple.

Eikian demanded, "How long have you left him down here?"

She did not look at him; her glare was on Shankan's rotting forehead.

She said, "Do not pretend you liked the weakling as if he were impressive now that he is dead."

"This is about respect! Human decency."

She laughed with her mouth wide open. "Human decency? Is that what they told the Centaurs when they murdered their fillies and burned their stallions alive for the last thousand years? I am just proving how very Human I am."

Eikian was silenced.

She knelt and looked into Shankan's sunken, gray eyes. "I am going to bury you tomorrow, Shankan. You can rest easy. No more lying down here like a dog. Teek. Pick him up. Do not damage him."

Eikian stepped back as the Darkhalk knelt down and carefully worked his hands beneath the corpse. Shankan's head fell back in the Darkhalk's arms. She led the way with his gray eyes staring like murky glass at the wall. Everything was silent and all around her were the deserted shanties. And she wondered, where were these people buried if they all died here?

She moved quickly and they climbed out of there in half the time.

She slipped the torch back into its sconce on the wall. She glanced back at Eikian who glanced back at the corpse that followed him. The Darkhalk had emptied the halls.

She pushed open the heavy door of the King's chamber and instructed Teek to lay Shankan down on his bed. Olisize turned from the window, his eyes hollow.

She looked at Eikian. "Get out of here."

He frowned at her before leaving. Teek shut the door behind him.

Olisize bent over Shankan's bloated stomach. "I am not sure if we can . . ."

Osondrous' voice was ragged. "What do you mean? You are a Healer!"

She stepped up to the bed and glared over Shankan.

Olisize said, "There needs to be some life left!"

"Speak plainer."

"I need something to heal, Osondrous. There is nothing left living here. I cannot heal it!"

"Oh, there must be something left." She motioned toward the body. "Life does not absolutely disappear so quickly."

"You obviously have not heard me, Osondrous. I cannot repair him; there is nothing left! Shankan is completely gone. He obviously was running for his very soul."

"Now what do you mean by that?"

"I saw what you saw. These Reapers, they are Grim's. They drove him to death. And the red man must be Grim!"

"You have no just reasons to suspect a myth like Grim! That is ridiculous. By this time tomorrow, nothing will change except this nuisance will finally be at rest!"

"You are only saying now what you want to believe. There is a darkness coming. The effort against your life and now the thing that drove Shankan away are the same. Something is affecting our lives very drastically. We are down to two Wards, Osondrous. We are weak."

She crossed her arms over her chest. "We still have to bury him." She motioned.

Olisize's voice was like a cough stuck in a charred throat. "Have you forgotten that the coffins Kings are buried in are glass-covered?"

Osondrous stared at him. "You want me to beg? I know there must be a way. If you need live blood, something living to heal him off of, then use mine."

Olisize looked down at Shankan's body and shook his head. "I cannot use your blood. Your blood is that of a Warlord. It would change his features when I heal him."

"Then what?"

"We could mix our blood. Shankan was no Warlord or Healer. If we mix our blood . . . I have no idea if this could possibly work."

Osondrous slipped a fine dagger from her belt. "How much do you need?"

"As equal amounts as we can manage."

Osondrous said, "Teek, measure for us."

Olisize held out his hand over Shankan. "Give me a dagger."

She handed him a second dagger.

The old man took a breath and cut open Shankan's robe. "Just going to lie. Bury his secrets. Oh, but you and I know. We will get to settle into this every night for the rest of our nights. Not that that would be anything new to you."

There was a flicker of sadness in her eyes that no one saw. "No. Nothing new."

He sank the blade down into the King Ward's skin. The concave of his chest gave in and slipped open. He nudged the skin back and revealed the decay of Shankan's bowels gone black and yellow in death.

They each snarled against the rising stench.

She held her hand aloft and slit a dagger across her wrist. Olisize slowly drew his dagger across his own wrist. His wrinkled face crunched. He held it out beside her hand and they watched their blood spill down around Shankan's rotten organs.

"Warlord, stop," Teek said.

Osondrous grabbed her wrist and held it to her chest. "You thought Shankan was a fine King."

Olisize sighed, "If he had had the support he needed, I think Shankan could have been one of the greatest."

"Olisize, stop."

Olisize pulled back and healed his own wrist. "But Shankan never had a real chance and so we shall never know which one of us was correct."

Sadness fell on them in a stone curtain. They did not look at each other.

"Will it work? Can you heal him?"

"Leave me alone. You are the ruler here now. Everyone knows. But let me heal your wrist."

"No, I will keep this." She turned to leave.

He called after her, "Why, Osondrous?"

She ran her hand down the rough surface of the door. "Do not stress your heart. Take as much time as you need. I am here if you need me." She shut the door behind her.

Eikian was waiting for her.

"You are really not needed anywhere else today?" She stared at him in disbelief.

"Your dramatics are far more interesting."

She turned to her chamber and let herself in. She poured a bowl full of brandy and washed her wound in the alcohol.

Eikian ordered, "Teek, send an Implin to bring some rags, Aloe, and a bowl of water." He snapped at her, "Stop that. You will just make it worse."

She glared at him. It was not long before an Implin entered the room and replaced her bowl of brandy with a bowl of water and a handful of Aloe and rags.

Eikian dug a plum from a little pouch he kept on his belt and leaned down to give it the Implin.

"Well done," he said.

The Implin grinned in pleasure, gazing up at him endearingly. "Thank you!" The Implin hurried out.

Eikian lay down beside her at the table and began cleaning her wound. He tenderly laid her wrist in the warm water and began rinsing the clotted blood from the cut.

He asked, "What happened to Shankan?"

"He was killed by Reapers," she said.

"Reapers? How?"

"I do not know. I believe that Grim is after the last Crystal shard. That is the only explanation I am aware of for the Darkhalks to abandon the Wards for Diggamara"

"And Karalay with them." Eikian held her hand as he patted it dry.

She shook her head, not seeming to notice her wound or Eikian's hands.

She ranted, "Why are Grim's Reapers attacking the Castle of the Wards? Why would they destroy the King Ward while what they seek is so far from us? There must be a reason, a connection. They tried to kill me and did not manage it. It feels like they are narrowing us down for some reason. But there is nothing here that they could want."

With his thumbnail, he opened a strip of Aloe leaf and squeezed all the gel into her wound.

"You cannot leave for Rayakdool," he said.

"I leave the day after tomorrow. After the funeral."

He finished the wrap, ripped the cloth down the middle and tied the ends.

She kept talking, "It would not be like this if he was here."

Eikian glared at her. "You do not need Telenay. You never did."

"You are charming, Centaur, but you are confused." She poured herself a cup of brandy and drank it down. "We need to dig Shankan's grave. Let us get it over with now."

Eikian nodded and they stepped into the hall.

She said, "Find Aerick, get some spades and remind him to send out ravens to Diggamara, Stonedowner and Willower informing them of the King's untimely demise. If he has not already."

They parted and she walked slowly down to the first floor. She pushed the door open to the bright white of morning. The blue sky above her moved with the waves of the great trees that guarded the graveyard. She smelled the crisp air, full of vanilla. The branches of the great trees were nearly bare. Their gigantic leaves marred the ground and the Implins were gathering them, to keep the graves clean and to use as kindling.

The wind shifted and blew across the thousands of graves toward her.

The white vanilla flowers' scent always reminded her of late nights as a child, curled up beside Olisize before the library fires. She had always hated it, and hated that Olisize always smelled like the graveyard.

Eikian stepped around the castle; the shovels on his shoulder clanked. Aerick followed.

At the back, the ground was raised into a great long mound. The trees spread their roots beneath it and leaned into it at either end. She climbed up and looked down the line of carved headstones. The stones of the Human King Wards. It was a long mound and could hold hundreds more graves. The first Wards had been a hopeful people to think that the Wards

93

would reign for so long.

She went down to the end of the line and pointed where Shankan would be.

Aerick took a shovel from Eikian and sank its tip into the soft ground. Eikian handed a shovel to her. The three began to dig and pretended not to notice as Olisize appeared and watched.

Osondrous focused closely on the hole. The old Healer climbed up the mound; Aerick reached down to help him. She ducked her head beside Eikian and they dug under the Healer's sad eyes.

24
Jezaline

The fire had died almost to nothing before Jezaline picked up the sound of Cousai moving swiftly through the house. The Centaurs slept soundly, on their sides, hooves jutting out from beneath their blankets. She crept to the base of the stairs. Away from the fire, her eyes adjusted and she caught the sight of light beyond the top step. Carefully she moved up the staircase, back to the wall, creeping until she finally reached the pitch black landing. A dozen steps away, she saw the flickering flame, clutched in Cousai's grasp.

Cousai opened the front door and whispered, "What do you want?"

The figure in the doorway was cloaked thickly in grays and greens. Her pale face was a sliver beneath a large hood. She stood as stone, regarding the other with menace.

The stranger said, "Let me in."

"I cannot. A Ward sleeps here tonight."

"A Ward . . . Why?"

"She is seeking Tarrick; he asked for her."

The other pushed past Cousai and the light flickered over her face. Her features were close to Cousai's but older and leaner. She pushed back her hood and her blond hair was a whisper tied at the base of her neck.

"Grim moves." And the stranger's tone allowed there to be nothing else of more importance.

Jezaline strained to hear and held herself absolutely still.

Cousai said, "I have nothing to do with the Fai anymore. Go back to your people."

"I am no longer queen of the Fai, Cousai."

Cousai gasped and dropped the candle. Darkness swept the room. They moved silently to a different part of the house. Eyes straining through the dark, Jezaline worked her way to the doorway. Abruptly a figure hurried past her. She shrank back, pressed against the wall and covered her mouth. The front door shut, the bolt was drawn and the shadow went back to the other room.

Jezaline let out her breath.

The noise of flint smacking filled the air and the room beside her lit.

"How could you step down from your birthright, Sicilia?" Cousai said.

"You knew I would have to desert them someday. I promised you the crown but you chose Tarrick!" Sicilia spat the name as though it were blasphemy.

"Quiet!" Cousai hissed. "Likely the Ward will kill you."

"Why?"

"Who did you hand the crown to? Tell me you did not give it to Rushel!"

"I had no choice; he is the last heir alive."

"But he will continue Father's war! He will go after the Draegoone again. Father poisoned him."

Sicilia said, "It will not matter anyway. The Draegoone will come after the Fai. The secret is out; the rivers grow weak when a new King Ward is called. The Draegoone know when they can traverse the black water without death. Our peoples will fly their soldiers to death and end this war, finally."

Jezaline squeezed her eyes shut. She knew no one in their land knew these things. When Shankan had become King, it had been with almost no turbulence. The fact that those creatures of the other realms knew now how to cross without harm sickened her with fear.

Cousai breathed, "Oh, the ignorance . . . "

"We have no choice but to fight back. This is the Draegoone in all of their *honor*." Sicilia spat the word in disgust.

"How long have you been in the middle realm?" Cousai hissed.

Sicilia hesitated. She finally said, "Nearly a hundred."

Cousai shrank back and stared; her eyes were hurt and filling. "And you never came to me?"

Sicilia reached out and Cousai let her pull her in. "How could I think that you would ever wish to see me again?"

"It has been a hundred and ninety two years. Please, let that be long enough to get over the past." Cousai looked into her sister's eyes; they were equal in height. She said, "Please."

Sicilia kissed her sister on the cheek. "I forgave you before you left."

Cousai began to cry.

Sicilia murmured, "Listen . . . I am sorry. This is my fault. I did this, all of it. This is a far more destructive shadow than this land has ever seen. Please, Cousai, you must help me undo this wrong. I have no one else to turn to."

Jezaline carefully turned her breasts to the wall, an eye slipping around the corner to look in on the two. She covered her mouth to silence her gasp as Sicilia flexed her wings in frustration. The wings of the Fai were delicate, thin as butterfly wings. They were spider-webbed with dark veins and wholly transparent. Both Fai's wings were taller than they were; resting now, they were collapsed back and fell from their shoulder blades like rivers to their heels. Jezaline had never before seen such creatures except for drawings kept in the library. They held themselves differently than Humans as well. They carried themselves with stillness and with movements that were quick and subtle.

Sicilia dropped to her knees before Cousai. "I beg you, come with me."

Cousai's shoulders fell, her wings hung sadly behind her. "What can two Fai do against such a night? I feel so old, Sister, and I yearn to be back with our people. When we are young, it is as though consequences do not exist."

Sicilia pulled her sister down and pushed Cousai's hair from her face. "Come with me."

"Where will we go?"

"We will go and protect the last Crystal shard in Diggamara. It is the only shard left that Grim does not have. I will not let him have the third; he must not make that Crystal whole again."

Cousai shook her head, wholly despairing. "But what if–"

Sicilia stroked her sister's cheeks. "I will let no harm come to you, little sister. Have I ever?"

Cousai sighed.

Sicilia said, "I need you."

Cousai nodded. "All right, I will go. But what of the Ward? She cannot return to the castle. She will be killed!"

"How do you know this?"

"Tarrick saw it. He told me that I had to convince her to go after him or she would die. But, but. . . I did not do well. She does not trust anything that I say."

Jezaline slunk away and slipped back toward the staircase, hurrying down the steps as silently as she could. Sethian shifted as she sat down beside him and his gray eyes opened to see her awake.

"Jezaline, you need your rest," he said.

She stared into the fire, brow furrowed. Sethian sat up, supported on his thick arms, frowning.

The sound of the door opening and shutting above them was loud.

He asked in a hush, "What happened?"

"Cousai is gone." She lowered her tone and quickly recounted all she had witnessed.

Sethian shook his head. "I had heard rumors that two of the three Crystal shards had fallen into a dark one's hands but I had not considered they were accurate."

"You trust their words?"

"Those sisters were not lying to each other."

"I have not heard these rumors as you have. How could a Fai have had anything to do with the Crystal and Lionel? And she could not have been very old at the time in Fai years. Even for Fai."

Sethian shook his head. "Maybe her father used her to get to Lionel."

"But that could not have happened," she snapped and glared at him.

"That is an age-old mystery, Jezaline. Karalay told me about it once. No one knows what happened to Lionel when he created the rivers with the Crystal. She was trying to find out . . . So what does this all mean?"

She said, "It means we go to the Krept, we go in search of the prophet, Tarrick. We go to the Draegoone."

"Where are the Draegoone?"

"How should I know?"

He got up. "I will search this place for a map."

"Be swift. Let me sleep some." She laid down her head and listened to the sound of him going up the stairs.

Everything was still and quiet. All of the doors along the hall were open and the rooms of Cousai's cabin were rampaged. Sethian had searched every conceivable space.

"Sethian?" She looked in on the sitting room. Dawn light showed around the edges of the shutters.

He glanced at her. "I think I found a map of the Krept, Ward. But it is old."

She knelt beside him and looked over the cracked parchment. Her chin rested on his bare, wide shoulder.

"Can we be sure it is accurate?"

"Why do you think that we should travel for the Draegoone?" He looked at her for the first time. His gray eyes were sharp.

"Cousai said her people would never forgive her for loving Tarrick. Could that not mean that Tarrick must be Draegoone?"

"He could not be Vamepire?"

She shook her head absolutely. "The Vamepire are corrupt. They would never be granted such a power of prophecy and no Fai, nor any female, could love one of them."

"But how could there be a Fai that could love a Draegoone? Have they not been sworn enemies for thousands of years? How is it they could even travel across the rivers to meet each other?"

She glanced at him. "Some say prophets have the power of a Ward. The rivers would let him pass if he had such power. And now I know how the Fai got across. She waited for the rivers to waver . . . way back, two generations ago. When a new King Ward is called, they know now that they can cross for a day."

He looked at the map in his hands. "The Draegoone then."

She stood. "Pack all of her food that we can carry and fill anything that can be filled with water."

"Are the others awake?"

"Getting there." She turned away, ebony hair falling down her shoulder, framing her narrow Willower features.

The Centaur's eyes moved down her body. She paused, glancing back at him. The Centaur looked down at the map in his hands, chewing his teeth. His gaze rose again to watch her eyes.

He said, "When do we leave?"

"Right now."

26

Jezaline had worked her way north for the Castle of the Wards, she and Carmin alone. It was a long journey for one girl. But she did not feel like a girl anymore. Packed with her was her father's bow and enough food for a week. Carmin grazed at night and seemed to take the change of his life easily. Often she would wake to his muzzle on her cheek, the horse sleeping over her. Every moment she thanked the sky she had chosen this strong stallion and if losing Carmin had killed her father, then all the better. But the farther she went north, the more the trees changed and the more her parents became the past. Willower became the past and she began to feel very old, very ready to start something that resembled life again.

In Willower, it had never felt as though she were going to stay. She knew now that the city had been her transition to this. Her break from the horses, from her home. Her final understanding that she could never go back. She only briefly worried of the Wards frowning upon her. They had sent the soldiers to investigate her and she had eluded them. Would this anger these Wards of high power? Would they question her or even deny her?

The nights were quiet and she did not dream with Carmin so close and the journey so endless and exhausting. She felt now, more than ever in her life, that she was running. With the nightmares held back, her thoughts were on her future and it felt damn good to have a place to go.

It was years later, while sleeping with the King, Shankan, when she had even thought of the red man again. The figment of her nightmares. It was on that one particular night when she had laid her hands over her ribs and understood that there was an emptiness in her and that she had not been running from her family, or her broken life, or the pain of it all. She had been running from the final admittance that the red man was real, and that one horrific moment in the desert had been no mirage.

27

Jezaline was standing in the wind watching the river, when Sethian touched her hand.

"Jezaline, you are certain?"

She did not look at him. "I have no choice."

In the morning, she had clucked to Carmin when she had first stepped out the back door. The horse had come to her and had hardly noticed as she removed his pack and bridle. Then she had said that he could not go with her and Carmin's eyes had widened. His nostrils had flared and his ears had flickered. He was an old stallion now and she felt she would be wronging him by dragging him along on this, no doubt, dark journey.

She had explained to him as best she could, but there were no words that mattered. She had to leave him and Carmin whinnied right into her face, piercing her and shaking his entire body. She raised her hand and was firm and told him absolutely in the Willower tongue.

The Centaurs had stood by, staring with their heads down.

The steed had touched her cheek, then rested his muzzle there on her shoulder and they had shared each other's breath with their eyes closed. She remembered waking to his muzzle as he had stood over her little girl body every morning on their journey to the Castle of the Wards. A long time ago but, she thought, probably not to Carmin.

And Jezaline had sent him away and the stallion had gone. A gray form along the horizon, moving doggedly, angrily. But he went and she was left in the wind alone, with the warmth leaving her shoulder and cheek, the smell of horse evaporating. Now she stood with Sethian, her new steed, with her heart barely contained behind her gritted teeth.

She slipped up on his back and laid her head on the Centaur's shoulder.

They left the little cabin without a word or a look back. The Centaurs lifted into lopes, long heavy gaits. Her hips moved into Sethian and they swiftly traveled. The river blurred beside them, blending to the dying greens of fall. Into the south, the wind was with them, helping them lift across the uneven ground.

Sethian's gait was that of a pony, sharp and hard. He was small though stout in horse terms, hands shorter than Carmin. Every time she had ridden a Centaur, she had felt as though her feet were going to hit the ground. She yearned for her stallion but when tears came fresh and cold, she pushed Carmin out of her mind.

They had traveled most of the day. With the wind with them, the Centaurs made ground. Quadik took the lead and angled closer to the river. They followed him and he began to slow.

The river had narrowed to almost half.

The Centaurs stopped and stared with no eagerness.

Sethian helped her off of his back. "I will be damned if you end up in that river. And me, too."

She unbuckled his pack and the other Centaurs distributed the weight.

Derkay said, "And I had made every effort to convince you to leave the extra arrows and blades at the castle, Seth."

Quadik nodded. "We shall be glad to have them now."

Sethian reached out his hand to her. "It is almost dark. I want to be able to see the other side of the river."

She got on his back. Her pelvis pressed into his spine, his hard hands gripped her thighs. He trotted down along the bank of the river, getting a feel for the footing and the mud. He slipped a little. She stared at the other side, squinting through the deepening of the twilight. Old and gnarled oaks covered the entire west bank.

He trotted away, hooves punching the ground. He counted out the steps, stopped and turned at the exact amount he was looking for. She shivered and gritted her teeth.

They both stared at the dark form of the river.

He propelled them forward with a single, powerful thrust. The wind whipped by. He speared them through the air, reaching his top speed in a matter of strides. Her eyes widened as they galloped down to the bank. Two strides and his fore hooves touched the water. His hindquarters bunched and coiled beneath them. They took in a single breath as he thrust them into the air.

They gripped each other. She closed her eyes. The night surrounded them and they flew.

Sethian reached for the opposite bank.

Earth came back to them in a mass of tangled trees. His hooves hit and she slammed into the back of him. Her chin snapped against his shoulder. He grabbed her as his momentum threw his body up the bank. She held on to him as he stumbled to get his footing.

She gasped, "Well done, Captain."

He stood beneath her, constantly shifting as the mud moved out from under him. Her knees shook as they gripped his ribs.

"Can you get through there?" Sethian pointed to a break between two trees. She slid off of him and pushed herself in. Branches clawed at her skin. Brambles cut past her face; she walked blindly. Slender shafts of light broke through the heavy brush ahead of her. She lurched for it.

She broke out with a gasp as her feet suddenly hit bare ground. The branches let go and she stumbled forward. Jezaline stood and stared. Her heart pounding, she tried to focus on those objects, those hills, those silhouettes of evening, those things of the Krept that were masked by the night.

How long had it been since a Ward had graced these lands? The Draegoone, the Vamepire—those names that were hushed when spoken by the Humans—this was their land.

The sound of ripping branches was behind her, stomping hooves slamming into the dry earth. She turned and watched as Sethian broke through the brush. He stood gasping, blood running down his thick forearms as his kin followed behind. Derkay's hindquarters dripped black water from a slip that had taken him halfway into the river. Sethian's grip loosened on a curved blade extending three feet from his palm. He sheathed it as he came at her, his hand open.

She helped the Centaurs quickly unbuckle their packs. No one spoke, everyone helped lay the wood for a fire. Ajax flicked the flint and they all breathed, relieved for the light.

She laid out her bed and sat, knees drawn against her breasts.

"You are bleeding." Ajax set a leaf of Aloe between them and folded a rag. He carefully rubbed the blood from her cheek, cleaning her face, then dabbing the wound. He went back to his bed.

She glanced up at the stars. Their light was lost in heavy clouds.

Sethian said, "It was a clear sky when we made that leap."

She turned away from him, pulling the blankets tightly around her.

The Centaurs tilted their heads, listening as the wind shifted the tops of the trees.

They could hear the river but nothing else.

"Never have I heard a night which rested in complete silence. There is nothing living here? Not even insects?" Derkay said.

Ajax shook his head. "When birds and insects keep away from a place, we should, too."

"Which is why we are just passing through," Sethian said.

Their Centaur tones quieted into their own language, voices hushing down like their bodies, hesitant to disturb the silence. They felt protected in the orb of their voices, as though they slipped to another plane when they used the language of their kind.

Quadik said, "She is quiet."

Derkay said, "Maybe she is distancing herself from those she knows she will lose. Remember our training, the words of our Warlord?"

"Those words were spoken long ago, Derkay," Ajax replied.

Quadik shook his head. "But he is right, Wards sense death; they know better than to pull close to those they are about to lose."

"It will not help saying things like this," Ajax said.

Derkay sighed. "We are speaking logic. Jezaline realizes the truth; she will simply not speak any more of it. Our decision has been made; she needs our protection. She will not argue."

"Aye, she needs us."

Sethian said, "She left Carmin. Jezaline is grieving."

Derkay said, "Yes, she left Carmin because she knows he would die like us if she had brought him."

"Quadik," Sethian ordered. "Take first watch."

Once Quadik was at post and the other Centaurs were sleeping, Sethian curled himself around Jezaline, more tender and protective in his touches than he had ever been. He kissed her neck despite himself, turned his nose into her hair and sighed. He knew she was not sleeping.

He whispered, "Will you do something for me?"

"What?" She turned in his arms to face him.

"Please do not ever get so far from me again." He touched her face. "When I asked you to get through, I was not asking for you to go for a run away from me."

She touched his cheek, then found herself wrapping her arms around him. And it was the embrace she would have given Carmin. The embrace of horse and woman that would have left her feeling as though they could survive anything. If her decision to cast Carmin away had been rash, she would have regretted it. And though she did, desperately, she knew it was the right choice. She did not want her wonderful old friend in this black place.

She had sent him back to the castle where he could live out his days in the best possible way.

But with Sethian in her arms and all the dark silence pressing in, she could not hold back her grief. Her tears turned to sobs held against his cheek and neck. She saw Carmin, head down, trudging on through the night, cast away by the thing he loved the most. She could see herself standing there, a cold statue, sending him as though he were useless to her. As though she hated him. And Jezaline's sobs intensified until she could barely breathe, having never considered until this moment, the one thing she had ever loved, all alone in the night.

She saw Carmin continuing on to the castle, as she had commanded, never considering that he might turn back.

When she fell asleep, it was uneasy and shifting.

Sethian tried to rest but his gray eyes opened constantly, disturbed by the silence of the night and always touching her to make certain she was as close as possible.

PART TWO

Karalay rose from her darkness in slow sweepings. First the dimness of light. Second the dimness of sound. Third the roaring taste of desperate thirst that brought her to full awareness. The room was slanted, an attic with one window. The floors were old and black with dirt. The bed was straw but not poking. Someone had taken the care to layer the blankets thick before they had laid her here.

Beside the bed, on the floor, was a cup of water. She moved with her mouth open, her stiff bones and muscles responding like ancient machinery. She fumbled for the cup, wetting her fingers before lifting it from the floor. She drank.

Out the window, more chimneys than she could count stood and spewed black smoke against a white fall sky. There were no clouds. Wind creaked the shutters tied outside and buffeted the thin-glassed window.

She was naked and her dress lay at the end of her bed. The smell of sweat was heavy. Not Human sweat. The sickening sweat of Barbakas driven hard for days. She could feel the grime beneath her fingernails. Barbaka hair stuck to the backs of her hands and ground deep into the insides of her knees.

She rose and sat on the edge of the bed, her breasts and hair hanging equally limply. Karalay spread her fingers over her chest and felt her heart beating hard. The cuts and bruises and muscle tears of her past days healed.

She took a deep breath and shook the hair from her eyes, feeling like she could breathe again.

At the side of the room was a basin not much bigger than a large bucket. She tested the water and it was not much warmer than the air. There was a block of crude soap and one threadbare rag. She stood in the basin and began between her toes, scrubbing even as her body shook wearily.

She had been days without food, that much she could tell. Karalay had no idea how swiftly Barbakas could travel a distance that usually took ten days. Maybe half that time, maybe less. Regardless, she felt the deep pangs for food right down to her very bones.

She finished by dropping to her knees beside the basin and feeling the wonder of water against her filthy scalp.

She slapped the majority of the water from her naked body, then grabbed her dress. Dropping it into the bucket and, with little more than stubbornness, she was able to get it clean enough. Karalay wrapped a blanket around herself and then opened the little window. She looked into the streets of Diggamara with wide eyes.

She had never been in any of the three major cities of the Humans. Diggamara sprawled before her with homes that had been stacked so many times and with so little care that they seemed to sway their chimneys into the wind. This was a place where growth had burst its seams. But the growth had been a long time ago and everything showed complete disrepair.

She could smell salt water and she could hear sea birds. The sea was to the north. They were close but she was looking west, to where they had come from. She knew, behind her in the east, the river would be running all along the banks of the city to the ocean. The black water would be silent and bottomless. She did not know how Jezaline had stood, not long before, beside the other river with the very same discontent.

Karalay shivered and pulled back from the wind. She hung her dress before the window by tying it to a loose shingle nail. She crept back to her little bed, holding her belly and her heart for warmth. There was no fireplace but there was an oil lamp. The room was bright enough but she lit it for warmth.

She stripped one blanket, the one fouled still with grime, and then curled into the bed. With the wind howling at the window, Karalay slept instantly.

2

Karalay held her cold, wet hair off her neck and tied it up so it would not drop on her sleep-warmed shoulders. She went to her dress and tested it. It was cold but dry. She closed the window with relief.

Beneath her, the sounds of a bar were clinking cups, a round of laughter and the boisterous noise of an endlessly opening and closing door. Before she slipped the dress on, she held it in the shifting heat above the oil lamp.

She wanted Jaridd. She would look for him.

She put on her dress, smoothed her hair from her face and opened the door.

The hall was dark and empty. Seven other doors no doubt went to other rooms with one bed and one lamp each. She wondered briefly what could be traded for such a place to stay. With her will, she knew all of the other rooms were occupied. She headed down the stairway.

The entire place reeked of fish. A long dark bar ran down the side of one wall. The other wall was covered in windows. Small, rickety tables, chairs, benches and stools were all filled. Men sitting at the bar were surrounded by men standing around them. Women in scoop-necked blouses and black leggings ran beer to calling patrons. They all had tobacco-colored skin and black eyes. These were Diggamara's fullbloods. She saw Telenay in all of their faces, though he did not share their eyes; his mother had been a Willower.

No one saw her or cared to. She walked down the stair and quickly weaved among them to the opening door. She stepped into the winding, narrow street and into the mass of fishermen heading home from the docks. The signs of stores, and the buildings they hung on, leaned over her.

She turned left, tried to see through the crowd, then turned again and stepped back in awe. She covered her mouth.

Down the street, no more than half a dozen buildings between her and it, was a tower. But it was not the tower itself that stopped her. It was the thing in the tower that made her stare. She could see it by feel, the enormous power thundering out of the last Crystal shard in Human hands. But it was not the light royal feeling she had expected. It was not the good of the Wards roaring there but something very sinister, very like the river she knew was there not far behind her. The two were the same and they were black.

A hand dropped on her shoulder. She whipped around.

Jaridd said into her mind, *I should have locked your door.*

She glared at him but did not say what he already knew; that she was not a child. But it was not over-protection she saw in his eyes or felt in his touch, but concern. He reached for her cheek and she flinched away before she could stop herself. His face was still a stranger to her and his eyes, so sharply and coldly white and blue, were nothing she had known of him. Not truly. This man may have been the Darkhalk she had wanted, but it seemed the Darkhalk showed nothing in the man.

She looked toward the tower and so did he.

She spoke in his mind, *It makes me ill.*

I know.

What is it? Why is it like this?

The intention of the Crystal was not what it became. Come, I have a dress for you and horses coming to take us to the castle.

She did not ask why there was a need for horses to walk such a short distance. Jaridd wanted her to arrive grandly as a Ward should.

He followed her upstairs and shut the door behind them. He handed her a folded package. She took it to find an elegant dress of green silk and lace.

"What did you trade for this?"

"I am still a Darkhalk."

"You stole it?"

He shrugged. "No one thinks that."

He walked to the window and she stared at his frame. He was standing in his resting soldier posture, the same one he had always stood in at her side. But she felt on her will his anxiousness. His emotions were roaring despite his relaxed pose. She tried to be polite, tried not to just blatantly read his thoughts, but it was obvious he regretted bringing her.

As she removed her tired dress, she thought that that was all right because as she stared at the darkness that was his silhouette, she felt fear. The river and the tower were as black as the Darkhalk and they were all keeping her.

She let her hair down. He looked back as she pulled up the shoulders of the green dress. He stepped over and began to carefully lace the corset. She pulled her hair around to her face, revealing her bare back. He stared at the curve of her long neck, at the profile of her lips and cheek. He stepped closer, felt her tense and stopped himself. He finished the lacing, tied it snugly but not tightly, exactly as he had done it for her for over a decade.

She said, "I had not known so many pureblood Diggamara were left."

"This bar is owned by a pureblood. Do not let the numbers here fool you."

"I had known that there was a sect of people after the war that had come here to keep the blood true. Is it good?"

"Not if you are one of them."

She combed her hair with fumbling fingers. Her hands shook and her gnawing hunger was painful. "How so?"

He walked back to the window. "Girls born pure-blooded are married at their first red month. They give birth until they cannot anymore."

She gaped at him.

He said, "It is why Diggamara has fought to keep slavery. They fear that the way they treat their children may then be attacked as slavery."

"Why do the Wards not know this?"

"This is how it has always been here. Tradition that was grandfathered in. Something considered a good idea and a necessity at the time."

She said, "If someone attempted to do such a thing to their daughters now . . . without tradition backing them . . ."

"They would be hung." He turned back to her from the window, head tilted to avoid hitting the ceiling.

He stopped at the door. "The horses are here."

She put her chin up. "The mayor is pure-blooded?"

He nodded. "Purebloods control this city. After the slaughtering of this place, it seemed only right to give it back to the last of the true Diggamarans. He is called king here, not mayor."

She said, "Tradition be damned. I will not like this king much."

"No. You will not."

"Let us get this over with."

Jaridd opened the door.

3

The streets were quieter when they stepped out into the oil-lit night. Four horses stood outside the bar, two bearing Darkhalks. It was Kackin, Jaridd's Second in command, and Brach, her guardian for a month. They did not speak but she felt their wills were close. Patrons were quickly emptying the street, seeing the Darkhalks, first with confused and then with terrified eyes.

The two riderless horses were old and sad-eyed. She touched the closest mare, seeing the tip was missing from one of her dowdy brown ears. The mare gazed back at Karalay, unimpressed.

They mounted and rode between the shadows of the window lights and oil lamps at the end of every street. She looked down unintentionally and could see the river water between the buildings. Like running oil, it reflected the moon and lights along the bank like stars that were being swallowed. It ran smoothly and quickly. She could not see its movement, but she felt it. Like a constantly running machine, it hummed out loud. She could not imagine living so close to it. Could not believe that it did not have some kind of effect on the people.

Ahead, the tower was a big black beacon. She looked upon it and swallowed hard as they approached.

She touched her mare's neck for comfort and unconsciously seeped her will into the horse to feel the easy spirit that was all animal. The horse's ears twitched as the mare listened to the Ward's will, felt the woman's kind hand on her neck and knew, suddenly, that she was bearing a Healer. A real Healer. Kindness far beyond anything the horse had ever believed existed. The mare lifted her head higher and snapped her feet with exalted pride.

The palace was a combination of three-story houses built around the tower. It squatted at the center of five streets. Compared to the Castle of the Wards, it looked like a construction travesty. Everything was dirty and full of shadow. The lamps let out a quivering, oily glow that made everything look greased and lit nothing. Around the palace was the only thing of decent making, a ten-foot rock wall that was topped in rolled, sharpened wire the likes of which she had never seen. Sentries stood with pure-blooded Diggamara eyes and harpoons strapped to their backs.

They rode to the iron gate and were greeted instantly. The guard's armor was made from a blue sea serpent skin. The harpoon on his back bore a hook on the end that was big enough to skewer a horse.

Jaridd had donned his mask without her noticing. The Darkhalks sat on her either side and very closely.

Jaridd said, "Open the gate for your Ward."

The guard stared at him suspiciously for a moment, then glanced at her, frowning. The guard pointed at him. "How do I not know you are just a man all dressed up? I must protect my king, ye understand!"

The arrogance in the soldier's voice appalled her.

She yelled at the guard before she thought better of it. "How dare you! Open that gate right now."

In the guard's mind she echoed her statement and fear finally registered in his black eyes.

She heard something one of the Warlords had said to her once. *Fear is better than no respect at all.*

The guard hurried to the gate. He scrambled with the key while they stepped their horses right up to his back. He swung the gate in and hustled out of their way.

Karalay looked up the tower and, as the gate closed behind, her heart began to pound. The white night clouds clustered around its spire as though the Crystal shard itself were conjuring a storm.

She heard the gate lock and her stomach knotted with it.

Servants rushed to the horses' heads, their own heads tucked so tight to their breasts that Karalay could not see their eyes beneath their ragged hair.

Jaridd took her hand and she slipped down from the mare with the two

Darkhalks stepping up behind her.

The servants led the horses away, their tiny bodies shrunken beneath brown rags. She stared as they moved, unable to register the extent of starvation that could cause them to be so stiff, so sickeningly like dead trees in a wind.

She stared open-eyed at Jaridd and he shook his head. *Now is not the time.*

Are the servants ill?

No.

It had also not been lost on her that those servants had been too light-skinned to be pure-blooded Diggamara. Of course, no pureblood Diggamara here would ever be a servant. That was left for the likes of the lighter-skinned and blue-eyed Stonedowners, or the bright-eyed Willower. Her teeth gritted and rolled. Karalay had no Diggamara blood in her in any way. She was mostly Willower and wondered how many pure-blooded Willower she would see soon, on their knees, scrubbing the cold halls with stomachs cramping for food.

Her rage killed her hesitation and she followed Jaridd with her narrowed eyebrows leading her grinding teeth.

At the door a guard greeted them and bowed. "The king's advisers just sit for evening drink."

The walls were mostly stone and the small entry was full of low ceilings and dimness. They followed the guard into a room that stunk with past meals. The table was small and above it hung a chandelier made of scales lit with large candles. The table was dressed with bowls of fresh bread, honey and butter.

Three men sat around the table; they all looked up with black eyes. Their dark skin glowed like dried tobacco in the candlelight. One of them held a strange look. As she gazed at him, he nodded slightly to her and she felt a pressure on her will.

I am Dind.

Yes you are.

Karalay put the man known as Dind from her mind and addressed the man seated in the middle. "Who are you?"

"Sit down, Lady. What can we help you with?" the eldest man asked and motioned to a chair opposing them.

A servant stepped from the hall and leaned over to fill his cup. Her dress was too big for her. As she leaned, it fell open at the bosom and the bones of her chest were a charade of death. The smell of the hot bread was thick and the youngest adviser generously covered a thick slice with butter.

As he put it into his mouth, Karalay slammed her hand into the side of the chair before her and it skittered and spun across the room with a bang.

She yelled, "I am a Healing Ward of the Castle of the Wards. I was sent to speak with your king. Stand and bow to me!"

Dind dropped from his chair to his knees. "Forgive us, Ward!"

The other two followed suit and silence fell after the crack of her lightning.

She caught her breath, licked her lips and nodded. "I wish to speak to your king. My business may be long here and I expect his full appreciation of my presence."

The eldest ambassador's chin shook beneath his thin, gray beard. "Our king is sleeping—"

She said, "Then you will have him awakened. I was kind enough to come to find such a rude welcome—is this how you want to be remembered by your children?"

The youngest of the three advisers stood. "Please, grace us with a long stay, Ward. I am certain your room will be prepared when our servants lead you to it. You will be informed the moment our king is ready for you." His voice shook audibly, begging for her consent.

Servants waited for her at the door. She glanced at them, then nodded at the king's advisers, paying an extra glance at Dind. She went to the servants and followed them down the hall.

Jaridd stayed close to her.

Her will was pulsating out from her. She found the king, awake and enjoying a second evening meal. The youngest ambassador hurried into the king's chamber and bowed before him, explaining her presence. She felt the king's contempt, fat and wet, for her interrupting his evening. The king took it out on his youngest adviser with a brisk slap across the cheek.

They moved down a broad staircase and a tall hallway lined with doors garnished in green scales. She was led to the first door, which Jaridd shut behind them. He took off his mask and rubbed his forehead.

She lost all composure. "What is wrong with this king? Who is he?"

Karalay paced and gasped, panic rising her heart to a beast against her breastbone.

She pointed at the one servant in the room and demanded, "How much are you fed?"

The question surprised both Jaridd and the servant. The girl's hair was thinning and her face was haggard in malnutrition. Karalay's gaze upon her left the servant shaking with fear. Her violet eyes scanned the room for help but she was the only servant left and Jaridd's fierce gaze terrified her.

She bit her pale lips and stuttered, "We—"

Karalay softened her gaze and said softly, "Tell me the truth."

The girl pushed her blond hair out of her face and wrung her hands. "Mostly, we get one meal a day. Sometimes not so much . . . "

Karalay looked at Jaridd. "This is how Diggamara is? Those fisherman in the streets were desperately poor. And those ambassadors and their king are eating better than Wards."

Jaridd shrugged, aggravated. "You are missing the point."

The servant ran from the room.

"How so?"

Jaridd approached her and she stilled defensively, keeping him two strides away.

He said, "The point is that we need to be here. You start condemning this king and you could be removed from this palace. We must be here. The Crystal is in the tower!"

Her eyes narrowed. "No amount of men could remove us."

"Maybe not, but we could lose a Darkhalk or two. If that happens, we are done. We are here for one purpose and that is to protect that Crystal."

"You would have me do nothing for these people? These are my people!"

Jaridd shook his head. "These are Diggamarans. If you ordered a change here now that conflicted with their traditions, they would not be your people at all."

Karalay glared vehemently at him.

Jaridd sighed. "You must pick your battles."

Karalay saw stress in every move of his body. His body which had been so hard and so impressively lean. She bit her lip and walked to the window. He watched her hips beneath the silk dress, watched it cling and release from her smooth skin.

She whispered, "Then what would you have me do?"

"Bite your tongue, bide your time. You are going to have to talk to their king tonight. Do it wisely."

4

The unique furnishings of the Diggamara people were narrow and tall. The blankets were mostly the thick hides and scales of sea serpents and more stretched hides were hung on the walls in blues, greens and golds. She rubbed her face, having tried to rest and finding it impossible.

The door opened and Jaridd entered.

Dind followed into the room, bowed and said, "Karalay, thank you for coming."

She stood and stepped to him, looked up into this man's face and scrutinized him without restraint and with great suspicion. His black eyes met hers passively and, she noted, very sadly. He was pure blooded Diggamara; yes, that was true. But there was something very odd about his face. She could not quite determine his age.

Finally, she nodded, "It is good to meet you, Dind."

He opened his mouth, then stopped himself, looked at his feet. The action was strange on this strongly built man.

Jaridd said, "Tell her or I will. Karalay, this is a man we can trust."

Dind said, "I was once a Darkhalk."

She took a step back despite herself. "How is that possible?"

"I was killed in battle and saved but the Cape and Sword were not."

She raised her eyebrows.

Dind said, "It was one hundred and seventy-eight years ago. I am here to take you to our king."

Karalay frowned. "What will be awaiting me?"

He said, "You are a Ward. Do you not already know?"

She looked down and away. "I suppose I do."

She followed him out of the room.

Jaridd covered his face before following her.

No one here knows of Dind's ancestry.

I will not speak of it.

Skeletons of enormous snakes lined the halls. They came from the sea where the Diggamara people sailed to hunt them. Their bones were held with string and they were hung as trophies.

She cringed away from their open jaws.

They walked up to the highest room of the palace. Dind knocked and entered at the beckoning of the king within.

She tilted her chin up as she stepped into the bright light of fireplaces ablaze on either end of the room. The man sat at an impressive throne, cast with brilliant red velvets and shining rows of scales. The king was enormous with rolls of fat. He was squeezed tightly by the throne. As she entered, he wrenched himself sideways to pry his hips out of the chair. His beard was cropped short and peppered with gray, black and brown.

He smiled joylessly, then struggled into a bow.

She knew that this was the first time in his adult life he had bowed to anyone.

He smacked his thick lips. "Ward of Healing. I welcome you to Diggamara. I ask what brings you to my halls?" His voice was slurred and wet.

She said, "Just Ward business. Nothing to concern you."

"You will not find peace here."

She frowned at him. "Is this not a time of peace?" She was thinking, *You are very right.*

He said, "Yes, of course. I do hope you find your stay comfortable here. How long do you think you will grace us with your presence?" His black eyes were tiny beads beneath his enormous brow; they stuttered and twitched fitfully.

"I am uncertain. My guardians shall protect me here." She glanced at her shoulder, feeling Jaridd's eternity behind her.

The king smiled. "Your guardians are welcome." He then spoke to Dind, "Make certain that all of her wishes are granted."

"Of course, my lord." Dind bowed.

Karalay watched the king hobble out of the grand room as discontent fell from him in slimy waves.

Dind murmured, "I shall take you back to your chamber, Ward."

She turned and left the room first, lifting her skirt to hurry her progress. The skeletons on the walls no longer felt like trophies but testaments to how these people worshiped death.

In her chamber, with the door tightly closed, she said in a frantic whisper, "How long has he been mayor here?"

Dind said, "Five years. Since his brother died."

Jaridd removed his mask and stood silent at the window.

She said, "He was not eldest born?"

"No, his brother was assassinated." Dind went back to the door.

Someone knocked. Karalay's face paled and she stepped back to Jaridd.

They entered on feet that were utterly silent. Hoods covered everything but their slender, white hands. They were small and, at first, she thought they were Human girls. The leading of the two raised her eyes and Karalay met them. They were ancient and gray and hard as metal. In those eyes, ash-colored bangs hung thinly.

The leader did not bow to her and did not remove her eyes from Karalay's face.

Dind held out his hand. "Karalay, Healing Ward. This is Sicilia and her sister, Cousai. They have come to aid us."

There was a tenderness in Dind's raised hand that was subtle and evaporated instantly.

Cousai was younger but otherwise they could have been twins. However, their time had been spent very differently. There was a gentleness in Cousai's eyes but the smile on her lips was merely courtesy; it held no joy. Sicilia did not smile, nor did she attempt any courtesy.

They both were lovely but their hardness, Cousai in her sadness and Sicilia in her wrath, made it impossible for them to ever be considered beautiful. Karalay immediately went to touch them with her will and was turned aside instantly. These were not Humans and the only possibility of what these females were left Karalay in disbelief.

Sicilia's gray eyes looked directly into Karalay's own, "We are not well met on a night as cold as this."

Cousai said, "It is fine to meet you, Healing Ward."

Karalay nodded to them. "Thank you for your aid."

Sicilia's eyes hardened but she did not speak. She glanced at Dind. Karalay read much in that glance .

Cousai said, "What did the king say?"

Karalay said, "I am a Ward. He could not deny me."

Jaridd spoke for the first time from the window. "What else, Sicilia?"

Sicilia said, "I have word from my general today. We will have more aid when the next King Ward is called. Though I do not know how many. And it is certain and set, the Draegoone and Fai fly to end the war and slaughter their soldiers as well."

Jaridd nodded. "Anything else?"

Sicilia shook her head and the sisters left.

Dind glanced at Karalay. "You must not have eaten yet?"

Karalay looked at him. "You and Sicialia are something?"

He stared at her, his eyes large. "Yes, we are."

She nodded. "No need to hide such things in our company. No, I have not eaten at all."

Dind said, "I will send food." He left.

Jaridd looked at her. "Telenay's party reached Addilade today."

She turned on him. "So soon? Why did you not stop them and bring them here?"

"It is not soon. Telenay has many plans that do not include this."

Karalay's chest clenched. "So you will let him die?"

"It is not certain Telenay will be killed."

She gritted her teeth and forced a shaky, humorless laugh. "Not certain?"

Jaridd shifted uncomfortably. "Telenay is the greatest Warlord ever to exist. I am certain he will live."

"You cannot be so certain." She rubbed her forehead very hard, fighting tears. "So you are waiting? You are waiting for war? For Grim to come and try to claim this last Crystal?"

"Yes."

"How can you wait silently for such things?" Her voice broke.

"It is my duty."

She looked away. "Telenay rushes to get to Addilade. I cannot understand why."

"He has . . . issues."

"Why do you not attack Addilade?"

"We do not have that kind of army. Our only hope is to settle in and fight with our backs against a wall."

She went to the window, her eyes narrowed. "How is it that Sicilia and Cousai crossed the river?"

They had two windows and many feet of stone between them.

"It was found out not very long ago that when a new Ward is called, the Crystal shards weaken and for one day after, the rivers can be crossed."

"Why would any Fai protect the Crystal shards? Would it not be in their best interest that the Crystals fell into Grim's hands, that the rivers would fall and they could continue their war with the Draegoone?"

"Sicilia's path has changed what she knows and she has convinced Cousai to aid her here."

She looked at him. "If they are royalty, then why are they not leading their people? Why would Cousai agree to be here at all?"

"Sicilia has stepped down from being queen. Her story is old and I am not the one to tell it."

"Then Cousai is queen?"

"Cousai was banished centuries ago."

"By her own sister?"

"Yeah."

She spread her fingers on the glass. "What did Cousai do?"

"She loved someone." Jaridd looked close at her.

"So we wait for Grim to come for the last Crystal shard."

"He will die before he gets the last."

She raised her eyes. "How certain can you be?"

"The Darkhalks are protecting it."

She looked away. "Shankan is young. He is strong enough. Another Ward will not be replacing him as King any time soon. And I believe in the Wards. If Shankan were to die when they are this weak, no one would be stupid enough to step up immediately to take his place. Certainly not Olisize and I cannot believe even Osondrous would be that ignorantly rash. So the Crystal will not weaken and when they receive our message, no Ward will ever step up to become King again. No war will be fought. Grim will never have his chance."

Her knees began to tremble. She leaned on the window.

Jaridd closed the distance between them.

He said, "How do you feel?"

"I feel very tired and very old." Her shoulders sagged. "Hungry beyond belief. What will happen?"

"Grim will have an army."

"How could Sicilia convince the Fai to fight for this cause anyway?"

"Some of the army of the Fai are still loyal to Sicilia because of her valor against the Draegoone."

"She was a soldier?"

"She was a general."

"How do you know all this?"

"The Darkhalks came after the rivers were created and I was sworn as the guardian of Lionel's son, Zaden. He traveled the whole land, not just middle realm. He spent his life researching the rift between the Draegoone and the Fai. He spent fifty years with the Fai and thirty with the Draegoone before his death."

Jaridd leaned close. His breath was without smell, like spring water. He pushed her hair back so he could see her face.

She murmured, "Why do the Fai and Draegoone hate each other so much?"

"You know most of it. The Fai and the Draegoone ruled the Humans. It came down to this city, the last of the free Humans. The Draegoone got to these lands first and, under oath, they left an army of Vamepire to protect the people here from the Fai. But when the Fai came to this place, there were none left alive. The Vamepire were gone after slaughtering every Human that lived here."

Karalay shook her head. She knew this story. She said the question that had already been asked for centuries by Humans and Fai alike. "Why would the Draegoone entrust such wicked creatures?"

Jaridd shrugged. "The Vamepire were not considered wicked until after this. The Fai swore that every Human killed here be avenged. So the war began."

She snorted and laughed bitterly. "What a lie, that the Fai ever cared for us enough to avenge us. They wanted war."

Jaridd nodded.

She said, "You did not answer my question. Why do the Fai and Draegoone hate each other so much?"

Jaridd said, "It is not about hate. It never was. Greed becomes hate. They each wanted what the other had."

She looked up at his face. "Lionel was such a great man. I do not believe any Human will ever have such power again. I understand Zaden's need to find answers to such questions."

"Scholars are given such questions to ask."

"If the Vamepires were not wicked, then why did they do such a thing?"

"The Vamepire are the only ones that might ever know that answer. The Draegoone are now their sworn enemy. They kill each other on sight. The Fai still believe that the Draegoone could not convince Diggamara to give in to slavery so they hailed the Vamepire to kill them all."

"And none of it is truth?"

"No one knows. Almost the entire species of Human Diggamara was killed. All that was ever written was that the Vamepire had left all of their weapons, every sword and every knife and bow, locked away in the dark in the Diggamara mines. The corpses were piled over the swords and they were never touched."

"They are still here?"

"Yes."

"Why have none laid them to rest?"

"None strong enough have been able to make the trek down into the pit of this place, open the doors and drag the bodies to be buried. Too many souls are screaming down there. Too many ghosts."

She closed her eyes. "Where is the opening to that place?"

"Here."

She stared at him. "In the palace?"

He nodded. "Beneath the palace."

121

"No, there is no peace here then. I have come to believe that there is no place left to rest in this land."

Jaridd said nothing.

Karalay asked him, "Do you know at any moment when Grim will attack?"

"You are tired. When another King Ward is called, the Crystal shards will weaken. It will be Grim's only chance to grasp this last one shard without having to become King Ward himself. We will see the flight of the Fai before Grim gets here. That will be our sign."

She grew still, then whispered, "The messenger to the Wards will be too late . . . will he not?"

He stared back at her. "I believe so. Grim's will is working against us."

She asked, "Are you a prophet, Jaridd?"

"No. I have no fore sense, unlike yourself. But I feel this is the final inevitable end of the Crystal. All of the Darkhalks do and if we are here, then there will be a war. No meager messenger will stop Grim."

"How is it you can be certain that the Darkhalks will not lose this battle?"

"We have never lost." His posture was strong even as he leaned. His head was up and absolutely certain in his words. She looked him over and knew that Jaridd believed what he said without hesitation or question.

She could not be so certain. "But if you do lose, and Grim gets this Crystal . . . what will happen?"

His face lowered and his eyes darkened. "We will not lose. If the end comes, we will destroy the Crystal before we allow Grim to touch it."

Knuckles tapped on the door and she went to it with relief. A servant held a tray up and, as she took it, she felt certain she would not be able to eat. She set the tray down and poured herself a cup of water which she drank and filled again. Her stomach rolled fitfully.

"You know what is strange?" She looked at him.

He looked at her as though he were fighting to pull his mind from something far more important. "What?"

She said, "The last free people. Diggamara. Those Humans who fought so desperately against slavery are now the last Humans to fight to keep their slaves."

He stared back at her and his emotionless face left her remembering him, the Darkhalk who had ever been at her side. The Darkhalk she loved. His eyes flickered fitfully and the Darkhalk was gone again. He looked away.

She opened the tray and, when the hot smell of food hit her nose, despite her reservations, she ate it all. Her first meal in many days.

5

She slowly undressed. Now full and hot with the wonders of sustenance, she could not ignore her weariness any longer. Jaridd was pacing broodily. His frame blocked out the light of the fireplace. But eventually her nakedness drew his attention. He watched in silence as she prepared for bed, brushing her long hair out and braiding her waves. Karalay took her time before the mirror, pampering her tiredness, enjoying the feeling of routine, even in this strange place.

She blew out the candles.

When she lay down, she asked him, "What do you remember before you were a Darkhalk?"

The fire had grown low by now and from the dark he answered her. "Not a lot. Some of it is coming back."

"What is?"

"I was Stonedowner. Mostly Stonedowner. I have no memory of family. I think I was an orphan. I have memories of living and fighting in the streets, learning things. It is all fragmented."

"Where did you go from there?"

"I joined in with a group of soldiers. They said that they were going to protect the first Ward. I had never heard of the Wards except by rumor. I remember the day the rivers came and the Draegoone holding Stonedowner fled. Some of them made it across the river, the rest died trying."

"Was there celebration?"

"At first people did not believe. They crept from their homes, jiggled their chains. I remember, we all wore hobbling chains then. They just kept waiting for them to come back. When they did not, Stonedowner erupted. The city was in a state of total joy. But not with the soldiers I was a part of. We moved quickly. Their leader was a man named Kackin. He sensed something was wrong with the rivers. We traveled to the Castle of the Wards and on the way picked up more soldiers who wanted to help. I respected Kackin. I remember the joy fading from city to city as we went. It turned to something else, something most people would not think about or maybe even believe."

123

"What?"

"Aimlessness. Humans had been slaves for so long. No one knew what to do. I followed Kackin. We had purpose. I felt fortunate."

"Kackin is your Second in command now."

"Yes, he is here."

"How did you become Darkhalks?"

"When we reached the castle, it was empty."

She sat up; her heart rate escalated. This was her mystery. This was the question on every scholar's lips. Where had Lionel gone? "Empty?"

"Absolutely empty. Lionel was already gone."

"You know nothing else?" she asked hopefully.

"Nothing. We stayed in the castle for a while. We did not know what to do."

Karalay sat back. She sighed, disappointed but not surprised. "What did you do?"

"I went to the library. The same library you have spent your life in. I went there and I began reading. I came upon something."

He was silent and she prodded. "What, Jaridd?"

He moved across the floor and sat down on the opposite side of the bed. He leaned on the headboard and crossed his arms over his chest. Her body nudged at her, reminded her of the night it had spent with him. Tingled that it had been good.

She leaned on her side, fingers lacing with her hair, waiting.

He did not look at her as he said, "The Broken Cathedral."

When the words were spoken, the air chilled and she stared at him. "No."

He nodded. "Yes."

"No, Jaridd. No one goes there. In the history of our land not a single Human being has considered entering that place. I have read numerous entries of people, even Wards, getting too close and always moving away."

He said, "I read them, too."

"What happened?"

"I told Kackin about what I had found. Just to tell someone. I never considered going there. He told some of the others and eventually we found ourselves thinking about it. Not all of us. Many of our soldiers were talking about going to Diggamara, to help rebuild the city. Diggamara needed soldiers and workers."

"How many of you?"

"Exactly five hundred of us could not get it off our minds. Then, one day, we all packed without discussion. I started packing, then Kackin came in and started packing. Before we knew it, we were all packed and standing outside the castle looking at each other. The rest of the soldiers left for Diggamara. They could not understand us and neither could we."

"The Broken Cathedral is south of the castle. In the hills."

He nodded. "It is not but a few days."

"What happened?"

"It was a broken place. It was the last place of a previous civilization of great power. Human-like but far beyond the Humans of today in ability. I know very little. Only what I was told."

"By whom?"

"The Broken Cathedral spoke to us. Told us about these creatures that came before. Our ancestors. All of our ancestors, the Vamepire, the Human, the Fai. The Rulers. I know they were not like us or anything left alive in this land. They were essentially powerful but that is all I know."

"What else was there?"

"There was very little left of the ruin. A cathedral to a king, I think. To the Rulers. I think it was the last place of life for the creatures that ruled before us. We all spoke to the cathedral; we told it we wanted what it had for us."

Karalay was silent.

He said, "We realized we were walking on the dead. The last of the soldiers of the Rulers. Exactly five hundred. From the earth, the Capes and Swords came for us. Rose from underneath the many layers of dirt and ash. Broke from the backs and the necks of those things that had worn them and fallen. The last of the Capes and the Swords came for us. I knew then, that there were many before the last five hundred fell. Can you imagine an army of thousands of Darkhalks?"

She shook her head. "That is not what scares me."

He looked at her.

She said. "Jaridd, what could kill an army of thousands of Darkhalks?"

Jaridd was silenced. She pulled her blankets up tighter.

"Sheer numbers," he said.

She nodded. "That would be the only thing. But, when a Darkhalk falls, the Cape and Sword die too. How were they not dead?"

"It is the place that kept them. Something running just beneath the surface. Something wet."

Chills raced down her arms.

Jaridd left sometime in the night and Karalay woke to watch the sun rise.

She closed her eyes and breathed in the still air.

Jaridd returned to her. He sat down at the table and poured a cup of water.

She said, "Are you going to drink that?"

"I poured it for you."

She dressed, then sat down across from him. "Where did you go last month when you left me?"

"The mountain of glass."

"Why did you go there?"

"That is nothing you need know."

"Why are you here?"

He glared at her. "You know why I am here."

"No, why do you come back to me? You stayed nearly all night. Am I wrong to say that you are no longer my guardian?"

He looked at her. She stood away from him, went to her window and stared at the chimneys.

His fingers clutched her upper arms.

His lips pressed to her ear. "I am sorry."

She shook her head. "For what?"

"I have no idea." His voice was exasperated.

She pulled out of his hands.

He said, "Karalay."

Karalay clutched herself. "There is not any love in this place. Do you feel it? War is already upon us like everyone I see is a walking corpse. The poor servants practically are already. There is nothing I can do here."

"You need more rest."

"I panic for Telenay and Osondrous. I feel our fate is resting in the hands of Warlords. And Olisize grows so old. I keep telling myself over and over that Shankan is young. But he was still missing when we left. What if he is already gone?"

"Their burdens will not be changed if you try to take them upon yourself. . . . My kindred only take their orders from me but without the Cape I am no match for their speed. That is why I am here."

"So you wait here with me? What will happen when we are attacked?"

"I will have to take the Sword and Cape upon me again."

She eyed the outline of the Cape in the corner. If she looked at it with her will she could see it clearly and always the Sword was on his back, whispering, pleading. She could hear it always, against her heart, in her will, their enticing voices, always speaking, never sleeping.

She blocked them out. "Why have you not taken them to your heart yet?"

He looked down. "I do not know."

"Do you not crave them?"

"With my whole being. But, I did not realize the longer I waited, the more difficult it would be to give them my life again."

"Yes, you did," she said. "You know everything."

He chewed his teeth. "Not everything."

"What do you not know?"

"I do not know the secrets of your heart as you have accused me of."

"You have not looked?"

He stared at her and there was shock in his eyes. "You are too strong, Karalay. You do not give yourself enough credit. You think I am so powerful. I am nothing but a Stonedowner orphan. At ten years old, you could have killed a man with a thought."

Jaridd frowned after her as she headed for the door to open it for a servant. The girl laid a large tray on the table and then left. Karalay uncovered it and sat down to eat her breakfast. He sat across from her.

She said, "You are no longer my guardian."

He sat forward. "I will still protect you."

"I did not think that was your objective."

"I will not stop protecting you."

Silence fell on them. She forced herself to eat.

He stood and left.

Her eyes moved to the ceiling and the whole of it was covered with a carving of the sea. She closed her eyes and wondered what it must sound like, the roar of a million tiny waves lapping at the feet of a sand shore. She had never seen it, despite that the Castle of the Wards was so close to the northern shore.

She lay down on the bed and stared up at the carving.

Telenay was an arrogant thing. Over and over she replayed their last moments of quiet together. The ride back. The odd feelings in the dining hall. His hands lusting on her hips. All for different reasons than she had suspected at the time. She felt stupid and blind and very, very immature. When Telenay had needed her the most, she had been too busy in her own pathetic little life. He could be at the castle now, certain to do the right thing.

Their lives were in the cold hands of Osondrous and the very thought made Karalay ill. Osondrous was almost certain to do the wrong thing, if only out of inexperience, or maybe just out of spite. Just as Karalay had done with Telenay that night. Her heart told her he would have left anyway but she still felt responsible. She wrapped her arms around herself and regretted.

6
Osondrous

The trees quieted above their heads with the stilling of the northern wind. In the air the only sound was the whimper of weeping, those that dearly loved their King. Osondrous looked over the lake of faces. The soldiers bowed in their brown leathers. The women went to their knees, staining their white cotton dresses.

On their shoulders, six of her Centaur Seconds carried the jewel-encrusted casket with the glass face. Carried it past the thousands of peasants that took their morning away from work to watch their King put to rest. They shifted the casket off their shoulders and she and Eikian dropped the chains across the hole.

They pushed her King toward her. The casket hovered on the chains. She stared at Shankan's pale face, hers a reflection in the glass over it. She focused on her reflection and their faces became one.

They lowered Shankan down.

Servants sang the wordless song to the dead and it was with their lilting tones that the people truly wept.

Osondrous covered her mouth and Eikian gripped his hands behind his back.

Olisize resembled ancient things; he was a relic of gray dust in the dawn light.

He said, "People of this land. You suffer as great a loss today as all Wards, as all Warlords, as all soldiers, as all servants. Mourn out the dawn with us for your fallen King. But sleep tonight knowing that the hands that hold you are still strong. Our Shankan's heart stopped for what seems too young a moment for him. The promise to us was that he would be our leader for longer than the sixteen years he reigned. Have faith, another leader will rise. Know that you can trust your faith, your Wards and your safety."

Osondrous reached out her hand to Olisize. She stepped off the mound

128

and helped him down. Women stood, knees stained green with grass and stepped back from their path. Her soldiers slammed their fists into their breasts.

She held her head high and Olisize's hand kindly.

Every eye of the kingdom stared now at her hard face. They saw her like she was too young, too tough, too severe. The women loathed her for being not a part of who they were. And the men looked on her with disgruntled uncertainty. She was pretty, but nothing about her was pretty. She was too strong for a woman of this land and too disagreeable. And, on top of it all, the Centaur stayed a little too close, was a little too comfortable touching her and the rumors about Eikian and Osondrous made everyone in their land uncomfortable.

And poor Olisize held on to her arm like he was barely able to keep himself upright.

Though, not even in the dark rooms of far away inns or brothels would you hear of the people's discomfort; their fear of Osondrous ran deeper than all else.

7

"You did well on Shankan, Olisize."

The King Ward's face had been pale and gray with death but not yet angry in decay. His hands had still been pink; even his eyes, though closed for the funeral, had returned to their sockets and been bright white.

Olisize leaned on his cane, sighing, "How do you think Shankan fell so easily?"

"They had to have driven him mad first . . . . It must have taken months. Our failure is that we did not notice. Why did he not ask for help?"

Olisize stepped into his chamber, shaking his head. As his door closed, she sighed and walked down the hall to her own room. Eikian followed her.

Osondrous sat down on the edge of her bed and put her face in her hands. Eikian spoke to her but she did not answer. He rubbed her back and smoothed her hair. He murmured something. Eventually he lay down to wait for her.

Constance ran out of the Centaur guard house, stretching out at a dead sprint. She gasped for breath when she swerved into the kitchen.

"Constance?" Relhie called. "Are there no Implins left?"

"No!" she said. "They all must be at Shankan's resting."

Relhie shook her head. "Why must have Shankan died? There are only three of us here serving and half of the soldiers are doing twice their share so the rest could go and mourn." Relhie's face was red from exertion; the bags under her eyes were deep and purple. She had not slept for over a day.

"Let me help, Relhie. Please."

"Oh, Constance! It is not so simple. The archers and watchers in the Human guardhouse are the ones most desperate and I cannot send you there."

Taking her guardian's sweat-soaked hand, Constance said, "It will be all right, I will take the trays. Tell me what I must do."

Relhie touched her cheek. "You are stronger than you look. Osondrous is wrong about your future . . . All right. Thank you."

The guardian handed her a tray packed with food and mugs of tea. "Take this to the third level of the Human guardhouse's watchtower. Do be careful!"

Constance weaved under the weight of the food and hurried toward the door.

She backed into the Human guardhouse, staring at the pitchers with wide eyes, willing them to steady. There she stopped and waited for her eyes to adjust. All the beds looked empty. She hurried to the back, passed the smaller Implin beds (all empty, too) and to the door that led into the tower.

Behind her, three men stepped farther back into the shadows to stay hidden. Their eyes were gleaming as they watched her.

Constance swallowed down her pulsing heart. She looked up the tight, narrow wind of the staircase above her. Slowly, she started up the steps, watching her toes, tray lifted above her head. She followed the stairs as they spiraled up in the middle, between the floors. She stopped at the third floor and squinted through the dim torches.

"Oh, Constance. Oh, thank you. Let me get that."

She jumped at the sound of a man's voice. She knew him from the dining hall. He was a captain.

"Tell Relhie thank you for us," he said and called upward. "Food!"

He was joined from above by half a dozen others.

She turned and hurried back down, into the warm light of the guardhouse.

The thick tower door shut tightly behind her; she hurried forward.

A man got out of a bed before her. She stopped, stared.

"Constance . . . What are you doing here?" he asked.

She backed up, remembering him. Marcus' eyes were black slits and his mouth was hanging open. The shirt he wore hung open and untucked; the tails were dirty with black smears of food and brandy.

She gasped. "I was needed here. The watchers needed food."

A man grunted from behind her.

"And you did not bring some for us? We are just starving from all of our mourning," Marcus sneered.

"I will go get you some." She swallowed to keep her voice from shaking. Her chest lifted and fell in quick gasps. Marcus rubbed his beard and glanced away from her. She turned to see what he was looking at.

A hand slapped her head back. Arms encircled her from behind, slamming her back into a leather-breasted chest. Constance kicked out, throwing her weight, kicking her heels into the man's shins. A grimy hand slammed across her mouth.

Marcus grabbed her hips.

She screamed, "No!"

Another man appeared from behind Marcus, eyes hidden behind strings of gray hair. He grabbed her ankles. She squirmed, clawing at the hand across her mouth. She stared at the door to the guardhouse; she stared at the door to the tower. She screamed into the palm as they pinned her to the floor and filled her mouth with leather.

9
Osondrous

Osondrous, startled, sat up. "Teek. What is happening?"

Teek answered in his drone. "Constance is being raped."

She stood with the sound of Eikian's hooves hitting the floor.

"Tell Aerick!" She sprinted down the hall, picking up speed with each connection to the stone. She threw out her will before her. Knew the names, the faces, the very thoughts of the gathering of her cruelest three soldiers. Soldiers she had not cared to know until this moment. This far away, she could not hurt them with her will. They scrambled around the corner, into the hall of silence. Eikian's hooves sparked across the stone. In front of them, Aerick was running full tilt. He hit the door of the guardhouse before them. They pierced into the darkness. Osondrous threw her strength outward, hitting the men with her will.

10
Constance

Constance cried, throwing herself against the arms that held her down. Marcus ripped her dress off. He pulled himself from his leggings and his cock jutted forward eagerly. She squeezed her eyes shut, tearing her face away. Marcus' hard callused fingers, wet sand paper, ran across her contracting belly.

"Oh, have we not all wanted you!" He grinned as he pushed his fingers between her legs.

She screamed, "No!" Bit the hands trying to cover her mouth.

He went down on his knees; the hardness of him probed between her thighs.

Constance's eyes opened wide as he pushed his thumbs into her softness, wrenching her apart. He wriggled with an uncoordinated thrust and jabbed it in. She writhed. She screamed. He pushed, broke her open. She fought and did nothing but make him grin, make him thrust harder and harder. He breathed hard with his mouth open, spraying her face with spit and sweat. She felt the soft, hot give that could only be the blood of her.

The others hooted and cheered.

Her blood lubricated him as he rammed it into what felt like no less than thick, down-to-the-bone burns lining all of the inside of her.

The door was outlined in white, outlined by the light of day, of salvation she could not reach. She knew then that women were born with an open wound. She squeezed her eyes shut and the tears sheeted her face as he continued opening that wound until she felt certain that the pain had been driven so deep that it would kill her.

She opened her eyes and everything had changed.

White fire burst into the guard house and licked up along the ceiling

132

and floor. A sword as large as a man entered at a throw, spiraling through the air. The light blinded her and she pulled away as the sword hit Marcus and catapulted him off of her. She saw at the door a filly made of scales and scars with feet like a dragon's; the fire was hers. Whips snapped around the filly's wild head; they slithered forward and wrapped around the heads of Marcus and his bastards.

Marcus and his men hit the floor around her, screaming and clawing at their eyes until they drew their own blood. Aerick and Eikian tied their hands and ankles, kicking their stomachs and backs until they begged for mercy.

Osondrous knelt at her head and Constance curled around the thing that she still felt, that had forced itself to a place within her. Her body wept as it tried to fill the hole that had been left, as it tried to undo.

Osondrous' cold hand pressed against her soaked forehead.

"Constance." Osondrous spoke softly. "It is going to be all right."

Aerick swept her up. He covered her with his arms and hands and took her away.

Eikian stood with both of his front hooves on Marcus' back.

Osondrous shook her head. "This is what my soldiers think about. Is this really what I train my soldiers to do?"

The Centaur said, "This cannot go unpunished."

"Oh," she said, "this I will deal with. Tie them to posts in the courtyard. Spread the news that those peasants who came to witness a funeral will have something else to witness today."

Marcus screamed, "She's only a servant!"

Osondrous said, "Gag them all." It would be the last time Marcus spoke.

11
Osondrous

In the courtyard the shovels of soldiers sank into the sand, digging. They dug until three feet of ten-foot posts were buried. By noon the sun had turned everything to gray stone. Tied so tightly to the posts that they could not move, the three men could only tremble and sweat.

The Warlord sat on the top step of the hall of silence. She stared unblinking with her jaw set. Eikian's hooves clopped to a stop beside her.

"Everyone is watching," he said

She strode down the steps and screamed, "Do you know these men?"

She landed in the courtyard's sand and three sets of eyes stared at her, brows pleated in horror. As she spoke, it was to the thousands of soldiers and peasants around her standing in stern-faced silence.

Her voice, with her will pushing, reached every ear. "You trained beside these men. You trained beside them and heard the same laws that they agreed to live by. They are just like you! They cannot hope to have a woman unless she is entirely willing. They cannot hope to have the servants of this castle for their beds. But they destroyed the chastity of a fifteen-year-old girl."

Osondrous drew a long, skinny dagger from its sheath. "Do you see what happens when my laws are not taken seriously? I do not ask for much. My men will not be animals."

Osondrous stepped to the first post of the three. She cut down his pants, released the pathetic little pink thing that hung shaking between his legs. His face writhed, sweat poured off of him. He began to sob as he begged beneath his gag. His mouth was wrenched open wide. Saliva melted down his chin as he gnawed the leather strap.

"Do you see what happens?" She grabbed him and his soft shaft and balls squished out between her fingers. She slid the dagger down his shaking belly and sliced it all off. He screamed. The blood gushed between his legs.

Osondrous held it up for all to see, scrotum and cock squeezed between her fingers. The soldiers on the parapet held up their swords and cheered. She tossed it to the ground where it rolled like a wet rag. Olisize stopped the wound from bleeding, completing Osondrous' orders that these men would be sitting to piss for the rest of their lives.

She went to the second soldier and did the same.

Her body was stained with blood and the two soldiers finished were being taken from their posts, when she turned her attention to the real bastard. Her face was cold and thin and, looking upon it, Marcus pissed himself. The fetid stench rose as it dribbled through his pants and down the post.

Osondrous laughed at him. "Are you sorry yet? Do not you dare to consider that your pain now could compare to the pain you gave that little girl. Oh, I am going to give you something that will, might, eventually compare." Her voice raised and she yelled, "His sentence will be to rot in Centmere until he is eaten by the turtles and water!"

Another resounding cheer erupted and her soldiers began to beat the parapet with their swords. The beat began to grow and resonate throughout the castle. Servants who could not bear to watch stopped and covered their ears. The cooks in the kitchen stopped stirring; they lifted their eyes. Everyone waited.

She looked at him. "The last man lived thirteen days before he finally rotted to death. But you get to feel death first, so you know what is waiting for you."

Marcus' bright Willower eyes were wide and rolling. She dug her dagger into the side of his throat and pulled it along with fluid slowness until the blood curtained down. The beating of the swords ended with a roar. Osondrous held her red dagger high. The roar grew and grew as Marcus trembled and gagged. His mouth opened like a fish toward the sky. The noise became one screaming monster until Marcus had been brought back to life, taken down from the post and chained from shoulders to feet. He was strapped, weeping, to the back of a Warbred. The cheers only died after he had been led out of sight.

The cooks went back to work and the servants continued their duties, relieved at the final fall of silence.

12
Constance

"Here," Relhie said. "Drink this."

Constance opened her eyes and sipped the hot drink.

She coughed. "What is it?"

"It will keep you from getting pregnant. You do not want Osondrous to have to kill it for you."

Constance took the cup and drank it down. Olisize had come and healed her earlier, leaving her feeling better, but still empty. She lay back and covered her eyes as she cried.

Relhie fed the fire, then sat beside her.

"I heard the beating from the courtyard. What did Osondrous do to them?"

"She castrated the two and then killed Marcus and sent him to the swamp."

Constance whispered, "Why did they do it? I am not so pretty."

"More than anything, what makes you so attractive is that you are entirely against the law to almost all of them."

Constance's hands trembled as she pulled her blanket close, looking as wretched and tiny as she felt. Relhie stood and her face was dark and desperate. She understood that she had a punishment coming to her as well. Constance never should have been in that tower alone.

Constance snuggled into her pillow. She closed her eyes and tried to sleep. The dull ache between her legs and inside of her pounded with her heartbeat.

The girl's eyes flew open and she snapped awake.

"It is only me." Relhie set a tray down over her legs.

Constance wiped the sweat from her face.

Relhie touched her forehead. Constance put her face down in the steam of the carrot stew. The hot broth soothed her throat.

"How do you feel?"

"I am better . . . is it yet past sunset?"

"Yes, it is well past." Relhie touched her cheek. "I need to serve tonight so I must go. If you need me, anything—"

She clutched Relhie's hand and nodded.

Relhie kissed her forehead and held her for a moment before leaving.

Constance sighed, curling back into her bed.

She awoke when it was deep into the night. She was alone and the fire had eaten itself down. Constance cried in memory; her heart was black and full. Her door creaked.

Her eyes wide, she gasped, "Who is there?"

Aerick stepped into the room. "Just me."

She held out her hands to him and he grasped them, falling to his knees by her bed. Constance buried her face in his neck and cried.

"I wanted to be first," he said and she heard the rage in his voice.

She nodded but could not speak.

"Come with me," he said.

Constance did not ask where they were going; she just went.

13

Osondrous

Osondrous glanced at Eikian sleeping. She dressed and pulled a cloak around her shoulders. The gate guards dipped their heads at her, watching her step out of the courtyard and into the night.

She had dealt with the Ring one last time before leaving. And, with the discipline she had shown Marcus and the others earlier, many had fled for fear of coming before her and the Ring problems had been few.

The gray grass cracked under her feet, frozen by the north wind. She jogged to the back of the castle. The road to Rayakdool slipped into sight.

She murmured. Tamarack stepped from the trees, ears pricked. He chuffed in a long intake of her smell. She touched his cheek, his black coat long since faded to gray around his face. Holjel followed him and Aerick nodded at her from the height of his red stallion. Riding behind him, clinging to his waist, Constance wore a cape that covered her and his horse's flanks entirely.

She mounted and Tamarack trotted up the road.

The feel of the animal beneath her brought Telenay back to her and it did not feel like a week ago, when they had left at dawn, and every part of her had been so aware of him behind her. It felt like both a decade and just a moment. The path was the same but could have been the autumn path the same time years before. But she could still taste him, see his rolls of smooth, lean muscle all brisked lightly with black hair.

The animals trotted along, through dawn and into the day. They turned off the road and onto the path to Rayakdool at noon. Eventually the day waned and, in the distance, Constance saw the straw rooftops of two immense stone buildings. The road cut down between them and two thousand horses looked out at them from wide stalls as they approached. The miles of pastures around were dotted by dozens of herds of more horses. Foals frolicked by their dams while the old brood mares looked on, blinking at them from a distance.

"What was that place?" Constance gasped.

Aerick said, "They never named the stables. It is where Telenay and Osondrous created the Warbreds." He patted Holjel proudly on the neck. Both horses moved with a frisk to their step, noses high, as they returned home.

It was not long before the forest fell back, opening to a clearing. The expanse of Rayakdool held no buildings. Black tents were set up randomly. Soldiers were everywhere. Training courses, stained with blood, stretched on for miles and miles. Constance had heard stories of this place, of the hell put to the soldiers training here. She had never wanted to see it.

They moved up to an outer edge of the camp, to a knoll surrounded by pines. A dozen large tents were staked to the top of the hill.

Two Centaurs and a man stepped forward and bowed down.

Constance had never seen a Centaur in the field before. Many of the Centaurs at the castle were tattooed but always clean with their hair tied back. These Centaurs' faces and bodies were painted with blue and white warpaint. Their tail and head hair was long and braided with beads and bones that clacked together when they moved. The grime on them was deep up their ankles, covering their coats completely and ingrained under their fingernails. The man standing beside them looked freakishly neat and feeble next to them.

"This is so unexpected," the man rushed.

"Silence, Irikus." Osondrous looked at the Centaurs. "How has he been doing?"

"Fine," they responded in one voice.

She looked at Aerick. "Take the girl and rest if you need to. Just make certain Irikus is doing better than 'fine'."

The Second nodded and took Constance to a tent. She caught a last glance of the wildness of those two Centaurs and Osondrous looking on with no expression.

Irikus paled and stared at his Warlord. Osondrous dismissed him and he hurried away. The two Centaurs flanked her.

The three of them used the Centaur language when they spoke.

Osondrous said, "Noran. How have things been?"

He shrugged. "The new recruits are pushing our limits. We could use a couple more Seconds."

"I will be sending our older men soon for a week or two of refreshment. If you find any of them of worth, you may appoint them and keep them."

"Thank you, Warlord."

She dismissed them and waited until she was alone on the hill.

Tamarack shifted eagerly beneath her.

"Yes, let us get away." The stallion and the Warlord hit the wall of trees and squirmed into the shadows. Their departure was unseen and Tamarack moved swiftly, his nostrils opening wide to pull in the heavy air of the wood. Osondrous leaned close to his mane and sucked in his horse smell. The ground turned to swamp grass and the trees began to change from leaf trees to pines and, finally, tamaracks. The trees she had named her stallion after.

The lake Centmere was a wink of blue through the trunks, where many of their enemies had starved. She and Telenay had thought clearly about where the real sentences should be carried out, where they would be useful. They chose in the lake beside Rayakdool, so the unrested souls could torment their men and their horses and make them stronger.

As they approached, she caught sight of him. Marcus, laying on the bank of the lake, a log beneath his head to keep it mostly out of the water. His body was half submerged in the sticky, green muck. His arms were in the same position they had chained them in, behind him. Black beetles were already settling in, leaving bulging, squirming pocks beneath the skin of his cheeks.

The smell of him wafted past. She moved on, never knowing nor caring if he had heard or noticed her.

Sunset came and went into the late night when a sound finally reached their ears. Tamarack perked up, his back tightened, nostrils widening in anticipation. She smiled to hear that sound.

Tamarack sank into the silty shore. His nostrils trembled and he breathed in the salty taste.

The waves crashed over his hooves.

She looked out into the emptiness. There was no horizon and with the stars covered in high, black clouds, it could have all been ocean.

She said, "Tamarack, when I leave for the castle, you will not be returning with me."

The stallion dropped his head as the waves came. He touched the water and snorted.

She rubbed his neck sadly.

They followed the sand bank, along the grassy ledge of earth. They stepped up on the road and Tamarack trotted forward. Midnight came over their heads and with it the cold. Tamarack's breath hissed out. She saw what she sought in the distance. A Centaur town.

The lights glowed through small windows held by mud and clay. Guardhouses rested on either side of the road ahead of them. A gate barred the road.

As they approached, the Centaur guards called, "Who comes from the sea tonight?"

She said, "No worry."

They knew her voice and opened the gate. "Good night to you, Osondrous."

The houses were built with extra wide doorways and straw roofs. They had many windows and most were open. Every house was well kept with a huge garden and a goat or two in the back.

At the edge of a row, she stopped Tamarack and dropped to the ground. She loosened his girth and removed his breast plate and croupier. She unclipped his bit and tucked it into his saddlebags. He shook his head in relief, his chains shaking with jingles. Osondrous grimaced at his noise, glaring at him.

The stallion ignored her.

She clipped him to a post out front and turned around as the door opened.

A Centaur stepped out and raised her hand in greeting. "Is that the young Warlord?"

Osondrous smiled and answered in the same Centaur language, "Yes, I am sorry I am so late. I had not meant to wake you."

"Oh, Osondrous! Come in." The graying Centaur ushered her into the warmth of fire. "Oh, I know you cannot resist the sea when your heart calls for it. Will you not stay the night?"

The Centaur's coat was faded with sun and time and her back was bowed.

"I hoped you would ask, Naycin. Do you mind?"

The Centaur shut the door behind her. "Of course not! I am alone here with Chake gone. Eikian's room is always empty these days."

They embraced. Naycin's blond hair was grayer than when she had last seen her. But her eyes were the same, hazel and serious, like Eikian's.

"It is so good to hold you again." The Centaur's grip was heavy with the old strength of motherhood. "Are you hungry, Warlord?"

Osondrous shook her head. "I do not want to impose on you."

"You look like you have missed half your meals! Come, have a seat and eat late with me. Why are you so pale?"

Osondrous removed her cloak and shook the chill from her bones. She paused by the fire, holding her hands out. The Centaur's tail swished busily as she pulled out vegetables and salt-cured meats. Naycin dumped them all into a pot of boiling water above the fire.

She inspected Osondrous' chest wound and tsked her for not getting it more healed.

They drank dark mead, made of honey, by the Centaurs. "Tell me now, how is Eikian?"

"Eikian's light always lifts my day, Naycin."

The Centaur lay down on a mat over the dirt floor and Osondrous beside her.

Naycin smiled sadly. "I miss his smile now that his father is gone. He

140

took so much after him."

"It is not too many years until he can retire and come back here."

Naycin laughed. "Osondrous, I doubt leaving you has ever crossed his mind."

"I think it has. He has earned a retirement from all the—from it all."

"Aye, I know my son has, but I do not think he sees serving the castle as work anymore. Many of the Centaurs that come home only come for a female to settle down with; otherwise they would never stop serving the castle. You are good to them."

"I trust Centaurs over Humans." Osondrous reached out, stirred the stew as it boiled.

"You have always been too hard on your boys. The Centaurs have not the temptations that they must try and stand. Unless, of course, you put them behind a cart of fillies in heat."

They belly-laughed together, long and hard. Osondrous wiped tears from her eyes and Naycin covered her stomach as she tried to get control of herself.

Osondrous gasped, "I had forgotten about that. How could I forget that?"

Naycin shook her head. "Those poor soldiers, stuck back there, following those pretty little Warbred fillies, swishing their tails and winking away at them!"

Osondrous caught her breath. "Oh, 'those poor Centaurs' is right. Eikian finally said something and I think having to admit it was the worst. I felt awful; I cannot believe I did not notice."

Naycin patted her knee. "Oh, you were so young. And it was good for them, builds character. Helps them remember how hard it is to be a Human man most of the time!"

Osondrous sipped her brandy. "They do not have it as hard as they make it out. I have known strong Human men; they could all be strong."

Naycin put her arm around Osondrous' shoulders. "How are Eikian and you?"

"I never know."

"You are both too strong."

"No, I do not think we are strong enough."

Naycin stood and fetched bowls and spoons. The Centaur filled them with stew and laid down, handing one to Osondrous.

"Thank you." Osondrous breathed in the steam. She tasted the goat and it was salty and wild; she ate ravenously.

"You saved this village so many times. I think it is safe to say you deserve another bowl of stew served to you."

"Have you ever wished you were born in a different time? Or as something else?"

Naycin sighed. "I think we all do, at some point in our lives. Usually when we meet a special . . . someone. Do you think, Osondrous, that my son has felt that way because of you?"

"It is the other way around. Eikian and I keep each other at arm's length in many ways."

"I remember when you two were assigned to our village. The night you and Eikian came here, my heart stopped when he said that you would stay with him, in his room, in his bed."

Osondrous drank the rest of her mead.

Naycin said, "But Eikian told me to have no worries, that it could be no other way between you. It was either this, or you two could not be anywhere near each other. I did not understand at the time, but I think I do now. You two have such rebellious hearts."

"Then you understand better than I do."

Naycin held back a yawn and finished her bowl of stew.

"Go on to bed, Naycin. Thank you."

Naycin touched her cheek, looked into her face. "Things will be all right."

Osondrous nodded and watched the Centaur go to her room. There was no door to shut on the bedroom, not in any Centaur houses.

She stared at the fire for a moment before raising the pot of stew up so it would only keep warm and not boil to nothing. She took the dishes to the basin under the window and washed them in the water kept there. Looked around the tiny kitchen and the dining table. Breathed in the smells.

Osondrous followed in her past footsteps, to the back of the house, to Eikian's old bedroom. She lit the wood in the fireplace and the candle beside the bed. Lay down, closed her eyes and felt sixteen years old again. Lying with her cheek on Eikian's chest, wondering if he would touch, if he would dare, and what it would feel like. No consideration of how fiercely she teased him, no consideration of the consequences he could have faced. But he had never touched her; he had always held himself back.

Jezaline sat up and stared, eyes wide, at the empty dark around her. She could make out no horizon. She could hear nothing but the crackling of the fire and the occasional whip of the flames. Her face was stiff from crying and the dull ache in her chest was a bonfire. But she could bear Carmin being gone now, if only because she had to. She had dreamed of the red man and was clutching her knees against the shakes of fear that clung to her back like sweat.

Beside her Sethian shifted. Sleep-hazed, he opened his eyes and looked at her.

Ajax woke and said something in the Centaur tongue to his commander. Sethian nodded and got to his feet. The scuffle of their hooves sounded loudly. Quadik woke, sitting bolt upright. His eyes scanned everyone for a moment, but there was no emergency. She understood exactly how he felt.

They had a cold breakfast and she helped them get their packs on. And then, taking Sethian's hand, she got on his back. They kept her in the middle and they stayed close together. She watched the dirt beneath them, waiting until the sun rose enough that she could see ahead of them. The Centaurs trudged on cautiously, having no trust for the footing. Their shod hooves rang out time and again on stones.

The flat expanse of the Krept reached out around them. Great shards of red rocks jutted out along the horizon. As the river distanced behind, sparse grasses and cactus stood as the last sickly sign of life. Jezaline had heard of the swamps in the northern half of the Krept but did not know of this desolate expanse of ground. Without trees to block it, the wind began to rise and picked up the fine dusting of red dirt that seemed to cover everything.

The Centaurs covered their faces and swept themselves up in thick leather cloaks.

"Is there anything on the horizon?" she yelled above the roar.

Sethian put his tail to the wind and pulled out the map from his belt. She squinted over his shoulder. The fine dust in the wind slaughtered her skin like living sandpaper.

"I had not expected flat ground!" he yelled over the wind.

"What are you talking about?" Derkay pushed beside them. Jezaline's thigh pressed between the two creatures. Ajax stood on the other side of them, putting his arm around behind her.

"By now I had expected to reach a mountain range. According to the map, the Stonedowner mountain range continues on the other side of the river heading straight west and it also cuts north, all the way up before our path!"

"Are you sure we can trust the map?" Quadik asked.

"It does not matter," she cut in. "We cannot stay in this wind forever!"

"Let's move!" Sethian pushed the map into his belt.

Quadik took the lead. The Centaur's wide hindquarters shifted and his hooves smacked the hard ground. She closed her eyes. The movement of Sethian pounded endlessly beneath her. His heavy, monotonous breathing throbbed between her legs.

Eventually, noon came and went and the wind grew more and more fierce with every step they took west.

Sethian said, "Once we reach that shade in the distance we will stop. It is already starting to get dark."

She said nothing, palms sweating on his sides, hot beneath the many layers of leather tied around her. She pushed her face deep into the neck of her cloak. She closed her eyes and leaned against his shoulder, focusing on the movement of his gait, pulling away from the only sounds, the pounding of hooves muffled beneath the roar of wind. She trusted him that there was something to be seen on the horizon, because she could see nothing through the dust.

Derkay took the lead, striding out into a canter, gaining more faith in the lay of the ground as he traveled over it. They left no hoofprints behind them. If they feared being seen or tracked by danger, they were wrong; here they could absolutely disappear and no one would ever find them.

It was growing later when it happened.

Jezaline was napping and the Centaurs were really traveling hard. Beneath their cloaks, sweat stained their bodies and red dust clung to every drop of moisture. In the distance there was something: mountains, trees, something. They were determined. When it happened, it was with the Centaurs running out with no caution.

She was awakened by the slamming of Sethian's hindquarters to the ground and she was being thrown into his back. Sethian held on to her as he skidded to a halt, his fore hooves leaving the dirt, his tail hitting the ground. She had a flash of Derkay's hooves as he hit something and flipped over it.

The wind whipped their dust past as they finally stopped. Ajax bumped her as he scrambled to stop.

Derkay lay on a line of wicked fencing. Every two feet, sharpened posts reached up from the ground. Too big to impale Derkay when he had turned sideways to avoid them, they hit him low and flipped the big animal over the top. The posts' sharp points had dragged down his sides on the way.

Ajax and Quadik pushed between the spikes and helped their comrade up. Sethian stared grimly at the two spiked posts beside them, wet with Derkay's blood.

She saw the blood and the cloak around her suddenly felt way too tight. Derkay groaned and Jezaline watched grimly as he tried to take on his own weight and hung on Quadik. Ajax worked fast, cleaning the wounds with their precious water. Derkay wrapped a blanket around his barrel, wincing and limping. He looked up at them and they all looked at Sethian.

Sethian was watching the fence stretch out beside them, infinitely, in both directions.

"Ever see anything like this?"

"No."

"Do not plan to again either."

The voices of the Centaurs to her blurred as they spoke like this. To her it was all of them speaking and none of them. They were shared thoughts.

She said, "Draegoone?"

They stood silent, shaking their heads. No one knew who built the fence, nor what it had been made to keep out, or to kill.

15

The sun began down on their third day in the Krept. Their water supplies were down almost to half. The wind continued to lash them. Sethian stopped and braced, reaching for a hold. Jezaline hid her face against his back. Quadik led them, following the grooves of stone made by the wind. The darkness in the distance had been a mountain range. A literal place of stone skeletons, shaped by sand and wind, contorted with endless paths surrounded by sheer red rock. Everyone was bleeding. Sethian shaved a sharp edge and it slit his bicep right open. Jezaline wrapped it and held it with him barely noticing. The bay form of Quadik she saw, briefly, over Sethian's shoulder. Her eyes were swollen from the dust and watered constantly.

They had stopped twice since the fire by the riverbank where the silence had made it impossible to rest. The Centaurs had stretched canvas over the ground, pounded it in with stakes and they had crawled beneath it where they rested only out of exhaustion. Jezaline pressed between two Centaurs, smelling Derkay's blood and all of their frantic sweat. The wind slapping at the canvas had made their ears ring. Sleep was impossible and they felt it now, right down to their very bones.

"I see something!" Quadik cried.

She looked up.

Before them they could see an end to the range of cliffs and rock.

As they emerged into open ground, the wind wailed like a tidal wave.

Sethian wavered, sidestepping before hitting against Quadik. The other Centaur braced and they moved forward together. She pulled her leg out from between them and coughed until her sides ached.

When the sun went down and everything was black, the wind was no longer a massive thing around and before them with nothing to stop it. The sliver of a moon was covered; the stars blinked in the clouds.

They could see something different in the distance.

They drew closer and it was most certainly a forest.

"Where there are trees, there will be water," Sethian said.

Agonizingly it came, the silence of life without wind, the feeling of walls again, the sound of noise echoing back to them. They stood in the darkness, unable to see the sky above them and they stood silent in the glory of the silence.

"Where are we?" she asked and the sound of her voice was now a curious thing. The sounds of the Centaurs' hooves on the path was a shockingly loud noise. Sethian set her on the ground. She did not let go of him. Her senses were tuned; there was the smell of earth here and of dried wood, dead trees.

Quadik and Sethian scrambled to get a fire started. The flint sparked, sparked again and then lit.

They were on a road, a mere slice cut out of the tight forest. The trees around them reached out and embraced the others with their branches. There was nothing living as far as they could see; the ground was parched and cracked. The trees were so long dead, there was no telling when they had grown into the massive forest that now stood.

Like refugees emerging from war, they began to unwrap themselves. Began to realize again what and who they normally were. Wounds were uncovered, grotesque and jagged cuts that had bled until they were done which had gone entirely unnoticed until now. She helped them unwrap their legs and hooves. No one spoke. They were revitalized for a second now, not having to fight to stand upright or to hear or to speak. But once the packs were on the ground and they were eating some and drinking a little around the fire, their exhaustion became too deep to ignore.

Before she faded away she wondered, had this been an Elvin forest once? Before the rivers had cut the land in three? She felt certain that it had been the rivers that had killed this place. Maybe they had stopped the spring, trapped it into the middle realm, and cast this place into wind-filled desert. She wondered how much else had been destroyed with the rivers.

They did not sleep restlessly. There was no amount of silence now that could keep them awake.

16

The desert was at the height of day, where every thing was moving and shifting and distorted by the heat. She was stumbling and the sand was spraying out before her tired feet. The river was deep in shade. Her mouth was broken and tasted like blood. Her throat was so dry she could not swallow. She could hear herself gasping and crying with each painful breath. She kept her eyes on the river and even as the wind picked up and the vision of shade blurred in red dirt, she kept going. The red dirt did not belong in the desert. The red dirt was of the Krept and the closer she got to the river, the more the trees faded from green to gray. And the ground changed from sand to the hard, thirsty ground of Dead Wood.

She stumbled beneath the trees and there was no water, no relief. She hurried on, searching, hoping that there might be something, anything to soothe her throat. She came to the dry river bank and across it the red stallion stared at her. His eyes narrowed and he glared with fiery intensity.

She pulled back.

He changed. His feet grew out into claws with each step before her and, as she watched, his mouth opened and mutated. Long sharp teeth grew and his bottom jaw elongated with a snap. Horns spiraled out from his head and his body went black and smooth like oiled leather.

He came upon her and she was unable to turn and flee. She felt the sharp ridges of the trees behind her. Where there was once a path, she was now surrounded.

147

He bent down to look her in the face. Saliva slipped down his long teeth as he opened his mouth.

"Go back to the castle!"

She screamed.

Jezaline opened her eyes and stiffly moved out from under Sethian's hands. He groaned. She reached for the water and took a sip. Red man did not want her to proceed.

"I will make you something to eat, Ward." Sethian's voice was heavy with sleep. He cleared his throat and coughed. He dug in Ajax's pack and found a cooking pot.

Jezaline held herself but would not be tamed. "When do you think we can get moving again?"

She would be damned if anyone told her what she could or could not do. She would not turn back, no matter the costs.

She dug her hands into her belly, into the dull ache that had been growing every single day since they had entered the Krept. Now, it absolutely sung. She felt it was almost penance, or maybe a reminder of owed debts. Maybe red man would come for her, come for some kind of payment for what he had given her. And always her common sense mind fought it. Continued fighting to believe that she had been born a Ward. But the long, slippery teeth of her dream remained printed on her mind.

Sethian dropped to the ground and set the pot into the side of the fire, filling it with water, turnips, dried meat and carrots. "We are going to have to use some of our water to clean our wounds or infection will eat us."

Sethian stirred the soup. He broke off a piece of bread and handed it to her.

"I do not know where the butter is." He shifted to look in one of the packs.

"Do not worry about it." She ate ravenously.

He dipped his piece into the pot and pressed it into his mouth, chewing slowly and deliberately. Every time he moved, he winced.

She rubbed his arm. "We cannot stay here forever."

His shoulders fell. "We have only been here half a day." He looked at her. "Do you need anything?"

She looked down at her dirty dress. "No."

Quadik shifted and painfully opened his eyes.

"How are your legs?" She looked at Sethian's swollen ankles.

"Stiff."

"Are they very sore?"

"Derkay has some Aloe in his bag. If we do not use it all on him, it should take care of it."

"Oh, that smells wonderful." Quadik cleared his throat and spat out a mouthful of blood.

Sethian spooned a bowlful of stew, handed one to her, then another to Quadik. Ajax and Derkay woke groaning and soon they were all shoveling food into their mouths. Each face haggardly bowed to the steam above their bowls. There was little talk.

After they ate, Derkay's three comrades lay down beside him and, using no tenderness that Jezaline could see, began cleaning the wounds down his side. They were deep, ravaged cuts, torn open more than sliced open, leaving broken bits of dying skin all along the edges.

Derkay hissed, "You could not have done this while I slept?"

"You would not have slept through this," Sethian said.

The sound of rain trickled down and tapped against the dead branches. Jezaline tipped her head back to feel it and felt nothing. The canopy let none of it through. The trees turned black.

They bandaged all of Derkay's wounds, then lay down and distributed what was left of the Aloe. The wind howled above them, the branches cracked and creaked.

She brushed out her hair, thick with grime, and plaited it tightly. The Centaurs doubled over on themselves as they brushed out their horse hides and tails. She changed into a clean dress, acting as though the Centaurs could not see her curves beneath her slip.

She moved beside Sethian and took the brush from him.

"No . . ." he protested.

"Yes," she said and started working on his side, her bare legs resting along his back, feeling his horse-heat. The sound of the weather grew loud but they felt none of it. In the circle of the firelight, she felt protected from the storm.

One of her first lessons as a girl was how to rub horses down to relieve their muscle pains and sores after hard work. Now, barely thinking, she started in on the long muscles down Sethian's back and the other Centaurs looked on longingly as he stretched out and sighed. It was healing for her, working her hands like the way she worked her hands as a girl, smelling horse hair, kneading horse flesh. And it was healing for Sethian. He fell asleep as she finished working her way down each of his legs.

It was easy to fall quiet now, as exhausted as they all were. She stood and went to each of her protectors in turn. Conscious of their wounds, she brushed out their coats and rubbed them each down with the linseed oil she had brought with her for Carmin. She unbraided, brushed out, and then carefully rebraided all of their tails.

Ajax sighed, rolled over for her to do his other legs and said, "You are an angel."

She said, "Angels do not exist."

He said, "I believe in angels."

"Do you?"

"Right now I do."

"You are all going to die on this quest for me."

Ajax was quiet for a time and the others frowned. She bent and straightened his right foreleg, working down the ankle muscles and knots. Her hands were strong and shining with oil.

"Well," he said, "could I see your breasts before I die?"

Sethian rolled his eyes. The other Centaurs sighed but Jezaline looked up at him and began to giggle. She laughed until the pain in her ribs made her cry. The sound of her joy lifted and entered the blackness of all of the dead trees. She laughed until she was bent over and gripping her belly and the Centaurs were grinning.

Jezaline wiped her cheeks, patted Ajax as she finished and said, "One more good meal, one more good rest and we need to go."

That evening, the air cooled down and she remembered that there was autumn coming. The weather had so completely changed with the wind that she had forgotten about autumn. She shivered beneath her blankets.

"Are you cold?" Sethian pressed his lips to her ear.

The snores of the other Centaurs around the fire comforted the air.

She moved in closer to him; his arm curled around her. Her back pressed against his wide, hard stomach. She felt him sigh into her neck and knew this embrace was as much for his benefit as hers. As strong and tough as the Centaurs appeared, they needed touch more than Human males.

"That was very good of you," he whispered.

"I love horses. It is in my blood . . . The one thing I was never able to deny of my upbringing."

"You have not been dreaming."

She said, "Too tired to dream."

She felt his breath on her back as he slept again. She pulled her knees to her chin. The wind blew above them.

17

There was no discussion about whether or not to continue on into the dead forest. Not a single word of argument or consideration that the place was narrow and without escape. Even as they gazed wide-eyed at the skeletal trees, none of them considered going back into the wind, or even voiced it. It was the worst decision that they could make.

Quadik made a torch and took it to their lead.

She rested her hands on Sethian's waist and her chin on his shoulder.

As he walked, she said to him, "Your gait is smoother."

"The sleep and you helped me." He patted her knee.

The Centaurs settled into the only sound: their hooves crushing the fallen branches and rocks that littered the road. The rain settled above them and ended with the sound of the wind until even that settled into the calmness of a dark, gray day. Sethian followed Quadik at a length's distance and Ajax and Derkay followed them.

She watched the light of the torch.

18

Sethian stopped. Jezaline raised her head and squinted forward, realizing she had fallen asleep again. It was dark out now and the only light was Quadik's torch. The firelight caught all of the tiny, wicked branches reaching out at them from above and around. Everything was in deep shadow.

Before them was an old bridge made of downed trees, still fully barked where travelers had not worn it away. There were no railings. Below it was a cracked and dusty riverbed.

Sethian motioned, then rushed to the side of the bridge; his hooves sank down in the embankment. They ducked their heads and stepped beneath the bridge and pressed back against the dirt walls.

Quadik put out his torch. The black was complete. Her heartbeat rose to her throat. Jezaline could not hear anything and did not dare speak. Sethian gripped her firmly.

Then she heard a sound in the distance. Like thunder. The sound of hooves. It began to roar. As it picked up speed and drew closer, she recognized the sound of a herd running. Dirt fell down on them as the bridge began to tremble. The hooves hit the ground in sprints. The hoofed creatures landed on the bridge in a thousand smacks; thunder surrounded them.

Sudden squealing pierced the night and she heard hooves scrambling and cutting into wood. A scream fell down at them and she cried out as something hit the ground close. One of the Centaurs slapped his hand over her mouth. She could feel his mouth pressed into the back of her neck.

There were struggles and whimpers in the dirt beside them. It stilled.

The sudden whisper of wings spread overhead. Screams in a tongue she had never known cut down at them, multiplied and then vanished after the hooves. Then the hooves distanced themselves from the bridge and the rhythm of those wings was gone.

They waited until there was nothing but the dark again.

Quadik lit his torch. Ajax took his hand off her mouth. She opened her eyes and stared at the black creature laying beside them, an arrow in its side.

"Black deer," Sethian said.

The small, cloven-hoofed deer had a smooth black hide that was bloodied. Its hooves were twisted beneath it and it stared at them, eyes frozen in death, blood dripping out of its nose.

"They did not come for this one." Quadik jerked the arrow out of the deer's side.

"They had enough to not have to worry for one." Sethian looked at the arrowhead.

Her eyes widened. "Is that a normal arrowhead?"

"No," Sethian said. "I have never seen anything like that."

Quadik touched it. "It is some kind of metal."

Each of the five razors were serrated and Jezaline swallowed down her queasy stomach. Sethian gave the arrow to Derkay. He tucked it into his sheath.

"Do you think it may have been a bad idea to hide from these folks? They may have right been the Draegoone," Ajax said.

Sethian shook his head. "I do not think that we would have wanted to run into this hunting party. Let us move."

Sethian took her up to the road, hands holding her knees. He adjusted her position, pushing her back off his spine.

"Sorry," she said.

He looked at her but said nothing. Quadik took the lead.

They walked until sunrise and the trees had thickened around them. She pulled her cloak tight, shivering. Sethian felt her tremble and asked her if she wanted to stop and make a fire.

"No, we must move." She looked up the road and it continued on, straight as far as she could see.

Ajax distributed bread and dried meat. They were all thinner by many pounds.

They went for another day before finally stopping when the sun went down. Sethian set a plate of dried fruit between them. She ate and the fruit stuck in her throat. She forced herself to only sip the portion of water offered her. Sethian drew close, put his arm around her and she laid her head on his chest.

She jerked awake.

Sethian said, "You did not sleep but a second."

She rubbed her face. She did not tell him that she did not want to sleep. The ache in her belly was a gnawing creature now and she pressed it against him. He held her tighter. They made no fire, their one little light was a torch laid down between them. Ajax, Derkay and Quadik should have been trying to sleep but they lay, eyes large.

She said, "Maybe we should just get up and keep going?"

Quadik said, "We are still resting whether we sleep or not."

It was beginning to occur to them that this was not a road but a corralling system. A place to herd whatever was being hunted at the time. A death trap with no end in sight. It seemed only a matter of time. They all lay there sensing the darkness around them becoming violent, turning them into the hunted.

Eventually she saw the other soldiers slip into their own worlds. They lay down, blankets drawn around them, close to each other for warmth, and gradually their eyes closed.

She turned into Sethian, looked up into his gray eyes and masculine face. Jezaline slipped her hands up around his neck and rose up to press herself against him. Sethian let her take him over and lay them down. Beneath the blankets she pulled her dress open and pushed his fingers down, filling his palm with her breast.

Sethian hesitated, his brow pleated and frowning.

"Touch me." Jezaline's voice broke. She pressed her face into his neck and began to cry. Sethian's fingers moved up and down her body, cupped her breasts and grabbed her thin waist. At first he touched with the force of a soldier doing his duty. Then he opened his mouth and kissed her wet lips. He touched the tears off her cheeks, kissed her face and her neck. His mouth moved down to her breasts and his fingers parted her wet grace.

He had her in every way he wanted. Embraced in the silence of Dead Wood. They made almost no sound. She pressed her mouth into his chest and took the pleasure even as she cried. Sethian was hot, unbelievable comfort and Jezaline had never been kissed so tenderly, so wantonly, but she had also never kissed a Centaur. She was on her back when his fingers sent her and she felt the tremendous tingle even through the ache.

She carefully pulled her dress back together. He did not let go of her.

Sethian held his lips to the side of her cheek and ear. "We failed you."

Tears threatened her again. She shook her head, covered his mouth with her fingers.

"I should never have brought you here," she said.

He lay with his head on his arm. She curled into his chest and Jezaline actually slept for a time. The heat of his comfort still clung to her. The heat of his body helped her ignore the sound of silence, the sound of their graves being dug around them.

After a few hours, Ajax finally sat up and rummaged around for something to eat. They all sat up, inevitably awake as well. The torch was still the only light and they sat, ate and waited for dawn.

When it finally came, it was in the dimness of browns and grays because that was the color of everything here. Ajax put out the torch and they sat, despondent, looking at each other.

The Centaurs suddenly grew still, heads tipped, listening. Jezaline held her breath.

"What is it?" she finally asked.

"It is voices; they are using a language as the one we heard."

She said, "Maybe we should go to them and tell them who we are. If this is their forest, we should not continue without their authority . . . if nothing else." She had no conviction and shrugged.

"It is your call, Jezaline." Sethian frowned.

Ajax said, "Maybe we should."

Sethian stood and glared at the other Centaur. "How can you say that?"

Ajax stood up and crossed his arms defensively. "I have been puking blood for a week, Seth. If this is the Draegoone and this is where she belongs, then a warm bed sounds all right about now."

Quadik raised his hands. "All right. Well, you are both loud enough."

Sethian glowered and Jezaline got to her feet and put a little more distance between herself and them.

The gray commander's voice lowered. "Quadik, you think it will matter?"

Ajax interjected, "It matters! If these are Draegoone, then we need to go to them."

"And if they are not? How long do you think it will take them to rip us apart?"

Ajax's hand went to his sword and he stepped toward Sethian.

Jezaline took another step back, into the road. Laying behind the standing Centaurs, Derkay had picked up his bow and his eyes were following something behind her. She saw Derkay's face and froze.

"We were ordered to protect her! Have you forgotten why we are here?" Ajax was yelling.

"That is exactly it! We need to protect her!" Sethian retorted.

She could no longer hear them as her heart began to pound against her ears and her blood began to flood her vision. Derkay began to fit an arrow into his bow. She turned around.

An army of Vamepire were flying toward her. They spanned the road with their mouths hanging open, grinning. Their wings were twenty-foot spans of black leather, appendages emerging from their backs in thick rows of sinewy muscle. Their leader was less than forty feet from her. His blond hair flew behind him in a tail. And closer to her than him was the long, jagged blade that he clutched in his left fist.

She turned and began to run toward Derkay, lifting her legs, urging herself to sprint. Everything was slow; her legs felt sodden.

Sethian drew his sword and was approaching Ajax; things had been said that she had missed. Quadik suddenly realized and his face paled and his eyes grew large. He gasped and drew his sword.

Then they all heard the rhythmic hiss of what could only be wings.

Sethian was turning as he and Ajax both drew their second swords, their quarrel forgotten. She sprinted by them as Derkay got to his feet.

Whap. Whap. Whap.

Vamepire arrows shot around them, hitting the dirt and the trees. She covered her head. Derkay let loose, fitted another arrow, let loose again. The sound of dead Vamepires hitting the ground filled the air. *Thud.* He fit another arrow. *Thud.* He drew back again. *Thud.*

Quadik stood before her, a sword in each hand. He was screaming something profane.

Ajax and Sethian barred the road, bracing for battle. They were hit

155

again and again by the wretched black arrows. They stuck and bled from their haunches. Sethian cut the Vamepire out of the air as they came at his chest. The Centaurs' forearms were bulging in intensity; they sheened in sweat. Ten feet from them, the Vamepire landed as another six had fallen to Derkay's arrows. Their jaws showed rows of black, long teeth. It was, at best, fifty to five.

"Draw my sword!"

She pulled Derkay's sword from his belt and held it before her two-handed.

Armored Centaurs were almost invincible in war. Her Centaurs were not armored. Vamepire tried to fly past the blockade and Quadik leaped and cut them from the air. Vamepire blood rained down. Quadik's face was a drenched mask of death. He was moving forward to get closer to Ajax and Sethian.

The Vamepire crouched low and cautiously. They snapped and shifted at the air like snakes.

Sethian was rushed.

She covered her mouth and screamed for him. Sethian blocked and cut them down but as five Vamepire fell beneath his strength, three others dove at him. They stabbed his arms even as he sliced through their wings. Ajax was rallying, fighting his way to Sethian. He screamed as a Vamepire lifted his blade and brought it down as hard as he could, across Ajax's back. The Vamepire died from Derkay's arrow.

Quadik reached Ajax. The two Centaurs ran side by side, cutting down the Vamepire. Ten feet seemed a mile between them and Sethian.

From behind, the leader of the Vamepire stepped into Sethian's space, his blond hair in its braid flying at his back. Jezaline screamed to stop them. Derkay fitted an arrow. Quadik dove to kill him and was cut short.

Derkay let loose his arrow.

Blondie dodged it and raised his blade. Sethian was overrun. The Vamepire were biting his wrists even as he gutted them with his swords. His blood sprayed down his arms in torrents.

Derkay fitted another arrow.

Blondie swung and drove his blade into Sethian's back. It split from Sethian's chest. She could not see her gray commander's face as his legs crumbled beneath him. Ajax went down. The Vamepire dove at him, mouths open. Quadik started pulling the creatures off of him like they were flies. Their wriggling wings fell to the ground like gigantic eels.

Derkay was out of arrows. He scrambled through Sethian's pack for more. Ajax was no longer moving. Quadik was cursing at the creatures even as he was being stabbed from behind. His horsehide was a canvas of blood and deep gashes, showing his bones beneath.

Derkay was screaming at her and she heard none of it.

He grabbed her by the shoulder. "Jezaline!" He pushed her up the road. "Run!" Derkay put his back to her and drew his last sword; he was screaming, "You are all going to die today!"

She began to run. Her legs were no longer in slow motion. Her body was a knife, cutting through all of the gray and the brown. Jezaline thought of the last time she had run like this. The trees whipped by her until they were nothing but seamless walls of her endless gray tunnel. Out in the desert it had not been like this. It had not mattered then where she ended up as long as she got as far away as possible. Oh, how she had run that day. She could see him clearly, the red stallion, moving upon her without making a sound.

They were gaining.

She could hear their feet hitting the hard ground behind her now. So close, the individual footsteps were fading to the sound of the sharp breathing through their teeth.

Tears were coming now; the violent pain in her chest from running brought them on in torrents. Her panic barely conceived of her cramping legs. For the first time, she would have given anything to be back in the desert.

He caught her by her streaming black hair. Waited patiently until he finally had a handful of it. She felt his knuckles on her spine and screamed. He fisted and yanked her back.

Jezaline's head snapped. She went down and dropped Derkay's sword. She scrambled to her knees and rose up, hand clutching the fist that was ripping her hair out.

Blondie bent over her until they were nose to nose. She could smell his breath that was fresh blood; it covered half his face and was still running and dripping. Her Centaurs' blood. Sethian's blood.

She looked him dead in the eye and ordered, "Let go."

He laughed and it showed every single, sharpened point. His face was young. He walked like a soldier off duty, with a slouch and a casualness. When he let go of her hair, he stepped away and rounded her like she was an interesting thing to look at.

From the ground, she snarled at him.

Jezaline got to her feet.

Blondie said, "I am going to take you to him."

At the mention of *him* she felt a quiver of excitement wash over all of the Vamepire around her. Her stomach turned over in nausea.

She grabbed her will, gritted her teeth and threw her hand into Blondie's chest. The physical act would have made him laugh but what hit him was her power. He was propelled backwards into the group of Vamepire behind him. Jezaline spun and cast the Vamepire behind her to the ground. Adrenaline raced through her veins and it powered her. They got up and kept coming and she kept them down valiantly, working her way backwards down the road.

If it had only been a few, she might have been able to force them to let her go. Or if she had been a Warlord. She knew Osondrous would have killed them with a thought. But the dozen or so Vamepire coming for her now, some walking, some casually crawling on their hands and knees, was nothing she was capable of stopping. Blondie walked before them all, smirking and flexing his wings.

He walked into her range. She trembled in hysteria; she threw her hand out to hit him again and felt herself go empty. Her fingers splayed out across his chest. His hand closed around her wrist and she looked up into his eyes.

Blondie struck her across the mouth. She hit the dirt. Jezaline spat blood. He pulled out his hunting knife, grabbed the blade of it and swung the haft hard across the back of her head.

It was painlessly swift. Darkness covered her.

He pulled her onto his back and held her hands together over his chest. He rocketed forward and quickly reached the end of the road. If Jezaline would have seen it, she would have been stricken. If they had kept going instead of lying down and trying to rest, they could have reached the end of the horror in less than a day.

Beneath them it all fell away, road, earth, trees. And finally it all became one gray sea as they lifted above the clouds. His powerful thrusts took them higher and higher and the sun encompassed the east in brilliant orange.

They flew south along the mountain range of the Krept. The Vamepire stayed close to the mountains because a good portion of the valleys north of the range were still enemy territory. Draegoone territory. They took no chances and watched the north warily.

They flew all day.

It was growing late as Karalay spiraled up along the inside of the tallest tower of the palace. Outside the wind howled in long, endless circles. The stairs were coated with a layer of dust that clung to the bottom of her skirt. She held her candle high and steady as she bypassed landing after landing. They were filled with furniture, ancient carvings and paintings that were broken and unkempt. Random pieces of life that had been left to die. She reached the second to the last floor. Her candle lit the books that lined the room. The laden shelves climbed with the spiral staircase that continued on along the inside of the tower to the top. A dusty table and two chairs sat, abandoned.

On the table was a single open book. Above her was the last Crystal shard.

Karalay glanced at the books momentarily before lifting her candle in front of her and continuing to climb, albeit cautiously. She squinted at the underside of the above floor. Thick steel spiraled to the center and reached out in massive beams on all sides. She lifted her head above the floor. A dome rose up in the center, steel-wrapped like the bud of a flower.

She felt the pulsing now. A clear push of noiseless power, radiating up and out. The steel helped block it from the castle but up here she now felt the constant howl against her will.

The winter wind hit the side of the tower and the empty windows yowled around her. She stepped nearer the bud, clutching her shawl against the cold. Holding the candle close, she ran her hand down the edge of the steel. She squinted at the etchings and they were carved in every language of the Humans. The same statement was repeated over and over again: *Bow down, Humans, before your savior.*

Chills raised down her back. Karalay realized she was not alone.

She stared around the bud. "Who are you?"

The shadow shifted. "I am Cousai. I had not meant to startle you."

Cousai stepped around the bud and her cold, narrow features warmed by the light of Karalay's candle.

Karalay said, "What are you doing up here?"

"I had thought that you might be here. Sicilia told me that you are a scholar. I assumed you would be drawn then to the ancient library here. Out of curiosity though . . . I could not help but come up to the highest floor."

"I read that mortals would have trouble being close up here . . . to this."

"Normal mortals yes, that would be true. But you are not normal, Ward."

"And what are you exactly, Cousai?"

"I can tell you already know I am a Fai. I am royalty."

"Why are you here?"

"It is Sicilia who is here; I am only aiding her. Sicilia was eldest, she was heir and served as queen for three hundred and eighty-two years after our eldest brother's death."

"She is no longer queen?"

"No," Cousai's voice grew sharp. "She stepped down from the throne to come here."

"And you will not tell me why?"

"No one has any right to tell Sicilia's story for her."

Karalay pulled her shawl closer, shivered.

Cousai lifted her hand. "Come, let us get away from this cold."

Karalay stepped down into the library, Cousai a few steps behind. They sat across from each other and the Fai pushed her hood back. Her face was pulled down by weariness and sadness.

"Why did you choose to aid your sister here?" Karalay asked.

"I was alone."

"Where were you?"

The Fai looked up. "I chose my love over the throne and I was banished from the east. I was in your land when she came for me."

"Why?"

"Because my love is the prophet your Ward Jezaline came seeking when he called for her. He left me with instructions when he departed months ago. And I . . . I had doubted him because I could not believe how ever I was going to come in contact with a Healing Ward to speak to her."

Karalay blinked. "Me? Why ever would you need to speak with me?"

"He left me with your prophecy and the prophecy for the Ward Jezaline and the apology that he could not speak to you both in person. He said, Karalay, that you need look to your guardian for ever those that are made of ice have warmth within them and a heart. There is love to be found and there are things worth giving up everything for, including life and love."

She looked down and rubbed her mouth.

"That was all he said." Cousai spoke softly.

"How was Jezaline when you spoke with her?"

Cousai said, "I did not have comforting words for her and I know her path will be filled with pain."

"Did your prophet tell you such things?"

"No, her prophecy drove her to the Krept. I would imagine no less from that wicked place."

Karalay drew back, appalled. "Why would she ever go there?"

"Her prophecy promised her death if she returned to the Castle of the Wards. I believe she sought my Tarrick out to make certain whether or not what I told her was true."

Karalay stared in shock at the Fai. "Your love is a Draegoone?"

"Yes. His mother, the queen, called for him to return to his people while they prepare for war. It was found out that when a new King Ward is called, the rivers weaken and can be crossed by those from the Krept and the Swoon for one day. When the next King Ward is called, the Draegoone and the Fai plan to send all soldiers in their ranks to die against each other. That is the promise; it will avenge all the deaths and finally end the Five Hundred Year War of the Fai and Draegoone." There were tears standing in Cousai's eyes.

Karalay took a deep breath. "If Sicilia were queen, would this still come to pass?"

Cousai shook her head. "The Draegoone will attack the Fai. It is no choice as to whether or not they will defend themselves. But the Fai are not a people to defend. They will meet them halfway and fight until every last soldier is dead. It matters not who is ruling." There was a very clear note of disgust in Cousai's voice.

"You were not a part of this war?" Karalay asked.

"I was too young. Sicilia is fifty years my senior." Cousai stood. "I will go now. Good day to you, Ward."

Karalay reached toward her. "Tarrick will be fighting in this last battle?"

Cousai's face flickered. "His father was a general. His mother is the queen. He will lead the charge."

"You will lose him?"

"He is a prophet; he is where he needs to be." Cousai lifted her hood to cover her face. Karalay watched her go until the Fai stepped beyond the light of her candle and Karalay stared at the empty darkness. She leaned on the table, head in her hands. Cousai's words came to her again and again, moving through her like an echo. She knew Tarrick was a true prophet, trusted that. But sitting in the dark, cold and shivering in this vile

161

place, she had a hard time believing that there could be any kind of love to be found.

A hand reached out of the darkness and touched her.

She gasped and jerked away.

Jaridd chuckled

She said, "How long have you stood there?"

"I had not intended to startle you so."

"You knew you would startle me."

He picked up the book and paged through it above her. "A journal."

"Oh?"

He tilted the book so she could look and set it back down. "It is that of the heir before the king now, his eldest brother."

Ignoring him, she stood, reached for her candle and stepped down the stairs.

He followed her.

"Why was all this left here?" She motioned toward a landing full to the ceiling of half-covered furniture.

"Diggamara royalty died and had no one to pass it on to. If they had not been fullblood Diggamaran, it would have been traded or burned but, out of respect for their heritage, it was kept here."

When they reached the first floor, she blew out her candle and left it at the base of the staircase. She took off her shawl when they reached her chamber and draped it over the edge of the bed. The fire beneath the basin was roaring. The water steamed. She dipped her fingers in and struggled to unlace the back of her dress.

He pushed her fingers out of the way and began to unlace the corset. She sighed as the dress loosened, slipped from her breasts, hesitated at her hips, then hit the ground.

His fingers touched the curve of her lower back.

She stepped away. "Thank you."

Karalay tied her hair up and eased into the water. Her breasts prickled in the heat. She leaned back and closed her eyes, her head dropping on the pillows that lined the top of the bath. The servants had left a pitcher at the edge of the bath and a plate of fruit. Karalay picked a piece of yellow fruit from the variety filling the plate. Gingerly she tasted a little and smiled in appreciation.

She washed her body slowly, taking care. She massaged soap into her neck and down her back. She rubbed her legs and feet. She let her hair down and dipped her head back, letting the water spill over her face. She worked her fingers through her thick hair and scrubbed her skull.

Jaridd watched her, leaning on a wall, his face a void.

She gathered a robe around her, sat down before the mirror and combed her hair.

She said, "It is amazing that I have come to be so used to your presence that I do not even notice you constantly staring at me."

She looked directly into his eyes in the reflection of her mirror.

Jaridd blinked and looked down.

She said, "With your mask, I did not notice your eyes always on me."

"I forget I am not wearing it."

Karalay turned around in her chair and stood. The robe slipped from her shoulders and hit the floor. Her pearly skin shone before him. Her wet hair was a cut of black hanging around her face and dripping between her buttocks. She pressed her hands into his flat belly and sighed her long frame against his hard form.

She said, "I like it when you look at me like that."

His fingers slipped along her left breast. Her head fell and he picked it up. Karalay's eyes were dark and veined, exhausted. She pulled away and went to the bed. The sheets had been warmed by hot shells the servants had laid between them earlier. She lay down and pulled the blankets up to her chest. She looked at the carving of the sea.

"What does the sea look like? I wonder what it sounds like. What it smells like."

Jaridd said, "Salt."

"And sound?"

"Like a war. You have heard the sounds of armor clashing."

"At a distance; you were beside me."

"That is the sound of the sea. Waves crashing."

"I would like to see it someday. I probably will not get the chance."

"No Healer will die in this war."

"You cannot know that for certain."

Jaridd glared at her and she put her back to him.

20

She woke at dawn. She was alone. A tray of breakfast kept warm before the fire. She wrapped herself in a robe and sat down beside the tray on the hearth. She poured a cup of cold tea from the pitcher.

The food was nourishing and good, though it tasted like nothing to Karalay. Waking alone left her feeling empty and already dead. She held herself and the events of her last few hours in the Castle of the Wards replayed for her. She could feel Telenay's harsh grip on her hips, the rock hard of him against her back. She would have given all of her days with Jaridd to go back to that moment, to melt into Telenay, give herself to the Warlord, and stay at the castle like they should have.

She dressed and was heading for the door when, *thud!* something hit her window. She jumped around and ran to it. She opened the glass carefully and ducked when the black bird flew in. It cawed loudly and flew into her. She grabbed it, holding its wings against its body.

She glared into the raven's black eyes. *What is it, Raven?*

Her heart began to hammer as she looked at his leg. Ravens were only ever used by the Castle of the Wards. Tied to the black, skinny leg was a message. This was no random raven. She set the bird down and fumbled to untie the message. Her fingers shook; she felt tears brimming in her eyes. Ravens were used very rarely, only with the most urgent of news.

"Please, tell me, Osondrous, that you received our message. Let that be these words."

But Karalay knew better than to hope.

She untied the leather binding and unrolled the small strip of parchment. Her eyes leaped down the message.

Karalay fell to her knees.

She gasped, "Shankan is dead!"

She fell to the stone floor as all blackness closed in on her. She could hear nothing but her shocking heart.

Jaridd was there in an instant. His hands went to her and pulled her against him.

"Do not cry," he said.

She pressed her face into his neck.

Olisize and Osondrous were entirely alone now and there was no King Ward to appease the ambassadors of Willower, Diggamara and Stonedowner. The ambassadors would push for a new leader to rise immediately.

They would push hard.

Karalay struggled from his arms and went to her open window. She clutched the sill and glared out into the day.

She closed her eyes and Jaridd stepped back as she pushed with all of her will.

Osondrous, hear me, do not become queen. On your life, you stupid girl, do not become queen.

The raven ducked down as her will passed him over. Jaridd waited silently, hands behind his back.

Karalay looked to him, shaking her head. "I just cannot reach that far."

He took her in his arms and whispered, "I must go. But I will be back."

She nodded, numb. She sat down on the bed and the raven settled in the quilts beside her. Karalay covered her face and cried hard.

21

Karalay had fallen asleep. Her eyes were grainy fire.

The raven remained in his place, wings and face tucked up in his ruffled feathers.

She washed her face. The raven took flight when she stepped into the hallway. He landed on her shoulder. Karalay started the journey toward the tower as a woman in shock.

The raven gazed around with wide eyes, silent.

She lit her candle with the torch in the hall, then wound upward, climbing the staircase and passing the floors until she reached the library. The wind whistled above her and stilled. She sat down because she had nothing else to do. The raven's head whipped around and he shifted nervously. The bird looked up and she followed his eyes, hearing a whisper from high up. She crept out of the chair and sat down at the bottom of the staircase.

"Someone has come."

"We are alone. Sicilia. You are too filled with worry."

"And perhaps you do not have enough."

Karalay recognized the voices of Cousai and Sicilia.

Cousai said, "This is your affair to worry over, not mine. My love is good as dead. Why can you not have some form of understanding for my grief?"

Sicilia spat. "How can Jaridd still protect her?"

"Are you speaking of the Healer Ward?"

"She may have will but she is too weak to deserve a Darkhalk's protection now."

"Sicilia, a Healer on our side might be the difference that will change our endings in this war. They say that a Healer's will is stronger than any.

They could kill with the strength of a single thought."

"Then she need not such protection."

"Strength is not always followed by heart, Sister. Healers have not the heart to kill, I think."

"Then she has not strength and does not deserve any protection! We need Jaridd as a Darkhalk. His mind is already reckless; he has not the focus he needs. Where could his mind be if he will not take the Cape and the Sword back onto him immediately?"

"Sicilia, there is time."

"What time are you speaking of, Cousai? The King is dead. It is only a matter of days until another steps up to be King and then Grim will attack from Addilade and kill us all."

Cousai hissed, "The Wards are not so stupid. I cannot believe they would be that reckless and ignorant with all that is passing that a new King would take his place so rashly."

Sicilia snorted, "Humans are greedy; they will always disappoint."

Cousai said, "Let us fly away from this tower. The blackness from this wretched thing taints my soul."

Karalay heard nothing more. She knew all too certainly that Osondrous would prove Sicilia right.

Raven lifted his wings and disappeared into the floor above her. Tentatively, she followed him. He stood on the sill of one of the tower's empty windows. He blinked at her before taking flight and disappearing into the sky. The white evening was beginning as the sun dipped past noon and the clouds cleared of rain. She looked out over the endless sea of chimneys and black and gray roofs. She half expected to see the flying images of Cousai and Sicilia along the horizon. But they were gone. It felt as though no living thing could grow in such a place.

Karalay turned and headed back down the staircases, winding her way along the inside of the tower. Guards stood at the end of the hallway, garbed in the blue scales of Diggamara armor. On their chests was their proud, white symbol: six sails with their tips touching, making up a circle.

They bowed to her when she approached.

"Where are the stables?"

One answered, "I shall show you the way."

She followed him. The walk took them into the streets. A block from the palace, the guard stopped at a long building.

She said, "Thank you. I need no more of your service."

He bowed to her. "I shall wait for you outside."

She knew he would wait for her regardless of whether she wished it or not. It did not surprise her that the king would keep her well watched.

She stepped into the stable. The back of the building was fenced off and the floor was sand. Half a dozen horses milled there, stretching their legs. Down the walkway, the few horses in their stalls kept their heads down. Their eyes held the look of captured things when their friendliness had been brutalized and they had been taught to make no friends. But when they caught her scent, they recognized the Willower in her blood and their ears flickered and they shifted. They did not understand that smell, but it called to a far distant memory for them. A memory of their ancestors of the deserts, of the Willower. Of kind hands and respect.

Karalay searched each face for the mare she had ridden to the palace. She found her in the last stall.

The bay horse nickered and tossed her nose a little. Karalay reached out and the big muzzle filled her palm with moist breath. She slipped into the stall and her fingers filled with the mare's mane and neck.

She needed to use her will. She needed to have hope.

She concentrated on her heart, on bringing her strength right up and out of her.

She focused hard and willed. "Help our messenger make it in time."

Karalay almost fell. "He will not make it?"

She clutched the mare and cold tears began to slide down her cheeks. It was absolute now. No doubts anymore. She knew for certain that no messenger to the Wards would make it in time. War was coming. She grasped her head and shook and shook. Her hands and body trembled. Her head bobbed as she tried to get control of herself.

Karalay needed to know what use there was for her in such blackness. She could feel the heat again but now it was blistering. She could see Diggamara burning with all of its people stacked in the streets, bloody and dead. She needed to know that there was a chance it could all be stopped. That her stupid actions with Telenay would not eventually be the start of her own demise. Of Telenay's demise. Of the falling of the great Crystal shards and the rivers and so many more dead.

The mare's ears flickered, for she had not the intelligence to know more than that the lady crying was the only Human who had ever been kind to her. The bay mare touched Karalay on the back, chewing her teeth as a Human would twiddle their thumbs when they knew not what to say.

Karalay absently rubbed the mare's muzzle. "What use is it to be a Ward, to know anything and be unable to stop it?"

She looked into the mare's eyes. "Thank you for keeping me company today."

Karalay patted her once more before tearing herself away, lost in thoughts of fear. The mare watched the lady go, while thinking deeper than she had ever thought in her entire life. Thoughts of stable life and food and the generalness of being a horse were gone. When Karalay's will had been out, when she had been trying to aid the messenger before understanding that it was futile, the mare had felt her raw power. It had pulsed through her and the mare understood now that she must help Karalay in any way that she could. As she watched the lady go, the mare hoped that she would not fail her.

22

The dining hall table of Diggamara was adorned with bright blue, aqua and green scales beneath trays upon trays of fish, potatoes, fruits and assortments of goat cheeses. The king sat at the head and was eating long before anyone else arrived.

His advisers sat beside him and Karalay took her seat across from Dind, glancing at the once Darkhalk. He dipped his head at her and she nodded at him. The servants skated silently around the tables, serving the diners as they went, filling cups with shaking hands. A small girl leaned over her and began filling her plate.

She stared, unable to take her eyes off of the servant's tiny wrists as the hands, lacking any kind of flesh, hefted the heavy silver spoon full of food toward Karalay's plate. This was no girl, but a grown woman. Karalay's stomach turned over and locked. She stopped the servant from filling her plate and waved her away.

The king looked at her. "Have you enjoyed our palace, Ward?" His jowls shone with a layer of sweat.

She said, "It would be kind of me to say that this place is anything but barely satisfactory."

He raised his thick eyebrows at her. "Is that so? And what could be done to make your life here more comfortable?"

"I am Willower. Your horses need to be treated better. I realize the Diggamara have little love for land animals but the Willower will not forever stand for their sad treatment."

The king's jaw muscles tightened; he looked at his advisers for aid.

Dind said, "Our horses are fed well, Ward. As of late, the servants of the barns have been recruited here, to help us better serve you."

Her jaw tightened. "I appreciate your measures to see to my comfort, Adviser, but those horses need not suffer. What they desire is not more care, just a place to stretch their legs in community on grass. Obviously nothing to that effect has changed with my presence."

The eldest adviser said, "No, there have been plans to give the horses a bigger place to run with grass underfoot, but our focus has been to the sea. I hope you would forgive us; we have been short-handed after we lost three of our ships and all the servants aboard to a storm not a month ago." He was lying.

"Your servants here are born into servitude?" she asked.

"Yes, our servants have it in their lineage. We feed them well and treat them right."

The king guffawed. "We feed them better than we should! How much do you feed your servants, Ward?"

"Enough." She smiled thinly. "But they do have names at the castle."

"Ha! That is a lesson you will learn the hard way then. Just like us. Give them no names and it keeps them in their place. Keeps them under control!" The king raised his cup, took a long hard drink and smacked his lips.

The eldest adviser said, "We have made tremendous progress with our servants, Ward. You must allow us to take you to their locked quarters sometime!"

"Oh?" she said. Her smile was a freezing thing that she held absolutely to her face.

The eldest adviser continued, "We have started locking the best of our male servants and females together to breed. We are on our third generation now and their children are stronger and smaller, so they can go longer with less food."

The king growled, glancing at a girl who filled his plate. "We already feed them too much. Look at the fat on that one." The servant girl's chest was so painfully thin that when she turned, every single one of her back bones could be counted at a distance, jutting out from beneath her thin dress.

The king said, "It is the modern way of dealing with servants."

Karalay drank from her cup, her mouth suddenly so dry she could no longer swallow.

They turned their conversation to fishing and she lingered as brief a time as possible, then excused herself. She pushed open her chamber door and was relieved to shut it behind her.

23

Jaridd was at her window.

She stepped across the room to him. "Is there any news?"

"Nothing. Have you not slept this last night?"

She looked down. "Sleep has not come easy for me."

He brushed her pale cheek. "What words did Cousai have for you?"

She shook her head. "Jaridd, please, must you ask?"

"If you do not want to tell me, say so, and I will not ask again."

Karalay looked up at him, the dark brown of her eyes as warm as the fire that reflected in them. "Cousai said to look to you for ever those that are made of ice have a heart and warmth. That there is love to be found and there are things worth giving up everything for, including life and love." She turned away and rested against her bed post. "I cannot see hope anymore."

"There is always hope."

Her brow furrowed and she looked back at him. "It is so odd for you to try to reassure me of such a thing."

"Why?"

"Because you do not need hope. You do as you are told and will die doing it. There is nothing else to your life . . . is there?"

He stepped close and stared down into her eyes until she dropped them.

He said, "There is you."

She sighed and when he rubbed her back, she let him.

"Why do you not take on the Cape and Sword again?"

He said, "Could you possibly understand how tempting it is to be a Human when the chance is there to take it? When the brain and heart are not locked to think and feel nothing but what is ordered? Do you have any idea how much you Humans take for granted?"

She tried to pull away. "Everything we are given comes with some form of pain. That is it."

His fingers tightened around her arm. "You are given choice. That is priceless. You cannot imagine how many races have longed desperately for a choice beyond living or dying."

170

She sighed. "We have choice now. But we fought and died for it."

"Karalay?"

"What is it?"

"Why did you seep your will into me those times?"

She said, "I needed to feel someone."

"Did you feel anything?" His fingers slid down her back.

"Yes," she murmured. "Through the Cape and the Sword . . . I did feel you."

His face moved down beside hers and she took a breath of his breath. Their lips brushed. She turned fully to meet him, opened her mouth around his lips and kissed him until their tongues met. It seemed their first night together, stretched out in the darkness on cold stone, was almost without merit now. It seemed then they had been half out of their minds. Now, it was a choice.

He laid her down and pushed himself upon her.

She looked at him closely then, looked into his eyes. "I have wanted you forever. I am glad you brought me."

Karalay pulled his face to hers, tightened herself around him.

He said, "I will always protect you."

She watched him strip off his armor. Pull off her dress. She touched his naked skin, stroked the muscles across his belly. Drew lines down his back. She sucked her breath in. He gripped her, hands shaking. Her heart raced. She lifted her knees; he clutched her hips. He buried his face in her hair and pulled her entirely against him. He pushed all the way in.

She felt the inches of his body grow hot with hers. The speed of their sweat mingled in their unique smells, until it was their smell that filled her. She cried out. All the embrace of darkness last time was a sweep of a sweet night memory.

I remember this, her body said.

His body said, *I want more.*

When it was over, she pressed her head against the damp pillow, staring down at them still locked. His grip slipped in their sweat. She caught her breath as he broke them apart.

24

Osondrous

Osondrous slept like death in Eikian's old bed. She dreamed of older days when she had still felt young. Her eyes opened and she looked out the window. Groaning, she rolled over. Outside her window, dawn was only just beginning to light the night. Naycin tapped on the doorframe before entering.

The Centaur looked at her, hands on her hips. "I just wanted to make sure you did not come here to die."

"Naycin, do I not get to sleep more than a moment? It is only dawn."

Naycin laughed. "Osondrous, you have the wrong direction for a sunrise. You have slept nearly a day away! And your stallion helped me earlier, by the way, in weeding my garden."

Osondrous rolled over and stared at her.

"You still look tired, Osondrous."

Osondrous looked out the window. Of course it was a sunset. She turned her face into the pillows; they still smelled of him. She wished he was with her now. She had forgotten how, back then, it had only ever been Eikian in her thoughts. Back when she had thought Telenay too stiff and full of honor and way too old. Back when the wildness of the Centaurs, with their tattoos, piercings and braids, had left her praying to God that he would make her one of them. Not long after, she realized that there was no God.

Osondrous dressed and stepped into the hallway and then the kitchen. The house was empty and dark. She lit the fire and shut the windows. In the front yard Naycin was bent over, plucking weeds. On the other side of the garden Tamarack was carefully walking between the rows, eating weeds as he went. The stallion paused and shook his head, hacking out a hunk of thistle.

Naycin stood up straight, hands on her lower back, rubbing her horse withers. "You know, I often think how much easier life would be if the Centaur diet could be as simple as a horse's. But then I think, no, that would not be good."

Osondrous crossed her arms over her chest, leaned in the doorway. "Yes, the appetite of a Centaur is truly impressive."

Naycin laughed. "I will be sad to see my garden gone. Will not be long now. The frosts have been hard and deep for this time of the year."

They shut the door of the house behind them.

"All of the stew is gone but my brother brought some fresh fish for us. Oh, and fresh tobacco! They took it down from the drying house yesterday."

"How is your brother?"

"He still has that gimp he whines about."

She smirked. "It has been nearly a decade."

"Oh, my." Naycin put her hand over her mouth. "It has been that long since the Keltch wars."

Osondrous took the knife and fish from the Centaur when she began to clean them.

Naycin chuckled. "All right, I will peel the potatoes and find some butter. My nanny had not produced milk the whole time she was ill last month. Was my bread dry those days!"

Osondrous cut the fish from the skin and bones, carefully removing the spinal cord.

Naycin smiled proudly. "No bones for us tonight!"

"Eikian never did do this well, did he?"

"Oh goodness no, I finally started taking the knife from him. And his father was worse! This job was yours in the field for so long, I bet Eik decided that he would have you beside him whenever he wanted fish, so there was little reason for him to get good at cleaning them."

Osondrous laughed.

Naycin said, "It is the only thing Eikian was not the best at. He is as bad as you."

"It was only his good nature that did not turn us into rivals. It certainly was not mine." Osondrous lit the fire in the iron bowl embedded into the counter. Naycin found her single iron pan and laid it in the fire. She dropped butter, oil and cracked a pigeon egg into it. Osondrous put the fish in and started chopping the sweet peppers. Naycin stood beside her, dicing the potatoes as the fish began to sizzle.

"I wish you would come here more often, Osondrous. I hate to complain in these times of peace but it is awfully quiet . . . I miss your cooking."

"You should visit us at the castle, Naycin. I know Eikian misses you."

"Oh, that is too long a journey for an old Centaur like me!"

After they ate they stretched out on the front porch, Osondrous seated in the doorway, long legs crossed at the ankles. They rolled the brown tobacco leaves with care, then lit them and puffed with the smoke hanging around them reverently.

Osondrous breathed deep and, with eyes closed, said, "I miss this."

Naycin only chuckled, sweeping the smoke around her face in a gesture so practiced that it had become a religion.

"Thank the mother land for a good tobacco year."

Osondrous nodded. When she finished her smoke, she made another for herself and Naycin.

The Centaur admired the roll and smiled. "You would make someone a good wife."

There was silence for a time until Osondrous just shook her head and started to laugh. Naycin coughed on her humor until she gasped and grasped her ribs. They grinned at each other, mouths hanging open, heads shaking.

None of it lasted long enough.

Naycin bid her farewell with a hug that crushed her.

"Thank you again, Naycin."

"Just come back soon and tell my son how much I miss him."

"I will."

Osondrous called to Tamarack, who stood dozing with his head between tomato plants. The stallion stepped to the gate. She adjusted his saddle and tightened his girth, reattaching his breast plate and croupier. He opened his mouth for the bit. She mounted. The horse jogged through the empty streets, his shoes and chains flashing in the random street lamps that were lit with fire.

25
Constance

"Call me Missy. It is what everyone calls me. The Southern-breds hail from the wild horses that run the desert near Willower. The Northerners have been bred for plow work and heavy pulling by the Centaurs for generations. Telenay built this place and brought the two breeds together. He wanted the strength, the bravery and the tolerance to winter that the Northerners possessed. And he wanted the endurance, the intelligence and the speed of the Southern-breds. The result of their breeding they called Warbreds."

Constance looked around at the horses surrounding her, eating their suppers of oats in their wide stalls. She was in the mares' barn, at the eastern end. Its one thousand stalls were nearly full. The entire stable was lit by the glow of firestone in the foundation and the walls. The stone was extremely rare and put off a fantastic warmth.

She stared at the ten pure-blooded Southerner mares. "They are amazing."

The lead stable servant glanced at her, continuing. "Legend always spoke of the horses of the desert having hollow bones like birds." The stable woman looked across the aisle to the ten pure-blooded Northerners that were eating their supper. "And the Northerners' bones filled with rock."

"They are as different as the night and the day." Constance stood in the middle of the aisle and stared between the two. The horses started watching them, their supper dishes empty.

This was Constance's second day here. Aerick had left her at the barn to give her something to do. The lead servant had been kind and had been showing her around. She was a tall, strong woman with dark eyes and hair. She reminded Constance a little of Karalay.

The servant stroked the cheek of an old Southern-bred mare. The Southerner's neck and back were hollow and her bones were narrow and sharp. The beautiful mare, and all of her sisters around her, moved as though they were afraid of waking someone.

She felt a touch on her arm and turned around. The huge face of a Northern mare blinked at her. She saw a smile in the big horse's eyes. She stepped closer and touched the horse's thick neck. The mare's hooves were the size of plates and they were covered by hair that reached up the backs of her knees and hocks. Her forelock was braided and tied back so her huge brown eyes could be seen.

"The servants call that mare Quiet."

Constance smiled. "Are these all breeding mares?"

"These foundation mares are of absolute pure blood, straight from the Centaur and Willower lines. They are not bred anymore. They earned their rest. The four hundred stalls at the other end are reserved for the youngest: the mares in training. The rest are filled with our breeding mares. Once gentled to the saddle and bit, the training fillies will be sent to Rayakdool and assigned a soldier. When the soldiers complete their training, the mares go with them to the castle. Same goes for the stallions."

"How many horses do you breed a year here?"

"It depends. We have been breeding less than a thousand a year."

Constance petted Quiet's muzzle when the mare offered it to touch. "What happens to them when their soldiers retire?"

"They go home with the soldier, unless the soldier does not want them. Then the castle keeps the horses and they come back here to retire."

"Does that happen a lot?"

"It has not happened yet that I know of."

"How long have you been here?"

The lead servant shrugged. "Awhile. Come on, might as well show you the stallion stable."

Constance followed the servant out into the evening air.

The wind was still. Aspen leaves crunched under her feet. She glanced up the road when they walked over it and she wondered how rarely anyone came through here.

The servant was greeted by the stallions when Constance followed her into the barn. Some of them paced their stalls. Jingling under their eyes were silver halters made of delicate chain.

Constance stopped half-way into the barn and looked closely at one face. An exquisite face. "Tamarack?"

The stable servant stopped beside her and looked at the stallion. "We lost a stallion a little while back and Osondrous chose Tamarack for his replacement. He really is the finest of animals. His height and build are perfect."

"Has he seen war?"

The servant's breath came out in a whoosh. "Tamarack has seen such war as you would not believe, Constance. But we do not talk about such things here. This is a safe place of peace and rest."

Tamarack watched them leave, his halter twinkling in the torches outside his stall. They stepped back out into the evening chill.

Constance sighed, her eyes dark and troubled.

The servant looked at her closely. "I want you to know that if you would rather not stay with Aerick, you could stay with us. If you choose to be a caregiver to the horses, you bow to no other but them and you will take care of them for the rest of your life."

"Where?"

Missy pointed skyward, Constance looked up at the barn loft.

"We servants stay above the horses where it is always warm."

Constance bit her lip uncertainly. Missy whistled. A girl from above dropped a rope ladder and Missy climbed up it. She waved before disappearing into the loft.

Constance turned and started back on the path to Rayakdool. Stared down at her feet, feeling the chill and yearning for a shawl. She stopped when she reached the place where the aspens grew thick and narrowed the road. She squinted into the woods. There was something in there watching her. She shifted nervously, trying to see. The sound of hoof steps in the distance made her jump. She stared with wide eyes through the darkness.

She focused on the image as it came to her, forming in the aspen shadows. It was Aerick.

Constance waited for him, glancing warily back in the wood, certain she had seen movement that was black.

She took Aerick's arm when he stopped and offered it. He pulled her up behind him.

"How was your day?" They headed back to Rayakdool.

"I spent it with the horses . . . Tamarack is there."

"Osondrous returned this morning."

"Where had she gone?" Constance shivered.

"Rumor has it she goes to the Centaur village, but no one has the courage to follow her."

"Why would she go there?"

"Osondrous has spent a lot of time there."

Constance gripped the sides of his belt, fingers shaking in cold. The soldier tents were dark around them. The men in training were offered no fire to see by or to keep warm beside. Constance was relieved when they reached the hill and Aerick motioned her into their tent.

She ran in and sat beside the fire in the middle of the floor.

Aerick had only touched her kindly since they had arrived. She had spent all of her time in the barns, with the horses. Now, she felt a flush on her face again. An old flush, something she did not know would come back again so soon. She was not thinking of Marcus in any way. Being away from the castle made that possible. Now when she thought of that tingle between her legs, the flutter in her chest, she was thinking about Aerick. And she was wanting again.

Aerick chuckled when he saw her by the fire. "Cold?"

The Second closed the flap to their tent and took off his sword. He dropped the rest of his weapons on the closest surface before walking to the fire. Looked down at her until she lifted her eyes to look at him.

He touched her cheek. "Winter gave you your eyes, Constance. I have never seen such an ice blue."

The Second sat down behind her and Constance hunched her shoulders as his thighs slid up either side of her own.

His fingers moved down her back. "Let me take your dress off."

She heard the familiar sound of his hard vest and leathers being removed and she felt his fingers tug at her cotton dress. Her heart did a stumble and she gasped. She hurried the fabric up over her head, leaving herself entirely naked. Her skin flickered with cold bumps. He wrapped his arms around her, pulling her back to his chest. She closed her eyes.

"Is that any better?"

She nodded. Turning, she tucked her feet under one of his thighs and leaned her back against his other. Constance knew what was coming and she felt fear and excitement. Adrenaline shook down through the middle of her. The wound that had become her sacred place had healed in the days at Rayakdool. There was no pain anymore.

She wanted.

The tips of his fingers ran down her shoulders. He picked her up. He laid her down on the bed and unbuckled his belt and leggings and unlaced his boots. Constance wriggled beneath the pelts and blankets. She watched him strip himself down to his skin, to his scars, with her eyes wide and anxious. The bed shifted when he lay himself down beside her. She clutched the blanket.

"Touch me." He rubbed her shoulder.

She looked down at all the length of him. He was hard and laying huge on his belly. She reached and closed her fingers around his skin. It was inexplicably, delicately soft and solid rock at the same time. It was not a weapon or in a shroud of fear or darkness. It was just a part of him. Her grip tightened. She watched his jaw muscles ripple, his eyes fall closed. Constance felt powerful, shockingly powerful. She saw now how he was not a master or a holder of a great weapon, but a slave to it. To her. His head fell back. She touched everything, every scar, every muscle. Always she went back to the hard shaft of him, twitching with desire, until she wanted him to touch her.

His fingers fell down her belly. He kissed her and their lips merged and their tongues met. She fell back and spread her legs. He swept her hair from her face and moved into the place she held open for him.

"Are you sure?"

She breathed. "Just go slow."

And he broke the tip of himself into her and her back arched. Constance knew then that she had not been born with a wound but a flower that was deep and when touched right, bloomed incredibly.

26

"Which horse does Osondrous have now?" she asked Missy.

The servant raised her eyes from the leg of a mare she was inspecting.

"The stallion has no name. The first best of our foals is held for Osondrous and any men she feels are worthy of them as mounts. They are named by their riders. Why do you ask?"

"Is she usually very cruel?"

"She treats her mounts better than she treats any Humans I know. But she demands perfection from them. Osondrous tells her mounts what they must do and how. She expects it. Horses sense that, and under her hand they are afraid to step wrong. But it is not because they are afraid of the punishment. The Northerners are such heavy creatures, I have seen their offspring take a beating without any kind of blink in battle. It is because they do not want to disappoint. When Humans get under such an eye of pressure, they tend to crumble but horses never will; they figure out what is expected of them and die trying to give it."

"Is that why you serve them?"

Missy ran her hand down the belly of the mare beside her. The mare was beginning to show the swellings of pregnancy. "Horses hold such unquestioned dignity. They give an equal, unwavering respect for everything and they always try to do what they believe is right. They never lie. They move on their hearts and trust them without any kind of doubt. If only we could have such honor." Missy smiled at Constance.

They stepped outside and an uplift of birds took flight in a horde to the sky. Their sharp wings pointed toward them, skimming the path.

"Whipper Willows," Missy said, watching the birds soar.

Constance held herself. "I have never seen them before."

"They followed the Northerners here, over from farther north beside the sea. Strange birds."

Constance watched the birds rise and dip with the rise and fall of the ground. They circled before they settled in a batch of frost-bitten flowers, their black heads all that distinguished them from the tall brown grasses. Constance glanced warily at the trees.

"Do not look there," Missy cautioned.

"Why?"

"During the Keltch wars, a pack of wolves joined Telenay's cause against the Keltch. Word was heard one day that the wolves' females and cubs were being attacked back at their home. Osondrous abandoned her post to help the wolves save their pack. The wolves swore an oath to Osondrous to repay her. She asked those wolves to make their home here beside Centmere and to protect her horses."

"It is wolves that I saw?"

"They do not recognize your smell, Constance. They will watch you close until they are sure of you."

"Would they try to kill me?" Constance glanced back at the trees, certain she saw the flash of yellow eyes.

"Only if you laid an evil hand on their horses."

Constance hunched her shoulders to the wind.

"A storm is coming."

Constance followed the servant into the barn, walking through the stable doors as servants opened them. The ten purebred Southern-breds rolled their eyes toward the ceiling, ears flickering as they listened for thunder. The Northerners across the aisle watched them, chewing their hay, unconcerned. Down the barn, Osondrous' Warbreds dozed.

"Why are the Southern-breds so bothered?"

"They come from the desert, Constance. It was long ago, but they were bred to the climate there where it rarely rains. It took four generations of crossing with the Northerners to get them used to rain."

They walked up the center of the aisle.

Missy glanced at her. "Come on upstairs with me. No need for you to walk back to Rayakdool in the rain. That apple cider smells good, does it not?"

Constance lingered, looking back at the mares before she nodded. "It does."

They reached the center of the barn, an opening cut into the wood and stone above them. A rope ladder hung down. Missy swiftly climbed up it and Constance followed.

The left side of the barn loft was stacked from floor to ceiling with thousands of thatched bundles of hay. The rest was swept clean and marked off by a line of blankets hanging from rope. Constance ducked beneath the blanket.

A dozen servants sat around a single fire, the hearth layered and layered by stone to protect the wood floor from the heat. Above it was a large pot of boiling apple juice. A woman tossed in cinnamon bark.

Each of the servants' separate rooms were large with straw-stuffed mattresses, separated by hanging grass blankets. Many of the servants were laying down, resting as the storm moved in.

"Here." Missy offered her a clay cup full of cider.

She smiled, taking it and closing her eyes over the steam. She sat down on a stack of hay beside two other servants around the fire. They all spoke with different accents; the women were from every corner of the land, of every age. They tucked their hair back into buns and braids. The eldest woman sat with white hair, enjoying the heat in silence, while the other servants murmured on about their days. One girl was bandaged with her arm tied to her side. She spoke of being trampled by the stallions earlier in the day. A trainer sat beside her, her leg heavily wrapped with blood stains on her leggings, having been thrown over a fence when she was trying to gentle a colt. Yet Constance heard no negative words spoken of any of the horses.

The storm fell above them. Hail pelted the roof. The sound of thunder made them each pause over their cider.

A woman with black hair was holding back tears.

The eldest of the women sat next to her and rubbed her back. "No more tears."

The woman covered her face and her shoulders shook.

Constance whispered to Missy, "What is wrong?"

Missy said, "She just came here a few nights ago. She was beaten and raped before she got away. She wandered a long time before she found us . . . A lot of us have been raped. We cast away the darkness of the world coming here. We are protected by the wolves and the horses."

Constance sat and, with sympathy, listened as the other woman collected herself.

The woman forced a watery smile. "It is just so warm here. And you are all so kind. Thank you."

A lightning bolt struck nearby and they all jumped. One of the younger servants stood.

Missy shook her head at her. "No, I will check on the old ladies."

Constance followed Missy back down into the dimness of the stable.

"They do not seem to hold anything against the horses that hurt them?"

Missy said, "Every response the horse gives is out of instinct. If they harm a servant, the servant deserved it for stepping wrong. It is never the horse's fault."

Missy reached out and touched the sweaty neck of the first Southern-bred mare that they came to. The other nine down the aisle looked out from their stalls, their eyes wide, their muscles twitching.

"You are all right," Missy said to them, then glanced at Constance. "I am heading back up; there is little I can do but let them weather the storm in their own way. You are welcome to join me or wait for Aerick. I doubt he will leave you here long with this storm screaming."

Lightning snapped. Missy grew small as she walked back up the aisle.

Constance looked at the Northerners that looked back at her. Quiet stood at the front of her stall, massive head resting on her stall door. Constance touched the horse's mane and felt tears in the back of her throat.

She could still hear the raped woman murmuring over the apple cider. She understood more deeply than she ever would have cared to understand. The castle no longer felt safe. Quiet gazed at her with one giant, dark eye. It felt like, tucked back here amid the aspens with these horses and their wolf protectors, that this was the safest place in the world.

Quiet turned back into her stall and laid her big body down with a grunt.

Constance jerked at the bang of the doors opening. Servants fought against the wind, throwing their bodies against the doors as ice bounced down the stone. Noon had been darkened to night by the storm.

She ran out and grabbed Aerick's hand; he pulled her up behind him on Holjel's back. She gripped the steed's slick sides. The horse leaped forward. Constance squeezed her eyes shut, holding Aerick with thin, shaking arms as the torrent drenched her.

The stallion ran, his big hooves holding firm in the mud. He reached the hill and Aerick dropped from his back, grabbing her, and ducking inside their tent.

Constance gasped.

"We need to get you something better suited for this weather, Girl."

They sat beside the fire.

She pressed her cold face into his collar. He rubbed her back and pulled off her shoes and rubbed her feet.

"Aerick," she murmured.

"What is it?"

"I see things sometimes."

"What do you mean?" He tucked her wet hair back behind her neck.

"I . . . I have not ever told anyone before." She glanced into his eyes. "When I first came to the castle, I saw everything strange for a moment. Like it was all spirit and real but not things that we should normally see."

He waited for her to continue.

"I saw Osondrous for the first time and she was a horse, a great animal covered in scars and she breathed fire. I was afraid of her for a long time after that. Eikian was a dragon." She shook her head. "I . . . I do not know what they are . . . they frighten me."

"Have you ever seen me like that?"

She looked into his eyes. "You were a sword. You pierced the man that was raping me."

He kissed her.

She looked down. "Is there something wrong with me?"

"You are special, Constance, like all Wards should be."

Constance sat up, alone, in Aerick's bed. The rain continued its unrelenting sound of war, crashing against the top of the tent. Tiptoeing barefooted over the dirt floor, she peeled back the flap of the tent and squinted out into the storm. The light of nothing showed past the clouds; she wondered if night had come. The ground was white with ice. Aerick's stallion stood with his head down.

"Holjel, come in!"

The big horse hurried forward; she pulled the flap open. The animal ducked his head; his withers brushed the top edge of the tent door. She closed it tightly behind him. He got close to the fire and his head fell to the ground. His wet forelock covered his eyes.

She sat down on the edge of the bed and pulled her knees to her chest. "I hope Aerick is all right."

He had been called by Osondrous' big horns of training not long after they had arrived. Aerick had left without hesitation, going out into the frigid weather without so much as a grunt of annoyance.

Constance bit her lip; her stomach growled. She poured herself a cup of milk and out of a floor cabinet she drew a wooden tray with a loaf of dark bread, butter and cheese. Sat down on the bed with it. She buttered the bread and sliced the cheese, eating them hungrily. The stallion glanced over his shoulder. She tore a piece of bread from the loaf and offered it. The piece shook in her cold, outstretched fingers. The big creature turned with a cross of his front legs and his massive lips snatched it from her.

With the sound of a flood, Aerick rushed in. The fire whipped back and forth. Holjel lifted his head. Aerick shook the water from his hair. He took off his sword and weapons, removed his bow and sheath of arrows. He sat down on the other side of her tray of food and slowly pulled his boots off.

"Do the men not get days like this to rest?"

Aerick shook his head. "Osondrous loves furious weather. You are Holjel's new best friend."

"I could not leave him out there," she said.

Aerick grunted and grimaced as he started to unlace his armor. She stood to help, reaching for the laces beneath his wrist guards and vest. His arms encircled her, pulled her tight. He breathed into her breasts and sighed.

She ran her hands through his cold hair. "I am glad you are all right."

Constance was beginning to understand what it meant to be a woman. She felt whole now more than she had ever in her life. She saw how Aerick needed her, was comforted by her and she suddenly was certain that she would sustain any amount of pain to continue giving him what he needed. It filled her, it made her proud.

He looked up at her. "Thank you for being here."

"Thank you for bringing me."

28
Osondrous

Noran limped slightly. "I am getting too old for your training grounds."

"You are not that old." Osondrous righted her horse's mane absently.

"I retire next year."

Osondrous looked at him. "It felt good to train again."

"Hell, you have only been gone a week."

"It will be longer next time. Is your retirement looked upon gladly?"

"Do you say that because Irikus needs replacing?" He pushed a braid of blond hair from his forehead and grunted.

She said, "So?"

He said, "I cannot wait."

"So you do not want Irikus' position?"

He kept walking, his hulking shoulders tightened and he rubbed his hands together. "I do not know."

She snorted. He stopped and her horse with him.

He locked his dark eyes with hers. "What about a little rest—huh? Is that even possible after Cobblestone?"

She snapped, "How should I know?"

His voice came out in a smolder. "You know."

"Maybe if we go back there. Put them to rest but not until and maybe never."

Noran nodded. They continued walking.

"I may very well be queen shortly, Noran. If that does come to pass, I will do whatever I can for Cobblestone."

The blue warpaint covering Noran was a snarling smear with mud all over. His white face paint gave him a look of death. She could smell his hot body from so close to her. One thing the Humans could never get used to was how close the Centaurs always insisted on standing. A group of them was like being beside a wall, only inches separating their bodies.

When she dismounted she landed right beside him, took that next step and pressed the side of her body against his. He looked into her eyes and she met his gaze gravely.

"You know the farther you are from Centmere, the more peace you will find, Noran."

He said, "If I retire, I am not going far."

She tried to hold his eyes but he looked away, so unmoved.

He said, "Why do they haunt us so? Above all others, they know that we had no ability to fulfill that promise. Why would they do this to us?"

"They are treating us as soldiers have always been treated. No excuses."

His fingers landed on her throat; he looked into her blue eyes.

She said, "I am going to miss you."

He nodded. "We will all miss you." He turned and walked away.

She watched his tail disappear.

Her horse had been watching her the entire time.

She said, "I like how you watch me."

She untacked him, then took his tack to her tent and returned and adjusted the thin chain collar that hung around his throat. He brushed her shoulder with his muzzle. She touched his cheek. His hot breath warmed the bare skin at the base of her neck. Their eyes locked.

She said, "I will call you Willan."

The Warlord fed her fire and closed her tent flap. She stripped almost naked and lay down on the rug. Looking up, she took a breath and closed her eyes. Felt each of her ligaments and tendons, throughout her body, start to hesitantly relax. She stretched out on her back and rolled onto her stomach. Raised herself up and tilted her head back until she could not swallow. Her breathing labored in the stretch, before she lay back down and curled her body in the opposite position. She raised back up and tilted her head back again, arms pushing, straining.

Fingers fell down her cheek; Osondrous did not open her eyes. The hands fell down the surface of her neck, along the ridge of the fabric around her breasts. The fingertips brushed the tops of her nipples, hard points.

She looked up into his hazel eyes.

"Sore?" Eikian said.

She dropped her head down and she brought her legs back beneath her, out from under him, out from between his hooves.

"Why did you come?"

His hands closed on her shoulders and rubbed her collarbone.

Her head fell back against his equine chest.

"Why did you come, Eikian?"

"I missed you."

She looked up at him. "You thought I missed you?"

"Even you get lonely."

"Lonely is dangerous."

"Everything with you is dangerous."

She got up with a grunt and poured them cups of brandy.

Her skin quivered at the feel of his breath on her neck.

She pulled away. He pulled her back and looked closely at her face. "You look horrible."

She pushed his hands away.

He shrugged. "There is not another tent for me to sleep in."

She scoffed, "Is that your way of saying that you want to lie down?"

His fingers closed around her neck; he forced her body against his. The riding all day, the smell of hot flesh and wild Centaurs was deep in her chest. Her heart quickened. She had found today, lingering there at the back of her throat, was Eikian's old smell from his old bed. The smell she had craved like a fever.

He smiled a little. "Is that your way of saying that I can stay tonight?"

"Oh, how lonely are you, Eikian?"

"I missed you."

She walked away from him, drinking the rest of her brandy in one long swallow before laying across the bed. He moved up behind her. She felt the heat of him along her exposed skin. She did not fight him when his fingers slid down the edges of her leggings and slipped them off. She did not fight him when he pulled off the cloth around her breasts. She did not fight him when he laid her on her back and looked into her eyes.

She asked, "And what is your intention now?"

"The hell, Osondrous. A few years ago you would have just fucking kissed me."

Her voice rose to a shout. "Is this really the only reason you came? How can this be what you want?"

He pinned her down. "I came to remind you that you have people that need looking after. We need you to come home."

Her fingers trailed down his long cheek. "My heart was born a woman's. She needs a man."

Eikian's mouth closed over her left nipple, slipping it between his teeth and tongue. Her breath emptied in a shudder as his fingers fell down the middle of her.

"Eikian."

He growled, "Shut up."

She squeezed her eyes closed. "Do not put your fingers inside of me."

He ignored her.

29

She opened her eyes when the fire dimmed and rose to feed it again in the cool air. Osondrous sat down in her place in the bed. Eikian's breathing was all she heard. His hazel eyes opened when he felt her touch down his arm.

"I need to tell you something, Osondrous."

She shook her head. She read his mind and already knew. "You could have retired, you could have walked away, you could have gone and had a family. You could have found peace!"

"Does any of that sound appealing to you?"

"It is appealing to everyone but me." She shook her head, eyes closed, seeing the yesterday of his life. Bowing to his sword before their Captains and soldiers, taking the oath before the Castle of the Wards, becoming a Warlord. Denying her all chance of preventing him.

"Not me." His hand stirred down her back.

Eikian was sworn to the castle now for the rest of his life.

"When did you decide to do it?"

"A long time ago . . . are you really angry with me?"

"Why did you not tell me?"

"You would have tried to stop me."

She bared her teeth, "You could have gotten out of this. This is how I was born; it was never my choice."

He said, "This is my choice. I am a servant of the blade now. There are no laws against Warlords touching, no matter the race." His hand slid down her arm, fingertips savoring the inches of her smooth skin.

She snarled, "Just because no one will speak a word now does not mean that it is not against our laws. It only means they fear we would cut out their tongues." She quieted to a murmur. "If you are a Warlord now, you are no longer named to serve me."

"You are my Warlord."

"Why do you love me?"

He looked close at her. "Cobblestone started us."

"It was never the same after that." She sighed and closed her eyes. They both saw the expanse of field, spotted with ruins that had been the darkest days of their lives. "Eikian, I need a man's body."

"Do not talk about him. You do not need him."

Osondrous touched his cheek and sighed. "Naycin wants you to visit."

"You saw Ma?"

"I went over there last night."

His hazel eyes looked away. "I do miss them."

"Well, you cannot go back but to visit now." Her voice was venomous.

He said, "The castle has been my home for twenty years. You think I could just go back? Your attitude of me is disturbing. You think I would just abandon my home of twenty years? Do you know how much I have changed since I left?"

She tried to pull away. His fingers were vises, digging into her flesh.

He forced her naked body against him and growled in her ear. "There is one place I want to be."

Osondrous closed her eyes. She ran her hands over his broad, hairless chest and thought of his childhood bed where she had slept the night before. He was still the same Centaur she had pined for so deeply, once upon a time. In all the right ways, he had not changed at all. At least not to her.

Eventually they got up to eat.

"You should wear your colors more," she said, referring to the warpaint of the Centaurs.

Eikian laughed sarcastically. "That would be wise at the castle."

She said, "The Centaurs should not have to change who they are. Humans do nothing to accommodate you; you should not have to do anything to accommodate Humans."

He shrugged and she watched him clean out her cupboard of bread and cheese, then finish off her brandy before he headed for the door. She went with him.

He rubbed his hand over her flat stomach and cupped her right breast.

In her ear he asked, "How far will you be behind me?"

Osondrous looked up at his eyes. "We will not be later than tomorrow."

She sat down on her bed and listened to the sound of him moving through the grass until there was nothing.

At dawn, Noran entered and waited for her instructions.

She said, "Noran, if your wish is to replace Irikus, you may. It is your decision. Kill him if he defies you. We are leaving."

In the new morning light, Osondrous walked with Willan following close. Her step slowed through the dew of morning, off the road, and she crossed her arms. When they stopped, Willan rested his head on her shoulder and her heart followed the quieting of his breath. She stared out over the length of land, between the tamaracks, falling to gold, and the quaking aspens, quivering their turning, yellow leaves. And the endless, endless, dark pines.

She breathed the air of tamaracks, autumn and the sweat and blood of her men. This was Rayakdool, these smells were hers.

30

Constance

The horses moved as harshly as the seriousness of Osondrous' frame. The Warlord pushed for speed. They beat on, past noon, past afternoon and into the evening until there was no more light to see by and it seemed they trotted blind. Constance, clinging to Aerick's back, slept the majority of the way.

They walked in, through the castle's two main gates.

Osondrous pushed back the hood of her cloak. The fires of the gate framed the Warlord's head back through her blond hair in a saffron ring. The horses carefully walked up the steps to the hall of silence and they dismounted. Without a word Aerick left them, the two horses in tow.

Osondrous said, "It may be time for you to make some choices. Life is very short."

The Warlord disappeared into the closest passageway.

Constance rubbed her arms alone and stared down at the stone. She slowly walked down into the heat of the servant hallways. The utter stillness made her hurry. In their chamber, she shut the door. The fire was out. She knelt before it and lit it; the fire quickly lapped at the dry wood.

189

She glanced behind her to make certain she had not woken Relhie.

Constance stopped. Stared.

"Relhie?" She crawled to the empty bed. Grabbed for the parchment laying where her guardian should have been. She read it, mouth covered in horror.

Constance – my dear child. I have failed you and have been justly punished. My duty as your guardian has been stripped from me. I am so sorry, my child. Such things should never have have come to pass for you. The entire room is yours now. You are old enough to be without a guardian. I hope to see you again one day. Push your bed into this that you may put our beds together and have a nicer place to sleep. Use your room as the closet it was supposed to be. I hope you understand that Osondrous had to make an example of my failing you. You shall always be a part of my heart— Relhie.

She fell into Relhie's bed where she pressed into her guardian's pillows and wept.

31
Osondrous

Osondrous washed the traveling grit off and pulled a slip over her head. She lay down to sleep away a few hours of morning before returning to the Ring, where she was certain she would have to remain for the rest of her life to make up for the days lost.

Eikian came to her and she pretended to sleep. He lay on top of the blankets and stared at the back of her head.

Thunder smacked overhead; she jerked.

"Osondrous?" Eikian's fingers closed over her shoulder.

"Did you ever consider that I simply do not want to be touched right now?"

He said, "I cannot welcome you back?"

Osondrous closed her eyes, pressed her cheek into her pillow. She felt his breath on her hair. Lightning snapped across the sky, thunder followed. The Centaur stood soon after.

"You are going to reinforce the watchers?"

"I do not know how long I will be."

"I need a man's body. Do not be offended if you find a man in my bed."

"He will be a dead man if he is in your bed."

She laughed as though he had made a joke. "I am going to ask Aerick to join me tonight. If there is any in this castle who could survive me, it would be my Second."

The Centaur chewed his lip as he reached for his swords. He strapped on his belts.

"Then you do not want me back?" His eyes were hard and pained. He looked at her, knowing what she was going to say and hating himself for having hoped for something different.

She flipped her hand at him. "Just get out."

32
Constance

Olisize's old hands stroked through the delicate strands of Constance's hair. When she had been unable to find Aerick, it was Olisize that Constance had rushed to.

He murmured, "Osondrous had no choice. Relhie should never have sent you there alone."

Constance wept until she choked herself to sleep and, in her sleep, she dreamed of graveyards spawned by the Healer's familiar vanilla smell. Servants brought their noon dinner in trays. The Implins stopped to touch Constance. Olisize shooed them away and tenderly woke the girl.

Constance cried over her soup when she tried to eat.

Olisize sighed. "I understand your loss, young one, but be done with the tears so that we may talk about this."

"I will never see her again." Constance covered her head.

"She is not dead. You could see her again. Was there no good in your time away?"

"There was good."

"What was good?"

"I was with Aerick. I met the horses."

"And you liked the horses?"

"Yes." Constance laid her head on the table.

Olisize tsked. "Come on now, back to bed for you."

Constance did as she was told. "I miss him."

"Who?"

"I miss Aerick."

191

"You were with him yesterday."

"I did not see him last night. I missed him. I miss him."

Olisize sat down beside her.

"I think he may love me."

"Oh?"

Her red-rimmed eyes opened wide. "I think I love him."

"You need to rest."

"He saved me, Olisize."

"How did he save you?"

"He stopped that man, he pulled him out of me. He took me away from there."

"From the man that raped you?"

"Yeah . . . I love him."

Olisize sighed. "Be careful who you choose to love, Constance. You must be cautious with your heart. Not all men are what they seem and Osondrous' Seconds—well, you know they are very hard."

"He is not like them. I know he can be hard, Olisize. He looked like a sword."

Olisize's brow piqued in interest. "A sword?"

"Yes, he came flying into the room, all in fire. I see things. Sometimes. Like of how people really are."

"When have you seen this?"

Constance sniffed. "When I first came here, I saw Osondrous and she was a monster. A horse, or a dragon I think, but I have only read of dragons. She was covered in scars. When they saved me, I saw them like that again."

Constance's eyes filled with tears. She squeezed them until the tears ran down her cheeks.

Olisize was looking at her closely. "How many times have these visions come upon you?"

"Not many. Sometimes I dream them, though."

The old man rubbed her shoulder. "You need rest. Is there no servant here whom you could stay with so that you need not sleep in a chamber alone?"

She shook her head, pulled the blankets to her chin. Olisize stared across the room, chewing his teeth.

He said absent-mindedly, "Go on to sleep, Girl."

The Healer stood and stepped to his window. He squinted into the cold, wondering. When she was finally sleeping, Olisize left her. He headed

192

down the hallway after he shut the door with care. But the silence of being alone woke her. She followed him the long way, down to the back of the castle and slipped through the doorway behind him. Squinting hard, she covered her eyes from the intense sun. The west wind blew plate-sized leaves against her. The trees stood barren of leaves from the unseasonably harsh wind. Shankan's grave was no longer dark and fresh. Olisize walked to the back of the graveyard, bent over his cane.

Constance dropped to the ground, hiding against a Second's stone, in a bed of vanilla. The flowers tickled her ankles and their smell engulfed her. She peeked around the edge.

Olisize stopped at the edge of the graveyard. He bowed his head and was still with a face of grief. Constance turned her back to the tombstone, looked up at the blue sky; wisps of clouds hazed the light. The west wind blew her tears as they trailed down her cheeks. She had lost one mother and losing Relhie was just as deep. She felt as though she were bleeding.

The Healer stood at the site until the sun dipped low and twilight concealed him. He walked slowly back to the castle and she lifted her head from the ground, watching him open and close himself into the torchlight.

Constance walked across the graveyard. She could make out in the grass where Olisize had left his footprints. She knelt down and looked close where his footprints stopped. A black stone lay, half grown over by grass and water-stained. She looked close, making out the only writing on the face. A name. Constance had been schooled in the library, just as all of the Wards had, by Olisize. She recognized all of the languages in the land, even of the west and the east. She had even learned those markings of the Vamepire and those names that were feminine to them. The name was written in Vamepirian, the name was female. The name was Lemira.

The trees groaned against the high winds. They rustled and screeched like owls. The moon had risen and was concealed; the clouds made it a wolf's eye above her. She hurried back to the torches and stillness of the castle.

Constance did not return to Olisize. She went to the floor of the Seconds and let herself into Aerick's chamber.

The room was empty.

She lit the fire. Fought tears. She needed him and cried at the emptiness. Constance took her dress off and lay naked beneath his heavy blankets. She closed her eyes and felt reassured. She knew he would come to her, knew he would come soon. She fell asleep thinking of how he would hold her and kiss her and tell her he loved her. It was the only comfort she had.

The day in the Ring had been endless. Osondrous was submerged in her bath. Her eyes were vacant, years in the past.

It was an empty day that was beginning to swelter. She stood, too young to hold such a huge sword that was gripped in her hand. Telenay introduced her to the newest Second he had promoted. The Centaur that would now, ever, be at her side. She stood, not bashfully like most teenagers, but with scrutinizing eyes. Eikian had stood before her, head tilted, eyes slanted, grinning cheerlessly. He had a single white sock, a marking on his left hind leg. He had been twenty-seven then, in the prime of his athleticism, the biggest Centaur she had ever seen. And even as she had stood there, trying to be so cool and easy, with a hand propped on one narrow, pointy hip, she had been taken aback.

Osondrous stroked the scar across her belly.

In her bed, Aerick shifted awake. The basin's water was light pink from blood. Not Osondrous' blood. She looked his way carelessly, then leaned back into her basin, eyes closed.

Her infatuation of Eikian had worn off in her twenties when she had set her sights on something she could actually have: Telenay, the most elusive man she knew. When he had nodded and reached out to really touch her, when he had laid her down and she had murmured like he had never heard her murmur, he had taken her. Finally, he had filled the gap between her spread legs. And the connection, Warlord to Warlord, had been beyond either of them. They had made it, not only physically, but every time with their wills pushed out as hard as they could. It had never occurred to her that they would not be together for their entire lives. It had not been a question or a want, just an absolution. Even when she had awakened and known he was gone, again and again, all last week. It had not hit truly until she had returned to the castle. On every single other return, he had been waiting.

She was frustrated, unsatisfied. She rubbed her face viciously. Aerick had done nothing for her. And had she really expected him to compare? To even give her anything that Telenay had offered? How desperate and pitiful was she going to eventually get?

194

"Osondrous?" Aerick's voice was strained. He worked his legs over the edge of the bed and sat up.

She stepped out of the bath and left a trail of water to the window. Osondrous opened it. She took a breath; the wind whipped at her. Her face was a rock and he saw it and quickly gathered his things.

She closed the window when he finally limped out.

Osondrous felt tears prick her eyes and she snuffed them back. She would not cry for Telenay. For the first time she felt livid for his betrayal. Real rage that he would dare do this to her. Her jaw muscles worked and her eyes narrowed to fine lines.

34
Constance

Aerick shut Osondrous' door behind him. Leggings, shirt and weapons in one hand, covering his bare rear and a blood-stained pillow in the other hand, covering his front.

Around the edge of the hall, Eikian watched him go. The Centaur's hands were squeezing and clenching in shaking fists. Eikian's eyes were black. The Centaur's head went down and he gnawed his bottom lip until he drew blood. With Aerick out of sight, Eikian punched the wall and stalked away.

Aerick tiptoed down a floor and tried to ignore the glances from the guards and their random smirks until he reached his chamber.

Constance woke. "Aerick?"

He grunted, dropped all of his armor, and eased down on the end of the bed.

"Aerick? What is wrong?" She reached for the pillow on his lap. He snatched her wrist, throwing her hand away. She stared up at him.

He glanced at her apologetically. "Just do not touch it."

"Aerick, what happened?"

Wincing, he took the pillow from his lap and pulled its clinging fabric free.

"Who did this to you??" Constance fetched a bowl and filled it in the basin. She soaked a rag and knelt at his feet. Aerick stopped her. They stared at each other.

His eyes darkened. "You have been crying?"

She looked down, his sympathy withering her defenses. "Osondrous had Relhie sent away."

He touched her face. "I am sorry. You can stay with me."

She reached out with the rag.

"No. Oh. Just. Please do not touch it."

"Aerick, let me soak it. The Aloe will ease the pain."

He took the rag from her, wrapped it around himself. "Thank you."

She drizzled water down the rag. The lump in his throat trembled. Constance fetched a bowl of Aloe, returned to her place, began to crush them. He eased himself down to the floor beside her. His head fell back on the bed. She touched his chest, lay against him, kissed his cheek. The Second stroked her back.

"I will go fetch Olisize."

"Not yet."

"What . . . What if it heals wrong before he can heal it right?"

Aerick said, "Go get Olisize."

Constance hurried into the hall and brought the Healer behind her.

Olisize laid his hand on Aerick's shoulder, focused his power and Aerick healed smoothly.

Olisize said, "You are lucky she did not kill you."

Aerick nodded. "Thank you."

Olisize left and Constance sat beside him. "Better?"

He took her in his arms and kissed her. "It was Osondrous."

"But . . . Why?"

"I do not know. I did not ask. Oh, you do not think she will again, do you?"

Constance's eyes were wide. "I hope not! Did Osondrous use a knife?"

"No."

"Then . . . How? I do not do this to you."

"She is a born Warlord. They are made different . . . With burrs, or something, down there."

Constance stared.

Aerick sighed. "I guess . . . she went easy on me. She has killed a lot of men in her time."

He lay down. She wiped her nose and lay down beside him, pressed herself along him, resting her head on his shoulder.

"I am sorry for Relhie," he said.

She embraced him. "I love you, Aerick."

He looked at her. "You do not need to say that."

"But I mean it."

"How could you love me?" He sat up.

Constance said, "I want to be your lover, Aerick."

He pulled her against him, kissed her neck. "I think I love you, too."

Constance listened to him sleep later, when she saw the sun begin to rise beyond the curtains. It shone blue in through the window frost. She tucked herself in tight behind him. Shielded her eyes from the sight of the cold window by turning her face into his back.

35
Osondrous

Someone was pounding on her door.

Osondrous yelled, "What?" She had not been sleeping for long and Aerick's blood was still damp on her sheets.

Prush, one of her eldest Centaur Seconds, ran in.

His eyes were frantic. "It is Eli."

She looked into his face and read his mind. Osondrous threw on her clothes and sprinted to the Ring of Wards.

Dawn was only a blush on the horizon. The Ring was packed with Centaurs, servants and soldiers, all wide-eyed, most disheveled from running out of bed.

"Tell me what happened." Osondrous' tone was tight and pinched, her eyes were sharp slits.

Five men were standing before her. They were all well dressed with gleaming swords, hilts plated in gold, hanging from their hips. Their leader stepped forward, the nephew of the mayor of Kamamine. His hair and eyes were dark and when he spoke it was in a barely controlled roar.

He said, "My name is Weslin. The Centaur Eli, one of your Centaur Seconds, was caught with the woman that is sworn to me!"

Osondrous looked around for Eikian and did not see him.

She sent back to Teek: *Bring me Eikian.*

A woman was brought into the room, fighting the men that restrained her. Her hair was mussed and there was a red bruise on her left cheek.

Osondrous said, "In detail. Tell me exactly what happened."

"I found that beast with his fingers in her!" Weslin pointed at a Centaur who happened to be standing in the crowd.

It was Cray, one of Osondrous' Seconds.

His red tail lashed and he growled. "Do not point at me, weak little

197

Human."

Weslin sneered at Osondrous. "Do you not teach your savages to keep their mouths shut when Humans are talking?"

She stood up and roared back at him, "Are you questioning my Ring?"

Weslin snarled. "I caught one of your Centaurs with my woman!"

Her voice dropped down with seriousness. "This is your one and only warning."

Eikian entered through a back door and stepped up to her side.

Weslin held up his fist and it shook. "Law states that the Centaur Eli be executed! You will lynch him. That is the law."

She said, "Bring the Centaur in."

Eikian took a drink of her brandy from the day before, touching her as he moved by. The men in Weslin's party brooded and motioned at her and Eikian, their voices growled in anger.

Weslin sneered, "Read my mind and see for yourself, Ward."

Osondrous frowned at him. She had already read their minds and knew Eli was caught with many witnesses. Eli stepped into the Ring without restraints, followed by two of her Human soldiers. The Centaur was a shade of cobalt gray and, as he walked, his salt and pepper hair hung in his eyes.

"String him up!" the men cheered.

Eli's face was dark and flat. It was lost on everyone else, but Osondrous saw the loving glance sent Eli's way from Weslin's battered wife. She saw in the woman's mind how they had first met in the street when Weslin had struck her in public and Eli and three other castle Centaurs had intervened. He had tenderly touched her swollen cheek. It had been the first kind touch the woman had ever had from a male of any species.

Osondrous said, "Take Eli to the dungeon and give the woman a place in the servants' quarters."

Weslin was appalled. "My wife comes home with me!"

Osondrous leaned forward.

The hall quieted when she said, "Your wife's choice."

Osondrous' eyes turned to the woman. *Stay the night. Heal here and decide then what you wish to do. Take our refuge.*

The woman gaped at her. She gasped, "I will stay here!"

Osondrous motioned. "Take her."

Weslin raged. "How dare you!"

Osondrous slammed her fist into the podium and her will hit Weslin in the legs. He fell to his knees.

She pointed at him again. "I can project every affront, every hit, every cruel word you have ever spoken to that woman into the minds of everyone here and I assure you the Centaurs will kill you for it. Or you can go and realize that this is a free land. Behind the gates of the Castle of the Wards, she is owned by no one!"

Weslin stared at her in disbelief. His eyes flashed viciously but he and his band left in silence.

Osondrous had the Ring cleared. Eikian finished her brandy. They did not look at or speak to each other. He followed her to the dungeons.

Eli was standing with his head down in the first cell. His gray coat was black in the dim light.

"What were you thinking?" Osondrous yelled at him.

Eli's face was stony. He said nothing.

Her hands were up and her fingers were curled into pleading claws. "I do not know how I can get you out of this! Do you realize that?"

Eli said, "You must kill me. You have no choice."

Osondrous ranted and struck the wall beside her repeatedly until her palm screamed. Neither Centaur spoke nor moved. Eikian stood apart from Eli, his eyes down. She and Eikian had not spoken since he had left her chamber the day before.

Eli said, "Osondrous?"

"What, Eli?"

"Will you make sure that Trailee is safe?"

"You know she will be fine . . . If she is smart, she will stay here."

Eli rubbed his head. She saw the scars down his left arm, jagged white gashes of lightning.

When Osondrous was fifteen, Eli had been the one to rally to her aid. Surrounded by Keltch, with Eikian lying in the mud barely breathing. Her big sword out with the tip shaking as she stood over him and those black things had begun to circle. Her will was gone. Her exhaustion had been absolute. Eli had come, a fierce blur that could not be stopped.

The gray grass of Cobblestone flashed behind her eyes and she turned away.

She ran up to the hall and sucked in the cool air.

Olisize rushed down the hall of silence. "Is it true?"

"Yes."

"What are you going to do?"

"I do not know."

"Osondrous, you have—"

She turned on him. "I do not *have* to do anything."

Osondrous ran into the castle. Everywhere she turned, servants were whispering about Eli. Guards were gasping together, heads bowed. They all looked at her with the same question: *What are you going to do?*

She reached her chamber and slammed her door, put her back to it. Osondrous gasped and gasped in panic. What was she going to do? The law wrote that a Centaur caught with a Human's wife was to be lynched, without trial. The only thing she could think of was that, if she became queen, she could change the law.

If she was going to do it, she needed to do it soon. Eli's prosecutors would not be silenced and would not wait.

36
Jezaline

The mountain range beside them lifted above the clouds. Another range formed into view from the east, lifting and growing until it met the mountain beside them and the two mountain ranges joined and ran south together.

They dropped, flying above the gray grass, dead from early frosts. And the wind from their wings rippled fresh water as they flew over it. Jezaline opened her eyes and saw her reflection. The lake was achingly blue. Her head was a blinding pain. Jezaline looked up.

The great black towers of the Vamepire rose before her, their base the shore of the mountain lake. Story after story rose to the sky, carved directly from the foot to the brink where the two mountains met. Endless doors flew up the towers, accented by little landing pads. He took her up and she watched as all his Vamepire minions fell away and she was alone with her face against his neck.

"Do not try anything." In such a murmur, his accent was beautiful.

She squeezed shut her swollen eyes and they cracked from old tears. He landed and entered the top of the center tower. The sound of torches was heavy and engulfing as he stepped into a tall, narrow hall.

He walked her before him, his hand in the middle of her back. They came to the last and only door. Blondie opened it into a chamber almost completely devoid of light. There were no windows, just endless, tall walls of black stone. He walked her in and in the center of the chamber was a bed. There was a small table beside it and on it was a single candle burning a tiny white flame.

Blondie pointed and she stared down at the black deer hides covering the bed.

She shook her head. *No.*

He grabbed her by the back of the neck and threw her down.

Jezaline's face filled with deer hide and musk. It was heavy, sickly. It filled her with dread and panic.

Blondie walked back to the door. She fought the primal urge to run after him and beg him to kill her now. Beg him to take her, to save her from the horror of seeing the thing that awaited her, in the dark, in this chamber. Blondie left. When the door clicked shut, and the last echo of torchlight from the hall was cut away, the chamber fell into the mercy of the candle. The flame was absolutely still.

"Stay there." The voice came from behind her and with it a chill of terror like ice water up her back. Filled with deliberate, essential fear, she could not have moved. Her head laid in doubtless the same place as hundreds, if not thousands of other victims. She waited for the teeth and the claws to work their way up her leg, then her neck and undoubtedly her throat.

He slipped across the floor like an arachnid. His minions had always brought him the very best and seeing her there in his candlelight, Waltruk could not believe his eyes. His excitement was so hard it was painful. He was already running his hands down her thighs and up and around her smooth, bare ass in his mind.

By the time he reached the bed, his hands were quivering. He had not eaten a Human in over a decade and then that had been a very ugly, very old man, nothing worthy of penetrating. Not that he turned his nose up at men; it had just been so long since he had tasted a Human woman.

He moved up and onto the bed like water running over stones.

Feeling the weight, knowing he was there, she whimpered. Waltruk grabbed himself, gasped and barely kept himself from climaxing. He laughed into the empty darkness of his chamber. It was a surprisingly light sound and it made her ill.

Jezaline gripped the blanket in her fists, panic containing her heart into a tighter and tighter cage. He grabbed her. His claws dug into her sides. She could not even get breath enough to scream. He flipped her over. She lay, paralyzed with fear. His eyes were black beacons beneath long, fine brows, watching her chest rise and fall in rapid, excessive jerks and causing her impressive breasts to quiver and bounce.

His long black hair escaped like a creature from a thick plait that ran all the way down his back. His face was the only part of his body not entirely covered in lines and lines and interweaving lines of tattoos that wrapped all over him. His face was wide and strong. His fingers were long and ended in sharp, black hooks that grew in severity down his hands. She felt them breaking the skin on her legs. But all she could see were his black eyes, filled with hunger, desire and the intention to consume her.

The room filled with the desert sun.

The king of Vamepire before her dissolved into red.

Jezaline rose up to him, feeling the blessed desert heat again. The fire in her past that was once her entire life, the sand, the sun, was all around her, filling her with the desert smells. Of all the darkness of the last day, it was not so hard for her to believe that this was real. That she was dead and she was now home. Jezaline reached out, tried to touch the red man's face. She tried to say *red man*, but nothing came out of her swollen throat. Before her was the Vamepire king with her hand on his cheek. She found her breath and groaned, not in fear of him but because, suddenly, the ache in her had grown into a culvert across her stomach and it was screeching as it never had before.

He said, "Red lady," and stared. "Who are you?"

She shook her head.

"You are the red lady?"

Her terror returned slowly, as though she was still trying to wake from a nightmare. She shook her head in confusion. He reached for her and she pulled back to try and stop it. But the Vamepire king clasped his fingers around her wrist and it hurt.

With his accent and his anger, his voice was without any kind of humanity. "How do you know of the red lady?" It was the voice of a wolf, of a hunter in the night.

She said, "Red man in my past."

He grabbed her head, pulled her face to him. "What do you know!"

"I do not know who he was!"

"Tell me what you know!"

Jezaline got it out, in sputters and gasps with his claws digging into the back of her head. She recounted how her fear had turned to need. "I was desperate for him. What was my getting raped became . . . I demanded him to enter me." She finally struggled out of his grip, fell to her knees and held her wet face.

"What did he do to you?"

"I had will after that. I am a Ward."

Waltruk's eyes widened. "A Ward of high power. What are you doing here?"

He reached for her. "Do you feel it? Do you feel the empty hole inside you?"

She pressed her hands to the place between her breasts and her belly.

"You feel it!" His voice was many things: frantic, excited and disbelieving.

She cried, "Yes."

"You were never able to fill it?"

She shook her head. *No.*

Waltruk sank down to his knees on the bed before her. His black hair lay in tatters down his cheeks. "If I had only known." He shook his head. "No, I could not have stopped myself."

"What?" She looked up.

He said, "I am king because of her but, if I had known what this would feel like, I would have tried to stop."

She said, "What is all of this?"

"Something changed our paths."

"Are there others?"

"Not that I have known."

He looked into her face and she stared into his.

He said, "I think it is Grim."

"He does not exist."

He ignored her. "Grim is on the move, right now. Why are you in the Krept?"

She felt herself standing on the blade of a knife. She had no idea what this thing wanted of her. What this king wanted her to do or say or what she could do for him. But there was something guiding her. Something dark, something empty. The same thing that had guided her to the arms of every man in her life. The primal thing in her, trying to find the piece missing that left the dire, empty ache. As the moments passed between them, where she could smell his body and his breath, where her own body reacted to the presence of his, she began to long to touch this king. She began to imagine what it would feel like. She was revolted. But, as she looked at his face, down his lean neck and strong hands, she could almost feel them on her again. Jezaline swallowed hard, forced herself to look away.

He spoke softly. "Talk to me."

"Or you will kill me?" she said.

"What are you doing in the Krept?"

She took a quivering breath. "The prophet Tarrick said that if I went back to the Castle of the Wards, I would die. I was looking for him. The Draegoone. Not the Vamepire."

The sound of Tarrick's name sent a jolt through Waltruk. He climbed off the bed and began to pace. His body faded in and out of the shadows like they were great swells and he a ship, long dead and left to drift. Jezaline sat holding the pain in her belly very tight.

"Are you going to kill me?" It erupted out of her ravaged throat like an animal tearing free.

He stopped before her and stood in the darkness, alone but not alone, as though the darkness was a crowded part of who he was. He said, "I think killing you would be very stupid."

Jezaline's heart was pounding hard. "Why?"

"Your destiny was changed by a prophet, Grim; now another prophet is trying to interfere. That much I can deduct. You are important somehow, maybe me, too."

"What do you know?"

"You and I, Jezaline, never should have met. This is another prophet that got you here. I know of Tarrick. He is the second youngest brother of the Draegoone royalty." He hissed it out in a long fluid jolt of malice. She watched him pace, sensing he would continue. He pressed his fists into his temples and his face contorted with anger. "We are at war with those cold-blooded things. I will kill them all. That was not changed by the red lady; that I will do before I die."

She said, "What will you do with me?"

He turned on her. "I want to drink you and then fuck your corpse for three days!" His teeth flashed and fell back into the shadows and it was all she could do to not run away. If Waltruk was right, which she seriously believed he probably was, it all still left her here in the highest room of the tallest Vamepire tower, completely surrounded by creatures she knew to be dark, wicked and unmerciful. But there was clear intelligence in his eyes. It had been there in Blondie's eyes, too. These were not stupid brutes as she had been made to believe and that scared her more deeply than anything she had ever known. These were conniving, brilliant creatures.

He evolved out of the dark, coming at her in three strides. His fingers moved up her face, pushed her to the bed. His weight bowed it next to her and he stretched out his body beside hers, touching her throat, her collarbone and lips. Jezaline squeezed her eyes shut.

She was overtaken by two polar opposites. The desperate, primal need to throw him off of her, run until she was overcome and die in hysteria when her heart finally burst in horror. And the other was to pull him against her. Embrace the darkness that was this king. Hold him between her legs, pull her skirt up so he could enter that hot place that was the ache the red man had left in her. Give this king the opportunity to fill it as no man had ever been able to. Because she knew somehow that this king could end her pain and give her what she had lost. She knew it because he had lost it, too.

He pressed his face beneath her breasts and his hot breath steamed her skin. "Right here."

The ache pushed up against her skin and screamed.

Her voice was strained. "Yes, right there."

"It has not yet engulfed you in the void. But it will."

"Like you."

He sighed and she felt his head relax on her body. The weight of his hands rested, one on her chest, one on her thigh. She stared up at the ceiling, though the darkness made it impossible for her to see anything.

He said, "Do you think we are missing our souls?"

She was stricken, left speechless.

"Prove something!" she cried out and her voice carried up and up until it was gone. "Anything, end this or something. Do not let me just be here in the dark. How has it engulfed you? How much does it hurt?"

His fingers slipped up beneath her and she felt them untying the back of her dress. She could not see his face. His hands slipped the fabric off her shoulders; his claws curled over the neck of her dress and with his face beside hers he pulled it down off her breasts. Then down, revealing her ribs, her belly, her hips and then the place that made her a woman. The dress hit the floor. She was naked before him, her breasts leaning back in their weight, her nipples dark perfections. He ran his fingers across her flat stomach.

When her hands raised, he waited for her to struggle, to hit him, to scream. Waltruk had never had another creature touch him in want. It never occurred to him that she was feeling the same pull, the same screaming need. Her fingers landed against the side of his throat, slipped under the collar of his shirt, pressed against his hard shoulder. She gasped. He was warm, not so different from a man. She bit her lip to keep from moaning. Jezaline rose before him, found laces with her fingers and began to tear his clothes from his body.

Waltruk froze.

The ache filled her entire mind and it began to pulse. The blood pumped through her in dangerous currents. Revulsion, fear, primal sense; it was all forgotten. Jezaline was who the red man had made her.

Her fingers worked down to the black hair on his lower belly that pointed her in the direction she needed to go. He was taken with watching her body work, her strong back pucker and move, her breasts hang and bounce. She ripped off his belt and when Waltruk was naked, she curved her fingers around his hard shaft and gasped.

The moan was nothing he had heard before, the same sound of pain filled with want. Her legs parted and she eased herself over him. His face was by the candle now and she could see his eyes and they were not entirely black. Jezaline stared, perfect lips opening, licking. He saw her tongue and his teeth gritted.

She came down at him, pressed her mouth against his. She forced him to learn how to kiss her, how to use his tongue. She parted herself with her fingers, drove him into her wet, red heat.

She had him, ground herself against him and he watched her, transformed by the act that he had never known existed. Watched a Human woman find something good in a Vamepire. She writhed. All the while, the ache in them both reached a piercing volume. It grew and grew with her until they were deaf to all but it.

Jezaline threw back her head and cried out as her climax unleashed. He felt the waves around his shaft, felt the hard pleasure and could not stop himself. They grabbed each other. Jezaline embraced the darkness, felt his wings around her arms and lost all awareness.

As fast and hard as it came, it evaporated. They were left listening to their own frantic breathing. The ache in them each was not gone, but silenced. She was holding on to him like he was a raft and she was adrift in a storm at sea, in the dark. They felt whole for the first time in almost their entire lives. He rolled her onto her back but did not break their hold. Waltruk pushed the hair off her face and looked into her eyes.

"It is so quiet," she whispered.

"Look at me."

Slowly her eyes turned and they were the eyes of a creature who had barely survived something. Her lips were scratched by his teeth. He licked his lips and tenderly touched them to hers.

Jezaline's awareness was returning to her faster than it was returning to him. She felt the rough pelts beneath her. She heard the silence of the room, the beating of their hearts. Most of all, she felt him inside of her. The long hard shaft of him, larger than any man she had ever tried to accommodate. It burned and she felt the awkward pain of it for the first time. When he kissed her, she closed her eyes and accepted it. They kissed easily, softly. She felt him twitch inside of her and she gasped.

Reluctantly he pulled out and the trail of wet stickiness that followed made her certain that she bleeding. It felt like a seeping wound and she closed her legs where he had been and moaned. This was a sound he knew very well but, for the first time, it bothered him.

"What is it?"

She reached between her legs, then held her fingers in the light. They glistened with blood mixed with something black.

"Is that you and me?" she asked.

He pulled her fingers into his mouth and closed his eyes, savoring. Jezaline waited for him to bite her fingers off. He pulled them from his mouth, wet and clean, and still intact.

He said, "I hurt you." His voice was strange and uncertain.

Her fingers closed around his hard shaft again and he hissed.

She said, "You are no Human man."

Their situation dawned on them both in the same moment and they were silenced in the dark. Waltruk lay in shock. Their aches were truly put to rest. The pain had become so much of who he was that Waltruk barely knew how to breathe without it.

She laid her hands beneath her breasts, whispered, "Yes."

She turned on her side, reached out and pressed her hands there on his chest. "Is it the same for you?"

"Yes." His fingers closed around her wrists and he pulled her to him. "Jezaline, I must have this."

Her head lay on his chest. She stared at the thing of him that was still long and hard as a rock. He could not see her eyes widening as he spoke, as she absorbed the implication of his words.

He said, "I can give you immortality."

She sat up. "I want to see you in the light. Real light."

He was up instantly and dressing. He gave her her dress and watched her slip it on. He tightened it for her in the back and ran his fingers over her shoulders. He took her hand and they left the candle and the chamber. They went up a staircase and emerged, suddenly, in the light of day. She was struck that this was the same day still that she had awakened with her

Centaurs. With Sethian.

She did not look at him right away. She looked out over the stone roof, at the mountain peaks that rose up and up beside them, at the clouds that drifted beneath them. She stepped out to the edge. Hundreds of Vamepire were living their lives, coming and going. Hauling food and water up to the towers. None of them knew of the Human that watched them from above.

She felt shaky, hungry, thirsty, tremendously deprived of her own living. She closed her eyes. Mustered her strength.

She turned and he was standing well back from her, arms at his sides. His face and body were intense, sharp and brutal. He was taller, far more powerful than the other Vamepire she had seen. And, she suspected, more so than all other Vamepire in existence. So many years spent locked away in his tower, trying to cope with the enormous pain, had left him pale and haggard. He looked desperate and at a loss. Where Humans were pink because of the red blood flowing beneath the skin, he was gray. She was certain every liquid in his body was black.

She felt real, knowing fear. In her fear before, it was of the unknown and this was far worse; her imagination could not compete with the scope of this king. The tattoos covered him with thin, intricate and weaving lines that made him look entirely armored. They tapered up to his chin and one line from either side slipped up, across his cheek bones and over the bridge of his nose. His wings were like the other Vamepire, like big eels that moved and twitched.

He saw the horror in her eyes and moved toward her. "Do not do that."

She took a step back and her heel slipped out over the edge. Jezaline turned, looked down at the thousands of feet of empty air beneath her.

He said, "I will only catch you."

She closed her eyes, put out her arms and jumped. The wind enveloped her and she felt the freedom of air. The roar encompassed all of her senses. Jezaline grinned and it was without cheer; it was savage.

He caught her by sweeping in from the side. He pounded the air with his wings and she was instantly moving at the same enormous speed in the opposite direction. He rose up above the tower and landed but did not let her go. He stared into her face as she trembled in his arms.

He smiled and it was a grotesque sight. "Do you like to fly?"

She touched his face with the lines of tattoos. "Will you fly some more?"

He launched them into the air and swooped above his kingdom. It laid out before them: his mountains, his range, his swamps, his Krept.

"Be mine. Be mine, queen Jezaline, and you could fly alone."

She squeezed her eyes shut, let the rush of flight fill her. He flew out in the wind and sunshine for a long time. Until the sun began to wane and the light turned from white to amber and he felt her shiver in his arms.

"Immortality," he said to her.

She said, "Live with this ache forever."

"Live with me, with no ache. We can fill each other."

He landed, held her against him before she finally slipped out of his arms. She held herself tightly, tried not to cry. She thought of Shankan, of Karalay, of Telenay, of Osondrous. But she no longer felt like she had ever been one of them. The Castle of the Wards was a very long way away. She thought of the Human peoples of the realm, of the people she had sworn to protect. She was supposed to have been a Ward until she died. Jezaline looked into the north, took the winter wind grimly on. When she breathed, her breath misted out.

Waltruk stood beside her, waiting, concerned to the point of barely being able to breathe.

Her shoulders dropped in defeat. "I am so hungry, and thirsty and dirty. Please, just, I need . . . "

He said, "Of course."

In his chamber, Waltruk lit the fire while she sat holding herself against the headboard. His servants brought meat and he awkwardly asked her if she needed to cook it to eat it. She did it in silence, holding the meat at the end of an arrow at the fireplace. They brought her water and she drank it greedily. They filled the basin with water and they started a fire beneath it. They brought her new dresses and warm clothes.

He watched her intensely.

Eventually, full and with her thirst quenched, she stripped her dress off and eased down into the hot water. While she soaked, Waltruk was devising his plan.

Eventually Jezaline rose from the bath, skin pink and deliciously smooth. She went to his bed soaking wet and pulled the blankets up to her chin. She slept instantly.

Waltruk went out and hunted while she slept. He savaged black deer and elk alike to quench his hunger. As much as she had satisfied him, he had been left desperately unsatisfied.

When he returned, it was after dawn and she was wrapped in blankets, sitting before the fire. Her hair was brushed and shining in glorious black waves. He reeked of elk and knew it when she winced. His clothes were soaked through with blood. She did not look at him. He cleaned up quickly and changed, then went to her.

He sat beside her and she looked into his face.

She said, "What did the red lady give you?"

"Our species has a connection through the mind. We can sense when other Vamepire are near. My power is many, many times beyond that of any Vamepire of all time. I can track another Vamepire across any amount of distance. I could tell you the count of all of the Vamepire here down to their very age. And I can tell you what anyone is thinking. I killed all of the predecessors before me, every heir to the Vamepire throne and any single Vamepire that thought to take it from me before they had power."

"You cannot tell what I am thinking though? I am stronger than you; I am a Ward."

He frowned and nodded.

"But within the Vampire you are unstoppable."

"I will be king for as long as I want it."

"And how long is that?"

He grinned. "Forever."

"You like power, do you not?"

"You do, too, or the red man would not have had you."

She moved closer and sighed into his chest, rested her head in his neck. Waltruk held her.

"Immortality?"

"Yes."

"Will I become a Vamepire?"

"Yes."

"Then what are we waiting for?"

He said, "I need you to do something for me."

She lifted her head away and looked at him sharply. "What is it?"

"Did you forget the path you were on?"

"What do you want me to do?"

"I want you to go find the prophet, like you are supposed to."

Jezaline opened her mouth to speak, then shook her head.

"Listen," he said. "We were never supposed to meet. You and I were given great power that essentially and completely changed our lives, even who we are. I believe Tarrick is intercepting something very dark here by calling you out. I believe this thing that changed us is Grim and he would not have done such a thing if he did not see something in us that would affect him very badly. If this other prophet is trying to right some wrong, and that I am sure of, then you need to go to him."

There were other things, many other things that Waltruk did not share. First and foremost was his hatred for the Draegoone. His people had been pushed out of the south by Grim's own warped breed of dragon that were feeding on them. Being pushed from the south, they had trespassed on what the Draegoone claimed to be their land. The war that was now ensuing was taking more Vamepire lives than were being born. His people were considered insects by the Draegoone and the feeling was absolutely mutual. He had fought in battle with the prince of the Draegoone, a really big creature named Kilikan, and had read his heart. Kilikan lusted after Humans, had seen and wanted Osondrous during the Keltch wars when the Humans eradicated the beasts from the Krept.

Waltruk was betting on Jezaline's beauty to move Kilikan to do something stupid. The Draegoone were controlled completely by honor. The Vamepire knew that the Draegoone still needed to pay for their ancestors' crimes during the Five Hundred Year War. Soon, a large piece of the Draegoone army would fly to die against the Fai. He was betting on the Vamepire winning a lot of ground that day. Jezaline could be his best chance at finding the last of the Draegoone royalty and wiping them out.

On top of it all, there was something else going on here. The dragons in the south, bred by Grim, were growing quickly in number. The prophet was growing himself an army and, though Waltruk feared it was going to be against his people, somehow he did not think that that was quite right. Grim wanted something else and, somehow, he and Jezaline were involved.

She gasped, "But they will kill me!"

"Not the Draegoone. They will not know that you are involved with me. They will take care of you."

Jezaline's eyes were confused and troubled. "I am not Vamepire. How will you know where I am?" It was now that her need was heard in her voice. She had given herself to his keeping, had given to the image of being with him for the rest of her life and now the idea of leaving his circle of power was terrifying. He softened, took her against him, spread her legs around him and held her tightly.

His breath was hot in her ear. "You will drink my blood, enough so there is Vamepire in you. I will know where you are at all times."

She stiffened but he did not let her go.

He asked softly, "Could we do it again?"

"Do what?" she whispered, peering into the fire over his shoulder.

"You know."

She felt him hard between her legs and sighed.

He said, "We do not have to . . . I know it can only be like that again, if you want to."

He held her for a time and then she said, "I want to."

37

Afterward, Waltruk saw Jezaline giving him a very odd, hesitant look.

"What is it?"

"Would you . . . Do you want to drink my blood?"

He stared at her. "Why?"

"Would it feel good?"

He sat up. "It would."

"How much pain would there be?"

"Some."

"Could . . . could we not use your teeth?"

He said, "Would that hurt less?"

"I think so."

"Then we do not have to."

"If I am going to drink yours, I think this would be fair."

"You like fair?"

She stuck her chin out. "I live for fair."

He took her hand. His claws wrapped around her wrists.

"When?" His voice was a hoarse whisper.

She said, "Now."

"Why?"

She said, "You do not get to have all of it."

He nodded but the prospect was making his heart pound, making his blood race with excitement. He grew still, turned her wrist over and pressed his lips to the veins.

She said, "Not there."

He closed his eyes. "Where then?"

She wrapped her bare legs around him and he adjusted to accommodate her.

She touched the side of her neck, "Right here."

"Is that where the Humans think we always feed?"

She smiled. "Yes."

"I cannot do it there . . . I do not dare."

She pouted and he knew he would be incapable of ever denying her anything.

He said, "I could hurt you."

"Prove to me you will not. I need to trust you like I have trusted no one else. You are asking me to give up everything I have ever known and loved." Her voice broke. She cleared her throat and would have continued except he covered her mouth with his. He punctured the side of her throat with his thumb nail and the blood dripped out.

She stiffened but did not pull away. He broke the kiss and covered her wound with his mouth. She gasped, held on to him, leaned against him and began to cry. She turned her face into his hair, squeezed her eyes shut and took the pain as though it were her duty.

When he lifted his face it was with a gasp of self-containment. Stopping was possible, but a torture. Her heart still pounded in the back of his throat. He pulled her face up and looked into her eyes. She was paler than before but her look was strong and he saw now the power in her that was entirely over him.

He pressed his face to the other side of her neck, savoring the last of the blood in his mouth. He drove his thumb nail into the side of his own throat.

She gasped, "Now?"

"For fairness."

"How much?"

"Just do it."

She covered the blood with her mouth, winced, took it on and swallowed. Sucked and swallowed. She shook her head as it hit her stomach. She grimaced, held her breath, took another swallow.

He pulled her back. "Good enough."

"I do not have to go yet though, do I?"

"As soon as we can bear it."

She began to cry, "Not yet!" She grabbed hold of him and cried on his shoulder. The smell of her blood was filling his senses. He focused on other things as best he could. Finally her wound clotted and the freshness began to fade.

38

A day passed and he offered everything she asked for and more. Food, wine, liquor of every kind the Vamepire made, trips kissing the sky in his arms. And everything she wanted of his body. She investigated him, his wings which fascinated her, his broad back, different than a man's, to accommodate those wings.

When the time came, it was with well-rested and well-fed healthy clarity.

She asked, "Will it hurt?"

He promised, "Only when you wake up . . . I will do it all. No other Vamepire will touch you."

She closed her eyes and nodded. "Then do it."

He picked up a mallet and slammed it across the back of her head. Jezaline went down and he stood over her shaking. He had promised her that only he would be the one to touch her and he would make right that promise. However, he needed supervision.

The Vamepire that Jezaline had known as Blondie came quickly to his side. The Vamepire's actual name was Makay and he was Waltruk's second general.

"What can I do?"

"Just . . . Just do not let me kill her."

"Are you serious?"

Waltruk glared at him. Makay shrugged.

Jezaline lay before Waltruk in her stained and ripped dress. He dug his claws in just beneath her left breast and filleted open her belly. He sank his claws in between her legs and Jezaline's blood began to drip on the floor. Makay covered his mouth and breathed carefully. Waltruk tore his hand across her eyes and opened up her face to the wind. He rolled her over, marked her back and stood back, panting, claws dripping.

"I need to bite her."

Makay's eyes widened. "Well, I cannot."

Waltruk sank his teeth into her shoulder and tore away without swallowing; he spat out a wad of pink flesh.

He picked Jezaline up and they raced out of the tower. With great speed, what was normally a few hours of flight evaporated quickly. She was paling, she was bleeding badly and as they drew close to the Draegoone line, he began to worry that he may have overdone it.

In the highest points of the rocky terrain, where the wind was at its worst, the Draegoone kept only one light post. Not surprising. They were buffeted hard and no matter how weak a place in the line it was, Waltruk knew that, in this wind, his light-weighted soldiers would fold quickly to the mass of the Draegoone. He used his senses to find a point between guards and flew right up to the wall in the dark. He laid Jezaline down. He reared back and let out the sound his species was most known for. A spine-crawling roar that was more hiss than scream.

The Draegoone guards responded instantly and he flew hard to get away. Makay flapped madly in the wind, waiting for him, bow drawn with an arrow fitted. The torches of the Draegoone narrowed in on Jezaline's location and Waltruk sighed in relief as their voices took on the urgent tone he was waiting for. They flew farther away and he pinpointed Jezaline. She was on the move. The Draegoone had her now and she was alive.

PART THREE

Karalay lay down for a time, wasting the morning until she could not rest anymore. She stood and opened the window. Her breath fogged out in the cold. Frost coated the sill. The sun broke through a pass of low hung clouds. She hoped Raven had found a place of shelter.

She jerked as Jaridd's will hit her. *Karalay. Find a horse. Come to the north entrance of the town. Now!*

Karalay threw open her chamber door and ran. She slipped when her feet hit gravel, regained her balance, and continued without caution.

The horses of the stable threw their heads when she hit the door.

"Friend?" She called in the Willower tongue and, through panting breaths, she begged the bay mare to take her to the northern entrance. The mare stood in silence, staring at her, waiting. Karalay snapped a lead to the mare's collar and pulled herself unto her warm, bare back.

The mare grunted and leaped out of the stable. Down the street the mare ran, hooves snapping against the stone. The buildings and docks of Diggamara flashed by in a blur. The mare scrambled through the back streets, avoiding the people. The mare roared on, pushing and pushing, lengthening herself flat out. Karalay supported her with her will. The horse's coat was black with sweat when the north entrance finally came into view.

Karalay knew what she would see before they reached the Darkhalks that were running into the city. The mare slid to a halt and she jumped to the ground.

The Darkhalks set a body down.

She collapsed to her knees beside him. "Telenay?"

His face was thick with grime. His swords were gone, his armor was beaten. The street she knelt on soaked her knees with blood as he bled it. She felt his life waning and she held his face and threw herself into the Warlord.

"Telenay?" She saw him in the night. He lay in black and white grass, a sword of blood in his hand. Slowly, his eyes opened as a shadow moved up his chest, to his neck. She grabbed him and pulled him back. He was screaming. She pushed him toward his sunset and jerked back, pouring herself into his bloodstream. She soared into his wounds, clogging the blood flow, stopping the pain.

She fell back on the street, panting hard, sucking in the air.

The Darkhalks lifted Telenay up and she stared into the Warlord's face.

Telenay's amber eyes opened once. *Karalay.*

Jaridd grabbed her and they ran back to the castle.

The brown mare, left with her muzzle hanging to the ground, slowly worked her way back to the stable, alone and forgotten.

2

In the basement of the castle, other Darkhalks brought the second and only other member left of Telenay's party. The Centaur was a captain whose wounds left her speechless. The many piercings across his chest and back left his Human lungs full of blood and useless. When she touched him and he murmured, blood ran down his sides and chin. From running, his legs had absolutely been destroyed. His right arm was entirely gone and the stub had been burned to stop the bleeding.

She healed him to a point but not entirely, needing to get his wounds cleaned first.

"Jaridd, tell the servants to bring rags and hot water . . . a lot of it. And as many blankets and pillows as they can find."

Unwrapping the Centaur's clenched fingers, she gingerly took a dagger from the his hand, his only weapon. The dried blood cracked and ripped when she pulled it away. She unbuckled the tattered remains of his belts and sheaths. With all of her willpower, she ignored the smell of the rotting blood that covered him.

Across the hall, she used the Centaur's dagger to cut the rest of Telenay's armor off. Karalay worked without hesitation; with a task like this, she was a warrior.

"Karalay," Jaridd said. "I must go."

She rushed him. "Jaridd, do not go where this was done to these soldiers."

He laid his hands on her shoulders. "There is the chance that more of his party survived; we must go look."

"I cannot lose you."

He touched her cheek, kissed her and left. She took a desperate breath.

The servants arrived carrying steaming buckets and armfuls of rags and blankets. They stared with wide eyes and covered their mouths against the stench.

She looked at the three women. "Will you help me wash him?"

The servants looked at each other apprehensively. They nodded and approached the Warlord together. Karalay slipped the rags into the hot water and ran them over his face. She washed his hair while the servants worked on his legs and arms. She cleaned his chest, then flipped him over. They did not stop until Telenay was clean and his many wounds pink and bright.

Karalay wrapped him in blankets and fed the fire high.

They stepped into the hall together, shoulders down and weary. The two women's and the girl's eyes were pained and uncertain. They glanced at each other and Karalay knew that these three were family. Born servants, the mother of the girl and the sister of the mother.

She said, "Please, tell me your names."

The oldest, the mother, shook her head. "Our masters do not use our names."

"I am not your master, I am your Ward. What are your names?"

The eldest sighed and made the decision with an uncertain glance at her daughter whose huge blue eyes had not yet left her feet.

The mother said, "I am Hracha, the youngest beside me is my daughter, Acasha, and this is my sister, Orac."

Karalay said, "I will not forget them. I am afraid I need to ask for more of your service today. There is a Centaur who went through as dark a place as this Warlord did. He needs to be bathed as well."

Hracha said to her daughter and sister, "Go, fetch us fresh rags and burn those that we have already used. Bring more water and let no one see you."

They sprinted away.

In the Centaur's room, Karalay and Hracha piled all the blankets beside him, making as soft a bed as they could. They stacked the pillows along one edge, against the wall.

"I do not think we are strong enough to move him," Karalay said. "But I hope he will wake up and not think he is in a cell."

Hracha shook her head. "This place is all a cell." The mother's face was lined far beyond her years; her hands were burned from being in boiling water so much that the cracks down them were permanent, weeping fissures. The other servants returned. Acasha set down two steaming buckets of water; the girl's tiny arms shook from the weight.

Orac brought an armful of rags and more blankets. "These are all the blankets that could be spared."

Hracha nodded and added them to the Centaur's bed. Karalay sank her tired hands into the hot water. Behind her, the girl, Acasha, stared at the

Centaur. No doubt it was her first experience with such a creature. Her mother, Hracha, snapped at her and Acasha leaped into action, moving the buckets closer.

Karalay asked the girl, "Have you not seen a Centaur before?"

Acasha stopped, staring at Karalay. She glanced at her mother. Hracha nodded that it was all right.

Acasha said, "No, I have never." Her voice was twisted and heavy with Diggamara's hard accent.

"They say," Karalay said, "that Centaurs were given the body of a horse because their own hearts were not large enough to hold their kindness. Instead they ended up needing two."

She saw warmth come to Acasha's cheeks; the girl looked at the Centaur and smiled.

Karalay tenderly ran her fingertips over the stub of the Centaur's right arm. It had not been cut off but hacked off by a dull instrument. Maybe an ax. It had been burned at some point to stop the bleeding. She ran her fingers over the jagged cuts and, now that it was clean, she healed the stub thoroughly. Karalay worked tenderly but none of them forgot the king upstairs. Without words, they scrubbed feverishly to finish without being caught by the guard. Karalay held out her will in the hallways, ever vigilant and ever aware that there was no Darkhalk beside her.

Hracha stood. "His Human part is clean but the rest of him . . . I do not see how we will reach his other equine side."

"Thank you," Karalay said. "I really thank all of you. What is left of the water we can just dump on him and hope it loosens the dirt on the other side."

"What is his name?" Acasha asked from her mother's side.

Karalay said, "His name is Jikrin. He is a captain of the Centaur guard."

Orac opened her mouth to speak but Hracha's sharp look stopped her.

"What is it, Orac?" Karalay said.

The woman glanced hesitantly. "Cannot restore his bones?"

Karalay sighed. "Centaurs tend to have very stubborn bodies, and he is not young. After I have rested, I will try to return his arm to him."

Hracha motioned and her sister and daughter left the room; then the mother paused before leaving and looked close at her. "You will stay?"

"Yes, I am going to watch over them."

"I will bring you a chair and dinner then."

The servant left before she could thank her and Karalay returned to Telenay's side. His face glowed from the heat. She pulled one quilt off of him and wrapped it around her shoulders. Karalay sat down on the floor and laid her head and arms on the bed beside him. She listened to his breathing.

The Healer closed her eyes and matched his slow intakes of breath.

She fell asleep for a moment and jerked up when she heard footsteps in the hall. Hracha set a chair down beside her and a tray on the floor at Karalay's knees.

"Oh, thank you, Hracha."

The servant snapped, "Please, let no one hear you call me by any name except 'Servant'."

Hracha headed for the door.

"Wait." Karalay stopped her and the servant turned cautiously back.

Karalay said, "Your daughter is not as thin as you."

Hracha swallowed hard and murmured, "I sneak her more food from the kitchens when I can. I cannot bear to see her stunted like all the rest."

She saw in the servant's eyes how desperately she wanted her only child to grow tall, to be beautiful and to have a chance to truly live without bearing the horrible scars of servitude.

Hracha left and Karalay watched her go before uncovering the tray and drinking deep from the pitcher of hot tea. Her back sighed in relief when she sat in the chair. She ate all the food that she could. Suddenly, the image of the mare, drooling, sweating and falling into the reaches of exhaustion, hit her.

Karalay bolted and gasped, "Let me not be too late!"

She ran out into the daylight, finding that the basement could be reached by a servant's entrance on the side of the palace. She entered the stable running.

Karalay stopped at her stall. No horse greeted her. The worst thoughts stopped Karalay's heart.

She rushed in and found the mare with her eyes squeezed shut, lying in the thick straw. Her breath came out in long-held grunts. Karalay curled her arms around the mare's face and pulled her big head into her lap. The horse looked at her, and there was gladness in her eyes. If the mare had been able to speak she would have said, "I knew you would come back for me."

Those torn muscles and splintered bones Karalay healed while she rubbed the mare's neck. The mare's breathing eased and the horse's body settled and relaxed. The mare slept with long easy sighs. Karalay stroked her cheek, leaned her head back on the stall wall. She closed her eyes and sighed but did not allow herself to fall into sleep.

Carefully she laid the horse's head back in the straw. Karalay left her and walked back out into the light. The white sun was just setting behind the rooftops. Her breath misted out into the cold evening air.

She went to Telenay and took his hand, feeling his steady heartbeat through his palm. With her will, she knew he was very far gone and long from waking.

"Thank you," she whispered. "Thank you for being alive."

She clutched his hand once, then crossed the hall to the Centaur's side.

Jikrin's breathing had lightened. She laid her hand on his bare chest. She felt his steady heartbeat and sat down on the make-shift bed of blankets they had made for him. Her weariness was making her emotional. It was becoming difficult to tell the difference between fear and prediction. With his severed arm so close to her face, she fought tears.

Karalay pushed her face into the pillows and fought herself. She quivered severely for a second, then she took a breath.

His sleeping was still, save the rise and fall of his wide chest. Karalay watched, taking in each breath with him. She fought the urge to will him awake, that she could know what had happened. She reached out and touched the stump of his arm. The greatest of Healers had strength enough to will lost limbs to regrow. She feared that she had not the skill for such a feat, yet or ever.

Karalay fought the sleep that transfixed her. She pulled a blanket over herself thoughtlessly. She looked at the Centaur until her body fell and she slept.

3

The Healer jerked upright before she woke. She opened her eyes and blinked to focus, staring at the Centaur's hooves. She had heard a scrape, a sound she knew well: a shod hoof moving across stone.

Jikrin shifted in sleep. She sighed and lay back down, staring up at the ceiling. She heard a murmur in the hall. She stared at the open door. Karalay slipped over the Centaur, stood and pressed herself to the wall. She stepped into the black hallway. Shadows flickered as people passed the fireplace in Telenay's room.

She heard Sicilia whisper, "When was the last time you saw him?"

"I have never seen him."

Karalay took a step to the side and caught a glance of the charcoal cloak of Dind, kneeling beside Telenay.

Sicilia's whisper was harsh. "He has done well without you; let us leave him alone. His mother is dead; nothing keeps you to him except you."

"He will always be my son."

"Let us go."

"I must thank Karalay."

"Why?" Sicilia's voice reached an inaudible pitch.

"She saved his life."

"She had best not hear you say that if you want some secrets kept!"

There was someone standing beside her. Karalay jerked back against the wall. Cousai glanced at her, then turned and slipped away. Karalay followed at a silent run. She squinted as the door to the outside opened and Cousai left the building.

She ran up and out and spotted the Fai walking down the edge of the palace.

"Cousai!"

The Fai stopped and waited.

Karalay said, "How did such things come to pass between Sicilia and Dind?"

"My sister does not tell me so many things. They are together, though I would not consider my sister ever having love for anything." Cousai's gray eyes were in shadow. "You best go back and get your rest, Healer. This wave will hit us soon."

"How do you know that?"

Cousai turned away. "Even immortals will grow impatient when they have been waiting forever."

"Are you talking about Grim?"

But Cousai was gone. Karalay scowled and walked back. Sicilia and Dind were gone.

She stepped up to Telenay's side. She looked at him and it was obvious now: a Darkhalk son. Telenay could go days without food, without sleep. Of course he was the son of a Darkhalk. A secret. How great a secret. And what a perfect Warlord.

She whispered, "Wake and rejoice, Telenay, you are the son of a Darkhalk. You met your father today; his name is Dind."

She sat down in the chair beside his bed. "Wake up."

She seeped her will into him and pushed, throwing her heart against the Warlord's being. She was grabbed. Black claws came at her and great red eyes screamed out a howl that sounded like an alarm. She cried as fear made her heart pound and Telenay's will leaped on her, claws out. She snatched herself out of the Warlord's body and fell. Darkness hit her with the feeling of cold stone reverberating off the back of her head.

4

She opened her eyes painfully. The back of her head throbbed. Karalay healed the welt that was growing beneath her hair and the pain subsided until she was able to sit up.

She snarled at Telenay, "Fine—I will leave you alone!"

She got herself up and glared at him a final time before leaving his room. She walked across the hall, still rubbing the back of her head. She stepped into Jikrin's room and stopped. The Centaur had moved from the floor to his bed and was stiffly trying to pull a blanket over his haunches.

He saw her and gasped, "Healing Ward."

She rushed to him. "Let me help you." She knelt and covered the Centaur.

His beige eyes were marked with streaks of blood. "Thank you."

He reached for her and she let him draw her in. They embraced and she reveled in the smell of a Centaur.

She said, "How do you feel?"

He closed his eyes. "As though all of me is numb."

"Those parts of you that are still healing will remain that way until they are entirely well."

"You saved my life." His voice broke; he coughed.

She noticed that two trays had been left by the door. She poured two cups of water and helped him drink all of one and half of another. She wiped the water from his chin, then poured a cup for herself.

His eyes were clear when they focused on her face. "My Warlord?"

"Telenay is in the other room. He will heal, but his sleep is too deep for me to do anything for him now . . . without his permission."

"I would never have wanted to wake if I were him."

"Why?"

He looked pained.

She laid her hand on his. "Do not start there. Start from the beginning."

Jikrin swallowed. "There are places of black where I do not have any memory, of hours, or days, I do not know."

226

The Centaur clutched her hand. "When we reached the forest, there was a very wrong stillness. No Elves. No life. Nothing. The Warlord split us into two parties. I was with my Second and four other Centaurs, one of them my brother. The first party, led by the Warlord, took a path straight into the center of the forest. We were not far apart when my Centaur leader noticed a smell. We did not go much farther when it became unbearable. Our decision was made to change our path and we headed to meet back up with the Warlord. But we could not find them. We . . . It doesn't make any sense. We searched and searched and screamed for them. We lost days, I think. We ran out of water. And things were quieter and closer and that smell . . . We did finally pick up their trail and followed it."

His voice broke. "Is there more water?"

She filled him another cup, helped him raise it to his mouth. Jikrin's hand shook and he spilled it. She used her skirt to dab up the water.

"I am sorry."

She patted his arm.

He said, "We followed their path and the tracks turned to those of war, as though they had been attacked. Telenay's Human prints disappeared, the Centaurs with him began to bleed and we followed their blood. They were practically running. We assumed, with no tracks from the Warlord, that he had been taken by something. We followed them forever; we did not sleep out of fear. We did not speak because we began to feel the eyes. I knew, we all knew, that those watching eyes had been watching us since we entered."

He drank from the cup again. "This is not the hand I was meant to use."

"I know," she sighed.

He continued, "I remember we found them, but we also found the heart of that forest. We found the place where they gathered. They were Elves once. I have fought beside Elves and these were once those creatures. But they are not anymore; they are dead and each battalion moved as though it was controlled by one mind. Female and male Elves, of every age, marched side by side. They knew we were there, but they did not care. But the heart was not where Telenay had been taken. No, their tracks broke away and they ran so we followed at a run to get away from that place."

The Centaur stared at her. "Karalay, thousands upon thousands, dead and walking. They moved in massive battalions and they . . . the wills that controlled them did not even look at us. Did not even care we were there. We were nothing to them, Karalay. Thousands."

227

She swallowed past her closed throat, was incapable of anything except pulling herself closer to him. He wrapped his good arm around her and held her tightly.

The Centaur stared at the fire. "Telenay escaped their clutches, probably with his will, I guess. I do not know. My comrades were with him and they killed those Elves that got in their way. Their will began to turn our way then and we could hear them. We could *hear* them marching behind us. There were Elves in front, too. We ran and ran, following Telenay's tracks. We heard them everywhere then. And the trees were all dead, their hearts were gone but we wondered if they still could see, if they watched all of this without the ability to stop it, and if that was what had taken their hearts away."

The Centaur closed his eyes. "I remember. I remember we caught up to them after we found most of Telenay's party dead. Most of ours had fallen, too. Friends. My comrades, once they were there and then they were gone somewhere. Dead along the way. We were out of our minds with that smell and that sound coming for us. I am shamed, Karalay. I am so shamed that I did not even notice when my actual brother, Chark, fell beside me and I do not even know when or where."

He covered his tears and Karalay clutched him. She listened with her ears and her will as the soldier mourned out the rest. "They attacked us from above and the darkness closed in. I do not know what became of this place in my mind, but the stink intensified and I lost my arm then somewhere. I woke and my Centaur Second was beside me; we were in a tree. We were the last, he said. He burned my arm to stop the bleeding and got me up. I had only one weapon left. He told me we were close and we were. I could hear the sound of slow cutting, that sound of torture. That sound of a Human being trying to scream."

The Centaur's fingers clutched her arm. "Telenay was laid out on a plank of wood, being slowly cut at as though he were nothing. The skin fell off of them, and their wooden bones were full of maggots and they fell on Telenay. We attacked them. My Second ordered me to do nothing but get to Telenay and run. I did as I was ordered and I cut the heads off of those creatures that hovered over him. I grabbed him and I ran in the direction that my Second had told me. I do not know how long I ran. I remember pain, in my leg and in my side. I remember I could barely breathe. And I am shamed to say that I was too scared to stop running. I want to say I ran out of duty but I was so scared. Telenay was dead weight and I was sure he was gone. I was sure we had failed him. I was sure that after we had all survived Cobblestone we were going to die here, where no one would know how our ends came. I could not let that happen to Telenay, leave him to end up walking around with all those Elves . . . I ran and ran."

Karalay held back his head so she could press her lips to his wet cheek. "You saved him." They held each other in silence though Karalay was far away. Her brow was tightly knit with fear. It would not take long for such an army to reach Diggamara.

5

She could see the sun between the houses, rising above the black water of the river, as it breached the horizon. The white sun rose before her on the ninth of the month of Qalin and she wondered if this was the day that would be marked as their end.

Karalay lifted her chin and thought of Jikrin's great courage and the stupid certainty of Jaridd. She felt there was little doubt and took a deep breath of the clean air. Her next inhalation was getting her closer and she straightened her shoulders. Her mouth was set in a fine line of finality. She could accept this fate if this was the last sunrise she would ever see.

The Healer stopped at the basement door. The sound of wings swept by her; she looked.

"Raven." She held out her hand.

The bird landed, settling into her hand. He cawed at her.

"Why did you return to me?"

The bird closed his eyes, puffing up his wings and snuggling down. She held him and walked back to her chamber. She set the bird down on her bed and looked at him closely.

"Will you take another message for me? It is too late to tell Osondrous not to step up to become queen. I know that will happen now . . . But, will you take a message to her?"

The Raven blinked. He looked away, then looked back at her.

She said, "Thank you."

Karalay poured a saucer with milk and another with water. Bread had been left on her table. She crumbled it all and set the meal beside the raven. Karalay picked up a piece of charcoal while he ate and ripped a narrow strip of parchment. She wrote in careful script, then rolled the parchment in leather and tied it to the Raven's leg.

"You must go back to the castle, my friend. Too late, but maybe not for

229

everything."

6
Osondrous

The rain came on the north wind with sleet and ice. It left the stone of the Castle of the Wards black and shining with fiery reflections. The very sound of the storm was cold. The servants and soldiers that could, stayed in their rooms, huddled up for warmth.

Eikian stood in dark silence on the parapet. He had not spoken to Osondrous today and did not want to. In the back of his mind, he knew Aerick was coming on duty as the lead Second. In the rain, Eikian's eyes were still and hard. He was waiting for Aerick and did not even know it.

7
Constance

Constance lay out in the blankets like a cat. Accepting her own beauty, her own sexuality. She murmured to him beside her, touching his slick sweat.

"Oh. . ." was all she could say. She was smiling and naked. She moved her smooth, thin thighs and they were slick with Aerick.

He ran his fingers down her; he growled and she quivered.

"I do not want to go."

She said, "Then do not."

He pulled her to his face. "I love you. Do you know that?"

She laughed. Ecstasy made her stunning. He swept her hair back and kissed her hard on the mouth.

He got up. The air was chilled with the storm and he got dressed quickly. She was a pink sweep of everything he wanted, topped in gold, and he had to leave for duty. She got up as he was heading for the door. Constance knew how good her breasts looked to him now, knew how to walk so she swayed. She parted her lips as she approached him and pressed herself against his hard armor.

"Do not go."

"Oh, I must."

He almost ran.

"I love you!" she called.

"I love you, too!"

8

Osondrous

Osondrous had sat long with her mouth around the rim of a cup of brandy, drinking away Eli's plight and her day in the Ring. She was exhausted but had completely surrendered to never sleeping again. Eikian was filled with anger and was avoiding her. She was sure his rage was over Eli and nothing else; she could not blame him for that.

A pair of Implins worked their way by on the seemingly endless task of scrubbing the dining room floor. She moved her stool closer to the dwindling fire.

The storm outside had worn out and she no longer heard the wind whistling by the door.

The smacks of wet leather feet were drawing near. She leaned back to see who was sprinting so hastily.

Majeik the Second spotted her and called, "Warlord!"

Her stool hit the floor and she reached him. "What is it?"

"Eikian killed Aerick!"

She followed him at a run. The sentence echoed in her ears again and again, as though trying to penetrate, though she could not yet, truly, comprehend what Majeik had said. The sentence hit with each pound of her feet as she drew closer to the truth, as she drew closer to incomprehensible. The air was so heavy that a cloud of breath hung around the cheeks of her soldiers. They parted as she approached. She could see Eikian framed in steam. His sword was drawn at his side, the brother to her own chosen weapon, still in hand even as Aerick had long gone cold.

Her stomach twisted.

Aerick was at their feet. His body wrapped around as though he had been struck so hard that his bones were unable to keep the impact from tearing him in half. He lay with his face slammed into the stone.

Olisize knelt at his head.

The Healer looked up. "He was too far gone. It had just been too long before he was found."

She opened her mouth to ask, *How can that be?* but nothing came out.

A soldier helped the old Healer up and away. Slowly, she knelt and touched Aerick's face. Majeik held close to her side and he motioned for the guards to grow near. They tightened around back of Eikian and reached for their swords. Centaurs stood behind them, some shaking their heads, some not moving at all.

She felt the fleeting warmth still in Aerick's cheek, or imagined by her palm. He was absolutely gone.

She stood and stared over Aerick's corpse, her jaw rolling, grinding. Her eyes lifted to Eikian. With her will she felt his breathing quicken, his heart begin to hammer. Her soldiers began to draw their daggers and knives, began to move in on him.

A sound shattered the air, something that was not all Human but that of an animal, desperate with disbelief. Constance emerged from the hall at a run, blond hair sticking to her face and in her opened, screaming mouth. The girl pushed through Osondrous' soldiers like she were running blindly through a cornfield. She dove for Aerick's body.

Osondrous turned and caught her, one arm down her chest, her strong hand wrapping around the girl's waist. Constance's fingers grabbed empty space. The girl's tears were hot and wet on Osondrous' cold skin.

Osondrous pushed her into Majeik. "Take her to your chamber. Be kind."

Majeik wrapped her in his arms. Seeing Aerick as he was, Constance dissolved to the other Second's touch. He took her away. Her weeping disappeared and the silence fell again.

Eikian's jaw muscles were locked, shaking slightly; she could not see his eyes but she had no desire to.

Osondrous said, "Take Aerick to the funeral chambers and get a hole dug; we will let him to rest tonight."

He was carefully lifted and hauled away. Aerick's eyelids fell open and she looked into his eyes as they passed her by.

She gave motion that stopped the progression of her soldiers in taking Eikian to the dungeons.

They stared at her, waiting.

She said, "Return to your duties. This was a terrible accident."

And they were alone and the cold night air dismissed the rising fog of breath. A mist had begun to fall that chilled her. He lifted his eyes eventually and she looked into them. As big and burly as he was, to her now, he looked small. But Osondrous did not attempt to read his heart anymore, nor press into him in any way.

232

She stepped right up to him and said directly into his down-turned face. "This is how Centaurs were given the name of savages. What right have you to chastise a Human man for his lack of control?"

She shook her head and left him standing there.

She went down into the warm rooms of the funeral chambers. Aerick was laid on a stone table. In the empty burial room, water ran in a well at the far end and her Captains were fetching buckets full. Servants had brought olive oil, soap and rags.

She touched Aerick's cheek. He looked almost well, the wound in his back covered by his clothing. He wore no armor, only his vest and leathers and high collared shirt and cloak. She lit the fire hole at the foot of the stone bed with flint. The dry wood caught and broke the silence with a crack.

Osondrous unbuckled his chosen weapon, a long sword, and set it against the wall. She searched his body for his dagger and laid it aside. Another two daggers she found, one in his boot and another at his hip. She used one of them to cut his clothing from him. She rolled his cloak beside his sword, dropped the rest of his clothes on the fire and the air filled with the sound of his leathers burning. She unlaced his boots and the fire consumed them too.

Aerick lay naked, hands at his sides. She held up the large wood needle and fine, leather thread. His wound ran straight across his spine, cutting him in half. She rolled him over, tucked in his bowels and organs that attempted to fall loose and sewed the wound closed with big crossed stitches.

Osondrous dipped a rag into a full bucket of water and she rubbed the soap between her hands. She washed his hair tenderly and with care. She sponged his broad, strong back, letting the rag slide from muscle to muscle. She washed his feet. She washed the bloody stitches of the wound. She turned him over again and she washed up his legs, his hands, between his fingers, over his muscular stomach and hard chest. She gently washed his face, along his forehead and down his cheeks. She shaved his face smooth.

The servants brought a leather body bag. They lifted Aerick up and spread the body bag beneath him. She brought his hands to his chest and laid his sword beneath them. They sewed him in from his toes up until she lastly touched his forehead.

She said to a servant, "Bring Constance if she is able."

The servant left instantly, just a flit of a girl at a run. Osondrous shook out Aerick's cloak, shaking out the dirt and rain. She carefully folded it and gazed at Aerick's still face.

She said, "No one knows that this is the reality. Just the dead and Warlords burying the dead."

Constance came with shocked eyes and face so starkly ashen that she could have passed for the dead as well.

"Come here," Osondrous commanded.

The girl approached without making a noise, without seeming to breathe. Osondrous stood her right beside Aerick and put a hand on Constance's shoulder.

She said, "Say goodbye now or you never will and you would regret that the rest of your life. Touch him, Girl."

Constance's hand rose, as if out of a trance, and lay down on Aerick's forehead. Constance swallowed and her dry throat clicked. Another servant stepped over to offer support and Osondrous gave her a warning look that kept the other away.

Constance whispered, "Goodbye." And her voice did not break.

Osondrous said, "Good. Now go back to Majeik and give yourself one day to grieve. Just one."

Osondrous gave Constance Aerick's cloak and the girl took it and pressed it against her heart.

Now Osondrous let the other servant come forward. As Constance was led away, Osondrous heard her begin to weep.

The Warlord sewed the bag over his face. The captains put him on their shoulders and carried him into the castle hallways and then out into the wet grass of the graveyard where they gingerly laid him down. They dug his hole among the line of Seconds' stones and laid him in it. She pulled out her dagger and raised it against the headstone, made a clear cut across the corner, so she would would know which one was his.

Osondrous helped her captains fill the hole over his body and packed it tight with their feet. It was all done in silence, out of respect. The soldiers left her. Their torch retreated into the castle and she felt the darkness of the graveyard close in. The pre-dawn cold was settling. She wanted to touch him again.

Osondrous squatted down and sank her fingers into the black dirt.

She went to her chamber, remembering how heavy her head had been in her brandy not so much earlier. She sat down on the edge of her bed, hoping the comfort would bring the weariness back. Osondrous caught a tear. She stared at it, rubbed it between her fingers.

She got up, cast a cape around her shoulders.

All was still and so cold that the stone had become slick. The stars were bright beacons, no clouds to cover or hold in the heat. She walked past the Implins on the parapet, scrubbing away the last of Aerick's blood.

Eikian was at the far end of the stone, hands flat out on the parapet wall. The peaks of his shoulders pointed over his spine through his thin cape. Beside him, she heard him breathing.

She said, "You will not speak of Aerick. There will be nothing from you to me or anyone else about this."

He looked at her; his face fell apart. He wanted to speak.

Her eyes riveted. "He was an innocent. You are not worthy of speaking of that boy! He deserved better than you. You are too bloody, too scarred."

She looked out into the black fields of Kamamine.

"And so am I," she said. "You and I are the exact same ugly breed of death. One day it will finally take us at the very same time and we will be buried together."

It was the first either of them had spoken, even in a subtle way, of the truth of their ties. Deep in Cobblestone, they had been truly fooled and had killed each other. Lying there dying, they had drunk and saved themselves. But at what cost? They were bound too deep. If she ceased, so would he, instantly. And though they had always lied to themselves that it had been only another hallucination brought on by the witches of the Keltch, there was no denying the gray scars on their bellies. Scars that would have killed them.

She touched hers now beneath her cloak and longed to touch his.

The night deepened after the moon set and the stars shone brighter and it grew colder still. The windmills and the town were all taken in the darkness. The last watch of the night came from their beds and relieved the watch of the guards before them. They passed the Warlords in silence. News of Aerick's death had moved through the ranks and the glances Eikian's way were unlike any looks he had ever earned.

"Go to bed," she said.

"I won't sleep."

"Standing here all night will accomplish nothing but making you cold."

She looked at him and Eikian nodded.

His departing steps were slow and heavy. She leaned on the parapet wall and blew on her hands for heat. The stars were so impressive that she stared at them, picking out the constellations she had learned as a child. There was the hunter, the huntress, the bear and the winged horse. She counted the stars to find the horse, his wings a cluster of five stars on either side. His head was held high and regal and she was reminded of Tamarack.

She made her way back to the hall of silence and wandered to the stable.

The horses were snuggled into their thick bedding, their heads down and they remained undisturbed when she walked by. In the back, in a long row of stallions, Willan was not sleeping.

He had caught scent of her before she entered and his dark eyes looked out in anticipation. He smelled the air. She placed her fingers over his wide nostrils. The stallion chewed his teeth, dropped his head to touch her. She leaned on his stall door, pressing her fingers beneath his black mane for warmth.

"You are the color of gold, not the polished gold of rings, but the real gold in its place in the mountains. One day you may see it, Willan. It is blackened and almost green; it is very dark."

Willan's huge eye stared intently at her. Both of his ears flickered as he listened.

Her eyes grew heavy in the stable warmth. Reluctantly, she headed for her chamber. The room felt large when she stepped into it. She stripped down to nothing after feeding the fire and lay down. She curled up tightly. She felt the empty presence in her bed as though she, as a whole being, no longer qualified alone to fill it up. She turned and tried to settle by taking deep slow breaths.

The sun had begun to rise in blue on the horizon.

She stood up and pulled a slip over her head.

She stepped barefoot into the cold hall.

She let herself in, past his heavy door. His fire was low, his breathing was lower. Parts of her still tingled with a chill; his bed was hot. She lay down and he moved. His fingers surrounded her and pulled her into his sleep. Her feet wrapped around his horse ankles; she laced her fingers with his. His breathing on the back of her neck lulled her. Osondrous slept.

9

It was late when Osondrous was awakened by the sound of the door closing. The windows showed no light. She knew the day had come and gone. The fire was high, just fed. She touched the place he had been and it was still hot. The Ring was overdue and there would be double work for her tomorrow because she missed today. But Osondrous did not think of that; she thought of Eli and her heart turned.

She thought of Aerick and her stomach ached.

The fire held her in a suspension, as though there was no time; it was only ever just the holy night and she the grave digger in it.

Finally she lifted herself from the bed. She dressed in her chamber. She made the trip to the dining room as though emerging back to civilization after having escaped for too long. She almost expected to see Aerick alive and well, leaning on a column, waiting for Constance.

The hall of silence was empty.

Her soldiers rose and bowed to her when she entered; there were few of them. She sat down at the long end of the table where they sat, watching them at a distance.

A servant came to her. "Is there something you wish for specifically, Warlord?"

"Hot tea and supper."

The servant brought a platter, a hot pot of water, two cups, one filled with herbs and a plate of dried fruit. She poured herself a cup of hot water, sprinkled the herbs until the water darkened and she could smell the headiness of the tea. The servant brought her a bowl of goat cream soup, seasoned with rosemary and filled with potatoes. On the side, a flat hard piece of black deer laid on a slice of buttered bread.

She ate it all and finished sipping her tea. She listened to the banter of the soldiers who ignored her because that was clearly what she wanted. They spoke of seeing Eikian, then stopped themselves before they said more, not wanting to speak of him with her listening, as if she could not read their minds. But she did not need to, to know exactly what they thought of Eikian.

Osondrous looked down into her tea and finished it.

She found herself actually wondering about Constance. The girl had lost everything in such a short time. She had never seen a place for Constance in the castle. The girl clearly was not Ward material. What was it that brought her here? What power did she have if it was not will? And how could it have been mistaken for the strength of a Ward?

From the hall of silence the head cook, Shrae, stepped into the dining room, arms opened wide.

"Boys!" he exclaimed. "The honey has arrived!"

Her soldiers leaped to their feet and raced for the door. She smiled at

Shrae who grinned beneath his big mustache. It had been two months the castle had gone without honey and her soldiers had pined for the healthy sugars in the sweet spread. She followed the chef and soldiers out.

In the courtyard, still unloading, was the long train of horses and wagons, piled down with barrels and barrels of honey.

She called out to one of her commanders, "Give them a hand."

A soft drizzle began to fall and she could hear the kitchen servants cursing the slippery barrels. Her soldiers filed down, men strong enough to lift a barrel by themselves. They rolled them on to each other's shoulders and hauled them in.

She leaned on a pillar.

Eikian stepped past her. Her soldiers rolled the barrels onto his arms and the massive Centaur stomped up the hall's steps, carrying two. His face was grave; he never looked at her.

Her soldiers made quick time of the five hundred barrels of honey. The drizzle had stopped, the night had cleared. Eikian leaned on the other side of her pillar.

Osondrous said out of the corner of her mouth, "Was it really necessary to show off your muscles?"

The Centaur did not smile, his eyes were down. "Why did you come to me last night?"

She glared across the courtyard and avoided his question because the answer was so obvious to her. "Something dark has entered my heart."

His face lifted with interest.

"I think Jezaline should have been back here by now."

"Do you want me to send riders?"

"Our lightest soldiers on our fastest horses, send five of them. Tell them to travel wide, cover as much land as possible. I want to know if there is any sign. Anything."

He hurried away, relieved for something to do. She looked at the sky; wispy little tendrils of remaining clouds covered the constellations. She meandered out onto the inner parapet, crossing the rope bridge, turning right and heading toward the gate.

She wasted the night watching her riders prepare in the courtyard for their journey in search of the Ward Jezaline. She hoped Jezaline had been hindered by too many good-looking servants and tasty liquor on her way back. But the hope of that good chance was dim and Osondrous did not think that that was what had happened at all.

Each rider wore light clothing, few weapons, and their tack was sparse.

238

When they mounted, it was with the reins in one hand and the lead of another Warbred in their other. The other horse packed their food and flint, the least amount for a two week journey.

She had never needed the other Wards in her life. Had often been heard claiming that the castle would benefit without them. Now she was desperate for just one more. She needed the strength of another Ward, any other Ward. And the Centaur Eli waited silently in her dungeon.

She watched them go, their urging pushing their fast horses whose tails flagged high. They cut off the road, spread out until they could barely keep sight of each other and they were taken in by the fields and the night to the west.

Above them the sky had entirely cleared of clouds. The horse constellation stood gallant. She thought of Tam again. One of the horse's wings blotted out into darkness. She frowned. High clouds she did not notice must be moving fast. The rest of the horse blotted out, then returned to clear view. She stood up straight, watched closely. Another batch of stars fell into darkness and then they began plucking out, closer to the castle, brilliant stars going black until reappearing.

The watchmen in the closest tower let out a call; he set the fire of war in his tower. A second watchman confirmed, another behind her did the same.

Osondrous flew over the slick stone. "Archers! Man the parapet!"

The castle erupted. The big basins every ten feet along the parapet were lit at sprints. The castle raged in light. The watchmen blew their horns for archers. They were from their beds and into their armor instantly. They grabbed their long bows and sheaths of arrows; they were up, into the towers. Her Centaur archers filled the courtyard with thunder as they filed down the inner and outer parapets, dropping to their bellies, resting their sights on the walls.

Eikian grabbed her hand as she sprinted by. "What is it?"

"Watch!" She yelled, "I run for Mlore!"

And she was in her chamber, grabbing her chosen weapon and belting it to her hips.

"Do you know what this is, Teek?"

The Darkhalk said, "They are dragons."

"Dragons?" She was throwing on her armor. "There is no dragon that could cross the rivers!"

"These dragons were made special."

She flew out the door, chain mail tight around her breasts and stomach.

Teek was at her back, his Cape a black swath through the air.

Her soldiers were screaming across the parapets at each other.

"They are dragons!"

"How can they be dragons?"

"They must be dragons!"

"They are dragons!"

She ran out along the outer parapet using her will to say to her soldiers: *Stay your arrows. Wait until we are attacked. They ARE dragons!*

She stayed on the inside, missing the tails of Centaurs as she sprinted. She rounded to the end of the parapet, turned hard and ran until she stood above the outside gate.

She waited. She watched.

The sky was all stars above her until a woosh of wings and they were all blotched out. Darkness swept over her. She ducked, felt the wind on her face, caught a glimpse of scales.

Her archers let loose, aiming at the black shapes that were too dark to be sky and too vast to be spaces between stars. An arrow fell beside her. Teek's arms surrounded her and dropped them to the stone. He covered them with his Cape. Arrows fell around them, bouncing like steel hail.

Her Darkhalk released her and she ran.

"Be careful!" she screamed.

Eikian was galloping up the other side of the parapet, waving his arms at the towers. "You are not hitting them!"

He faltered and stopped, looking around at an arrow sticking out of his left arm. He jerked it out.

She screamed, "Eikian. Find your shield!"

Teek grabbed her arm, slammed them down. A black claw slapped over her. She swung at it and her knife landed a blow. A roar enveloped them. Teek held her down until the dragon passed. She pulled out her two short swords.

Osondrous sprinted along her line of Centaur archers. "Get up! Go to your swords!"

Her Human soldiers poured out of the guardhouses, fully armored, gripping short swords and shields.

Her commander of the archers ran to meet her screaming, "I do not think we can penetrate them!"

"You light your arrows on fire!" She ran across the hall of silence to the other side of the castle and the parapet where Eikian stood, swords out, dripping black blood.

"Bring out the oil!"

He ran from her and she ran for Majeik. He stood dripping in dragon blood and panting.

"How many are there?"

"At least a dozen."

As he spoke, she turned and a dragon the size of ten horses attached itself to the side of one of her towers. His head lunged deep into one of the windows.

Majeik said, "There are six doing that!"

She dropped to the parapet with him as a dragon swept overhead. They both swung hard and missed. When they stood, Osondrous caught sight of the old Healer in the hall of silence.

"Olisize?"

The old man stood in the midst of the hall, Constance quivering at his side.

She sprinted to him. "Olisize, have you lost your mind? I need you healing my soldiers."

"She is a seer!" He lifted Constance's arm.

Osondrous stopped short, stared at him, at the girl, and back again. "Are you certain?"

He nodded. It made sense. The girl was no Ward but something else entirely.

Osondrous grabbed Constance and threw her over her left shoulder. The Warlord ran over the bridge to the outer parapet, all the way down past all of her soldiers, took the turn without slipping and set the girl down above the gate. Constance stood shaking and covering her face.

Osondrous said, "I will not let harm come to you. Now you must see!"

Osondrous pointed the girl toward the castle and pinned her arms down to her sides. She delved into Constance and searched and searched until she found the outlet in the girl's mind. A gift that was not the will of a Ward or dictated by distance or strength. From the outlet she saw what she could not reach with her own will: the dragons, hollow skeletons against a dark sky, ridden by black Reapers, wrapped up in gray cloaks like corpses.

Osondrous opened her eyes.

"Majeik!" She dragged Constance to him and pushed her into his arms. "Get her out of here!"

She ran back to the castle and into the stable where the ruckus of Warbreds smelling and hearing war echoed off the stone. Willan whinnied when he saw her. She opened his stall and threw herself onto his back. She pushed him to run and the Warbred galloped out of the stable, took a turn at the hall of silence and crossed the narrow, swaying bridge without question. She clutched her dagger in one hand, his mane in the other.

The stallion picked up speed down the parapet.

The dragons were swooping by the gate. Willan galloped faster and faster, his nostrils showing red. They reached the end of the parapet. The stallion made no hesitation. He hit the end running as hard as he could. Willan lifted off, forelegs stretched out before him, reaching for stars, for sky. He leaped for her.

A dragon flew, claws spread as though to embrace them. She gathered her feet beneath her and jumped off her stallion's back. The dragon opened his mouth to snatch Willan from the air.

She hit the dragon with the thud of her sword smacking bone. The dragon reared back with a scream. Willan fell to the darkness of land. Her will was out, her eyes tight. She clung to her dagger and grappled with her other hand to get a hold. She pushed into the dragon and searched until she found what was not reptilian, nor scaly, nor cold-blooded. She found the Human, the Reaper, that controlled him.

Mlore in hand, she rose out of the ashes that was the dragon's soul.

The Human sat in utter stillness, engulfed in concentration, unaware. She came down on him with all of her rage. His scream shattered the sky that was black and it all came tumbling down. The Reaper vanished, dead. She was jarred out of the dragon's mind as he began to thrash. Osondrous pushed into him again, soothed him, shut him up until the dragon flew smoothly. She slowly climbed up his shoulder, got to the base of his neck and threw her leg over him.

"Now you will help me, Dragon."

She felt the animal give to her will so easily that it was as though he were bred to do so. She felt him tilt as she pushed him to turn and the animal gave himself to her. The sun was rising in the east and the sky was steely blue and she could see the stark outlines of the other dragons. Another twelve in total. They gave no notice or interest in her direction. She pushed the dragon forward, urged him with rage and horror. The dragon reacted, bringing out his claws, opening his jaws.

Another dragon flew by and her dragon turned on it. Ripped open the other dragon's throat. Dug so fast that the other creature did not fight at all. The huge body fell with a devastating quiver into the wheat fields. She pushed him for more. The dragon lifted higher into the sky, spread out his wings and turned back toward the castle.

Dragons attacked the towers like wasps. Eikian had the men throwing oil at the dragon bellies as they flew over and the archers' fiery arrows were spreading throughout the sky like comets. Her dragon carefully swerved, avoiding the arrows. He went at a dragon on the tower. They picked up speed and she braced.

They hit the other animal broadside; it flapped its wings and the wind threw her back. Her dragon clawed at the other animal's face, biting at its flailing claws.

The roar of the night dimmed to the screaming of the two in her ears.

She turned to see an approaching black blur, wings flapping. The third dragon bore down on them. She gasped, preparing to leap. The third hit them, mouth opening up behind her, grabbing her dragon's spine. He screamed, threw his head back and she lost her grip. He fell out from under her.

She leaped toward the tower, hands out. And her archers saw her fall; they were leaning, fingers out. She grasped nothing but air. They all missed. She thought that it might be the end. Her forward momentum evaporated and she fell straight down.

She was caught. Osondrous recognized the distinct smell of a Darkhalk: old, oiled leather.

Teek set her down and held her up.

She had fallen between the outer and the inner parapets. Bodies littered the causeway. Above her men were screaming, fighting and falling dead. She ran toward the gates of the castle, the only escape. Over their heads the dragons, balls of fire, flapped their wings at their burning bellies. Her feet slipped and crunched in the stone. Teek kept a hand on her elbow, rushing her along.

His grip screamed *danger, danger, danger.*

She reached the gate and flew into the courtyard. A burning dragon tumbled down. The beast's impact threw her and she hit the sand sliding. Centaurs, legs flailing, flew by her, hides ripped as they slid across the sand. Black dragon blood poured from the beast's belly. He swatted at her Centaurs like flies, held one between his teeth. She heard the crunch, could feel at a distance the breaking of the Centaur's bones. The dragon threw the body across the courtyard.

The dragon was getting to his feet even as her Centaurs were trying to weigh him down. She was getting to her feet. Teek was going at the animal's head, the Sword of darkness a black swath through the air.

She stared as the Darkhalk and dragon parried and Teek resiliently held

243

on, stabbing at the animal's eyes. The dragon did not fall. *What great will could possibly hold on to their life that they can fight without breath?* She raised Mlore and ran to her Darkhalk's aid.

The dragon's body was a rolling sea. Muscles, light bird-like bones, all bending beneath soft scales. She dove in to the animal's shoulder, hacking away. Osondrous desperately rose to join Teek at the animal's head, holding on with a knife in the dragon's ear, trying to saw through the thing's throat with Mlore. Teek moved. She whipped her head around, watching the black Cape rising and swirling, lifting the Darkhalk through the air. A dragon was there, brimstone and coal. His jaws open, she could smell his breath; he was hurtling toward her with all of his speed. She turned to take his attack, though she did not have enough time to even raise her sword.

His toothy image in her face became the black sweep of the Darkhalk. The dragon's mouth closed it down. Teek's blood burst black and red all over her.

Rage took her.

Her exhausted will surged with adrenaline. Osondrous grabbed hold of the dragon beneath her, she killed the will that was controlling him. And in her will the dragon turned, raised his mutilated head and opened his mouth to take the head of the other. The dragons hit, making their bodies look like one.

She fell to the sand, rolled tight, covered her head.

The dragons writhed. She opened her hand and she took Mlore to them as they faltered, came down on each other, and her. The war for the second dragon had exhausted her will. But fury was still powering her. In one last monumental effort, the last of her power, she grabbed them with her will and tossed them toward the wall. The dragons were airborne and the castle seemed to hesitate with a breath as they flew. A ton of muscle, bone, teeth and claws with blood spraying.

They hit with a thunder of horrendous sound. The bodies compacted to a quarter of their size. Cracks spider-webbed out as the inside parapet walls caved in to the force. Osondrous shakily got from one knee to her feet. In her head there was a thought emerging. Something of suspicion. This Grim, this red man held the will, the power, the prophecy of the greatest of Wards. Back in the time of the rise of Wards, this was the kind of power that they had held. She could not believe he was born in darkness, not with this kind of power.

Who was Grim really?

She could imagine the Reapers somewhere, all wrapped up in blankets, safe in some place no one knew about. Warm and happy beside a fire as they surged outward with Grim's tremendous power behind them. As her will was decimated to the physical toll, they just kept roaring on. And anger now, pure white anger, drove them into a higher level of power. Her will was done and dead, and they were stronger than ever.

She raised her head. Dragons flying had turned to the sound of the impact. They swept their wings around, snarled and dove to meet this woman, this Warlord who claimed to have such power. The two dragons were dead but there were ten others coming for her. They climbed down from the towers, dove from the sky and Osondrous raised Mlore and braced herself. Will of a Ward or no.

She screamed and it lifted from her in a long cry that everything and everyone heard. Her soldiers' bodies littered the walls, the courtyard and the parapet in thousands. They would be left until this was over. The Centaurs saw her in the midst and they leaped from the inner parapets, emptying the walls of strength, throwing it all down, onto the backs of the diving serpents. In the towers her archers, the smallest of her men, dropped their bows, unsheathed their short swords. They leaped out of the windows of their towers onto the beasts as they flew by. And they and the serpents went to their final doom.

10
Constance

No one heard Constance's cry in the healing chamber of the castle. The walls were lined with wounded soldiers, bleeding on the floors and dripping dragon blood everywhere. Sweat slipped down their bony faces, into their eyes and off their chins. There were no windows to offer a breeze. They were deep in the bowels of the castle, underground and cold before the room filled with gasping soldiers. Osondrous' stallion stood in the corner with his head between his knees, shaking with shock. He was healed only enough to survive.

Olisize had stopped healing those soldiers that could live through their wounds, no matter their agony. The old man had fallen farther to the floor with every soldier he had healed and the strength the healing of the stallion took from him showed in all of his bones.

Majeik had caught Olisize when he had collapsed. He was picking the old man up when Constance reached him.

"He is still breathing," Majeik said.

"Take him to his chamber!" She pushed open the door. Majeik, limping, left a footprint of dragon blood as he made his way up the hall. He laid Olisize gently on his bed. She grabbed Olisize's hand.

"Constance, the soldiers need tending." Majeik grabbed her shoulder.

"Leave me alone!" She pushed him away.

He pulled her around to look at his face. "I need tending! What did Olisize tell you to do before he collapsed?"

She gulped. "He told me to go get all of the servants, the seamstresses and the dining workers and show them how to make tourniquets and how to bandage."

"That is what you are going to do!"

"He could die, Majeik!"

"Many could die! Many are dying!" He was pulling her toward the door. "Do you know what we are fighting out there? Constance, move!" He had her down in the servants' chambers in minutes.

She called out, "All of you, we need you in the healing chamber!"

And they gathered all of the Implins and dining servants. Tears streamed down her face when she told them what they had to do.

"But where is Olisize?" they all cried.

"You need to just wash their wounds and stop their bleeding!" she ordered the Implins, pointing at the growing number of soldiers, some falling down, some laying down.

The servants looked horrified. "What happened?" they all asked her. And she cried harder and they cried with her because, if Constance was crying, there was only one horrible reason. Olisize was not able.

"Stop crying!" Majeik shrieked. "There are people in this room that deserve to cry today. It is none of you!" He pointed at the wounded soldiers, faces bent in pain. He perched on a stool and watched unwillingly as an Implin pushed his pant leg up and ran a rag over his jagged, foot-long wound. Majeik gagged, wiped his mouth.

Constance gathered all of the bandages she could find, stealing the fabrics from the seamstresses' chambers. The castle was not equipped to handle a war without a Healer. The healing chamber had only two hundred beds and they were all full. The men were dripping Human and dragon blood all over the castle, dragging in chairs from the dining room so they could sit.

They started a line. Implins ushered in the soldiers, removed the armor they needed to reach the wound and washed out all dragon blood and debris. The servants then tied the bandages.

Eikian slammed into the room, the first of the Centaurs they had seen.

"Someone get this arrow out of my back!" he roared, unable to reach it even as he kept trying.

Majeik leaped to his feet, hopped over to his Warlord and inspected the feathered end poking out of the Centaur's left shoulder blade. Another hole from another arrow, much shallower, bled from the Centaur's other arm.

Eikian said, "My boys are going to be coming in soon enough, patch them up first. They are not waiting in line! Majeik, you send any Human soldier able to stand back out. If they are stable, send them back to the guardhouses. The hurt need these beds!"

Majeik nodded and, as Eikian talked, the Second jerked the arrow out of his back. The Centaur grunted, shook his head.

Eikian bandaged his other arm himself, tying the knot with one end between his teeth. "Where is Olisize?"

"He could be dead," Majeik said.

The Centaur cussed, turned and cantered out of the room, favoring two swollen ankles and layers of burnt and missing skin. When the Centaurs started arriving, the Implins went to them straight. Their wounds were hideous, many with broken legs came into the room hopping.

"Where is Olisize?" The chorus echoed from wall to wall. Those Centaurs bleeding bandaged themselves as fast as they could and they were in and out of the chamber before the Implins could try and clean them up. Dragon blood became the floor and Constance began to hear exclamations on how the dragons seemed to live now, without breath. She knew it had been hours, could feel it in her legs and ankles. She sat down on the edge of a bed. Tried to wipe the blood off her hands.

The soldiers had quieted, their faces were drawn. Many of the soldiers were coming in second and third times, their wounds more heinous than the first time. Majeik hopped around the room, grabbing soldiers who could still walk and sending them back out.

Constance hurried to the door. Majeik did not see her leave. She ran up and out of the lower levels, gasping for clean air. The sounds of war were like a storm outside. The dragons were screaming. She covered her ears; she reached the Ward chambers running. She heard Osondrous roaring louder than any Human could, her voice twisting into something God-like. "Do not let them run! They all die today!"

She ran to Olisize.

The old man was still. She lay down in his bed beside him, took his hand.

"Olisize," she said. "You cannot leave me."

She watched his breathing bring little rise to his chest.

11

Constance jerked awake, hurried to the window. It was already dark.

The entire day was gone and evening had come deeply. She looked back at him. Olisize was no longer breathing. His thin face and features were cold and still. His short gray hair looked too thin and his entire body seemed to have collapsed down to a pitiful, shriveled form, as though his very will before had kept him strong enough to walk.

She rushed out of the room, down past the hall of silence where everything was quieter but not over. She covered her mouth; the smell of the healing chamber was rotten meat and dragon blood. She went from bed to bed.

"Majeik!" she cried, searching the faces of the soldiers in line, who were leaning on walls, looking at her bleakly.

An Implin took her hand, pulled her out of the room.

"Brandy, is Majeik all right?"

The Implin grabbed her waist and embraced her; her huge black eyes looked up. "Scared!"

She knelt down and held the Implin tight. "Osondrous will kill them all. You know nothing can beat her. Everything is going to be all right. Where is Majeik?"

The Implin pushed tears off her green cheeks. "We took him to his chamber."

"Do you want to stay with me?"

The Implin nodded. Constance took her hand. The Implin's hand was cold and sticky with blood. They reached Majeik's chamber as fast as they could.

Constance's heart pounded. He was as still as Olisize.

"Majeik?" She crept up to the side of his bed. She had slept there the night before, and remembered the smells of his chamber. He had not pushed himself on her, only gave her a place to sleep off her tears of Aerick. It seemed a century ago.

248

She took his hand. "Majeik?"

He groaned. "What?" His eyes did not open. One of his arms was bandaged to his chest, it was a different injury than he had had before. With his bad leg, he must have still gone out to fight again.

"Olisize died," she whimpered.

Beside her Brandy began to cry.

Constance kissed the back of his hand and begged. "Please, I do not know what to do."

He sighed and it was a wretched, gurgly sound. "Find a servant or soldier who is still capable. I will meet you there."

"Thank you!" She gripped his hand. "Brandy, you stay with Majeik, help him if he needs you." The Implin stayed at the bedside as she left the chamber. She searched the halls of the castle, calling out. Up in the royal chambers of the Wards, she found a soldier running.

"Wait!" she screamed.

He was an old man, carrying an armful of Osondrous' swords. "I am on a mission for the Warlord!"

"I need a man. Olisize is dead!"

"I will send one of my kin to his chamber." He turned and continued running.

Constance went back to Majeik's chamber, finding him creeping out, one hand on Brandy's head, one shoulder on the wall. She touched his good arm; he wrapped it around her shoulders and leaned on her.

"Thank you," she whispered.

"You should have found someone less wounded."

"I do not think there is anyone else who is less wounded."

Brandy shook her head. "Everyone is hurt!" Her little voice broke and Constance fought tears. It took a good part of the night to get Majeik up the stairs. Waiting for them was an old soldier, a large piece of his legging was missing and beneath it was a new bandage, wrapped tight. His hair was the color of slate. The man took Majeik around the waist and helped the panting Second.

Majeik said, "You came out for this battle too, Steini?"

The man just grunted.

"Brandy, go fetch a bucket of water and soap," Constance ordered.

Brandy ran off. In Olisize's chamber, Steini leaned Majeik against the wall.

Majeik said, "We need to take Olisize down to the burial chamber and prepare him. Are you not so wounded you could lift him?"

Steini tested the weight of the old man. "I can carry him."

Constance's legs shook under Majeik's weight as they worked their way into the hallway. Olisize's body led them. The old man's head fell on Steini's chest, his eyes closed.

"Poor old man," Majeik grunted between breaths.

"Do not speak. How is your leg?"

"Do not talk of my leg; it is my ribs that are the problem. That damn dragon got me with his tail, threw me twenty feet."

Steini growled, "One of them got my leg with his mouth."

Majeik winced.

Constance began panting. "You are really heavy."

"You came and got me out of my wonderfully soft bed."

"Your bed now covered in dragon blood."

"I was passed out when they took me to my chamber. If I was awake, I would have taken my clothes off." He gripped her shoulders defensively.

"Lean on the wall, Constance." Steini glanced back as they fell behind.

They worked over to the wall, she put her hand on it for support. Brandy ran up, a bucket of water sloshing and a bar of soap clenched in her green fist.

Constance said, "You do not need to spill."

Brandy's lower lip trembled; she stared at Olisize.

"Do not cry!" Majeik snapped. "Steini and I are the only two here who deserve to be crying right now and are we?"

"If you do not shut your mouths, I might start!" Steini snapped.

Majeik glared at the back of the other man's head. They reached the stairs to go down to the burial chamber.

"Oh, for fuck's sake," Majeik grunted.

"You need to get some of your armor off!" Constance realized why the Second was so heavy. Majeik leaned on the wall. Constance pulled out the last weapon hanging from the Second: a small dagger.

"I forgot about that," he said.

She used the dagger as best she could, cutting off the Second's thick chest armor and the rest of the armor over his thighs. She pulled his chain mail over his head. It all hit the floor with clunks and they left it. Beneath the leather, Majeik was a much skinnier, younger man. She wrapped her arms around his thin side. She only briefly thought of the difference between this skinny man and Aerick's muscular back.

They worked their way down the staircase with grunts and Brandy's splashes. When they reached the burial chamber, Constance cried in relief.

Majeik crumpled to the floor and leaned back against the wall. Steini laid Olisize down. Brandy lit the fire and pushed the soap into her hand.

Brandy said, "There is a well here." Her voice was devoid of care or emotion.

Constance's breath came out in a woosh. "I am sorry, Brandy. I had forgotten."

Constance took Olisize's cold hand. She cried on the leathery white skin as Steini cut the Healer's clothes off.

"Please help me," she said to Steini.

Steini took the soap from her, rubbed it between his hands and dipped them in the bucket of water. She took off her apron, ripped rags from it. Majeik watched, head back. Brandy tucked herself under his good arm. Constance wished that it was her. Steini began scrubbing off Olisize's chest. Feebly, Constance began to help, rubbing a rag up and down his side, smearing the soap in long white swashes.

She began to weep. "Olisize—" Her voice caught, her shoulders and hands shook. She became blind and began to sob. Steini reached out, stopped her hands from scrubbing.

"I will do this for you," he said to her.

"Come here, Constance," Majeik ordered.

She dropped the rag in the bucket, fell down to her knees and crawled to him. Brandy pushed herself into Constance's lap and wrapped her arms around her waist. The Second put his good arm around her. She wept and Brandy cried with her. Majeik said nothing. Steini cleaned all of the old man, his face, his hands and feet. He washed the old man's long hair, then braided it back.

"He looks good and dignified." Majeik nodded.

"I need help turning him over," Steini said.

"Help him." Majeik pushed Constance up.

She went to Olisize's side.

"Just push," Steini said.

She lifted up on the Healer's side and pulled him over. They gasped. They stepped back from the slab and stared.

"What is it?" Majeik asked.

Constance reached out to touch the old man's back. "How can this be?"

Scars, half the width of her hand, ran from the tops of Olisize's shoulders to the lowest part of his back. There was one specific thing that made scars such as these.

Steini ordered, "Implin, you cover your ears and hum or you must leave the room."

Brandy's huge eyes opened wide.

Majeik said, "Brandy, just leave; you can come back."

The Implin did as she was told.

"Constance," Majeik said.

She did not move.

"Constance!" he snapped.

She whipped around.

"Help me up!"

Constance eased the Second from the floor.

Majeik saw and said, "Vamepire."

"No!" she cried. "Do not say that!"

Steini shook his head. "What else could have made these scars?"

"Nothing," Majeik said.

"That cannot be true!" She glared at Majeik.

"We must tell Osondrous."

She gaped at Steini. "You would not!"

"I will be right back."

Steini left and Constance stared at his retreating back. "How can he do this?"

It was not long before he returned.

Steini said, "The dragons are defeated. The Warlord is on her way."

Majeik shook his head. "In the time it took us to go down a staircase, Osondrous won a battle." He was leaning heavily on his good arm; the hand was blistered and red.

Constance shook in panic. "She will destroy the memory of Olisize! She cannot know."

The sound of footsteps was working its way slowly down the hall toward them. It was a step, drag, step rhythm. Majeik grabbed her from behind, arm across her chest.

"Shush," he ordered in her ear. She held her breath.

Osondrous appeared in the light, limping down the wall. Constance had never before not sensed the Warlord from her powerful will. There was no feeling her will now; there seemed to be no will left in her. She was a ghost, a shell of the thing of rage she had become during the day. Her skin clung to her mortal body, covered with the blood of her men, the blood of dragons and so much of her own.

Osondrous sighed. She leaned on the stone slab over Olisize. "You finally went and died. Now I am totally alone." Osondrous touched the scars, leaving a smear of dragon blood on Olisize's pasty skin. She looked back at Constance and Majeik. "Impressive scars for a Healer, huh? I did not even know he was scarred in war."

Steini bowed to Osondrous. Majeik nodded.

"Bury him," the Warlord said. Then she left.

Constance gasped, "How—"

Majeik leaned back on the wall. "Osondrous has more respect and honor than you give her credit for."

Constance touched Olisize's hand. Steini cleaned off the smear Osondrous had made. They managed to get the old man into the leather bag made for the dead.

She sewed him in. "I know where we need to bury him."

Brandy glanced into the room. "Can I come back?"

Steini sighed. "I have been able to rest. The graveyard is not far." He picked the old man up with a grunt and Majeik leaned on Constance. Brandy followed as they gimped out into the hall and out the back door. The graveyard was lit with torches. Across the graves, servants were digging holes.

Majeik snapped at one of them, "Follow us."

Constance pointed to the far corner and eventually they found the overgrown grave.

"I think he would want to be buried beside her," she said.

No one argued with her. Majeik pointed, motioning. The servant started to dig. Steini laid Olisize down and sat beside him. Majeik sat down with Constance's help and leaned against a gravestone. She sat in the crook of his good arm.

"Where is Aerick buried?" she asked.

"Osondrous marked it with a cut across the stone of his grave."

"She can do that?"

"She can do anything she wants."

Constance lay down, head in the grass. Majeik brushed her hair off her neck, closed his eyes. It was overcast. There were no stars out. The servant kept digging.

"Been like this all day," Majeik said.

"How late is it?" she asked.

"Very, the moon has already set; we are close to dawn now."

"How many died?"

"I do not know."

She noticed Brandy's head falling in exhaustion.

"Brandy," she said, "go to bed."

The Implin did not argue. She got up out of the grass, embraced Constance, then hurried back to the castle. Steini became unresponsive, sleeping beside Olisize's body. She took Majeik's hand, felt tears surface.

"With the way you have cried today," Majeik said, "I would have thought you more wounded than me."

"I miss Aerick."

"He was a good soldier."

"He loved me."

"You loved him?"

"I love him."

He rubbed her shoulder unconsciously. She used her hands as a pillow.

"I have one all right leg." He patted his thigh.

She laid her head in his lap.

"You are beautiful. When I am well, would you come to my bed?"

She turned onto her back, turned to look him in the eyes. His eyes were dark blue, not striking; they were swallowed by black eyebrows and a deeply lined face. He had the look of a man who had spent too many days in the sun. He was a farmer's boy before he became a soldier—that was all she knew about him.

"You are a Second. I am a servant. You do not have to ask."

He smirked. "If I did not ask, you would cry the whole time."

She glared at him. Majeik laughed, then grabbed his chest and whimpered. She turned back on her side, pulled her knees to her chin. The grave was half dug and the servant was panting and sweating.

"Yes, I will come to your chamber when you are well."

"Too bad that will not be for a while." He closed his eyes.

When the grave had been dug, Majeik was sleeping and Steini remained still. Constance helped the servant lower Olisize as gently as they could. But the old man was heavy and landed with an undignified thud. She winced.

The servant got to work covering the old man.

Majeik woke with a start. "Is it over?"

"He is being buried."

She held out her hand to him. He got up, using her and the gravestone.

"My chamber?"

She said, "Yes."

They gimped through the graveyard as the sky began to feel the effects of dawn. Exhaustion was beginning to pull down her head.

"Is it the ninth of Qalin?" he asked.

They began up the staircase.

"I think so," she said.

They reached his chamber. They sat down on the edge of his bed and breathed together.

"You need to get your clothes off. You need a bath."

"I need rest first."

"Before the bath or the clothes?"

"The bath."

She helped him out of the rest of his clothes. She burned them along with the majority of the blankets on his bed. She covered his bed with new blankets, then stood by the door and watched him lay down.

"What are you doing?" he grunted.

"Could I sleep here, tonight?"

"You mean, this morning?"

"Yes."

"Come lay down, Girl. You slept here last night. Maybe I will die. If you are here, then I will not be alone."

She bit her lip, then nodded, took off her dress and slid in to the other side of the bed. She pulled the covers up to her chin. They slept immediately.

12
Osondrous

Mlore was the only weapon that returned to Osondrous' chamber with her. She unsheathed it after she shut the door. She dunked the blade in the clean water of her bath, then wiped it down until its black blade shone. She laid it in its place before the fire and slowly got down to her knees.

Osondrous put her forehead on the floor. "Thank you for your strength."

She crawled over, beside her bath. The Warlord took hold of her boot, took a breath for strength and pulled. She screamed, slammed her hands to the floor as darkness cascaded down her eyes. She crawled laboriously to her bed, fumbled beneath it and came up with a dust-covered knife. Slowly she cut the leather boot down her calf. She gritted her teeth, peeled the boot off her foot, down off her toes. Her blood dripped on the floor. She leaned her head back and gasped for air. Her leg lay limp. With her

255

boot constraints gone, her ankle began to swell. Osondrous cut off her leggings, her shirt and vest.

Puncture wounds slaughtered her right side and hip, her right thigh, all the way down her leg to her ankle. Her stomach was queasy. It was stupid to want a bath. She should have gone directly to the healing chamber but after she saw that dead old Healer she needed to be clean, to be hot and feel life pump through her again.

She tried to get to her knees and she dry heaved in the effort.

She clutched the edge of the basin, stared at the hot water longingly. She got up on her left foot, hopped twice to get her balance. She braced herself, tried to sit on the edge. The Warlord slipped. She hit the water falling. The bath overflowed. The water flew across the floor and the fire sizzled.

She sat up, clutched the sides of the basin gasping and coughing. She choked on her cough, dry heaved again. There was no food or water in her system to throw up. Her chest ached. She wanted to ask Teek to help her. She wanted to ask him for a cold drink.

He was dead, dead, dead. *Dead.*

She lay back and tried to find a steady place. Her hands shook as she gripped the sides of the basin. Her fingers slowly relaxed. The water finally stilled. It was a long time before she could move without her world tipping. When she was able to sit up, she slowly washed her skin and her hair, all of her wounds. In the heat of the water, the pain was beginning to lessen. Rest nagged at her. She shook her head and sat up before it could overcome her. The water was red; every wound left a tendril of bloody silk floating around her.

She got to her bed slowly, like an old woman on ice. She sat a long time before she caught her breath, holding her right foot off the floor. She pulled a shift over her head, fetched a clean set of clothes, clutched them to her heart, and then finally really looked at her right foot.

The back molars of that dragon had crushed almost all of her toes, right up to where the next tooth had shattered her main ankle bone. Everything was black and oozing. She told herself to not look at it again.

"All right, I am going to go out that door, down the hallway to the staircase, down to the healing chamber so I can be treated."

She recognized the wooziness of her head, the clench of her stomach. She needed her bleeding stopped.

Barefoot, she hopped into the hallway. The Warlord made her way. Hop, hop, stop and breathe. Hop, hop, stop and breathe. She set the big toe of her injured foot on the floor to rest. Her heart was hammering in her ears. She reached the staircase while holding onto the wall with shaking hands. Her wet hair fell in her face. The pain heightened with every step and oozed from each wound. The white shift was now a shade of bronze. Sweat ran down her body. She made it two steps before her left knee began to shake and threaten collapse.

She stood hard, teeth gritted, knee locked.

When she reached the bottom of the staircase, she stood utterly still. The darkness was flickering all around her now, endless fluttering, threatening. The long hallway was empty and growing farther away. She stopped after every step. She choked on her breath and swallowed down her parched throat. Her fingers curled against the stone; her entire left side shook under her weight.

Finally her fingers felt the side of a door jam. She could no longer hold back the cry that emerged from the back of her throat with every pull for breath.

Her soldiers saw her; those that were awake gasped. "Warlord?" "Osondrous?"

She held out her hand in response, to shut them up. Hands took hold of her, eased her toward a bed. A Centaur moved over; she was laid down in his heat. He stared at her, hand out.

"It is not so bad, Cray," she said to him.

"It looks bad," he said, his voice hoarse with an infected fever.

She grabbed his hand out of the air and held it on the bed beside her. She was aware of the cutting off of her shift, of the murmurs, of the demands for water, soap, clean fabric. Then she felt herself fall off the cliff.

13

Jezaline

Her skin was paler than starlight, and beside it were the bleeding wounds made of her eyes. Kilikan, heir to the Draegoone throne, touched her cheek and whispered, "Hold on, Gorgeous. Do not let us be too late tonight." The lady lay like death in his arms, a drapery of silk fabric blowing in the wind.

"She is going to die!" he roared, rushing her to the bed.

Kilikan had taken on the woman when his guards flew her in as fast as they could. He had brought her immediately to their Draegoone Restorers. She moved, moaning a moan that gave no sound. They stared between her slender thighs, all that had been ripped apart. They ordered him out. The prince left the sight of beauty dragged through hell and stepped back into the wind.

His brother, Tarrick, dropped down beside him.

"It is a woman?"

Kilikan nodded. "Is this the one?"

"I do not know . . . It must be. Brother, this fate was brought to her because of me."

"Are you certain of your visions?"

Tarrick was distraught. "I am a prophet! I am never certain of my visions."

Kilikan growled, "Stop it! This is not your fault; we had patrols out. She must have gone to the dead forest to get out of that hideous wind. She is going to be all right."

14

Jezaline remembered the feeling of warm water being poured down her throat. She remembered the taste of winter fruit that had melted on her tongue. She remembered she was blind, with bandages covering her eyes, keeping her from opening them.

"Where am I?" She tried to open her eyes.

Kilikan watched her hand raise weakly.

"You are in Lousen, the First Moon of the Draegoone." He stood beside her bed.

"How long has it been?" Her voice cracked.

"It is the fifth day of Qalin. How long was it since you were taken by the Vamepire?"

"Five days." She turned her head. "Are we alone?"

"Yes."

"There is the breathing of many here."

"Only me . . . But I'm big."

The sound of claws dragging across the marble floor was a shriek.

She shivered. "What happened?"

"You will not be hurt here. You are protected."

She faded away and he left the room. He stepped down the arched hallway, lit with white torches and the sun. He looked out the window and took a breath of the cold winter air. Snow fell from scattered clouds.

Tarrick was waiting. "How is she?"

"She is awake."

"You saved her."

Kilikan nodded. "Why do you not go in now?"

"I do not know if I have the courage."

"She is not frightening." Kilikan chuckled and jumped from the window. A thousand feet below him a winter river wound its way through the rock. Few trees scattered the landscape. Everything was concealed in snow.

Tarrick rubbed his claws together as he watched Kilikan fly. Eventually, he went to her room and sat down by her bed. The servants came in with the evening and she woke when they fed her.

"Who are you this time?" she asked.

"My name is Tarrick."

"Tarrick?"

"Yes."

"Are you Cousai's Tarrick, the prophet?"

He said, "Yes, I am Cousai's."

"She said I could not go back to the castle."

"How was she?"

"Her sister came and begged her for aid. They left for Diggamara."

"You said Diggamara?" His breath hissed through his sharp teeth.

"Yes."

Tarrick turned and took flight out the window. His wide leather wings slapped the air, gained him altitude. He began to weep; his body shook. How could such a fate have come?

No one was aware of the torment in the prophet's heart. So much of his visions were blind dreams that seemed to have so little merit in real life. But there were a few dreams he trusted, a few visions that he believed to be true. Jezaline needed to come to the Krept and to be taken to Grim, this he was certain of. His wonderful wife, his lover, his perfect friend Cousai, would die in Diggamara. He did not know when, did not know if it was tomorrow, or a hundred years from now. But despite it all, the sound of Diggamara and Cousai in the same sentence left him barely able to breathe.

15

Jezaline slept past the day and woke when the servants came again to dress her wounds. The Draegoone murmured in their soft tongue, spoken not from their guts, but from high in their throats. And they exclaimed at her immense healing.

The lead female touched her shoulder. "Is there anything you long for?"

"I want nothing." She rolled away from them.

She wanted Waltruk. This was all in the plan. This had been explained to her, but he had not told her the scars she would have to endure the rest of her life. The beauty of her body, the one power she had always had and been able to use, was gone. Waltruk did this to her and she was beginning to wallow and, regardless of whether or not this turned out, the damage was done.

The Draegoone exchanged a glance over her body, leaving immediately. "Wait."

"Yes, Lady, what do you wish?" They returned to her side.

"How was it that I was saved? Do you know?"

"Kilikan brought you to us."

"He saved me?"

"His guards on the outskirts flew as fast as they could. They took you to him because Kilikan is the fastest flier in all of the land. He brought you here. His speed saved your life." The lead Draegoone lingered briefly before leaving with the vast echo of the shutting of the doors. Jezaline slept soon after.

She woke, startled at the sound of footsteps. "Tarrick?" she asked.

"No. I am not Tarrick."

"Who are you?"

"We met before. I am Tarrick's brother. My name is Kilikan."

"It was you that saved me."

"Yes." He watched her hand as she reached for him; he raised his palm to touch her fingers. Their skin met.

She jerked back. "What are you?"

"I am Draegoone. I will not harm you."

Jezaline shook her head. Her mind was fuzzy and ill. She was trying to remember what the Draegoone were sketched to look like in the library of the Wards. Demons? Dragons?

The Draegoone stared close at the bandages that covered her eyes.

Her hand returned again to touch his, touching his rough, scaled fingers.

"How can you be?" she asked.

"How can you, with soft skin, be?" He chuckled and it was a sound like a purr.

Her fingers moved down his wrist, the heavy muscles there as wide as two of her hands. Her fingers moved up, along the scales of his forearm where they grew smaller, suppler, like Human skin. She touched his shoulder and pulled back, intimidated by the sheer size of it.

He watched her hand linger in the air, move hesitantly. She touched his cheek.

She jerked back. "I am sorry."

He carefully took her hand and pulled it to his cheek. "We are not demons. I met some of you Humans years back. Osondrous, Telenay."

She said, "I know them well. I am a Ward."

"Maybe we can get you back to them soon."

She touched the bandages around her face; her body began to shake. The idea of going back had never occurred to her. It overwhelmed her with shame and guilt. She had tasted Waltruk's blood—there was no going back.

"Oh, do not weep." He touched her to console her. She shook her head. Kilikan ran his finger down her cheek; she jerked away.

"I will not hurt you."

She put her back to him, her shoulders shaking. The Draegoone moved closer; the bed dipped under his weight.

"Please do not cry."

"Leave me alone." She squirmed out of his reach.

The prince stopped, hand closing into a fist.

He drew back. She listened to the sound of him leaving.

16

Later, Jezaline stood in the window, breathing deeply. The wind was cold, smelling of salt. She recognized the sound of the sea. She had once seen this northern sea, in her youth. Beyond the Castle of the Wards, through the villages of the Centaurs, was this same northern sea. Though she was much farther north than the Wards now, she could walk down to the shore here and follow it all the way to the castle.

The call of seagulls flew by. Jezaline turned from the window and pulled her shawl closer. She felt her way back to the bed. Sat down and sighed. She scratched at the bandages holding down her eyes. She yearned to see this place. The floor felt like marble. She wondered if all here was made of such precious hard stone.

She felt her way to the wall from her bed. She ran her spread fingers up and down the smooth surface, feeling the carving of a braided rope at her shoulder's height. She followed it along the wall, skipping over the window and into the corner and out again. Her fingers landed on wood. She gripped the door handle, pulled and moved out, into the rush of cold. The wind whistled to her left. She tilted her head, able to sense she was in a hallway.

She could hear nothing else.

She reached out and took a step into the unknown, took another, and another. She found the wall. She reached an open window. The wind chill cut through her; she moaned but stood before the north with her chin up. She could feel the wind down to the tips of her bare toes. She knew this window was a door for Draegoone. She thought of the jump she had taken, the moment of pure weightlessness.

Jezaline leaned out into the wind.

There was a growl to her right and a loud word spoken in Draegoone. She sprinted back, grabbed open the door to her room and slammed it shut behind her. Head pressed against the door, she gulped at the sound of claws on marble in the hall. They moved past as she held her breath. They faded.

She rushed to her window and shut the shutters, gasping.

Moments later a tap, so light she barely heard it, came outside her door.

She sighed. "Yes?"

"Are you all . . . right?"

She recognized the sound of Kilikan's accent; his tone held mirth as he stepped into the room.

She asked, "Why?"

"I had an odd request come to me not moments ago. One of my guards said 'the Human' snuck up behind him. He requested I come immediately to make certain that you had not actually managed to do him any harm."

Jezaline laughed despite herself. "And did I?"

"He seemed quite intact. What were you doing outside your room?"

She frowned. "I am no servant here."

"You are a guest. Listen, you can wander as much as you like. But you are twenty levels into the sky and your bedroom has the only windows that do not reach to the floor and they are the only windows with shutters. One wrong step."

His head was down beside hers. "I do not want you to get hurt. You may have frightened him but he is your guard. If you would ask, he would gladly be by your side and walk you around this tower."

"I have the power of a Ward. I need no one's aid . . . nor do I need to be walked like some kind of plow horse."

She felt the Draegoone's grunt more than she heard it, a growl so low that her heart skipped a beat.

"You are the only occupant of this tower save your guardian. I will tell you that so when you run into him, you will know who it is."

Jezaline did not respond. She kept her head away from him, face down, until he finally left. She clumsily found her bed and undressed, looking forward to the heat that soaked up through the feathers from the frame of firestone.

She slept hard.

The sound of wings. She jerked awake and turned as clawed feet landed.

"Jezaline?"

"Kilikan?" she mumbled.

"The queen wishes to dine with you tonight, joined by my brother and me."

He sat down in the chair beside her bed.

"Is he eldest to be king?" She cleared her throat and licked her lips.

"No, I am."

The Draegoone stood and turned away. He gave a call, in his own language, making her jump.

He said, "Servants will be here shortly. I will return to guide you."

She shuddered as the cold wind that followed swept her face. The servants entered the room. They greeted her and helped her out of the bed. She let them wash her and brush her long hair.

"Such lovely hair," they murmured.

They put her in a heavy dress made of thick fabric and boots that reached past her knees. Kilikan returned then, a loud thud landing on her windowsill and sweeping in on the floor. The servants left immediately.

He said, "My hand is out."

She reached until their hands met. He walked her to the window and heard her breathing quicken.

"May I lift you up?" His hand tightened, moving around her shoulders.

A gust hit them, slamming her body back against his leather breastplate. She cringed.

Kilikan lifted her up. She bit down on her tongue.

He chuckled. "You have flown with me before. You were safe with me."

He stepped up onto the window ledge. She put her arm around the back of his neck and gripped the leather cloak over his shoulders. He was very hot.

"You are Human Willower. You are wind friends."

"This is not my wind."

"The wind does not change." He stepped off the window sill. The great spread of his wings unleashed and he gave a heave, throwing them up. And they plunged and he pushed again, taking flight with another grunt. The wind threw her hair back. She turned her face in and held tight. Where Waltruk's flight had been as easy as gliding, this flight was work. Kilikan weighed a ton and Jezaline could only imagine the width his wings had to be, to be able to hold him up. He stopped them in midair and her breath was jerked from her as he hit the ground.

She lifted her head. The sound of waves was close.

"We are on the ground?"

"We are on the ground."

She swallowed. "How close are we to the sea?"

"Do you want to be closer?"

She breathed the air as the wind turned, whipping up the smell of silt. "Yes."

Kilikan held her firm and she swayed to his long strides. The sound of waves crashing intensified. She lifted her head up and listened.

"Are the waves all around me?"

"You are with me at our point. On our sacred beach. We call it Morning here. You are surrounded almost entirely by the sea. Behind you are great cliffs. I do not know how well the Humans know of this place—"

"We know nothing," she interrupted him.

"Our land is filled with mountains. Behind you are cliffs taller than any towers I have seen Humans make. They are sheer and fall to this small stretch of beach that cuts out to the middle of the sea."

"Do all the Draegoone live on the sea?"

"No, this is the only beach in this land and only the royals of us live in the ancient white towers here."

"How high do your towers climb? As high as the great three?"

"You speak of the Vamepire towers?"

She turned her face away. "Yes."

"You remember them?"

"They were black as the mountain."

"Once the Draegoone ruled all of this land. We were the most powerful until the Humans rose. They became Vamepires and Fai. And though we are to end our feud with the Fai . . . Our opinion of Humans is not well."

She said, "Why do you tell me this?"

"You dine with my queen tonight, my mother. She will not be kind."

"Though you are kind enough to warn me?"

"It would be unfair to anyone to send them to the table with my mother without proper warning."

The Draegoone turned his back to the waves and looked up the steep cliffs before him. His eyes reflected the blue sky. It began to snow and Jezaline felt the prickle suddenly on the back of her neck. He walked up the bank. She heard the sound of a high door open and close. And the welcoming touch of warm air. She recognized the heat of firestone.

Kilikan set her down. "You will not be expected to bow to her."

The Draegoone's arm remained tucked around her waist. He sat her at the table. His attentions were not lost to Jezaline. Had Waltruk mentioned that Kilikan would be very interested in her? She could barely remember. She felt foggy and dark and, left without sight, she felt like she had not yet awakened beside Sethian in Dead Wood.

"Are there no walls here?"

His face dipped beside hers when he pushed her chair in. "The floor beneath you is made of firestone, the chair and table are of cedar and there are pillars of firestone holding the glass ceiling. Our south wall is the mountain, our north wall is the door to the sea. The east and west are without walls."

The sound of wings threw the air around and Kilikan spoke in gruff barks. The sound of doors banged open. Silence fell and was held. The footsteps echoed around them. A tone rose in the ever-complicated language of the Draegoone. It held a feminine stir that cut short of delicate and precluded harsh. This must be the queen.

Kilikan sat in the chair beside her.

He said, "No, Jezaline does not speak Draegoone."

"Jezaline?" the queen snapped. "You call her by her name?"

Kilikan cleared his throat. "Jezaline is her name."

"She is a Human! Her people are slaves, they do not have names! It is only by my kind graces to your brother's ludicrous visions that I even allowed her to stay in a place out of my dungeon."

Jezaline swallowed through her cold throat. She felt Kilikan's eyes on her.

"Kilikan?" the queen demanded. "Are you listening to me?"

"Yes, Mother, there has not been a time when I did not hear you. Jezaline is a Ward of high power."

"High power? Then she could have killed you by now?"

The hulk beside her shifted, picking up his cup and gulping. She sipped from her own cup; the alcohol was smooth and sweet.

"And she has said nothing of her Vamepire encounter?"

Kilikan answered, "She is sitting beside me. You could ask her."

"I am asking you, Prince!"

He sighed, "No, she has not yet spoken of it."

"Why has your brother not interrogated her? The Vamepire are our enemies. She slept with their king! She could know something vital!"

"We do not know if it was their king or even that she saw the great towers. It was probably just his minions having their fun. They got too close so they dropped her to die. We were fortunate that she was saved." Kilikan drank again from his cup. When the queen heard the word *fortunate*, she snorted her retort.

More wings filled the air.

Kilikan growled, "You are late, Tarrick!"

The queen said, "Tarrick, your brother was telling us how we are lucky to have saved this Human whore."

Tarrick said, "I apologize for my belatedness. Jezaline, how are you?"

"For a Human, Tarrick, I am apparently doing astoundingly well here."

"Indeed," Kilikan said.

"Shut her up." The queen's low growl seemed to shake the table.

Jezaline snapped, "I am afraid I was unaware that your custom was for your guests to have no voices after you invite them for dinner."

The queen slapped the table. "In this place we eat our Human guests for dinner!"

Tarrick roared, "We do not need more enemies! Let us not forget what their Warlords accomplished." And to Jezaline he added, "Neither Kilikan nor I nor anyone of our generation has eaten a Human."

The queen sighed and, in a tone of patience only reserved for her sons, she said, "Yes, I remember what their Osondrous and Telenay did."

Jezaline asked, "The Keltch have you remembering our Warlords?"

"Yes," Kilikan said. "They came with an army that was too small and yet managed to destroy the home of both of the two Keltch queens in our lands. They killed them all without our aid and without ever asking for it. They were the only Humans that the Draegoone had seen for nearly five hundred years."

Tarrick said, "Until then, we would not have welcomed any Humans here."

"They are a filthy kind." The queen spoke in a tone that carried above both of her sons' voices.

"Those not of our ways are not necessarily filthy," Tarrick said.

"Do you forget where the Draegoone once were on this island? What we once ruled and who bowed to *us*? They were barely good enough to be our slaves. Now they are the Vamepire and Fai!"

"Things always change." Kilikan was drinking hard now. His cup was filled for the fourth time.

The queen continued, "We were called to be rulers! It was the rising of their greed that brought them into the thought that they could be as strong as we were. Their sacrifices to the dark one gave them their power. It is wicked—it is wrong!"

"I was not speaking of our enemy the Fai or our enemy the Vamepire. The Humans rose as Wards. Jezaline could flatten us with her power as we speak. But she does not." Kilikan snapped his teeth together.

Tarrick said, "And it is our own fault that we bow now."

"Silence! You are a shame to me—once our kind ruled on honor and it is the falling of that honor that we are dying off now!"

Tarrick yelled, "Sending our troops to die to face the Fai over a war five hundred years old, while we fight a real war here, is insanity!"

The queen's fist landed hard and silenced the table. Jezaline could hear Kilikan's infuriated breathing.

The queen hissed, "It is our last chance to bring honor to our people. There are some of us that still remember that honor had us as rulers of every wretched kind on this island. It was the warped choice of Humans to save their pathetic little lives with the creation of the rivers, another bastard thing done to *our* land. If this act of honor for the memory of the Five Hundred Year War does not salvage our status as kings, then we shall at least die with dignity!"

Tarrick and Kilikan were silenced. They were joined by more Draegoone and Tarrick stood to change seats. The prophet sat on the other side of Jezaline, murmuring that it was him. She sipped more liquor. It was then removed from her and a steaming cup and large bowl were placed before her. The soup was of a meat and vegetables she had never eaten. The drink made her stomach burn in the best kind of way.

The Draegoone language lofted over her head and beneath her in wolf-like growls that raised the hair on the back of her neck. Somehow, she sensed, she heard very little of what was actually said. With her will, she listened to what they were saying and noticed immediately that no one spoke politics here. As soon as others arrived, the conversation about the Fai was over. But she saw that, in their hearts, each and every Draegoone at the table, male and female alike, were thinking about the upcoming war fearfully. Between the Vamepire and the Fai and the arguments that were erupting over what to do, all of them were afraid. Most of them did not think they should send their troops to die when the Vamepire were so powerful and so close, but the queen's choices were not doubted.

Kilikan whispered, "We shall slip away soon."

She smiled, drinking her hearty drink again.

Five courses followed the soup, brought quickly and eaten by the Draegoone in startling silences that were replaced by their gulping and then the conversation would suddenly continue. There was a reverence that came between the fourth and the fifth courses with the rising and leaving of the queen. Jezaline felt the rolling drunkenness around her. Could feel it in herself. Tarrick rose and left. Kilikan's hand moved around her waist. She rose with the Draegoone and knew only the wind as it rushed at her. They lifted and she turned into him, allowing his arms to conceal her, to protect her from the north chill.

She asked, "Is the moon out?"

"It is concealed tonight. The clouds are deep with snow." He stepped into her window and set her down. She felt her way across the room. She sensed him diddling without purpose by the window, understood he was trying to come up with a good reason to remain. She wondered what the gargantuan Draegoone could look like while he diddled. She thought of Waltruk and pushed it away. The ache was returning to her chest, becoming impossible to ignore. She had not forgotten her ways of forgetting it in the past. She was terrified of sleeping alone in the dark and now she was eternally in the dark.

She smacked the stool beside her bed, screeching in a cry of pain. She grabbed her shin as she went down. The Draegoone swept her up. He set her down on the bed.

"Are you all right?"

She sighed. "I am afraid of the dark."

"I wish I could see your eyes."

"The scars terrify me."

What could be wrong with being as honest as she could with this big creature? She knew he meant her no harm. Where in Waltruk's presence, she knew she was food, here she felt like a woman. He touched her cheek, his thumb moving down along her jaw.

Kilikan whispered and she could hear and smell the intoxication on him. "No great scar could hurt your beauty."

"I can only imagine what your culture would consider beautiful."

"Well, it is not smooth skin." He chuckled.

Her head bowed. Jezaline scratched at the bandage on her face. "I remember the Draegoone are something like Human but with no Human blood. Our library holds some memories of your kind and then there were Osondrous' stories, of course." She laughed. "Is there any Human in you, you think?"

She realized she was drunker than she had thought. It felt good. It felt fantastic.

"If there is any, it is very little." Kilikan's voice drifted off into a growl.

She shivered.

He noticed. "I am sorry."

"Sorry?"

"For making you so uncomfortable. I know I do not sound like something you would want to talk to."

"Your growls, they remind me of a predator that we used to abhor."

"Oh?"

She rubbed her hands. "The predator of part of our island is a type of wolf. I was raised a horse maiden; the wolves killed many of our horses."

He said, "What do you remember of the Vamepire?"

Lying to him was going to be hard. There was the tantalization, the promise: he could take her home. And the Wards were very strong; they would protect her from the Vamepire. She stood up and walked toward the wind as it whistled into the room. The Draegoone followed her.

She said, "I remember no pain, no wind. It was stagnant. There was no sky, no earth. There was no life, Kilikan. It was as though the very mountain had died too long ago for even the stone to remember."

He stopped her when she reached the window.

She asked, "Why did you lie to the queen about my seeing the towers?"

"I was not looking to give her an excuse."

"And you trust me when she has good reasons for you not to?"

"I have met the Vamepire; they are wicked. They are. I cannot imagine any creatures wanting to be near one of them. They eat everything. Nothing is beneath their appetites. They are entirely without the ability to understand another life."

The wind died down and Jezaline's hair fell to her shoulders. "I have nightmares . . . It has been a long time since I slept alone."

The Draegoone reached out of the window and pulled the shutters closed. He moved around to stand between her and the window. His fingers slipped up her back. He touched her shoulders, swept back her hair and stared down into her face.

He said, "I will stay with you tonight. Or, I could call a servant."

"You can stay."

He looked into her bandages. "Then I will stay. Come back to your bed."

She shook her head. "I am not tired, Prince. What I am tired of is resting."

"It has been so few days for you to long for a run."

"Maybe a walk, could we walk?"

He said, "I think there are reasons why we live in this northern corner of the isle and the Humans live in the center."

"And why is that?"

"Because the living rock here makes for difficult walking ground, too rough for Humans. But this tower is filled with endless hallways."

"Let us walk down a hallway then. It is not as though I need a view."

He led her through the door.

"Do these hallways you speak of lead to nothing?"

"More towers," he said.

"Does no one live here?"

"Not any more."

She left the topic in the hallway behind them when they turned the corner into another. A gust of wind shook through her. Kilikan put his arm around her.

"Tell me what I should see," she said.

"This hallway is narrow and long and perfectly straight. Empty windows were carved out of the stone long ago. They stand in rows, all the way on either side."

"What does your craftsmanship look like?"

"Our ancients carved with scales and dragon teeth in patterns around large square doorways. But we have begun curving our craftsmanship. We find it shows a greater talent."

She thought of the grotesque carving of the Vamepires. She gritted her teeth against the shivers that ran through her.

He pulled her closer. "Let us go back."

"All right."

She reached over and covered his hand. "Do you want to be a king?"

"It is my duty."

"Do the Draegoone live on duty?"

"We first live for duty and honor."

"And what of love?"

"Love?"

"Do you have love here? Do males and females have love between them?"

"Oh, yes, there is great love here."

"Do you not have a love, Kilikan?"

Jezaline sighed when they turned back into the enclosed hallway. The relief showed across her.

He stared at her soft pink skin. "I have no love here."

He opened her chamber door and led her inside. The wind howled against the shutters. She rubbed her arms, stopping in the middle of the room so she would not trip on anything. "Have you never had a love?"

"Have you?"

"A lot of men. No love." She laughed. "I have loved Centaurs deeper than I have loved any man." At the thought, she felt tears and tried not to let them show.

"Neither have I. We train in the army here when we come of age, both males and females. We have a very equal diplomacy. Sometimes it seems our females try too hard to be strong, and some males here long for something . . . a little more feminine."

She said, "Oh?"

He led her forward, turned down the heavy blankets and guided her down on the bed.

"It supports my theory that perhaps it is why our ancestors mated with Humans to create what we are today."

"Is that a fact?"

"Only my own theory—we used to be real animals. Very intelligent, but animals none the less, hairless animals."

"You have hair?"

"On my head," he said, "I have a lot of it. And now, we are truly warm-blooded."

She turned her face up toward his. "Are you one of them?"

"Of what?"

"A male that longs for something a little more feminine?"

Jezaline felt his fingers move down her spine. He opened his mouth to speak, gritted his teeth and finally said nothing. Out of almost no inclination of her own, Jezaline reached out and touched his cheek. The liquor was wearing off now and so was her time with Waltruk. She shuddered at the thought of the last nightmare she had had in Dead Wood. She did not want to be alone to curl around her empty ache and wish she were with Waltruk when this Draegoone promised he could take her home.

"Your skin is not so rough," she said.

"We are softer than we may look."

Her hand fell to her lap. "I did not even have to see you to assume that your kind did not have soft skin."

"Our scales are hard down our arms and legs, across the tops of our shoulders."

"You are well armored."

"It does not stop Vamepire arrows. Jezaline, tell me how you came to be here."

She started with her receiving of Tarrick's letter and the travel to Cousai's home. She went on until they were attacked in Dead Wood, giving no details of the deaths of her guardians. Kilikan showed particular interest in her knowledge of Cousai as well as Sicilia.

"Is it not forbidden for a Draegoone to love a Fai?" she asked.

"It is more than forbidden. It is so far beyond treason we do not even have a punishment for it."

"And Tarrick is forgiven?"

"Not even I knew where Tarrick was the past decades. He came and went, as much as he was needed. I never knew he had found someone to love."

"She seemed devoted."

Kilikan stood. "It is growing late. You must have your rest."

"There a place you need be?"

"I must go for a while."

"But you will come back?"

The Draegoone stared down at her, his eyes wincing, thinking. He chewed his lip. "If you want me to."

"I would not have asked otherwise."

He began to say something, then the Draegoone turned and left.

When Jezaline was certainly alone, she undressed completely. When she lay down, she stretched out, head back in the soft pillows. She held sleep away for a moment—that she could enjoy the heat a little while longer. The wounds on her back and stomach were healing in long fine lines. Waltruk had made certain that she would heal perfectly and quickly. This she did not know and the scars remained terrifying to her.

17
Karalay

Beside Telenay's bed sat buckets of hot water, a bar of olive oil soap and soft wash cloths. Karalay gathered her skirt and knelt, dipping the rags, wringing them out. Lifted his hand, washed between his fingers, up his wrist, up his arm. His scars stood out white on his tanned skin, some new—some old. She soaked his body until, scars and all, his skin was soft and clean.

She rubbed a rag down his forehead, washed his cheeks, his neck. She lathered the soap between her hands and smoothed it over his cheeks and the scruff of a beard that was growing there. She fetched a razor blade. The sharp edge caught the light and she ran it expertly along his cheek, his jaw, his upper lip.

A servant stood in the doorway.

"Karalay?" The girl's voice was just above a whisper.

"What is it?"

"Jikrin is ready."

She nodded. "Thank you."

The servant watched her finish shaving the Warlord.

"What is it, Acasha?"

"Could I watch?"

"Of course." Karalay smiled back at her but on returning her gaze to Telenay, her smile faded. A quiver of uncertainty passed over her expression. She set her jaw, swallowed it down. Washed the razor in the bucket and soaked a rag. She cleaned his face and neck. Wrung out the rag, hung it on the side of the bucket.

She went to the servant.

Acasha asked. "Will it be hard?"

"It will be very hard for me."

"Will you be able to do it?"

Karalay touched the girl's shoulder, turned her into the hallway. Shut Telenay's door behind them. "I do not know if I will be able to do this today or ever. This is a greater form of healing. Few have ever had such strength."

"You will fix him," the girl said. "I know you will."

The girl's confidence was not reassuring but gut-wrenching. The servant followed her across the hall into the Centaur's room.

Karalay said, "Jikrin, how are you feeling?"

The Centaur's eyes were bright. "I feel my heart healing, Ward."

She knelt beside him. "Today I shall try to make you whole again."

He rubbed the stump of his right arm. "It would be grand."

The Centaur sat up, pulling his legs beneath him. She took his hand, let her other hand fall down his rough cheek. She cupped the side of his neck and closed her eyes. Acasha watched. She strained; sweat dripped down her cheeks, onto her chest. The flames of the fire blew over. Acasha squeezed her eyes shut as the Healer's power tightened around them. Jikrin's teeth gritted and his jaw cracked with the strain. No one breathed. Karalay snapped backwards and fell. He grabbed her, pulled her to his bed.

"Acasha, fetch water!" he gasped.

The Centaur scooted himself out of bed, laid Karalay down. He touched her forehead, wiped the sweat off her eyes. Acasha returned, pitcher sloshing. He dipped his fingers into the water and ran them down Karalay's cheeks and across her lips.

Karalay opened her eyes. She saw the stump of his arm, unchanged. "Oh, Jikrin, I am sorry. I have failed you."

He shook his head. "You saved my life."

Acasha gasped. "Are you all right?"

Karalay sat up. "Yes." She held her swimming head.

The Centaur reached out to her. "Are you certain?"

She stood. "Yes, Jikrin, thank you. Acasha, fetch his dinner when he is hungry."

The servant nodded.

Jikrin frowned. "You should rest, Healer. You do not look well."

"I am perfectly fine, Centaur. You are the one who should be resting. I must go check on Telenay." Karalay hurried from the room, ducking down the hallway, up and out, into the cold.

People saw her scuttling through the streets, a great mass of dark hair behind her like hawk's feathers in the cold. She flew to the stable. A nicker echoed up from the arena to her. The mare had been let to run on the sand with two others. Karalay leaned against the fence and the mare came to her.

She sucked in her breath. "A great war is coming and you are looking at a Healer who is going to be of no aid in any way."

The mare gazed into her eyes, listening.

Karalay heard the stable door open and close and knew it was Jaridd.

"Are you all right?" he asked.

"I finally have Telenay and there is nothing I can do for him."

"Yes," he whispered. "You have him."

Karalay stroked the mare's long neck.

He ran his hand down her back. "I want you to myself; will you promise me that?"

"Who else would there be?"

He embraced her. "I understand why Dind abandoned the Darkhalks now."

She stiffened. "He said that he had died, was brought back and the Cape and Sword could not be saved."

"Half the truth. The Cape and Sword were saved. He chose not to return to being a Darkhalk. He chose to abandon the Darkhalks."

His tone sent a chill through her; it held a very old anger. She could only imagine the terrible things the other Darkhalks must have thought and spoken about Dind.

"You have not used that word before."

"He could not bear to return to being unknowing. He found that he was loved."

She could not say, *Abandon them for me,* because she knew she would not abandon the Wards for anyone.

She said, "I love you."

"I love you, too." The Darkhalk sighed. "We have to go."

"You said there is an Elf?"

"Yes, we found an Elf."

"There are still living Elves in Addilade?"

"No, he is not living . . . But there is life still in him somehow."

"Where is he?"

"They will be here momentarily."

The rear of the palace was deserted. They waited by the basement door.

"How long has his body been dead?"

"Awhile."

She shook her head. "This will be beyond me."

Jaridd growled, "Nothing is beyond you unless you believe you cannot grow. A Ward must be bold."

A Darkhalk rounded the bend, the masked figure slowed to a jog from a sprint, a long body draped over his arms. The smell met them before the Darkhalk. Karalay covered her mouth. The Elf's eyes hung open, showing a shade of tempest's purple gone pale with death. His wooden bones showed through the skin on his knees. His arms crumpled together on his chest.

She stepped back.

Jaridd turned into the basement; the Darkhalk followed him. She stayed at a distance. Jaridd entered an empty back room; he lit the fire and the Darkhalk laid the body on the floor. She put her back to the wall. The Darkhalk left and Jaridd shut the door behind him.

Jaridd said, "Tell me what you need."

"There can be nothing left to him."

"There is. You must look."

Karalay stared down at the purple eyes. Held her breath to stop the gag that was rising in the back of her throat. His lips were drawn back in a wide death-snarl. Karalay reached out, touched the Elf's arm. The skin slipped back; she jerked.

Jaridd knelt by her. "You can do this."

"I hate death." She gritted her teeth, touched the Elf's hand and squeezed her eyes shut.

The darkness was sharp, filled with things that froze until they were broken, shattered to points that scattered across the night. Treacherous dead things lay severed, blue-purple held open with ice. Human things and yet, not Human. She climbed through the freeze, pulling herself upward until she reached the top and burst through to the white light of day. She perched at the top of the dead tree and across the frozen leaves at the top of an endless canopy. There was no horizon, no color to the sky.

Hanging from a string was a single crystal.

She touched it and it began to sway, began to twirl. She pulled back.

The crystal spun, taking off and then it screamed. She felt cold on her fingers. It began to creep up her arms. Karalay smacked at it. She stepped back into the darkness as the crystal became a light. With each pass it flashed across her face, blinding her. Then she saw the purple, frozen eyes.

She reached for him, took his hands and pulled until they broke free and the crystal shattered.

She stared into his dead face. "Are you all right?"

The Elf looked around but could not speak.

Karalay pulled back and staggered.

Jaridd grabbed her. "I can feel you did it; you awakened him."

"The frost almost got me, too."

"You are all right."

"Jaridd, I have never seen anything like this. How can he still be here—look at his body! Get me out!"

Jaridd lifted her up and ran her out into the back lot. She scrambled out of his arms, to her knees in the crunchy grass. She dry-heaved on the cold air until she gasped and gasped and clutched her ribs.

Jaridd rubbed her back. "You saved him."

"I am too old to be this weak!"

"There are few that could will an arm to regrow, Karalay. You cannot blame yourself."

She cupped her face in her hands. "I never will be. Why do you care for me at all?"

Her heaves turned to wretched, tearless sobs.

Jaridd sat down. "I love you, Karalay."

"How?"

"I want you."

"You are stupid to want me."

He pulled at her until the wind could not blow between them.

He said in her ear, "I am not going to become a Darkhalk again."

She shook her head. "You cannot abandon your post for me."

"After this war—I am done."

"But we have not been together very long, Jaridd. How could you do this for me?"

"This is for me. And we have been together a long time."

She touched his cheek. Her face lit. They grabbed each other.

She cried. "We can go and find peace? Get away from all of this?"

He said, "That is my plan."

Karalay kissed him and held him against her. Their wills were out and they felt each other's hearts.

Jaridd sighed. "First, Karalay, we need to deal with this."

"The Elf."

"What can we do?"

She pulled away. "He may be there but his body is ruined, Jaridd. There is no life left, it is too far decayed. I cannot heal that which is no longer alive, whether his spirit be willing or not." She looked away. "That poor soul, he has held on this long and I just . . . I do not know. The only thing I can think is to fill a basin with water and bless it."

He nodded. "Then we will do it."

He pulled her up.

The Darkhalks hauled a basin out of one of the unused palace rooms and dropped it down beside the Elf. They put him in it, then began the slow process of hauling water down three floors to fill it. Acasha, her mother and her aunt helped in line with the Darkhalks. They did not stop until the Elf was completely submerged.

18

The cold light from the small basement window silhouetted the steel as a non-threatening block. Karalay approached slowly, each step revealing the painted white inside of the basin—the black hair—his rotting forehead, his eyebrows peeled back. His throat—hanging open. His hands—skeletons beneath ragged shards of skin. The skin of his knees, just beneath the water, flapped in the last of the ripples as the water stilled. She rested her hands on the edge of the basin, stared down at the top of his head. She felt the wet of the splashed water and the remnants of old oil under her fingertips.

Her knees shook when she knelt.

She opened her mouth and began chanting in the tongue of the Healers. She reached out and her fingertips brushed the cold water. Her voice closed and her tone quieted to a hoarse whisper. Her voice quivered only once and it was at the touch of slimy flesh. The water began to ripple. Her voice rose. The water began to tremble and the servants in the hallway fell to their knees and bowed their heads.

Karalay's voice broke—the water boiled.

Her voice stopped and the water stilled again.

She sat back on her heels, breathing hard. Jaridd helped her stand and she leaned on him. "Keep the door closed—we shall leave him be."

Jaridd led her out into the hallway where she stumbled into the heat of Telenay's room.

She grabbed his hand. "Telenay. Telenay, I need you to wake up. Please,

Warlord, we need someone of strength . . . I do not have enough." She leaned forward and kissed the Warlord's cheek. "Please," she said in his ear. "Wake up!"

"Karalay." Jaridd stood in the door.

She went to him.

He said, "You need rest."

The Darkhalk took her by the waist, ushered her into the hallway and stared over her shoulders into Telenay's suddenly opened eyes. The Warlord focused. Karalay's head fell, bowed in sadness as she stepped into the hall. Telenay blinked once, twice, opened his mouth to speak and Jaridd quickly shut the door before she could hear.

"You need your rest," Jaridd said.

Karalay let him lead her upstairs.

She poured herself a cup of wine and drank it all the way down.

The Darkhalk smiled. "Sometimes I wish I could join you."

She shook her head. "No. You do not."

She pulled her dress off and stood naked across the room from him. "You will stay with me if we live through all of this?"

Jaridd removed his armor and then reached for her. "Yes."

They moved to each other and he laid her down. Jaridd wrapped himself around her and she grasped him. Closed her eyes and in the dark she heard his steady breathing, his ever-pounding heart, felt his throbbing need.

I want you.

His will was a deep knife in her. She held it in her hand and trembled before him. She felt his fingers around her heart and she stiffened.

I want you all the way.

Her heart started to pound.

"Jaridd. I—"

Yes.

She slipped into the world of will and stared at him, her mouth open with uncertainty. Her heart became a vibrating beacon of her fear, of her uncertainty and of her excitement. She had read of this and it came back to her as she felt his will begin to part, begin to surround her, begin to let her in. And she broke herself before him. Tore down her own defenses, stripped her walls until she felt him enter her own spirit where she had allowed no other thing to touch. She tasted the bitter linger of the Cape and the Sword and the power flooded her fragile self.

He entered, not with the brashness of a lover, or the callousness she

279

might have expected from a Darkhalk, but with tenderness and confidence that left her still and merely desperate for him. He entered every place, poured throughout her bloodstream. She felt him drench her physical skin with a tremendous tingle. She moaned. He heard it with his ears and hers and with the depth of both of their wills.

Do you feel it?

Yes, Jaridd. Yes.

She felt him part and she slipped into him with will wide open and gasping like a girl. Never before had she been in these depths of another person. The defenses were carnal; everyone was born with them. As a Healer, she could bypass so much but not like this. Never like this.

She tasted his eternal mind and spirit and it was cold and clear. Absolute and honest. It raged with need for her and she felt it too. As she slipped her fingers around his heart and pushed out, she became a part of him. And she heard his moaning, felt his moving with the same senses of her own body but now also with his.

She cried out for him and the throbbing thing pressed tight against her wet skin and she heard it with his ears, too. She parted her legs and he felt it both ways. When he screamed, *I love you*, it was with her voice and his.

She felt his awesome power of will out from his fingers, her fingers. He entered her and she felt the sensation of her own tightness, gripping and slipping around like a sheath of lightning.

She screamed as it began. He moved, hard and soft, trembling, gripping, dripping and thrusting for her. She felt his climax rising. Karalay's own became a magma of force. She could not scream, could barely breathe as it came. Her physical body was a mere figment before them, a mere outlet as it rose. He ground against her, grabbed her hips and forced it.

Karalay reached above her for a handhold to brace. He reached for her fingers and they gripped. She threw her head back as it hit her. He pressed his face into her breast.

It flooded her, not with the delicate Human moaning of all of her past encounters. But this. This was a light. This was a storm and the thunder filled her ears. Her will erupted, passed through him as a wall of roaring. His heart stopped. She went stiff; she opened her eyes and saw nothing. Her breath stopped.

Karalay screamed; Jaridd gasped as his heart started again. She writhed beneath him, almost sobbing, almost laughing. Karalay took him in her arms and pressed her face into his neck. It began again. He could not stop now. She wanted it with his need. He pushed and thrust. She braced and as he came she felt the very eruption as it began to tear forward through him. It was the same and like nothing she had known. As he came, so did she again.

Their wills ignited as it happened and they both froze, physical bodies momentarily incapable of surviving such a force. And their wills lifted out of them, embraced, entangled, with unthinkable impact.

They fell back and it was with the reality of wet, hot bodies that were shaking in exertion.

"Jaridd."

"I know."

"Oh, I do not."

"Karalay." He whispered her name as though it were sacred and she could hear something like tears in the back of his voice. "I love entirely."

They lay still for as long as it took for the recovery.

"I have read of what we just did."

"Yes."

She just shook her head, strength only enough to pull the blankets up over her chilling body. He tucked her in.

"I do not know," she whispered.

"What?"

"You held back."

"Yes."

"I am no match for you." She licked her dry lips, ran her fingers down his back as he sat up.

He shook his head. "The Cape is beginning to really leave. You will not say that tomorrow."

"I do not care. I love you." Her head dipped down and she closed her eyes.

Jaridd's hand laid flat out over her stomach. "I shall keep your nightmares away tonight."

Karalay barely breathed. A smile curved her lips; Jaridd kissed them. The Darkhalk guarded her throughout the night and, as the sun rose, he stood to watch it out the window. He glanced at her; in her mind he shushed the dreams that were beginning to surface. Dreams of Telenay. He pushed the memory out of her mind, leaving Jaridd thinking of the evening he had stood outside Telenay's chamber door and she had remained all night within, many years ago. He glared at the rising sun.

Do not forget your promise. I will not share you.

Yes, it was dawn already. Help was coming in from Kamamine. The servants chatted ceaselessly, creating a low comforting murmur that filled the healing chamber. Osondrous squirmed to the edge of the bed. The Centaur beside her, sweating in his fever, was making her boil. She looked at his red face, sheening in the firelight.

Cray's eyes painfully opened.

He took her hand. "You are in bad shape."

"No," she said. "You are."

"I will be fine." His eyes closed again.

Spotting her clean clothes, she eased her feet to the stone floor. The coolness felt good. She pushed herself up and sat and breathed. They had wrapped her all the way around her ribs and breasts. All of her wounds were bandaged. The pain had relented to an all-encompassing ache.

She stretched out her left foot and toes. She carefully moved her head back and forth. Her right foot and ankle, twice their normal size, were completely wrapped in bandages.

"Osondrous!" A servant hurried to her. "You must not get up. You need rest!"

Osondrous turned her head as quickly as she could and glared at the woman. "Go away."

She pulled her shirt on over her head, fumbled with the laces until it was closed enough. She sat down to ease herself into her leggings. The cleanliness and softness of the clothes felt good and cool. She smoothed her damp hair back. Osondrous worked her way out of the healing chamber, using the wall for support.

The servants had been right, the sun had risen another day. There were no clouds, just crisp, endless sky. Seagulls had journeyed from the oceans to pick the last of the grains and grubs out of the fields and now the corpses of the dragons. The farmers were turning over their finished crops. Work horses were grunts in the black of farm ground. The gulls flashed their white bellies over the castle.

In the kitchen, Shrae and many servants were working on huge pots of potato and goat cheese soup, seasoned with rosemary, lavender and chamomile for the sick. The smell was hefty. Osondrous limped around them, going unnoticed. She poured herself a cup of water and drank it empty. She poured herself another.

Osondrous was making a pot of tea when Shrae gasped, "My Warlord!"

She steadied herself against the counter. "Yeah."

"Would you like to sit?"

"No."

"Could I make your tea for you?"

"You finish that soup, Shrae. Make my boys feel better."

"Is it true—Olisize is dead?"

"Yes." She sprinkled the dried leaves in the pot. The water boiled, the leaves dissolved.

Shrae shook his head. Osondrous watched them slave over the soup, peeling potatoes, boiling them, mashing them. Adding the white cheese and goat milk, the dried rosemary, the fresh lavender and the chamomile leaves. She followed after a tray full of bowls that was balanced on an Implin, back to the healing chamber.

Eikian was awake; she went to him.

"I lost sight of you." She sat at his side.

"I watched them bandage your foot. It is nasty."

"How are your legs?"

"I am going to sleep it off."

"I could not." She reached for a bowl of the soup, stirred it a little. "Want a spoonful?"

He slowly sat up with a determined wince and took the whole bowl. He ate tentatively as she watched him.

He asked, "You are thinking?"

She said, "We were so ill prepared for this. Half our Centaurs are dead. I cannot bring myself to go to the back of the castle and see all the bodies."

"And Humans?"

"Four thousand . . . at least. The Centaurs were valiant."

"We always try to be."

She covered her mouth, shook her head; she was looking at all the men around her. "This castle was not built for this. Not in any way."

"That has always been obvious."

"We must do something about it."

Eikian licked his lips. "What could we do?"

"I am going to redesign the castle. Rebuild it. It will be bigger, better designed for war."

"Like we always used to talk about. Over in the rockiest region of

Barbaka?"

She nodded. "Remember that hill? It was practically a mountain. And not too far from here."

"That was a decent place to make a stand."

"And big enough for a castle twice this size."

"That would be too big." Eikian laughed, then groaned and held his side.

"It cannot be too big." She stood up. "I am going to the Seconds."

He nodded. "I will be along."

"Do not hurry those legs, Eikian."

Osondrous worked her way up the stairs, passed by Implins and servants taking soup. The servants left the empty chamber doors open; those with occupants were kept closed. Half the doors hung in. She sat beside them all morning, dribbling cool water on their brows, fulfilling their most mundane of requests: open a window, bring another blanket, wait until I sleep before you leave. She found her Human Second of the archers, Crik, dead in his bed. Had servants take him to the graveyard. Majeik slept in a treacherous fever with Constance beside him. Osondrous did not disturb them.

The last of her Seconds, wounded the deepest, was one of the eldest of the Centaurs still living in the castle and the Centaur she had awakened to that morning. She had heard from the servants that Cray's fever had reached a violent rage. His soup sat untouched by the bed. She felt his heartbeat to be certain he was alive.

He did not respond to her.

She leaned back in the chair, closed her eyes for a moment, bad foot propped up on the edge of his bed.

"Sure be a shame to die now, Cray," she heard herself say. "Another year and you could retire. Go make babies."

She yawned.

A servant woke her with a cry. The woman held Cray's hand. The servant shut Cray's eyes and bowed her head over him, then she left to fetch help to take the Centaur's body to the graveyard. Osondrous stiffly stood and patted the Centaur on the chest. She pressed her face to his and kissed his cheek.

She took his soup and shut his door behind her.

It seemed a long journey for Osondrous to finally make it outside again to feel the warmth of the sunshine on her skin. She was finding she could put a little weight on the bad foot now. She got herself down on the top step of the hall of silence, legs stretched out in front of her, soup steaming in the noon sun. It was a warm day for early autumn. No wind. She sipped at the bowl, having dropped the spoon far back behind her somewhere, no doubt on a staircase.

She heard him coming, his horseshoes dragging and scuffing on the stone.

"You sound awful," she said.

Eikian leaned on the pillar over her head. "I would sit with you but I do not think I could get back up."

"Do not sit with me. I am in no state to help you get back up."

"You could have helped me up if you had not let that dragon mutilate your foot." He leaned down, looked at the bowl of soup. "You know, that soup is for the ill, those men lying in sick beds. You are not lying in a sick bed."

She continued eating the soup. He leaned heavier on the pillar. He struggled to get comfortable.

She said, "The sick who this was brought for will not be missing it."

"Who was it?"

"Cray."

Eikian whispered, "It could not be worse than that."

"Oh," she sighed, "you never know."

A guard named Grey approached them. He bowed. "Warlord?"

She looked at him.

He said, "I have a report about the dragons. Would you like to hear it?"

"I would like to see it. Help me up."

The guard took her hands and eased her up onto her good foot.

"I can carry you," he said.

She looked down the long staircase, thirty-two smooth steps, to the mass of sand that swept the length of the courtyard. All the way across, near the front gates, the dragons were being gutted, skinned and butchered.

She said, "Carry me."

He picked her up and limped down the staircase.

"You were injured and you are carrying me?"

"My leg is not too bad and you do not weigh much."

She grunted.

Her able men had gutted, skinned and cut all the meat off of seven dragons and were working feverishly on the eighth. There was not a single soldier in her castle that did not limp or have a bandage that could be seen beneath his clothes.

"Four left?" she asked.

"Only three."

"I thought there were thirteen?"

"One of them lived. He has not awakened yet."

He set her down at the side of the eighth dragon, opened up and gutted. They were working at a desperately fast pace. A line of tables was covered in mounds of salt. Men packed as other men cut and threw them meat.

The guard pointed to the animal's open chest cavity. "It is huge," he said, holding his arms out wide. "This animal had three sets of lungs."

She stared at him. "How is that possible?"

"They must have been bred to cross the rivers. To go high enough and hold their breath."

"This was planned for a long time." She shook her head.

A guard ran up to them. "Grey!"

Grey turned. "What is it?"

"The Dragon awakes!"

"Take me!" she gasped. He picked her back up.

They hurried around to the side of the castle. Before them rose the dragon. His gray eyes opened and closed, opened and closed, trying to focus. Beneath him was the huge black stain of his blood.

Grey hesitated.

She ordered, "You put me down and stand away."

He set her down, his eyes worried. He could feel her exhausted will. She was only a skinny woman now. She was not even carrying a weapon. He bit his lip but did as he was ordered.

She gimped up to the dragon, negotiating the hard grass and bumpy ground. His head tilted to stare at her. His brow furrowed as though squinting. The animal was missing a horn; hideous scratches and tooth marks ran around his neck, all over his belly and across his back.

She recognized him.

He said, "Where am I?"

She said, "You are at the Castle of the Wards in the middle realm."

"I do not know this place. What is my name?" His voice ran like molasses, so deep Osondrous had to listen hard to understand. The way his tongue formed each enunciation, it was as though the dragon had only just, in that moment, learned to speak.

She said, "I do not know your name."

The dragon lifted his claw and pointed at the dragons being gutted and cut on behind her. "They are me. You are going to eat them. Will you eat me?"

Osondrous stepped closer to him, said directly up and into his wide face, "Dragon—are you my enemy?"

He pulled back. "Should I be?"

She glared at him. "Dragon, if you are my friend, you are welcome here. We will not kill and eat you."

His head tilted at her. He pointed at the dragon behind her again. "You killed and ate him."

He lowered his head and looked close at her glare. His head was three times the width of her. She could have comfortably lain out on his tongue as if it were a bed.

She crossed her arms over her chest. "I killed the man that controlled you."

His head went up. "You are her? You are her! What is your name?"

"My name is Osondrous. You may call me just that."

He smiled at her; missing teeth completed his grin. "What will you call me?"

"We will find you a name."

"Will I like it?"

"You may choose it."

He looked around at the castle. "What will I do?"

"You are welcome here."

"Stay here. With you?"

"If you are my friend, Dragon, we will take care of each other."

She turned to the guards standing behind her. "Get this dragon whatever he wants, treat his wounds if they need it and feed him."

Grey stepped over and picked her up, clearly nervous being so close to the dragon.

The dragon frowned. "You are hurt. Will you die?"

She grinned. "If I die, Dragon, you can skin me and eat me."

Grey took her back into the courtyard where Eikian was gimping through the sand.

"One day," she said, "we will not have sand."

Eikian's face darkened. He was looking over her shoulder. She pushed out of Grey's arms and got her balance. Up the street from Kamamine, the Ambassadors of Stonedowner were rushing toward her. Eikian stepped back as they ran through the gates.

The eldest Ambassador exclaimed, "Osondrous! You have defeated a great threat!"

She raised her eyebrows at him. "What was that, Lortie? Say again."

He bowed down. "You vanquished the dragons, Osondrous. My people are crying out for a queen!"

"This is not a private place!" She motioned to Grey. "Take them to the Ring."

The guard stepped behind the tall men and nudged them across the sand. They bowed to her before consenting. Eikian grunted when they were out of earshot. She raised her hand to keep him from following as she went after them.

The hall of silence, all of the castle, was quiet, as though everyone was pained to disturb the rest of the wounded. Osondrous limped her way down the hall, taking her time, body throbbing from the long climb up the staircase. Her teeth were set and she glared with concentration at the floor. She entered the Ring at the far door. The Ambassador was standing, arms crossed; the other was right behind him.

When the ambassadors saw her, they smiled and bowed.

She glared at Lortie. "You left days ago, Ambassador. What are you doing here?"

"Osondrous, you are a true asset to our kingdom. You proved that yesterday."

"I proved nothing yesterday that was not already known."

"Telenay is gone. You fought yesterday alone, Osondrous! No Warlord has ever won a battle alone."

She motioned at them. "I am sure you are wrong about that, too. Sit down."

He sat across from her, perching on the edge of the chair as though to spring from it. He tried to sound reasonable. "Osondrous—the people of Stonedowner have long respected you. This kingdom needs a queen!"

"Ambassador." She spoke slowly. "The people of Stonedowner have never respected me. You among them."

He opened his mouth to deny it; she stopped him. "Is that all, Ambassador?"

His head fell; he nodded.

"Then I expect you to return to your capital." She stared at them until they stood, bowed, and left. Osondrous sat down and stared long at the door closed behind them. In his mind, she had seen little black swooping creatures with teeth. The same darknesses in Shankan's heart and in the hearts of those men that had tried to kill her. The same creatures that had held the dragons in an iron fist of control. Red man whispering in his ear.

An Implin entered the room. "Would you like something?"

Osondrous could not help but smile. She shook her head and escorted the Implin out the door. They hobbled to the kitchen together. Osondrous poured herself a cup of brandy and tried to drink away the sick taste in her mouth.

Eikian was leaning against a wall and eating soup. She sat down beside him.

"What was that about?" he asked. "What were they doing here?"

"They came to encourage me to become queen." Before he could react she asked, "All of my Centaur Seconds are wounded?"

"I just helped Prush upstairs. They are all staying in one chamber."

"One chamber?" She took a drink.

"They did not want to be alone if they were going to die."

She nodded. "If I were worse, I would join them."

"I am worse—I think I may join them." Eikian winced between spoonfuls of soup and bites of bread.

She sighed.

He said, "There is something on your mind besides the Ambassador."

She touched his arm when she stood but told him nothing and hurried on. The all-encompassing pain of her right side left her with the echoing replay as the dragon's mouth opened up from beneath her and she slid into it like a grilled morsel. Her right foot slipping all the way back and setting in between those last two molars, his snout ending past her head where she was frantically stabbing at his nose and kicking his eye with her left foot, panicking as she tried to jerk away. Then, he snapped and tossed her. The last tooth had broken through three of her ribs, just beneath her right breast. She had been aware of the entire toss, all the way through the air and the shocking roll through the sand, thinking the entire time: *The last dragon gets me, just my fortune.*

Osondrous worked her way up another floor to her Seconds' chambers, her energy beginning to flag. The hall echoed her steps back at her. She followed the murmurs of laughter. The Centaur language rolled out from under one door and across the floors. She let herself in.

They had arranged the five beds in a U around the fireplace and they were cozied with blankets, pelts and pillows. They cheered when they saw her and she could not help but grin at them.

"Osondrous, come sit." Minre motioned beside him.

She went to him and sat down, accepting the blanket and arm he put around her shoulders.

"This is the last of you?" She looked at the five faces.

They all looked down.

Minre said, "Cray died today."

"I was with him," she said.

"I am glad he was not alone." Minre looked at his hands.

She said, "All of you, how sick are you?"

Now the eldest after the death of Cray, and with Eli still in the dungeon, Prush said, "The five of us will be fine, Osondrous."

"If you were more well, I would have called you to a meeting in the Ring."

"Eikian should be here."

"Aye, where is Eikian? Is he all right?"

She said, "Eikian does not need to be here."

Their eyes hardened; they looked close at her.

"What is this about, Osondrous?" Prush asked.

She said, "The Centaurs fought valiantly."

They did not smile.

She said, "I came to speak with the five of you for two reasons. The first is that as queen I will decide to begin plans to build a new Castle of the Wards. You are the Seconds I trust the most. You have all cursed the shortfalls of this wretched place. I want all of your thoughts."

Prush nodded. "The Second reason, Osondrous?"

She sighed. "Let us talk on the first, Prush." Her voice said, *Please*.

"Give us the second reason, Os. We deserve that." Dade, the youngest Centaur among them, sat across from her, his blue eyes filled with worry.

She said, "The second reason is that the Centaurs fought so valiantly. You are five left of those that I will miss the most."

His blue eyes darkened. "Os, we are right here. No more Centaur death today. Not today."

"She is not talking of death," Prush said. He murmured, "Finish your words, Osondrous, so we know where we stand."

She said, "The Centaurs here, after this, deserve to be released."

She remembered Jeday so specifically by his dark skin. In the night he was the most camouflaged of the Centaurs. He was also the softest spoken as well as the biggest besides Eikian. She had a distinct memory of being pinned under the Centaur in battle when he had been knocked out. His mass had protected her and they had each been left for dead and,

290

eventually, saved.

Jeday said, "You would have been slaughtered without us."

Their chorused voices raised,

"What would you have us do?"

"How could you ask us to leave?"

"This is our life, Osondrous. We trained together!"

"You cannot do this without us!"

She sighed, looked into the eyes of Prush, who had not yet spoken. She laid her hand on his arm.

"We trained together," he said defensively.

"I remember." She looked at all of them. "Of course, I remember! Could you forget me so easily? Do you remember who *you* are talking to?"

They looked down.

Minre said, "Forgive us."

She said into their eyes, "Those reasons, all of them, are the very reasons why I should release the Centaurs. It is dangerous for the Humans to be so reliant on another species. We are entirely weak without you. That is not something I can tolerate and I cannot use that as a reason not to release you when it is so deserved. That would be the mark of the worst kind of leader. That is not how I should start my reign."

"When will you take on the crown, Osondrous?" His hair had been blond as the sun; his name was Serkin. He had saved her from rape when she was thirteen. His hair had turned ash and grayed around the edges now.

She said, "You are the first to know of my decision. It is not something I do willingly; I just see as I have no other choice. It will be done soon."

Prush said, "Does Eikian know?"

"No. And I will be the one to tell him."

"He should be here."

She glared at Minre. "You leave Eikian out of this. I came for the five of you that are left."

The Centaurs said nothing for a moment.

Dade said, "Poor Noran."

Osondrous frowned. "What?"

Prush said, "We just heard word. Noran took command of Rayakdool. He cannot go home now. Even if he wished to. Osondrous, you understand—"

"Of course I do. I may not bunk with you anymore and we are considerably past our training days and I know I am about to become a queen, but I am still your Warlord."

"This is our life."

"What do we do?"

"What would you do?"

She smiled wryly. "Go home. Make babies. Is that not what we all want to do?"

The Centaurs laughed at her.

Prush asked, "How would you go home?"

She said, "I have no other home . . . after the Keltch wars—." She winced.

Prush said, "It must be brought up."

She said, "There are few of us left who survived the Keltch wars. If it is only those others that can go home, then they can."

"What do we do?" They stared at her intently.

She snapped, "Do you think I want you to leave? Have I not already said—you are the Centaurs I will miss the most . . . if you choose to leave."

"Then we could stay?" Prush said.

"I want you to stay." She spoke softly. "I would be glad to see all of the Centaurs stay. But that is not the outcome I am seeing."

They shook their heads.

She said, "I will only do this if I can give you a guarantee that there will be a place here for any Centaur that wants it, forever. And if you stay, I am forever in your debt."

Minre said, "I do not know how I could not go back. My ma would never forgive me."

Prush said, "We are your family, Minre."

The Centaur sighed. "It has been a long time."

She said, "It has not been long enough if every Centaur does not receive this news gladly."

Implins entered carrying more soup. They froze when they saw her.

"Come in." She waved.

They gave out the bowls and cups of tea. When they left, the Centaurs ate silently and she sat staring into the fire, rubbing her tired left knee.

"You are thinking of the stony hill, in the Barbaka fields?"

"Hmm?" She looked at Prush.

He said, "That high hill, in the Barbaka fields?"

"Yes," she said. "The new castle will be built there."

"We will give you any aid you need."

"You bring me any ideas you have, Prush. I want them all. Think on it, all of you, every short-coming of the castle, where things can be improved, where things need to be entirely changed. I need it all."

Minre grinned. "No more stairs?"

She nodded. "No more stairs!"

Everyone cheered.

Prush spoke just to her. "What about Eli?"

Her face clouded. "I do not know yet."

"You cannot change a law for just one Centaur."

She nodded but did not agree and said nothing.

Later she slipped down into the dungeons to see him. In his cell she leaned on the wall beside where Eli lay. The only time he had spoken was in trying to convince his guards to release him to help fight the dragons. She slid down and sat on the cold stone.

"I am going to change the law, Eli."

"You cannot." He shook his head and looked up for the first time.

She said, "I will become queen. Nothing can stop a Warlord queen. I will not see another Centaur die."

His eyes were as gray as he was and, in so little light from torches, they were black and fierce. He sighed and shook his head when she would not relent. She left him and slipped into the hall, pulling her cloak around her. A hand closed like a vise around her upper arm and jerked her around.

He pulled her face up to his.

She said, "Eikian. Let go of my arm."

He hissed, "You will have rioting!"

"I will be queen. They can lay down and bow to me."

"Osondrous, I know that I am no prophet but something is not right here. Stonedowner's Ambassador coming back just to tell you how much he loves you? There is something going wrong and it is pushing you to become queen!"

She wrenched out of his hands. "Then you would have me cut off Eli's head?"

His face contorted savagely. "You cannot change a law for one Centaur! You will have rioting."

Her jaw set in defiance. "No one will tell me what I can or cannot do."

20
Constance

She had dreamed of Aerick and tamaracks and quaking aspens turning yellow in the fall. The smell of apple cider was still with her when she rose. The rape, the horses, Aerick's death. It echoed in her like she had died. She could still see him, still hear him say *I love you*.

When she woke she whispered, "I love you, too."

Majeik murmured beside her but did not wake from his fever. She brushed the hair off his boiling forehead before slipping out of the bed. The servants had left a vase of chamomile flowers. Their smell was the smell of the sick. She stared out the window with the darkest feeling she had ever had.

"I cannot stay."

Constance wrapped Aerick's cloak around her shoulders, savoring his smell. It dragged on the ground and completely covered her cotton dress. She went to the graveyard with a chamomile flower clutched in her hand.

It was dawn; the horizon was blue like a lake. The clouds were gray and thin. Mist clung to the castle walls and moved down between the graves. Against the parapet the bodies were stacked. Servants and guards were furiously digging.

She found Aerick's grave, sank her fingertips into the cut in the stone. She knelt in the soft black dirt. She wanted to tell people that Aerick, the great and powerful Second, had chosen her to be his love. She laid the flower down, wondered how long it would last out here, if it might seed and chamomile would grow only on Aerick's grave.

"I love you." She touched the soft black dirt but did not let herself cry again. There would be more tears, endless tears, but not yet. Constance got to her feet before the cold of the ground reached her. She had heard that Osondrous was being crowned this morning. So, when the great roar of celebration rose from the front of the castle, Constance knew the reason.

She crept through the castle and worked her way toward the courtyard. In the center of the hall of silence, looking down on all of her people and servants, Osondrous rose from her knees. Eikian slashed the sacred knife across her palms.

Constance hurried behind the crowd.

Osondrous' blood ran red down on the steps.

Eikian bowed to her.

The crowd applauded and cheered. Constance reached the gate panting, running. She looked back at Osondrous the queen and her sight changed. Her stomach clenched, fearing what she would see but she could not look away.

Beside Osondrous stood a man with red skin. He was nude and his mouth was open and salivating. Black things flew around Osondrous' head, bat-like wings flapping and tails whipping. The red man's eyes were empty and his teeth were sharp. He turned slowly and deliberately. Over the thousands of people, he looked directly at Constance and grinned.

Constance flew through the gates, around the front of the castle, past the corpses of dragons and working men. Past the parapet, the castle, all the way down the hill and into the quaking aspens. She ran until she could no longer suck in the cold dawn air, until her legs threatened to collapse beneath her.

On the road to Rayakdool, she stared back at the castle, expecting to see the red beast coming for her, naked and grinning. But Constance was alone in the chilling wind. She was a small figure up the road, beneath the canopy of fall yellow leaves and white bark. The wind was beginning to pick up and the leaves were scattering.

The hoofprints of Aerick's and Osondrous' Warbreds were still the last steps on the road. Her feet fell into the big holes. She had heard the whispers about Grim and his Reapers but had no idea the power that made them what they were. It was all him, all the red man, all of Grim. And what Creator or God would give such a wicked creature such enormous power? She hurried on, determined to get back to the one safe place she was sure of in this land.

By noon the sun was shining and warm. She wondered how long it would take her to reach Rayakdool. For the horses it was half a day to a whole, depending on pace. For a Human, three days, she guessed. She had no food nor water and, as the evening sun dipped down, she began to peer into the woods with wide, white eyes, wondering if she dare stop or keep moving. Animals could smell up to miles away, brush wolves, fire lions. They all hunted here.

Her stomach growled; she thought of the hot potato soup at the castle. The chamomile tea and water. Blessed, wonderful water. She thought of the warm place beside Majeik where she could lay naked and sooth his fever. Feel needed like she knew now, she needed to be needed. Giving Aerick such pleasure had completed her. Without him, she was an empty vessel and it felt as if the wind blew right through her. She could be tending Majeik's fire now, laying in his hot basin.

Her ankles stung with cold. She could no longer feel the tops of her feet. Her toes were stiffening. She stubbed her heavy foot on a rock, tripped, grabbed at the trees to catch herself and missed. She went down crying. When Constance touched her swollen toes, she felt the sticky warmth of blood. She looked up and searched for stars but the overcast night had closed in.

Constance got up and kept going. She made herself think of pots of hot apple cider, stirred with cinnamon and the smell of horses. Made herself keep walking, using the trees beside her as leverage as she gimped. Her feet had begun to ache under the skin, so deep it felt as though her very bones throbbed with cold. She could no longer feel her fingers. She held them against her belly, chilling herself through and through. She licked her parched lips, attempted to swallow but her mouth was too cold and dry.

She knew dawn was coming when the temperature dropped furiously and she could no longer bear to move. She hunkered down against a tree and pulled all of her inside the cloak. Her ankles throbbed again, as they had not been anything but numb for hours. Her eyes were heavy. She could almost see the fire in the dimness of dawn, could almost smell the embers beside Aerick.

"Aerick?" she whispered

His eyes were there, like grace, like kindness. He touched her cheeks because he loved the feel of her skin. He kissed her lips because he loved her. They laid down beside the fire. She felt him behind her with the strength of a tree and felt safe.

A snow began to fall, so light at first it was a mist. The cold of dawn burst the mist into flakes and as the sun rose and everything was gray, the white flakes covered her still form. She became a log, a rock, an object that would or would not be noticed at the side of the road. The snow covered and froze her bloody tracks until there was no sign of her.

Constance heard a sound that roused Aerick.

"Do you hear that?" he asked.

"What is it?" She looked at him over the fire.

He said, "It is a wolf."

She jerked. The snow shattered from her.

It was finally morning. The light of dawn reflected off the snow and everything was dove gray. She looked down the road toward the castle; there was nothing and no one.

Behind her, big and black, he stepped silently out of the aspens.

Constance did not look at her feet; she avoided them by trying to will her frozen joints to move, to stand. She gripped the tree beside her, lifted herself up. Her legs shook.

He watched her.

Constance stared back the way she had come; her stomach ached with hunger and regret. The castle was as far as Rayakdool now. It did not matter where she turned.

Constance pressed herself against the tree to turn around.

She froze. Her breath came out in a puff, a gasp.

He was the size of a small horse, covered in long black fur. In the night, he would have been a shade darker than anything else. He was coming toward her.

Her heart pounded in her ears.

"No!" she cried. "Please!"

She hurried backward, numb feet dragging in the snow. She tripped, hit the ground with a thud. He watched her try to get up, try to crawl away. Her bare hands filled with stinging snow.

"Stop," he said. His eyes were yellow and without any reflection of light. They were wells and they stared upon her intently.

The wolf said, "What is your name?"

"Are you going to eat me?"

"What is your name?" he growled.

She whimpered, "Constance."

"Do you come to protect the horses?"

She stared at him, blue eyes wide.

He sat down. "I am leader of the sixth clan of the second ancestry of the black wolves of Centmere. My name is Morgan. We protect the horses. We protect the servants of the horses. I have come for you."

He moved close to her. She stared at him.

"I am warm." He lay down.

She sank her fingers into his fur and felt his heat. She pushed close and slipped onto his back. Her face parted his fur and his black skin and undercoat smelled like smoke. He entered the trees and his black mass became the aspens and the snow and the blue light of the sun.

Morgan murmured, "You are a servant of the horses now. We will protect you."

Constance was taken away and the castle that was her life evaporated. All she took with her was the memory of being loved and loving with every desperate part of her. She held Aerick against her heart as she held the gigantic wolf beneath her. Her choice to leave would haunt her for the rest of her life.

"Kilikan?" Jezaline said, "Is that you?"

"Yes, I had not meant to wake you."

"I did not sleep."

She got up on one elbow, face turned in his direction.

"How late is it?" she asked.

"It is morning."

"You said you would return soon last night."

"Something came up . . . perhaps you can help me?"

She pulled the blankets up tighter to cover her breasts. "How so?"

"Do the Humans still ride horses?"

Her breath caught. "Yes. Why?"

"I had my scouts find your last location in Rhechk or . . . Dead Wood, as you called it, to recover your belongings. They did find the remains of your Centaur guardians as well as all of your packs and . . . a horse."

She gasped, "Where is he? Is he all right?"

"He had tracked you well and hidden himself well—it does not look like the Vamepires had known of him. But he has sustained serious injury from the Vamepire traps . . . we think."

Jezaline gripped the blankets. "How is he hurt? Tell me!"

"He is raging with sickness of the wounds."

"Is he here?"

"Yes."

Jezaline threw back her blankets. Kilikan's mouth fell open. She leaped naked from the bed.

"You must take me to him!" She dressed and ran at him. He grabbed her fingers and swept her up. The Draegoone took two strides, held his wings in and threw himself out the window. He stretched them out and caught the current with two deep pushes against the sky.

Jezaline's fingers clutched his skin. "Hurry. Hurry."

The last time she had seen Carmin, he had been walking away in the opposite direction, as she had ordered him. She wondered how far he had gotten before he had turned around to follow her. They had been too focused on the horizon before them to have seen the stallion in the distance. And he too shamed to tell her, *I am here. I am here. I have always been back here for you.*

Had he been afraid to show her he was there? Had he honestly believed her punishment would be so severe that he could not have stepped to her side and told her he could not leave her alone? Any time they had stopped, he could have come to her. Or had it been too late? Carmin too hurt so soon to ever catch them. Had the great wind blown something up, taken his legs out from under him?

She wondered what last glimpse he had had of her: on a Centaur's back, instead of his own. Touching Sethian over touching her Carmin. Had the pain of seeing his replacement kept Carmin from ever catching them?

Kilikan let them drop down low and fall from drift to drift until his wingtips smacked snow-covered ground and he landed with a jerk. She pushed from his arms.

Jezaline sensed walls around her and the distinct reek of sickness hung in the air.

Her throat closed. "Carmin!"

He said, "This is one of our sheds. The walls are of stone and the ceiling is high. There is nothing to trip on."

She pulled away from him. "Carmin?"

Kilikan followed her.

The horse lay on a pile of blankets. Two of the soldiers held buckets of wheat and water—desperately trying to get the stallion to eat. Kilikan swallowed down hard, relieved that Jezaline could not see what was left of the animal.

Carmin lifted his head with a grunt; he threw himself onto his stomach. The animal gave a call none of the Draegoone had heard before. A throaty nicker that shook the animal's entire body. He struggled to get to his feet, hooves kicking out.

"Do not get up!" She ran until she fell to her hands and knees and crawled until she felt the touch of his whiskers on her cheek.

The stallion breathed and gasped her in.

"How could you follow me?" Her shaking fingers cupped his cheeks.

The three Draegoone stepped back. They spoke in their language in a tone beneath what they knew Jezaline's Human ears could hear.

"How is he still alive?"

"It has been weeks since he has eaten or drunk anything."

Kilikan repeated himself. "How is he still alive?"

"Prince, he should not be alive. You saw his wounds—they are furious—they should have killed him by now."

"Has he eaten anything?"

"He will not eat."

Kilikan stared at Jezaline. "Bring our Restorers back here. I want this horse saved."

"They have already done everything—"

"Bring them back here. Now."

His soldiers bowed and ran out.

Jezaline wrapped her arms around the animal, her fingers felt down his body, tenderly touching his quivering muscles, his taut skin.

"He followed me." She was stunned with grief.

Kilikan stepped closer to her. "Why did he follow you?"

The animal hid his head up against her arm, muzzle in the crook of her hip and thigh.

She said, "He is my heart." She felt the bandages around the stallion's neck. She felt his legs and hooves, brow furrowing.

"Jezaline," he said.

"You said—." She swallowed. "You said you thought that it was a trap?"

"Yes."

"What is left of his legs, Prince? Tell me."

"We do not know how he managed to get himself to your place in the dead forest. We know he could not have dragged himself, but his hind legs are broken. No animal could have walked on them."

The stallion raised his head and glared at the Draegoone prince across the room, his tattered ears turning back against his head. The stallion chuffed.

Jezaline said, "You should show more respect, Prince."

Kilikan blinked. "Can he understand us?"

She ran her fingers over the stallion's nostrils, his muzzle, up between his eyes. The animal's head fell down onto her thighs. Carmin settled. She helped him ease back onto his side and she followed him, holding his head until he was laying in her lap. She traced the lines of the stallion's face. Around his eyes, around his cheeks and throat.

"I am so glad to see you," she whispered. "I am glad you came—you were so strong—you did so well." Her voice broke and she squeezed her eyes shut. Tears fell down her face. She curled herself around the stallion's neck and head. "I love you."

Carmin heaved a great sigh, nose tipped up, eye opening to look at her, memorizing her in near disbelief. She began to quietly sob into the horse's thick neck.

Through the gloom, Kilikan hurried away for fresh air. When he reached the doorway, Tarrick was waiting for him.

"What do you want?"

Tarrick said, "Is the stallion broken?"

"Any animal with such heart is at least worth all of our efforts to save him."

Tarrick's eyes reflected the cold grayness of the day. He stared at the few snow-coated trees and across the rocky ground and jagged horizon.

Two of Kilikan's soldiers landed. One said, "The Restorers are coming."

Kilikan ordered, "Make no noise but guard the Human and the stallion. And get some blankets for her." He turned back to his brother. "What is it?"

Tarrick said, "I had a dream, Kilikan."

"All my life, Tarrick, I have bled for your dreams."

"My dream was about Jezaline."

Kilikan waited.

"I dreamed long ago about a broken desert stallion crossing the mountains alone. He walked on dead legs and without blood to sustain him in the name of love. It would be a sign of what I must do and ask you to do. It made no sense at the time but I learned long ago to write all of my dreams down to remember them."

"And what of Jezaline?"

"I saw a woman, a warrior wearing Draegoone armor and our queen's crown. But not just a warrior, Kilikan. She went and cut the head off of Grim and burned his castle to the ground. The woman was Jezaline but not the Jezaline you have met or a Jezaline that she could ever become."

"Then why was she shown to you?"

"Because it was the Jezaline she should be. She should be the killer of Grim. She should not be a Ward of high power."

"You sense her power as well as I do. She is a Ward. The Humans deemed her so!"

"Did you not wonder where her Darkhalk guardian was, Kilikan? If she were a Ward, why would no Darkhalk be by her side in her time when she would need a Darkhalk the most? No one may have ever known but the Darkhalks that her power was not born to her. Grim is stronger than I ever imagined. He saw his own future, he saw who would bring him down. He changed Jezaline's future that she would never be here, that she would never know of the Krept or the Draegoone or of him. This is why I was given the dream to bring her here."

"So he gave her the power of a Ward?" Kilikan smirked in disbelief.

"Yes," Tarrick snapped. "There was no other way to change her life enough."

"But she is here, Tarrick."

"Exactly—Grim did not account for me. He did not know that another prophet would interfere. We cannot see other prophets."

"So Jezaline is here. She must then become our queen and defeat Grim?" Kilikan was mocking.

"I believe that you may be the only one that can take her to Grim's castle and finally end this."

"But she is no warrior. She cannot take on Grim!"

"She will not have to. This is the largest reason I am here. Grim is long gone from his castle. The two Crystal shards are in his hands and within the next days he will attack Diggamara for the last Crystal. He and his Reapers are out of their bodies, controlling his armies."

"And what of his dragons?"

"I wait on word. They are his reinforcements. He waits for another King Ward to be called for the Crystal to weaken—otherwise he cannot get anywhere near it."

"Tarrick, are you telling me Grim is just going to walk through Diggamara and become all powerful within the very week?"

"He will try."

"There is not anyone guarding it?"

"The last of the Darkhalks, a Healer, a Warlord and two royal Fai as well as a Fai army."

"How large of a Fai army?"

"I should have said a small Fai army. They all should be flying to meet us. Every Fai that chooses to stand by Sicilia and Cousai and not fly to meet us will be deemed a traitor . . . so there will not be many."

"The same day this is all going to come to pass?"

"Grim has but a short walk to the door of Diggamara when a new Ward is called, and we have a three day flight."

Kilikan looked into his brother's eyes until Tarrick turned away.

Kilikan said, "You are still going to fly with our army? You could just disappear, Tarrick. You have done it before . . . Cousai is there, standing against Grim!"

Tarrick's eyes snapped at his brother. He growled, "How do you know of Cousai and me?"

"Jezaline told me." Kilikan folded his arms across his chest.

Tarrick's tail hit the wall beside them with a crack. "Cousai does not matter anymore."

"Tell me how that can be. I do not see how you could abandon her for this bastarded Five Hundred Year War! Jezaline said Cousai is yours."

Tarrick looked out over the expanse of their land made fuzzy and blurred with the falling snow. "When you are a prophet, you know in your heart that you can only change those things that must be changed and you can change nothing else or it could doom us all. But there is always the temptation to see your end, to see the end of those that you love and, if it is an end that you can change, the temptation to save them or yourself is devastating." Tarrick looked at his brother. "I saw my Cousai's end and I could fly now and I could save her but the consequences of changing a fate . . . well, there is no telling. It is the reason that prophets exist: to make certain that things happen as they would naturally happen."

"Tarrick—"

"I do not need your sympathy. My Cousai is dead and so I shall fly and die to help end this ridiculous old feud with the Fai. By next week, she and I will be walking in the reeds together."

The brothers stared into the distance, so still a layer of snow began to settle on their shoulders.

Kilikan said, "When will you know what needs to be done?"

"Soon." Tarrick lifted off and was gone.

Kilikan ducked back inside the barn. His soldiers and Restorers stood with their shoulders bent and their faces still.

He approached cautiously, smelling the death in the air. Jezaline's hands tangled in the horse's mane, strands wrapped around her fingers as she twisted. Her hair spewed forward, covering the stallion's face.

"Jezaline?" He crouched down.

Her shoulders trembled and she made no show that she had heard him. The blankets brought to her lay in a pile, offering no warmth. He glanced at his soldiers for aid but their eyes were on the woman, their faces sick.

Kilikan touched her arm. It was ice cold. "Jezaline?"

She pulled away, her hair parting to show the horse's white eye, glazed with death. The wind outside cried around the building, threatening it, whistling in at every gap in the mortar.

Kilikan commanded, "Leave us." His soldiers and the failed Restorers left in relief.

He spoke in her ear, "Jezaline, you are going to freeze to death."

She held tight to the stallion. If Kilikan had let her be, she would have died the horse maiden, the Willower with the future lost in a breath of red fire. With Carmin dead before her, Jezaline felt the missing piece of her deeper than ever before. She wanted nothing less than to finally just let it kill her.

"I am not going to allow you to die here," he said.

Her head snapped up. Her will hit his chest and the Draegoone flew back and slid across the floor. She tucked her head back into Carmin's thick neck.

He got slowly to his feet and limped back cautiously.

It did not take long.

Her head slid down behind the horse and her body followed down onto her side, curving along the animal's back. The prince stared at the bare skin of her legs. Raw and red, spotted with white. She shifted, murmured something. Her body gave a last shiver before growing still.

He inched closer. "Do not sleep."

Her lips moved but he only heard her answer in his mind. *This is my end.*

Her face was covered with gray mane. Her fingers grew still until they stopped moving entirely.

He moved around behind her and knelt over her body. "Jezaline, I am going to take you in now."

She did not answer. He unwrapped her fingers from the animal's thick mane. With one arm beneath her, he tipped her into his chest. Frozen tears covered her cheeks and neck.

He picked her up, sprinted into the night and took to wing. Snowflakes falling on Jezaline's skin did not melt. He whispered her name in her ear, felt the vague stir of her taut body trying to respond, trying to push him away. He dropped into her chamber as a dozen Restorers were filling basins and feeding roaring fires beneath them.

"Get out!" The servants scrambled out the door.

He knelt down beside the coolest of the waters and lowered her in. Her feet disappeared, the water began up her ankles and she gasped.

Jezaline screamed.

Water hit the floor and the fire sizzled as she struggled. He held her down and pressed her into the bottom of the basin. Fresh tears broke down her cheeks. She smacked pathetically at him and just as quickly collapsed onto his chest. Jezaline's sobs racked her.

He whispered, "The pain will not last forever."

He pooled water in his palm, raised it and pressed it against her cheek.

She screamed, "Stop!"

He washed her face, wetting her hair and combing it back with his claws. Her body quaked and then went limp over his arm. He gathered her up and lifted her to the next, hotter basin. He lowered her down again and felt her tense. He picked her up, moved her to the next and laid her down against the basin. He untied her boots and tossed them across the floor. He used his claws and cut her dress up the middle and snipped the sleeves off her shoulders.

He slipped his fingers down between her back and the dress. He lifted her up. Her breasts and arms came out of the wool and he snuck his hand beneath her thighs and the dress fell from her feet with a wet flop. He walked her to the last basin, the hottest of them all, and laid her in it.

She murmured.

He said, "Just until I can feel you warm again."

He pulled his arms out from under her and stood up, unlacing his wet armor and wool tunic. He laid his breast plate to dry by the window. He whisked the water off of his scales.

He pushed the hair off Jezaline's forehead, tucked it behind her ears and sat down beside her. He touched her feet. She kicked at him. He grabbed and held one until she gave up and he massaged until she no longer moaned. He rubbed up her ankles, over the strength of her calves and her knees and then beneath her, submerging his arms up to his shoulders.

She moaned. He worked his way up her back, moving to alongside the basin. He touched her stomach, mindful of her still healing wounds. He did not touch her breasts. When the prince's fingers filled with her shoulder blades, he lifted her off the back of the basin and cradled her on his arm. He rubbed down her shoulder, pushed his fingers between her fingers. He ran water down her face and soaked her hair, combing it with his claws.

The Draegoone finally lifted her up and held her over the basin to let the water drip off of her. He held her at arm's length, chewing his lip, mindfully looking over her every curve. Her skin had not returned to its dusky hue but was all bright berry red. He knew that meant life and that it was a good sign.

He laid her down and tucked her in until he was sure the blankets were doing all they could.

Of his training against the cold, the first most important thing had always been to get close to the person afflicted and let them share your body heat.

He stood there for a while, mulling it over. He bit his lip, then finally sat down and removed his boots, his steel leg armor and rough wool leggings. His eyes moved down as she curled into a ball for warmth. A tremble shook from the tips of her toes to the top of her head.

She looked tiny.

He got into the bed beside her.

"No. Stretch out or you will hold the cold in. Come here."

He turned her over to face him and pulled her stiff body apart, stretching her arm over his chest. He grabbed her tight until he felt her finally give in. Her wet legs slipped over his thighs, her head lay still on his chest. He felt her steady breathing.

Kilikan stared at the ceiling, hoping he might be able to sleep before he started panting.

22

Sometime before dawn, she ran her fingers across his smooth skin. Jezaline opened her eyes to darkness, touched the bandages wrapped around her face. She pushed her fingers back into the firm skin, felt a heartbeat.

"Carmin?"

She shifted her face into the beast beneath her and felt him move. Her nakedness felt his inhumaness. Her thighs felt the pinch of scales that lifted ever so when she brushed up them. His hands spanned the width of her back. She smelled the scent of honey, sweet water, winter. He smelled like the north. She raised herself up on her elbows to reach his neck. Her cheek brushed his chin, her nose brushed his cheek.

She rested her hand in the center of his chest.

"Carmin." She heard herself in the utter silence.

He murmured and she grew still beneath his growl.

23

The next day they brought her everything left of her journey and her Centaurs. She pressed her face into Ajax's leather pack and breathed it in.

Jezaline lifted out the heavy cooking pots and spoons. They still smelled of the fire. In the darkness of her sight, she saw all of her lost Centaur guardians. She put aside the pack for another. Pulling it up her thighs, she reached into it and murmured with pleasure when she felt the softness of one of her own velvet dresses. She pulled it out of the pack and shook it out.

When she dressed in it, she twirled around with her arms out, tilting her head until she felt her hair fall off of her neck. She smoothed the dress down her breasts and thighs.

She sat down on her bed and wept. She wept for more than her guardians. She wept for herself. As every day went by, her need for Waltruk was growing. Even as her heart began to beat in a way it had never beat for another thing except Carmin, none of that power was enough to stop the pain of the ache left in her. She could almost believe that this was where she belonged. Such a different life than the one she had led as a Ward. It seemed absurd, but it was true. Maybe this had been destined to be her home. Kilikan, the only biggest, most powerful thing that could ever attract her, bridle her. And even as she still felt and smelled Kilikan beneath her, even as she began to not consider but *know* that this was the place for her, that empty piece in her belly called the name *Waltruk*, over and over again, and louder each time.

The wind outside her window heightened. She froze when she heard a thump. Kilikan peeked in the room before entering in a gust and locking the shutters behind him.

She had awakened that morning to the feeling of smooth scales under her fingers, against her stomach.

She sat on the edge of the bed.

He gasped. "The storm is intense."

He sat down beside her, carrying a cloud of cold with him. "How are you feeling?"

She raised her hands. "They still tingle a little."

He took her hands and pressed the tips of her fingers to his lips.

Her face had been pressed against his cheek when she had awakened and she had felt all five claws of his right hand spanning her lower back.

Jezaline pulled her hands out of his.

He said, "They are warm now, though."

She headed for the window. Her fingers hit the shutters and she spread them out wide to feel the cold.

Kilikan laid his hand on her shoulder. "It is going to be severe."

She pulled her hand back and pressed it against her heart. "It is like the very north has frozen over and this wind is like nothing I have ever felt."

Kilikan cupped her shoulder in his hand and pulled her back toward the bed. "You should stay away from the north today." He looked at her. "That is very beautiful."

"What is that?"

"Your dress."

She touched the pleated velvet skirt. "What color is it?"

He murmured, "Like a midnight sky. Our females here do not wear such fine things as that."

She felt the brush of his fingers as he stroked the fabric.

When she had awakened, her hand had been pressed into his chest and she had felt his heart beat.

She flushed.

"Jezaline?" He said, "The Restorers here would like to remove your bandages tonight."

When Kilikan had awakened, her hair had been tossed across his face and he could feel the weight and the softness of her thigh between his legs.

"What did—." She gritted her teeth.

He finished for her. "What did we do with your stallion?"

She whispered, "Yes."

"He was floated to sea and a stone was picked for carving of his name. His incredible strength will not be forgotten here."

He pressed into her hand two long braids. She could smell Carmin.

"One is of his mane and the other from his tail."

Jezaline pressed them to her cheek.

He touched her back, moved closer. "I am so sorry."

She breathed deeply and the Draegoone's eyes moved to watch her chest lift with each gasp.

She touched her dress. "A friend gave this dress to me."

"A friend?"

"Karalay. She is a Healer, a great Ward."

"I recognize her name. I believe I heard the Warlords of your people talk of her."

"I miss her. We are near the time to dance with the wind."

"The dance of the Phoenix?" he asked.

"You know it?"

"There was a Human prophet that came to our people once, a good man. He spent years here and he spoke of the beauty of the Willower

308

people."

She smiled.

Kilikan said, "He stayed here, but that was generations ago for your kind. He spent days writing about us. About our customs. He wrote about the Humans, too, for our own knowledge." His voice quieted. "I have read many times what he wrote about the Willower. About your relationship with the wind. I read that there were few who could actually hold the wind's hand, feel it like he were another Human, trust him entirely. Dance with him. He wrote so much about the beauty of the women."

Jezaline could feel the Draegoone staring at her.

She lifted her head up to meet his stare. "You would like to see my eyes?"

"Yes . . . he wrote especially about the colors of the eyes of the women. He wrote that it is the Elvin blood in your ancestry that comes out ever so rarely for the most awesome of colors."

"This prophet knew much about us."

The Draegoone squeezed her hand. "My mother may not feel that the Humans should ever rule here. Up until this point, it is only Humans with the power of Wards; I believe that that is a sign, you have been given a powerful gift."

"When will you rule here, Kilikan?"

"My mother is very old. My rule here will be soon."

"When she dies?"

"When I overrule her."

Jezaline raised her brow. "You just overrule her?"

"Yes, I make the decision when her rule is over."

"And you have not yet?"

"No."

She could feel the Draegoone shrug.

"But why? You could be all powerful here."

"I have no desire to be."

Jezaline shook her head. "Our species is very different."

Kilikan stood and walked across the room. He poured two cups and brought them back to her.

He said, "Our brandy is better than any Human brandy."

"What makes you say that?" She took the cup and smelled it tentatively before sipping.

He said, "Your Warlords told me that. Osondrous was taken with our brandy."

She smiled and nodded as the hotness reached her belly. "I do not blame her."

The Draegoone's eyes watched her hair toss down her back. He lingered on the velvet fabric that was pulled tight across her backside. That morning her face had been against his, her breath had been on his cheek and she had been murmuring something. When he had tried to speak to her, to move her gently off of him, her mouth had closed his mouth. Her body had slid on top of him, so smooth that he could not let go until she realized what it was her lips were kissing and she had pulled away.

Kilikan watched as she spoke of the days when Osondrous had tried to make her own brandy and attempt to outdo his own. He laughed when she laughed and could not help but let her cheer lift him. When her talking turned to Karalay, her brow furrowed.

He said, "You miss her."

Jezaline nodded. "She was my friend."

"Is she not still your friend?"

Her lips parted but she did not speak. Jezaline did not say, *No, I do not think any of the Wards will ever care to see me again.*

"You said you danced with the wind with her?"

Jezaline smiled. "Yes, every month for years and years." She frowned again. "It is funny though. I have not felt the hand of that wind in a long time. Not since I left the castle."

"That is not so long." He touched her hand.

"It feels like a very long time."

He murmured wordlessly. His tone dropped so low, it pulsed and she shivered.

He said, "I am sorry."

She said, "I shiver because I like the way you sound."

She felt his exhale of breath. Kilikan's hand fell lower down her back.

"This morning," he said.

She shook her head.

"What is it?"

She said, "I am embarrassed and I apologize for this morning."

"For what?"

"I had not meant . . ."

His fingers pressed into her back again. "I liked it."

She lifted her head. "How?"

"All of it."

She felt his breath on her mouth. He watched her tongue press out to moisten her red lips.

Kilikan touched her cheek. "I want to kiss you."

"I know."

"Can I?"

Jezaline's lips parted and she pressed them against his lips. His forked tongue slid up her mouth.

She drew closer. "Kiss me more."

She climbed onto him and her fingers dug into his shoulders. He could feel her breasts against his chest.

"You will not like me." He broke their kiss.

"What?" She frowned.

"If you see."

Kilikan looked across the room at the mirror on the headboard; a monster holding an angel. He almost left—could see himself get up and get out.

He said, "I am a monster to you."

Her legs parted around him, "I want you to touch me, to see me." She did not say, *So the ache will leave me for a little while.* Even though she knew it would not be the same, knew the ache would not be touched by this Draegoone as it had been by Waltruk. But she needed this. Needed to know that she was still Human, still alive, and not yet a Vamepire. Needed, most of all, the comfort. It was as though she was on the ground in Dead Wood again, laying with Sethian. She felt despair coming for her and needed something to remind her that life was not all death.

Jezaline pressed herself down so he could feel her heat, so she could feel his desire. She sighed in his ear.

"We cannot," he growled and she felt the vibration through his chest and felt it reverberate throughout her entire body.

His arms held her back.

"Why?" Her body was rank for him, it pulsed through her every pore. She needed this. She needed him.

He touched her cheek and lowered her to the ground.

He said, "Not now. When you see me. If you still want me. I have to go for a while. I will return with the Restorers."

She heard sadness in his voice. Melancholy, need and weariness.

She reached out to him and he stopped on his way to the window.

She said, "Do not bring the Restorers. I can take the bandages off myself."

He chuffed once, low in the back of his throat, a purely dragon sound, and was then gone.

She stood at the window a long time, feeling the darkness of her sight deeper and deeper. How could Waltruk do this to her? Certainly, he would not leave her blind. Of course he would not. But her memories of their brief time was less than a drunk binge one night with Centaurs. Had she? How could she? Maybe it was a nightmare. But her heart was shrouded still in his black embrace. She could see him clearly, shifting from shadow to shadow, an animal born to the black of deep places, where no light ever shone. And if she had been able to deny her words to him, to deny the making their bodies had shared, she could not deny her craving. The ache would not be denied now. She was the red man's creation of a living wound, a person missing something. A spirit? Was that what Waltruk had said? Was she now without a soul? It was not a question but a cry in the night of her blindness.

She was scared to her core. She pulled away from the window as though Kilikan could be coming right now, this very moment to tear her bandages down. What if she could never see again?

And it dawned on her. She probably would be able to if she became a Vamepire. Was Waltruk that clever? Yes. That cruel? She had no idea.

She went to the table and laid her hands on the smooth marble that was every surface in this place. Flat, perfect and very cold. She imagined hearing him outside already and whipped around with a gasp.

Just the wind, and not her wind.

Jezaline turned back to what she felt certain was a mirror and her hands shook.

When Kilikan returned, it was late and she was still standing there. He closed the window against the wind and stepped toward her once before stopping.

Her right hand opened and from it fell her bandages.

He backed to the wall.

Slowly, she opened her eyes and looked upon her own face. It was there and tears pricked her green eyes. She rubbed them and smoothed her hair back, blinked hard to see clearer. And she could see clearly. She gasped and laughed, touched her own face in relief. Her face was thinner now, more lined but prettier to her eyes; thinner was always prettier.

His breathing drew her and her smile faded.

Jezaline slowly turned. She gripped the table behind her with white knuckles.

His size was three times that of any Human she had ever seen. He was massed in nothing but muscle and over them his scales glistened dully in the light. His hair was thick, unbrushed and full of tight braids; it fell down to his shoulders and his wings, which he held behind him almost defensively.

As she stared, he pulled his arms across his chest and looked down hard. She could see his jaw muscles working, his eyes squeezing shut as he took her gaze. He tried to hold in his frantic panting but the sounds that resulted were hard and hot huffs.

She moved across the room as fast as she could.

He held up his hands uncertainly, fingers spread; sharp talons on the ends were green and pointed.

Jezaline gasped and threw herself against him. He caught her and his face pressed into her sweet hair. She looked into his eyes. They did not seem to have color; they reflected her eyes back to her. But beneath the reflection was a darker color, almost gray, almost blue.

She murmured but could not speak. She pressed her face against his and listened to his relief.

He gasped. "You—"

"I cannot believe you."

He shook his head in disbelief.

She said, "You are the most incredible thing I have ever seen." Her throat closed and she desperately swallowed past her tears. He set her down so he could touch her face.

He said, "You have the most beautiful eyes I have ever seen."

His wings lifted. She reached out and touched them. At the base they were almost the length of his spine, a mess of muscles that ran into his back, shoulders and hips.

She moved against him again and he took her tightly. Jezaline took in the profile of his face. His nose was strong, broad and long; his jaw was square and full of muscle. His mouth was longer than a Human's, faintly hinting of what Human breeding may have done with a snout.

His eyes fell at her scrutiny and uncertainty returned to his face.

She took his cheek in her hand and pressed her mouth to his long, pointed ear. "Take me to the bed."

He moved slowly, setting her down and following her as she moved backward up to the pillows. He moved over her, resting on one gigantic fist. His eyes ran over her breasts and belly and she stared at every single inch of this beast.

He smiled at her, almost hopefully. She stared with mouth open at the row of sharp, straight teeth, top and bottom.

She pressed her hand to his chest. "How did I not feel them when you kissed me?"

He looked down. "I did not want you to feel me a monster."

She felt the back of his neck, his cheeks; she looked in his eyes. "You are incredible."

She saw the bones in his wings bend beneath him and the paper thinness of their skin twist and pinch without complaint. The fire caught hold of a particularly big piece of timber. Jezaline pushed aside his vest and sank her fingers into the eight separate mounds that made up his flat stomach. Her hand moved down into the V made beneath his belt. He licked his lips and she stared at the bright red-forked flicker that emerged.

"Let me see," she gasped.

He looked at her. "What?"

"Your tongue!"

He shook his head.

She stuck out her own and swept it along her bottom lip. He drew her face closer to his and pressed out his long, red tongue, as wide as hers but smoother, wetter, longer and forked at the end. He swept it along her bottom lip and she opened her mouth to meet it with her own.

Jezaline stepped from the bed, from beneath him and stood before him. She unlaced her corset and watched as his eyes widened. The dress began to drift down. She pulled it from over her breasts; it caught at her hips, then slipped all the way down.

She stood before him in her nakedness and asked, "Do you like any of what you see of me?"

He grabbed her and pulled her back. She felt the singing ache that was endlessly in her chest and her heart began to sing with it. A chorus of desperation. A chorus of pure want. Tears choked her throat as she moved over him, took in his wide hips with her thighs and spread herself around him. Her fingertips grabbed and grasped his clothes, pulled them off of him. She moaned hard and it brought forth from him a long essential growl that vibrated all the way down, between her legs.

He watched in awe as the pleasure took her. Felt her mouth open on him again and again as she gasped for more.

She let herself forget, let herself be lost by his guttural roar that filled his being and her being. He was deeper, heavier, harder than anything she had ever been able to take. She could see, if this had been her destiny, then she had found exactly what she had always wanted. The way he felt inside of her, the way he felt under her fingers. The way he kissed her. The way his growl made her feel. Yes, this was it. This was what she had always wanted. If things had been different. If things had been how they were supposed to be.

Jezaline started to sob.

He gasped, "I hurt you."

She lay in the warmth of the bed and in the arch of his body until her heart slowed down. Until her sobs stopped racking her and her stomach ached from them. He rubbed her breasts and kissed her belly and chest.

She whispered. "I think I love you, Kilikan." She ran her fingers over his horned and scaled face. "I have never loved anyone."

25

When Kilikan left her she was sprawled out, naked, over the bed. She watched him go. She reached for her robe and tentatively peeked out the door. The hallway was empty. On the floor was a tray of breakfast and two tall pitchers. A delicate strand of steam slipped out of the mouth of one.

She poured herself a cup from the steaming mug and breathed in the smell of leaves and roots. She smiled, understanding the cup of honey sitting beside the pitcher. She stirred in a little and sipped deliciously.

Jezaline rubbed her lower belly, between her legs, to help sooth those things that were still trying to settle. She sighed, leaning back in the bed. She cupped the tea near her mouth and tried hard to let it calm her. She noticed the length of Carmin's hair where it had slipped out from beneath the pillow. She pulled it to her heart and squeezed her eyes shut.

She jerked at the smack that blew her windows open.

Kilikan stepped in and locked the shutters behind him. She rose from the bed and hurried to him.

"Kilikan?" She laid her hand between his wings as they folded down his back. She turned around his shoulder, looked up into his face.

"Kilikan? Is everything all right?"

The Draegoone's shining eyes opened; he touched her cheek with a hand that was wet with cold. Kilikan sighed. His teeth flashed when he opened his mouth to speak but he did not say anything. Jezaline pressed her cup of tea into his hands. He drank. They sat down beside the bed.

He said, "My brother was waiting for me."

She held her breath.

The Draegoone looked into her eyes. "He said many things."

"Good or bad things?"

"He spoke of war."

"What kind of war?"

"What was it like when you left?"

"Left where?" She licked her dry lips.

"When you left the Wards and the middle realm."

She shook her head. "We are in a time of peace, Kilikan."

"Tell me of the Wards that were there."

She said, "The Healers, Olisize and Karalay; the Warlords, Telenay and Osondrous; and our King Shankan."

He said, "I do not know how most of these things have come to pass but in this moment there are only two Wards at the Castle of the Wards and the King is dead."

"Dead! No! Shankan was young."

Kilikan said, "Osondrous is the only Warlord protecting your castle now. The old Healer is by her side."

"What of Karalay?" She gasped, "Is she all right?"

"Karalay is at the heart of Diggamara with the last of the Darkhalks, a small Fai army and two royal Fai and the Warlord, Telenay."

She felt ill. "Why Diggamara? What reason would the Darkhalks abandon the Wards for Diggamara?"

"Grim has risen."

"Grim?" She frowned but said nothing. Waltruk's words were an echo in her heart but she held it at bay.

Kilikan growled, "We have all warred against Grim. Vamepire and Draegoone alike. We are trapped in the west realm and it is not big enough for the three of us. We know not how he came to be, or how such power was given to such a creature. But he does have power. Our sources informed me of the taking of the second Crystal shard decades ago. I knew he would rise for the third but I had not known its location."

"Diggamara." Jezaline closed her eyes. "Grim has risen for the third Crystal?"

He nodded.

She said, "If he accomplishes reaching that shard . . . Kilikan."

"I know."

"How long have the Draegoone known that he would rise for the third?"

"We have suspected it for decades."

"And you did not try to inform us of this?"

"We did not realize until this year we could ever cross the rivers. How would we have gotten that message across? And are you really considering the Humans would have taken our word seriously?"

She put up her chin. "Our Warlords would have."

"Yes, the Warlords of this generation. You forget the Wards of this year have only been of power for a short time. This has culminated too quickly for mortals to keep up. We could have done nothing with the last generation Wards! Or any generation before them."

"So what do you want from me?"

"You are a Ward."

Jezaline said, "I have lost all control of any life I thought I had to live. I should have just gone back to the castle and died like your brother said I would."

Kilikan's hand ran quickly up her back. "I believe Tarrick. This is where you are supposed to be. He told me things about you . . . and me."

Her heart stopped. She glanced sharply at him.

He said, "Why you need to be here, why you need to be with me and where we need to go."

"No, Kilikan."

He said, "In the morning I will come for you and we will fly and end all of this. I want to give you a life to live with me. Do you believe my brother? Do you believe in the power of a prophet?"

She stood up and paced a little. "I never doubted until now. I want to say I do not believe him. I want to say I am uncertain of his truth and be able to live with myself and just not go. Go back to the Wards . . . or something."

"I think we must go." He stood up and went to her with his hands out. She looked down at his claws, grimacing but she let him pull her to his chest.

"There was good," he said into her hair.

"Tell me."

"Tarrick said that Grim has been waiting for hundreds of years for this opportunity. He has destroyed the forest and the Elves of Addilade to use as his army. He has been warping and breeding a form of our dragons to be able to fly so high, to be able to pass over the rivers at any time. These dragons are his strongest army. He does not have many, three in Addilade to help control the army and thirteen or so in reinforcement, settled down in the Barbaka fields nearby. But Grim is going to grow anxious and he will make a mistake. To kill those Wards that may be left at the castle and encourage Osondrous to become queen, he will attack the Castle of the Wards with his reinforcement dragons."

"And what will happen?" she asked.

"You cannot guess?"

Jezaline shook her head. "I do not think even dragons could touch Osondrous."

"You are right. Tarrick said before Grim can pull his dragons back, she will kill them all."

"Of the very small amount of sense I have heard tonight, that makes the most. I guess that is where I would have died if I had gone back . . . Osondrous rises to be our queen?"

"Yes."

"She does exactly as Grim needs her to. He can gain all power of the third Crystal shard then."

He nodded. "Only in its weakest state can he get it under his full control, when a new ruler is called."

"So Grim will attack Diggamara, but without most of his dragons."

"Yes."

"Did Tarrick tell you the outcome?"

"I do not think he knows."

"Where is he sending us?"

He said in her ear, "We go to Grim's castle."

She startled in his chest. "I am no warrior!"

"Tarrick said you will know what to do."

Her eyes sparked. "You just told me of a thing with such power and now you and I alone are going to go tap on his castle door?"

Kilikan shook his head. "Tarrick said that all I had to do was get you there and you would know what to do."

"I would like to see your brother say that to my face!"

"Jezaline." He grabbed her arms.

"Let go of me!" She jerked out of his grip.

He put out his hands pleadingly. "Do you think I would ever let anything hurt you? He swore to me that you would not be alone. It will be

318

me, I will be with you. Can you imagine anything more frightening than me?"

She looked at the reflection of her green eyes in his. Jezaline went to the window, pulled open the shutters and gasped. A gust of snowy wind threw her hair back and pressed her robe tight until her nipples shone through hard and fierce. She gripped either side of the window in her hands.

She said, "Your brother is wrong about me. But I will go. I have done all else."

PART FOUR

Jaridd kissed Karalay's cheek and she smiled. "Have you watched over me all night?"

She pushed the blankets down and slipped to the floor. She washed and dressed while Jaridd watched the sun rise.

Naked, she stepped to his side.

"Beautiful," she said.

"It is so warm." He glanced at her.

"Last night . . ." She shook her head.

He smiled. "Was the greatest thing I have ever felt."

"I know." She kissed him before turning away and getting dressed. "I must go check on Telenay. Will you come with me?"

"No, I am needed elsewhere this morning."

Her face fell. "All right, then I shall see you tonight?"

He kissed her lips. "Oh, yes." In her ear he said, "I think it is time you put aside the tact of Wards. We are in a time of war; use your will wherever you feel the need."

She looked at him closely. "I will, Jaridd."

He squeezed her hand before he left and she touched her face as the door closed behind him. She brushed out her wet hair with oil and, with sticks and cloth, tied it up.

Before she left she went to the window, opened it wide and clutched the sill.

She spoke out loud as she began to push even as she knew it was useless. "Osondrous. Do not do it. Do not be so stupid and rash, no matter the cause. Do not become our queen."

Her power, pressed so hard and held as far out of her as possible, stopped many Diggamarans in the streets to look up and wonder.

The halls were quiet.

She paused outside Jikrin's chamber, hearing voices within.

Acasha said, "Do Centaurs have loves like Humans?"

"Oh yes, Centaurs are actually a lot like Humans."

"Well—" Acasha started. "But . . . you could not mate the same. How do you?"

Jikrin choked. Karalay covered her laugh.

"Do you mate like horses?" Acasha continued.

"Something like that," Jikrin stuttered.

She stepped across the hall to Telenay's chamber and into the heat.

The Warlord's scarred features were placid. He remained on his back, arms at his sides, as he had been for the past days. She sat down and took his hand, rubbed his wrist and laid her head down on the bed. Karalay closed her eyes and breathed all of Telenay's distinct smells. His hand lifted behind her head. His eyes opened and they blinked, then focused on her. He reached into the pile of her hair, his fingers curled.

She jumped. "Warlord?"

"Karalay?"

"Telenay, you are awake!" She threw herself to his chest.

"I thought I would never speak with you again." She wiped the sweat from his brow and stroked his face.

His voice was hoarse and husky. "How long has it been?"

"It is the tenth of Qalin."

"Who else is alive?"

"Jikrin. And an Elf was found yesterday; I do not know if he will survive."

"That is it?"

"And you, Warlord. Thank everything. You are alive." She laid her head on his chest and embraced him. He smoothed her hair and patted her until she rose.

He said, "You must send messengers to the castle. There is an army—"

"I know. A messenger was sent days ago."

Telenay's face tightened in pain.

Her brow furrowed. "How are you healed?"

"I am only stiff. You saved me."

She helped him sit up with her arms around his shoulders. "You must eat something. I will send for food."

Karalay stood for the door.

Telenay grabbed her wrist and pulled her back to him. "Wait."

His grip became fierce.

She frowned, still as though she were suddenly in the presence of a wild animal. "Are you all right, Telenay?"

"I should have known," he growled. His eyes darkened from amber to black in the shadows; they moved into the corners to stare at her.

She pulled back, her heart began to pound. His grip tightened.

He said, "Why did you come here?"

"What . . . are you?" She pushed against his chest, leaned away.

Telenay snapped, "You abandoned your people for him!"

324

Karalay broke away—backed to the wall. "You are one to talk!"

"I saw you yesterday, Karalay."

"You were not awake yesterday!"

"That Darkhalk took you in his arms."

"What do you mean? What does it matter?"

Telenay tried to get out of bed. He wavered, grabbing the bedpost before he would fall.

Karalay ran and held him back. "No! Not yet! You are too weak."

He grabbed her and snapped her back, onto the bed, pinning her there. "Karalay, you must listen to me. You cannot be sleeping with that Darkhalk!"

She screamed, "Telenay, you are hurting me!"

"Karalay, we need our lead Darkhalk! Do you have any idea what we are up against?"

"Let me up, Telenay, please!" Tears began streaming out of the corners of her eyes. His grip eased. She slipped out from under him and hit the floor at a run. She reached for the door. Telenay caught her and threw her around. She hit the wall. His fingers spanned around her throat.

"Karalay, I am not going to hurt you."

"I am scared, Telenay. Please . . . let me go."

"Do you hear me?"

"I do not know what is wrong—what are you are trying to tell me?"

"We need Jaridd. We need him a Darkhalk."

She felt his breath on her neck. Karalay knew his head was spinning. He closed his eyes and pressed his forehead against the stone.

"I do not know what I can do," she whimpered.

"Why is he not a Darkhalk?" His fingers moved up her neck. He pushed her tears away with his thumb.

She whispered, "For me . . . He promised . . . He told me, Telenay, that he loves me. He loves me."

"Karalay, do you know what kind of creature you are talking about?" She pulled away but he did not allow it. "Karalay, a Darkhalk and peace is like trying to make Osondrous a brood mare. Do you even know who you are talking about? They are designed for only one thing. They are not Human. They cannot love!"

"He loves me."

"He cannot love you. Not like I could love you—like a Human could love you. You know this." His voice was muffled.

She turned her face against the wall and he rolled off of his forehead.

They stared at each other over the stone.

She said, "You could never love anyone."

"Imagine how little love a Darkhalk could have for you then."

Karalay started to cry. She covered her face. "I love him."

The Warlord let her creep into his chest to cry and he rubbed her back.

He said, "Jaridd must become a Darkhalk. He must. Do you have any idea of what we are up against?"

Her wet face pressed into his hot skin.

"You must convince Jaridd to become a Darkhalk again."

"How?"

His grip tightened on her shoulder. "You must find a way."

The door opened and Acasha entered, platter of food and pitcher in hand. She stopped short, stared with shock at Telenay's naked body. "I am so sorry!"

Karalay said, "It is all right, Acasha. Telenay, let me help you back to bed."

The Warlord let her lead him back.

She said to the servant, "Acasha, bring the food. It shall be our Warlord's breakfast this morning. It is wonderful that he is all right!"

Cheeks flushed with embarrassment, Acasha handed Karalay the tray, then ran from the room. Not looking at Telenay, Karalay laid it over his lap, poured his cup and unfolded his napkin.

Telenay's hand closed around her wrist. She froze.

"Did you hear me, Karalay?"

"I do not know what to do." Her voice shook.

"You will know. You are a Ward, you must do this. Or I will have a far greater chore . . ."

Karalay was swimming in his amber eyes. They were bright and fiery, the color of a fierce sunset.

Her stomach turned and her face paled. "You would kill me because I am the only reason he is not a Darkhalk?"

He said, "We need our lead Darkhalk."

She hurried out of the room, ran out of the basement and past the guards that called out when they saw her distraught face. She ran until her lungs burned and she reached the bottom step of the tower. She went up. Up until the sweat from her exertion stung her eyes.

Karalay stumbled, her tired legs not lifting high enough, toe caught on the edge of one of the last steps. She landed hard and burst into sobs.

She was a lone figure, a floor away from the great, last Crystal shard, whose power she had felt every waking moment in this wretched place.

2

On the sill of the tallest window, dust moved. It shifted from one edge to the other, then dropped to the floor. A little stone kicked, tumbled down, one, two, three steps. Skipped off the edge and landed in the library with a tink. Rolled along toward the lady with her head down on the last step before being left behind.

She lifted her head when she heard that howling sound. Her tears swept off her cheeks, her hair flew out of her eyes. She breathed in the smell of fall from outside, dying leaves, the blooming last of the wild flowers. She scrambled up the wall to her feet, up the steps. Her dress swayed, the coolness pushed up her legs, between her breasts, dried the sweat on her forehead.

She climbed until the light of day filled her face and covered her body. Karalay searched the room, window to window, until she saw the slit of light across the bottom of a door. She pushed it open.

The sun reflected from the copper roof. Karalay covered her eyes. She tentatively stepped out on the slanted metal. The door slammed shut, the gust swept up from behind her and lifted her feet off the roof. She reached out her arms, felt her hands held. She closed her eyes and stepped up, turned, twirled above the roof. Her stained dress filled, twisted and unwound in a sweep around her ankles. Her hair gathered, lifted up and was tossed from her face.

Karalay and the wind danced in long slow drifts until the sun headed toward noon and she was tentatively let down. She could see in her mind the arms around her waist. She could see the lips kiss her cheek. She could hear the laugh in the howl, the whisper that she was a wind child and she was loved.

Karalay took a breath and opened her eyes, stared out over the expanse of Diggamara and the empty roof.

She whispered, "Jaridd."

She closed her eyes. "Jaridd."

She gasped, "Jaridd."

She screamed, "Jaridd!"

She sat down on the ridge in the center of the roof and waited.

"Jaridd, I need you," she said.

327

Jaridd stepped out of the door behind her.

"Karalay!" he gasped. "Are you all right?"

"No. I am . . . I am all right."

"What is it?" He touched her shoulder.

She pulled away. "Jaridd, I need to speak with you."

He reached for her. "What is it?"

She stepped out of his reach. "You hid Telenay from me."

His blue eyes darkened. "What are you talking about?"

"Telenay was awake last night. You took me away from him before I saw."

"You should have—" He stopped himself.

She snapped, "What were you going to say? That I should have simply known . . . you are right. I am a Ward and I was blind last night. I let you take me away. Last night I did not think he would ever awaken. My job is the upholder of hope and I failed as a Healer and a Ward."

Karalay covered her mouth to hide the tears.

Jaridd said, "I do not know what to say."

She spat, "You failed me. You lied to me."

He looked to the north, his jaw muscles working.

She said, "You were right to hide him from me."

Jaridd glared at her. "What are you talking about now?"

"I love Telenay. He is the man for me, I—"

Jaridd cut her off, "You promised me!"

She did not look at him. "I am sorry, Jaridd."

The Darkhalk paced to the tower. His rage began to show. She moved her lips in the words she wanted to speak but did not say, *You know I am lying, just read my mind.*

The Darkhalk quivered. "I had known this would happen. I never should have trusted you!"

She covered her mouth to keep from screaming. *Read my mind, Jaridd! Read my heart! You are the only one for me. You know I am lying!* He stared into her eyes. She held back her will, held back from touching him. She waited for the sensation of him seeping into her, of him reading her.

Jaridd looked away. She saw his lips move.

Karalay gasped and rushed out to stop him.

The great black Cape appeared like smoke against the cloudless blue sky. It jumped between them.

"No!" she gasped.

The Cape leaped on Jaridd's back and the Darkhalk hit the copper with a jolt.

"Why did you not read my heart?" She screamed at him, "Jaridd, how could you do this! You knew I was lying!"

His figure did not move; the Cape covered his face and body from all light. He masked his face and gloved his hands. His movements became eternally deliberate. He stood and called on the Sword and it jumped from the sheath on his back. The great black beast slipped between his fingers.

Her mouth twisted. "Who is the betrayer now, Jaridd? Who is the liar now? I thought you loved me!"

The Darkhalk slipped into the tower and she stared at the shut door.

"All you had to do was read my heart. It was right here." Her trembling fingers slipped down the splintered wood. She covered her face. She stood as still as she could, afraid any movement might spring forth her grief. Karalay held herself tight.

3

The echo of a bright horn blew across the rooftops.

Karalay snapped up and stepped away from the tower. The horn blew a second time from the forest on the other side of the black water. It was a long, cheerful wail that cut the air. She jerked as a second horn answered and lifted into a scream from the tower behind her. It vibrated across the city before blowing again.

Across the river the thrum of wings grew into a thunder. From the trees rose an army garbed in jade armor. They came in a horde, flying side by side, twenty across and many deep. The river water trembled beneath them. They lifted above the buildings like wind. Her dress snapped back as they swept overhead and she was surrounded by the thunderous thumping of their wings. The Fai army entered Diggamara; no power of the river stopped them.

Karalay sprinted back to the tower. Cousai and Sicilia stood at a window, cloaks cast on a sill, no longer hiding the wings that fell to their knees. In Sicilia's hand was a horn.

Sicilia looked back at her. "Healer, a new King Ward has been called."

Cousai looked on with sad grimness.

Sicilia kept talking at Karalay. "You are strong to do what you did. You did the right thing. This war will need its lead Darkhalk. It is amazing—" Sicilia continued. "How their addiction of the Cape is so strong that even Jaridd, in love, would choose it over you."

"Sicilia," Cousai snapped. "There is no need to rub salt in wounds."

Sicilia turned her fierceness on her sister. "But it is incredible, Cousai. I have never before witnessed such power. He truly loved the Cape more than he loved her. What a remarkable power—"

Cousai glared. "That is enough."

"But do you not agree?"

They watched the Fai sweep into the city and the people of Diggamara run in fear and confusion. Karalay sat on a windowsill and let the north wind run her cold and finally numb her from the salty build-up behind her eyes.

She whispered, "Osondrous, you are now our queen."

Sicilia overheard her. "I suppose that probably upsets you."

Cousai glared at her sister.

Karalay said, "I have no love for a Warlord leading my people."

"Then why are you not leading your people?"

Cousai hissed, "Sicilia, there is a war coming. Must you?"

Sicilia blinked uncomprehendingly at her sister.

Karalay said, "Because I abandoned my people for disgusting, selfish reasons and the truth is that young, stupid little Warlord whore is more fit to rule than I am."

Sicilia took a leap and was gone out the window without seeming to have heard her.

Cousai sighed. "You are stronger than you may think, Healer, or your faith has no bounds that you were so able to do what was right today."

Karalay looked upon the city as Sicilia's Fai soldiers vanished beneath the roof tops.

"They must hide," Cousai said.

Karalay frowned but, before she could speak, she was silenced by the sudden roar. They turned and from the east came the real bulk of the Fai army.

"And here come the martyrs." Cousai's mouth was tight.

The sun was blotted out before them as the horde crossed over the city. At a distance, the army was a storm. Above them, it was a machine of war flying high and swift.

Karalay asked, "How long will it take them to reach the Draegoone?"

"They will fly about the same speed. They will meet midway."

"Over the castle?"

"Probably."

They watched in silence as the army passed.

330

"Just thrown away?" Karalay gasped.

Cousai nodded. "If they do not die in battle, they will be expected to die by their own swords. If they return alive, they will be executed."

Karalay said, "I do not know if what I did today will matter. It may very well be that we are all going to die tonight."

"Most of us." Cousai's gray eyes reflected nothing in the sky or along the horizon.

Karalay said, "I am sorry."

"You need not be. Our lives go as they go. There is nothing that can be done. I will meet Tarrick in the field of reeds. Much will be put to rest today. Many will die for old feuds. I do not think there will be a soldier flying today of my people who will actually know why they need be dying, except the soldiers here, of course. How was it that Jaridd uprooted you from your quiet castle to bring you here?"

"Maybe he knew they would need a Healer here. Maybe he just wanted me. I really just made him bring me." Karalay leaned against the cold stone.

Cousai picked up her cloak. "Here, wrap this around your shoulders."

Karalay accepted it and wrapped it around herself. "Thank you."

Cousai said, "But why did you come?"

"I was lonely," Karalay snorted. "How well ruled the Humans are. A Ward moves on her own pathetic needs."

The Fai did not look at her nor respond. She tilted her head to the sound of steps beneath them.

Karalay pushed out her will and read the minds of those coming for her. The steps brought faces up over the edge of the steel floor. Three Diggamaran soldiers. The man in the front wore a silver shoulder guard with a sail carved into it. He was the general.

Karalay stepped forward to meet them.

The general looked at her. "You are the Ward?"

"Yes."

"I have orders to arrest you."

The two other soldiers began at her.

Cousai stepped forward. "Who gave you these orders?"

The general focused on Cousai for the first time; his eyes widened at the sight of her wings. "You are Fai?"

"Why is this of concern to you?"

He growled, "The Fai are trespassing!"

Cousai's eyes narrowed. "When did Diggamara become private

331

ground?"

He pointed at Karalay. "You are coming with me."

Karalay spoke softly. "Soldier, if you feel that by following orders you are doing what is right here, then you have been lied to. If you take me away, there will be no Healer for this war tonight."

Cousai stepped between them. "Whose orders are you following?"

"The king demands she come and be questioned."

Cousai said, "This Healer will be busy all night. Call on her tomorrow."

The man looked close at Karalay. "What is happening?"

She read his mind. "Your name is Gidon. You are the general here." She spoke into his mind. *Gidon, do not do this.*

He said, "I cannot just ignore orders."

Karalay said, "You and all of your soldiers will be needed tonight. Your king believes this Crystal is in no danger and no harm is coming but I tell you that war is on your doorstep and it will be for this Crystal shard. If it is lost . . . "

"But who is this enemy?"

Cousai's hand rested on the hilt of her sword. "Grim is your enemy, Soldier. Grim already holds two of the three Crystal shards."

The general snorted. "Grim? The myth?"

"It is too late to still believe him a myth, General." Cousai said, "Tell your king you could not find Karalay. The Fai are here to fight for your lives, to protect Diggamara. If I were you, I would send my soldiers to help build the roadblocks and evacuate the villagers to the south."

The general eyed the Fai skeptically.

Karalay rested her hand on the side of Cousai's arm and stepped around her. "General, please."

He shook his head. "I must follow my orders."

Karalay said, "I know the heart of the Diggamara people is not to lie down and pretend a war is not coming. Do you know the power of the three Crystal shards?"

He nodded.

"You know they control the rivers? You know they divide the land?"

"Of course, Ward. But . . . how come the Fai crossed the river today?"

Karalay said, "A new King Ward has been called. For an entire day the Crystal shards and the rivers will be weak, the rivers can be crossed, the Crystal shards could be taken by a new master. And then, those three can be made whole again."

"You say Grim has two?"

332

"That is right. You must believe us. You have seen the shrinking shadow of Addilade. The great forest has fallen, the Elves there have been lost and you know the great power of the Elves."

The general stared to the north.

"If the Elves could be lost. . ." He paused. "Then how could Humans survive?"

Cousai glared. "We are not all Humans, General. And the last of the Darkhalks are here to fight."

The General squinted hard at Karalay. He shook his head and gave motion to the soldiers beside him. The two men stepped forward, snatching at Karalay's arms.

In a blink Cousai held the tip of a sword to the general's neck. "Take that order back."

Karalay cried, "No! There will be too much blood today, Cousai. They will need me eventually and they cannot hurt me. I am a Ward of high power. I will not let them."

Cousai's eyes narrowed but she made no move when the general stepped back from her blade. Karalay let them take her down. The general kept to their backs and there were no words, no motions, no actions of any kind exchanged. She held her breath when they reached the chamber door of the king.

4

She read the minds of the men around her. They were shifting nervously. The general opened the door and guided her away from his soldiers, dismissing them. The king sat, leaning against his throne. The huge room was full of his sick rage. She read into his mind without tact or reservation, remembering what Jaridd said.

She demanded, "On what grounds do you feel you can arrest me?"

The king hefted himself to his feet. He raised his fist and it boomed onto the throne. "I want respect!"

His eyes bulged. He got up and moved quickly toward her, raised his finger and shook it between her eyes. "You little sneak, I know why you are here. You are treacherous. You are a liar! You came here to uproot me!"

The king's mind was a boiling black sea. In it she saw the corpse of his brother, the real king, knocking around in freezing waters. The veins across the king's forehead bulged like blue rivers. He leered over her. She stepped back until she bumped into the general. She saw it in the back of the king's mind, in his darkest place. His younger self, with his fat shaking and sheening with sweat, as he carefully slipped the poison into his eldest brother's drink.

The king's mouth hung open. "You ugly, wretched sneak! Did you think I would not know? I have called my advisers here; we will take you to our dungeons. No one will hear you, no one will know. We will do away with snitches like you just like we did away with my big brother!"

The general beside her gasped. He pulled her back. She saw a flash in the general's mind of him finding his beloved king, blue and bleeding out. They had never found out who had committed the murder.

The general shook in outrage and put himself between her and the king.

The king stared in shock. He raised his finger and pointed directly into the general's face. "You will not get in my way, Gidon. She will not take away my crown. I earned this crown."

The two advisers of the king entered and stared. Dind had not come or had not been called. Her stomach tipped in disappointment.

The king snapped around. "You are here to see the demise of this sneak. She calls herself a Ward. She is trying to take my crown!"

The general reached for his sword.

The advisers' faces darkened and the eldest spoke at her. "That is why you came here? To hide behind a ruse and try to take our king away?"

She held her will back, not wanting to waste her strength.

The king unleashed a sword. "Gidon, you will now move!"

The general backed her up with long deliberate strides. She worked her way down the wall, glancing frantically around for a door. The advisers drew their weapons and moved on them.

The king held up his sword. "This is my crown!"

Karalay gasped, hands flat out on the walls of the corner behind her.

The king bellowed at his general, "I thought you were loyal!"

The general growled, "Your brother was my king. I loved him. This is my Ward. This is your Ward! You should bow to her!"

"You will die for her!" The king raised his sword and the advisers hunkered low.

Dind ran into the room. He held a long sword and Karalay stared at its bloody tip, jutting out of the king's chest. The advisers stepped back in shock.

Dind held their king erect for a moment, taking pleasure in the sensation. He released the king with a long stream of blood. The king fell and his crown clattered across the stone.

The advisers lunged at him, daggers held high. Dind moved down, cutting up and the general moved out, cutting through. Karalay covered her face. They let the bodies down gently and used their backs to clean their swords.

"Karalay," Dind said.

She lifted her eyes over the edges of her fingers.

The once Darkhalk held out his hand. "We must hurry."

She took his hand and carefully stepped around the body of the king.

The general whispered as she passed him, "I am sorry."

Dind said, "Gidon, rally your men, aid the Fai in the roadblocks and start evacuating the Diggamaran people."

Karalay paused only to pick up the fallen crown.

5

Sicilia stood in the royal dining room of Diggamara. Gone were the dishes and feasts of the king. Dind and Cousai stood beside the Diggamara general and his highest ranking soldiers. Sicilia's own general stood at her elbow with her sergeants standing around the table, leaning over the high-backed chairs to see Sicilia's map of the city.

"There are five streets leading into the palace. Each of the five roadblocks have been constructed and our archers stand ready. Does anyone know where the Darkhalks are?"

The leader of the Darkhalks entered with her words. Jaridd stepped in, his Cape still despite his moving, untouched by any kind of wind. When they looked at the black leather covering his face, their hearts stuttered. As the leader of the Darkhalks, he was the most powerful thing in the room and he said nothing.

Sicilia said, "We have done all we can. The roadblocks will hold."

The Darkhalk said, "We will know tonight if they will hold."

"What do you think we are up against?" the general of Diggamara asked.

Jaridd said, "The entire population of Elves in Addilade."

A reflective gasp echoed around the room.

"How?" Sicilia's voice was bound tightly.

"Grim's Reapers are controlling them."

335

The Diggamara general said, "But the Elves are dead?"

"Yes."

The room filled with murmurs and glances of dread batted across the table and over shoulders.

Sicilia's voice stilled the room. "Is that all we are up against?"

"We shall see." The leader of the Darkhalks left.

Sicilia snapped, "That is all Jaridd has to say?"

Dind shook his head at her. "Darkhalks do not waste time."

Their conversation blurred into a litany of stressed voices.

"Will they have weaponry?"

"We have no way of knowing that."

"It is likely they will."

"We will need strong stomachs tonight."

"How is it that such a powerful race can be utterly destroyed?"

"We will know tonight."

Karalay stood at the doorway, staring after Jaridd. She heard the words behind her. Each one a soldier's voice, male or female. They all sounded the same to her.

"Karalay," Dind said from beside her.

Her head snapped up.

He said, "You, Cousai and Sicilia will be in the tower, guarding the Crystal."

She said, "No. You will need a Healer on the ground."

Dind shook his head. "It will not matter tonight." His eyes were sad and hard.

She pushed her will into him. *You do not think there is hope?*

One Healer will not help us enough tonight.

Sicilia commanded Cousai, "Go now. Take the Healer with you."

Karalay dutifully followed Cousai out and they made the trip up the long, spiral staircase. They saw no guards and no servants. The Diggamara palace was deserted.

They stepped past the Crystal and to the tower windows. The wind had died down.

People looked like insects. File by file, step by hurried step. Farmers and wives and children. The huge fishing ships of Diggamara ferried people south, down the black river, to the closest town. The soldiers of Diggamara ordered all possessions left behind except food and water. Farmers carried lambs over their laps on horseback as they evacuated their herds and the smallest babes were not old enough to keep up. Those stragglers picked up their strides when the shadow of Addilade seemed to reappear and the darkness began to take shape.

The Fai emptied the buildings surrounding the palace. They had ripped out doors, shutters, tables; anything made of wood they brought to the streets and piled and tied into the roadblocks. Above the roadblocks, the archers laid out their arrows in long stacks.

It was sunset and the clouds were gray and low when the Humans reported that the city had been emptied. The last full fishing ships headed south.

"Half a day," Cousai murmured.

"What?"

The Fai looked at her. "It is nearing sunset, Karalay. The clearing of this great city began just half a day ago and it is already empty. That is impressive."

"What is impressive is that the Diggamarans never asked what their king thought."

"You think many had already left?"

"Yes."

Cousai's gray eyes were the color of the sunset. She gazed at it, as though keeping her face turned away from the north would make her strong.

"Cousai?" Karalay stood beside her.

"Yes."

"You are thinking of him?"

Cousai chuckled. "I am always thinking of him."

"Tell me of him."

Cousai smiled a little. "He was always too good to me. Right now he would look at me and tell me that nothing can touch us. And I would believe him."

A tear trembled down Cousai's cheek and she left it until it either sank in or the breeze blew it away. Karalay touched her hand.

Cousai said, "Tarrick spoke in his dreams."

"Did he?"

The Fai nodded. "He spoke every night, all night sometimes. You could sit and listen to prophecies spoken over the forked tongue of a dragon ancestor. He would remember so little and cling to those memories. It was a never-ending cycle. I was tempted to tell him once that I heard him—I knew he had asked of my fate."

Karalay looked close at the Fai. "You know your own fate?"

Cousai smiled and tears spilled out of the corners of her eyes to round her cheeks. "It is the prophet's duty to know and to do nothing. He never spoke of it, never told me that Diggamara would be my grave, Karalay. That is how I know he knew for sure. If word reaches him that I am here, I hope he comes to save me. But I hope he does not. I hope he remains true to being a prophet, that he does nothing. He must let me live out this fate here . . . and I must let him live out his fate there. It makes sense now, why he went to his mother queen to fly and die. He knew he could not save me."

Karalay longed to touch the Fai, to seep into her and comfort her. She held herself to quell the urge. She understood that Cousai needed to be left standing alone in the cold wind. And so did she.

6

It was nearing nightfall. The clouds cleared out. In the circle of roofs that surrounded the palace, the Fai's torches blazed and whipped. The moon was rising on the horizon and cast white light across the city.

"Find a way to appreciate the sky or the cold night will kill you," Cousai said as though speaking the verse of a song.

Karalay looked at her.

"Do you know who said that?" Cousai asked her.

"No, who said it?"

"When your great Human warriors destroyed the Keltch, my people heard rumors from Diggamara. They were described as the cold on a clear night, barely tolerable until you see the vastness of the sky. They were a truly grotesque bunch. But they ended such a vile race. They created greatness."

"Osondrous and Telenay? Grotesque?"

"Oh, yes. When they were seen . . . it was after Cobblestone. Do you know what came to pass for them there?"

Karalay frowned at the mention of that place.

"No," a voice spoke from behind them.

They jerked and turned.

Sicilia stepped up the stairs. "No, I do not think anyone will know of that day and those Humans. I do not think anyone should know."

Karalay said, "Why?"

Sicilia glared at her. "I have traveled through the field of Cobblestone and what came to pass there . . . Some scars should not ever come to light."

Cousai did not look at her sister; her eyes were seriously in the north.

"Something is coming," Sicilia said.

"Yes." Cousai nodded. "It can be seen."

Karalay squinted past Diggamara's last houses and there was a shadow as wide as the city, where the forest should have been. Her heart quickened.

She gasped, "Sicilia?"

Both Fai stared at her.

"Why are you helping us?"

The two sisters stared at her until Sicilia's eyes fell to the floor and she leaned against the side of the window. The sound of the wind whistled above them. They watched as the blackness took shape.

Sicilia sighed. "It will all be over soon. My stupid father . . ."

Karalay waited for her to continue.

Sicilia sighed. "I want you to remember something for me, Karalay. Something that happened a long time ago and it is the great mystery of the fate of Lionel."

Karalay's face drained of color.

A wrinkle of pain split Sicilia's brow. "I was a warrior once of great power. The royal Fai ancestors favored me when it came to the degree of royal power that I was born with. It was great. I was great. When the Five Hundred Year War came, when we began the fight against the Draegoone, I became a general of my people. My father was king and I was unbeatable."

Sicilia's eyes never left the northern horizon, her voice did not waver. "I took thousands of lives over you Humans . . . but I had an acquaintance among the Humans. Your great Lionel, not revered back then, he was nothing to your people, powerful as he was, nothing but an old man. One night I visited him and he was full of fear for you Humans. He was devastated over our war. Your Lionel told me that I would fetch a Crystal from our most sacred mountain and give it to him with my power."

Sicilia chuckled, looked at Karalay. "You may imagine how I ignored him and forgot about such a ridiculous statement. But, then I began having dreams and I began to realize that there was a plan to end my father's war and it required the great power held inside of me, my people's ancestral power. My birthright power. The dreams intensified. Until. Until I fetched the Crystal and I gave it my power.

"My father was a great Fai, the greatest of Fai. But he was power-

339

hungry, he was blood-thirsty, he wanted everything destroyed that he could not have. I was his daughter, I was his general. I told him what I had done and what I was going to give to Lionel. I betrayed your old King."

Sicilia bowed her head. "My father did not punish me. He hated Lionel. He hated anyone who did not want his war as much as he did. He bastarded that Crystal and I took it to Lionel."

Sicilia's eyes wavered. "I took it to Lionel and he took the Crystal and I hid. I waited for him to use it and when he did—he used it and the two rivers emerged. The war ended and it happened. My father did something crueler than I could have ever imagined. The Crystal broke with the impact of the curse and it pierced that old Human. Things happened to Lionel's body, to his life, that were not natural and he became something else."

Sicilia looked at Karalay. "Lionel became Grim that day. In a split second, he was no longer Human or anything that ever existed. Your great Lionel was absolutely destroyed. I was only able to recover two shards of that Crystal. Grim got one and he was just gone."

Karalay found her voice. "And if he recovers all three Crystal shards?"

"I do not know."

"He could destroy us all?"

"I think his heart bleeds for revenge. I fear for my people. I even fear for your people."

Karalay whispered, "But Lionel was a great man."

"It is as it is. I am the only witness to the depth of my father's wickedness."

Cousai's eyes never left the north.

Karalay said, "But if the Crystal shard is destroyed?"

"If we destroy one, the others will shatter and Grim will die, too. They created him."

"But then the rivers fall and that could mean the war between the Fai and the Draegoone may commence?"

Cousai shook her head. "It may mean worse things than that, Karalay. Tarrick told me of the great masses the Vamepires have grown. They have become more powerful than the Humans. The Draegoone themselves have been slowly losing ground to them for years."

"Then we must kill an immortal for things to remain?" Karalay stared at them.

Sicilia said, "I will kill Grim at the end of this battle. This night will be the last that I see. It will be a good end and I can go to the reeds and say that I am worthy."

Karalay shook her head. "How did Grim ever get the second Crystal from you?"

Sicilia laughed, "I was a stupid girl once, too."

Cousai stepped over to Karalay. "Sicilia trusted a Human to protect one of the Crystal shards and he betrayed her. He is one of Grim's Reapers now."

Karalay stared out the window. Cousai stood beside her and they watched the night grow darker.

7

It came portraying the rainbow of colors in long deep and seeping, rotten skin. It came with the smell of flesh having been left to bloat and go black in the sunlight. It came all around them in a swath of horror that reached as far as they could see. Their mouths hung open, though they uttered nothing. The only sound was of their soft, ever-forward progress. Their hands clutched swords, spears, broken bones, anything. They walked so close together that they were a river of rotten flesh.

The Fai lined up around the roof edges of each building that shouldered the five blocked roads. The Elves entered the city streets, twenty blocks from the palace.

"Brace yourselves," Sicilia murmured.

The Fai soldiers each pulled arrows into their huge bows.

Horns stood poised in the hands of the Fai positioned at the farthest accurate distance that the archers could fire. The army spilled into each of the five streets, rounding the city, surrounding them.

The Fai readjusted their arrows, wiped their palms of sweat as the Elves began to descend upon them.

Nine blocks.

Eight blocks.

Seven blocks.

Karalay pressed out her will. "Let no harm come to us today."

Six blocks.

Five blocks.

"Steady their arrows, give them strength."

Four blocks.

The horns, one after the other, sounded as the Elves stepped into range.

Three blocks.

Karalay whispered. "There are thousands of them. There are children."

Cousai clasped her hand. "Do not despair."

The sound of the arrows cast. They flew straight up to their full height, then their tips turned down and the arrows began to fall. They picked up speed and were direct when they hit.

The Elves walked on.

Sicilia gasped, "How can this be?"

The Fai soldiers fired again. The Elf army continued on, arrows sticking out of them. Sicilia raced from window to window, scanning all five streets, hearing the cries of her soldiers.

The Fai general dropped into the tower. "What do we do?"

Sicilia screamed, "Keep them firing!"

Two blocks.

The general gasped, "We will run out of arrows. Then what?"

Sicilia grabbed her general by the neck. "You keep them firing!"

The Elves reached the roadblocks.

Cousai and Karalay gasped and whipped around at the sound of metal meeting metal.

"What are you doing?" Cousai screamed.

"Help me!" Sicilia snapped, "We must get this shard into a position where it can be easily destroyed!"

"We have not lost yet!" Cousai pulled her sister back.

Sicilia threw her off. "There are too many!"

Cousai stared into her sister's eyes, then nodded and unsheathed her own sword. The two Fai began hacking at the metal bud.

Karalay cried, "No! Wait. You must wait!"

Cousai looked at her. "We must be prepared for this."

A cheer rose outside.

Karalay raced to the window. "Jaridd!" she cheered.

Behind the barricades, the Darkhalks stood with their swords drawn. Behind them the bulk of the Diggamaran army, every soldier, every guard stood at the ready.

Karalay gasped, "The Darkhalks have come! Do not destroy it yet!"

Sicilia said, "Both of you, help me."

Cousai said, "Help us get it open. We need to be ready." She handed Karalay her sword and pulled another from her back. Sicilia and Cousai jammed their blades into the metal bracing and with the first cut, they stumbled back from the light. It pierced out like a beacon, so bright it was physically tangible. Not hot, but skin-numbingly cold. Sicilia grabbed the cut metal and threw her weight back.

Slowly it began to tear free.

Cousai joined her sister, pulled at the other side. The Fai rested, then pulled again, feet braced at the bottom, heads back, arms stretched. Karalay grabbed the metal corner and they strained, eyes squeezed shut, the metal cutting into their palms.

The bud ripped with a steady groan and they pushed the metal to the floor.

Sitting in a bed of steel, the Crystal was a broken shard with an edge sharper than any sword. From within it, the light poured out of the tower and reflected from all of Diggamara's copper roofs.

A warped form of daylight fell upon the dead armies.

Sicilia sat on her heels awash in the light. Her haggard face, stretched from lack of sleep, food and readiness for death, looked suddenly beautiful. The once queen of the Fai reached out to touch it, her head tipped, entranced.

"Sicilia," Cousai cautioned.

Sicilia laughed; it was a sick sound. "Do not worry, Sister. It is mine. My great birthright power, that I gave away for a stupid Human. Oh, I have missed it . . . I know it must recognize me—"

Cousai said, "It is also the great wicked our father cursed Lionel with."

Sicilia's hand fell; she brought it to her chest in a fist.

The general of the Fai smacked into the window. "We are taking some of them down at the gates!"

Sicilia jerked up and ran to the closest window.

Karalay stared at the fourth gate and she could see the Elves had begun to finally fall at the onslaught of the Fai arrows. The Elves behind them continued walking on. When they reached the bodies, they began to climb.

Sicilia screamed out the window, "Stop!"

The Fai general swept back. "We are taking them down!"

"You are creating a ramp!" Sicilia pointed. "Stop them!"

Cousai and Karalay began circling the tower, window to window, speechless as they stared. The Elves at the gates began climbing, then collapsing and the Elves behind them stretched back for miles, pushing.

The Fai soldiers stopped firing, mouths open, devastated.

"What do we do?" The cries rang from the roof tops.

"Sicilia!" the general ranted. "What are your orders?"

The once queen of the Fai took a step back from the window and she turned on the Crystal.

"Not yet, Sicilia!" Cousai grabbed her sister's wrist.

Sicilia did not shake her off. "What else would you have me do?"

Cousai's mouth set in a fine line. "I think you should burn them."

The light of the Crystal lit Sicilia's eyes like stars. She ran back to the window. "Dump the oils! Light your arrows. Burn them all!"

The Fai began to fly in surges, fetching all the oil in all of the palace in all that they had brought for timber and the drenching began. Lit arrows were shot through the sky. Rivers of fire surrounded them and the sky filled with black smoke.

A smell began to rise.

The stink of dead flesh burning, the sickening sweet smell of rotten sap on fire. Karalay and Sicilia, their eyes watering from the smoke, stared at the gate with the Elves nearly up to its very height.

"Do not destroy that Crystal," Karalay urged. "Not yet. Not yet."

They covered their faces against the stench. The Elves suddenly turned around. Sicilia gasped. The Elves switched directions. They headed away from the west gate, back up the street.

"They are retreating!" Sicilia cried.

Cousai screamed. They raced to her side of the tower.

The general of the Fai sounded a horn. "They have breached the southern gate!"

The fire-backed Elves spilled over the roadblock toward the two Darkhalks standing with a horde of Diggamara men behind them. Elves turned around, headed for the southern gate and pushed until a dozen fell over it at a time. The Fai frantically lit their arrows, flying overhead, shooting their fire down.

The Darkhalks raced for the southern gate and they attacked first, hacking away as the bodies came at them.

8
Osondrous

Their nostrils filled with the smell of dragons. Their ears having heard the sound of war, the Warbreds screamed from their stalls.

"My queen?" The lead servant of the stable hands bowed to her. "The Warbreds need a place to run."

The graves were full, the last remainder of war was buried. Osondrous closed off the cemetery and the horses ran between the gravestones. She stood with Eikian on the parapet, watching it all.

344

"The Wards down to one, and you crown me. How ironic." Osondrous fiddled with the bandages around her hands.

"As though you needed more scars." Eikian leaned on the parapet wall.

"It will be a good day when our horses are taken to the new castle. They will have paddocks and green grass."

Led by a stable hand with a gold chain, Willan limped onto the turf. He was ignored by the frolicking others. The stable hand unclipped the lead. Willan dropped his head and stepped forward to nose the vanilla around the stones.

She said, "When are they leaving?"

Eikian sighed. "Right now."

"You knew already."

"Prush told me."

"I thought as much." She shook her head, had yet to look at him. "The rioting in Kamamine?"

"We did not give them time to rally. We killed anyone who stood against your decision to change the law. Most of them just scattered. No longer can a Centaur be charged any differently than a man in trial. All laws treat them as equals now."

She said, "Eli is staying, at least. You should not sound so glum."

"Something about this is not right." Eikian stared at the back of her head.

She snapped. "I'm sure you would have enjoyed cutting off Eli's head."

The horses powered around the graves, leaping and snapping at each other.

Eikian said, "Constance is missing."

"Missing?"

"Do you want me to send out a party to find her?"

Willan wandered to Aerick's grave and lifted his head when he found a long stemmed chamomile flower, its petals still new. The horse chewed on it, throwing his nose to get it down.

Osondrous said, "No."

As they stood in silence, the line of Centaurs began around the castle. Four across, marching solemnly past. Their faces were set. Their hoof steps stomped the ground and created a vibration that everyone felt.

"You should have gone with them," she said.

He glared at her. "I suppose you would rather I had just left."

She walked away, rounded the graveyard, not looking down on all the fresh graves, not looking out at the line of Centaurs she would never command again. The castle walls closed the sound of marching out and her chamber was quiet.

9

Osondrous unwrapped her hands and stared at her perfect, unscarred palms. The cuts made there by the dagger to bind her to the Crystal shards had disappeared three days earlier on the tenth of Qalin. She had told no one. Osondrous feared she would no longer be considered queen, as though the Crystals denied her. She had sent her fastest horses and riders to the rivers. She needed to know if the Crystal shards still held power or if something terrible had come to pass. She had still heard no word of the riders sent for Jezaline.

She walked down the empty halls to Majeik's chamber. Soup had been brought for him and was sitting on his bedside table. Osondrous picked up the bowl and stirred the hot dragon broth.

Majeik opened his eyes. "Constance?"

"She is gone."

"Gone? Where?"

"No one knows. Here, eat." She offered him a spoonful.

His face filled with worry. "She said nothing to me."

"Majeik, it has been four days. How much have you been awake?"

He grimaced.

She said, "You need your rest."

"Why do you come to me?"

"You are the only Second I have left, Majeik. All of the rest are dead or gone. The whole floor is empty. I am the last Ward. That whole floor is empty."

Osondrous stirred his soup, fed him.

He said, "You should rest too."

"They brought you bread." She offered it to him.

"Thank you." Majeik ate his bread and the rest of his soup.

"Where could she have gone?"

"Constance?"

"She said she would come to be . . . be with me."

"Maybe you scared her away." Osondrous set up the empty bowl.

"No, she—I do not know."

She sighed, looked the Second in his dark eyes. "Majeik, she is not your

346

worry. You leave that girl be, let her die wherever she is, or live."

"You are not going to mark her a traitor?"

"No."

He touched the tail of her sleeve. "Thank you."

Osondrous fed his fire and closed his shutters as the sun turned over to face his windows. Majeik was snoring when she left.

The castle was quiet. Those men that were the most hurt had either died or recovered enough that few needed constant care. There was less to worry about. Food remained bountiful. The dragons were full of fat and strength and they had enough to feed her armies for months. She had already traded some of it for extra honey, cheese, brandy, oats, alfalfa, deer, goat, apples and dried grapes. A variety of other fruits would be sent green to ripen when it reached the castle from Willower and Diggamara. There were rumors of Diggamara having gone under siege but she had received no absolute reports.

Her soldiers had picked up a dead messenger that had been sent from Diggamara from a Darkhalk. She knew he had been sent by the Darkhalks only because the leather he held was ripped from the black leathers only the Darkhalks wore. Inside the leather was parchment and on it had been written something of great importance, she guessed only because the Darkhalks never sent messengers. The parchment had been saturated with rain and dew until it was unreadable. The messenger had lost his mount at some point and eventually had frozen to death in the Barbaka fields. Tragically, he had fallen only just out of earshot of a road and had died long before he had been found.

She unwrapped her foot and soaked it for a time, sitting on the edge of her basin. The pain of the joint eased from the heat and she got into bed. Her ankle and foot were green and blue from bruises. The many other punctures that the right side of her body had sustained itched from their stitches. Osondrous lay out flat on her back and closed her eyes.

She slept hard.

It was afternoon and a silver fall day when she got out of bed and got herself dressed. Osondrous combed out her hair and braided it. She bandaged her foot.

Someone knocked. She called them in.

A guard bowed to her and said, "The Human reinforcements from Rayakdool have arrived."

"Why are you telling me this? I am a queen now. Go tell the Warlord Eikian."

"Noran is with them."

She stared in surprise. "Well, where is he?"

"The graveyard."

She limped out the door in a hurry.

The castle was still and the graveyard was even more so. Noran was looking down. His tail, in a set of many braids tied with beads, clacked in the wind. He had washed out of his warpaint to come to the castle.

"Noran?"

"Do you know where they buried Cray?"

She said, "Yes."

They walked across the yard and she counted down a line of stones to find Cray. Noran stepped up beside his brother, laid his hand on the blank gravestone.

She said, "I wanted to—"

"I know," Noran sighed.

"Who is handling the training while you are here?"

"The Centaur Seconds with me stayed. They can handle it."

"All of ours left."

He looked up. "Even Eli and Prush?"

"Eli stayed. A girl of his is a servant here now. Prush went."

She touched Cray's gravestone beside Noran's big hand.

Noran said, "They will come back."

"I hope that you are right."

"We stayed for a reason. They will come back for the same reason."

"You had to stay."

"I would have stayed anyway."

They looked at each other.

"Come on," she said. "Come have a brandy with me."

They sat in the back of the kitchen and Osondrous fetched them two large mugs, filled to the brim. Shrae and the servants left them alone.

She said, "You are the first Centaur to see me gimping around and not offer me a ride."

"You are getting old if you would have accepted it."

"I did not say I would have accepted it."

They drank deeply and Noran murmured with contentment. "This is why I came back."

"You are right—I am getting old."

Noran leaned forward. "Where is Eikian?"

"We are in a phase."

"So you are not talking?"

"He did not agree to my releasing the Centaurs. . . among other things."

"It was not his decision."

"Did you see Prush on the road? Did you pass them?"

"I did not see Prush."

They finished their brandy and she filled the mugs again.

"If I drink that, I will need to stay the night."

"Then stay the night." She smiled.

Osondrous eased herself back on the stool, wincing.

The horns of her sentries sounded. Her head snapped up. They sounded again. Noran jumped to his feet. She hobbled at a sprint out of the kitchen, through the dining room.

They joined a host of men standing in the hall.

"Get out on the parapets!" Noran roared at the gawking Humans.

Eikian galloped down the outer parapet, stopped above the gate. Osondrous ran over the rope bridges, looked to the sky. She had a very subtle inkling of what was coming and, when she saw the mass of Fai, a great gray storm of hornets to the east, she screamed, "Do not fire! Do not fire! Do not fire! This is not our war! Put out the flags!"

Eikian echoed her. Noran yelled at the Humans up and down the parapets. Out of the tower windows flew the yellow flags of cease.

Eikian yelled, "What is happening?"

"It is the Draegoone and the Fai."

"How did they get across the rivers?"

She just looked into his dark eyes and shook her head. The implications left Eikian speechless. Noran stood beside her, big shield on his arm. They stood on the outer parapet, watching the west and the growing cloud of Draegoone that approached.

Their hearts began to race.

Noran said, "Maybe we should get all the men off the parapets."

She shook her head. "I am not certain we will not be attacked."

"But you are fighting wings again."

The storms approached and the sound of their wings reverberated the air. The Draegoone powered forward, massive leather pounding. The Fai were flat out on their bellies; their wings buzzed. Following them was a great shadow sweeping across the land. The sun was blotched out and an eerie gray darkness fell.

"Osondrous." Noran started twitching. "Osondrous!"

She yelled, "Take cover!"

The Humans dove into the courtyard, pressed themselves against the inner parapet walls. Noran grabbed her and galloped up the parapet. They reached the hall of silence as the sound approached a deafening roar. Eikian stood beside her, breathing hard.

They braced. All eyes stared into the skies.

The two powers collided with the sound of sheet lightning.

The bodies began to torrent down. Fai and Draegoone hit the parapets and splashed in the courtyard sand, sending blood and weapons flying.

She said, "Start digging the pits. Take the survivors to the dungeons."

Eikian was gone at a gallop, shield above his head.

Her soldiers kept low and fast, sprinting from body to body, checking for a heartbeat. Her men, four under each massive Draegoone, began bringing the still-breathing up the steps. There were not many.

"This is not going to take very long," Noran said.

Osondrous stepped to the edge of the hall and looked up into the entire heavens filled with war.

Noran said, "They are very good."

Osondrous shook her head. "Go help my soldiers, Noran."

She turned her back on it all.

She entered the dining room where servants were gathered.

She said, "All of you, anyone capable, I want the cells in the dungeons padded with blankets and pillows. I want a jug of water in each cell and bread. Is this clear?"

The servants nodded. Their faces were gray as they hurried to do her bidding. Osondrous limped out to the hall. In his arms, Noran held a Fai whose armor was bloodied, his wings cut to tatters.

"This one fell on me. He is alive."

She went to the dungeons and Osondrous helped prepare the cells. Noran laid the Fai down. Osondrous stripped the armor off the male. The largest of the Fai men were not much bigger than she was. Their bones were hollow, their wings delicate and opaque.

Soldiers brought the living Draegoone and the Fai as quickly as possible. She set the Implins to cleaning them and the servants to stitching their wounds. Noran and Eikian directed her Human soldiers in digging the pits. She sent men out on Warbreds to search for survivors. With no Healer, she called on all of the Restorers of Kamamine.

When she returned to the cells, a woman was crying hysterically. Implins and servants crowded around her.

"They are covered with scales! They are demons!"

The servant shook, her hands covered her mouth and face, fear slashed her eyes. Osondrous rushed forward and smacked the servant across the cheek. The woman hit the floor. The servants and Implins stepped back and stared.

She put out her hand. "All of you listen to me. I will have none of that tonight. These Draegoone and these Fai need care. You give them the best you know. Is that understood?"

The servants rushed back into the cells. None of the Draegoone or Fai had awakened yet. The Fai suffered the least from the fall. Their light bodies took the brunt like a leaf might falling from a tree. But the Draegoone did their damage and the death of Fai was, at first, more immediate.

"How many are down there?" Noran asked.

"Twenty-five or thirty each . . . if that." Osondrous crossed her arms over her chest. Leaning on a pillar, she watched her soldiers checking bodies.

Noran said, "What do you think they will say when they wake up?"

"I really do not know. You were there when we went to the Krept. The Draegoone are absolutely controlled by honor. I think this is their last act to finally wash the Five Hundred Year War from their ancestry. I think they may kill themselves if they do not die in battle."

The last Fai fell with darkness. The night came clear and warm.

Osondrous could see a few Draegoone soldiers still sweeping the skies, looking for an enemy. She sent out riders to collect the bodies and, most importantly, the weapons and armor on the bodies.

She worked her way back down into the dungeons. The servants' dresses were stained with the dark green blood of Draegoone and the crimson blood of the Fai. Their faces were grayer than they had ever been, now haggard with exhaustion. Few of the servants had yet entirely recovered their strength from the fight against the dragons. It showed starkly in the lines of their faces.

The dungeon was filled with the hefty smell of the dragon ancestors. Osondrous knew the Fai would wake enraged and she began locking their cells the minute her servants could do no more for them. Osondrous looked for familiarity among the Draegoone faces. One particular Draegoone caught her attention immediately. He wore the bronze armor of a leader, of royalty.

"Bring me Eikian," she ordered a servant.

The Draegoone was a shade of gray like a deep lake. He was muscled tremendously like all of the Draegoone. She looked close at his armor, lying in a mangled heap at the edge of the cell. It was absolutely royalty.

Eikian stepped in.

"Do you recognize this Draegoone?"

Eikian stepped closer. "He was wearing royal armor?"

"He had to have been the general."

"Kilikan was the general."

"It looks like him."

Eikian frowned.

She shook her head. "Was he not bigger? Much, much bigger?"

He nodded. "Kilikan was the biggest Draegoone I ever saw."

She motioned at the Draegoone in the bed. "This is not."

"This makes no sense. He has to be a prince."

"I thought Kilikan was the only prince."

"That is what we were told."

They frowned at each other.

Noran appeared at the open cell door. "Osondrous, there are Draegoone that want you."

She stepped by the Centaurs, hurried up to the hall.

She could hear their panting. They leaned on the pillars in the hall of silence. Half a dozen of her men gave them their space.

"Osondrous the Warlord?" one of them gasped, holding his side. Blood oozed out between his fingers and was pooling at his feet. Their wings were tattered but not disabled. Their faces and bodies were bloodied and much of their armor was dented or destroyed.

Osondrous got so close she could look right up, into his eyes. "I am Osondrous."

She held out her hand.

The Draegoone took it gently. "I remember you."

She said, "You need help."

He nodded meekly, his face down.

"I cannot treat you better than the Fai. I am sorry, I cannot afford it. I am offering you comfortable cells, water and food."

"Cells?" The Draegoone glanced at each other.

Her Humans shifted uncomfortably. Her Centaurs hovered over her back, arms crossed.

"For now," she said, "this is what I can offer." She lowered her voice and whispered, "No one need know we did not take you by force, like your brothers."

The Draegoone was failing, his face was drawn, the blood ran down his leg. "We will speak for each of ourselves. I must accept your help or I will die."

She motioned to her soldiers. "Help him!"

Eikian reached out, let the Draegoone lean on him and led him down.

The four other Draegoone watched, their faces long and heavy. They each nodded in turn and gimped after the others.

Osondrous said to them as they passed her, "I will need to speak with you."

They nodded wordlessly, heads down. The Implins and servants stepped back, covering their mouths, eyes wide open.

Osondrous snapped, "These Draegoone need water. Help them remove their armor! Help them lie down! Get them anything they need."

She followed the blood trail after the five. The one that had spoken first was in his cell, reaching to untie his armor, moaning.

"Wait." She went into his cell and pulled out her dagger and began cutting his armor off. The Draegoone tipped toward the cell bed, staring down at the soft, long surface.

"Wait—Wait—Wait!" she growled through clenched teeth, sawing through the leather ties. She cut off the armor over his back, shoulders, neck and chest. He teetered deliriously. She ripped off his leather vests and chain mail. He fell down on his back, gasping for air.

Eikian watched from the door. A servant brought her thread and a needle. The Draegoone was littered in wounds. The worst in his side pierced through his rib cage. Eikian held the wound to stop the bleeding. The Draegoone's eyes shut.

Osondrous said, "I want to look at those Fai weapons. We have nothing that could have pierced his armor."

"You are right." Eikian shook his head, inspecting the wound. "Look at how perfect it is. Clean through."

"One very sharp weapon."

"How did any of them live through this?"

She shook her head. "They were not supposed to."

Eikian murmured, "There are always survivors."

Osondrous washed the Draegoone's wounds, sewed them shut, left him with bread and water.

"Did you remove all of their armor and weapons?" Osondrous asked the servants in the hall.

The servants nodded.

"Take it all to the guardroom at the bottom of the staircase. If any of them start to wake, alarm me. Do not speak to them or open their cells until I am here. Is this understood?"

They all nodded.

An Implin tugged at her hand.

"Yes?" She looked down at him. He held up a steaming jug.

Osondrous smiled. "Thank you."

She went to the guardroom. The small chamber was larger than the cells. In one corner, two dusty chairs sat around an old table; in another corner the armor was piling up. The table was stacked with knives, daggers and swords.

Osondrous eased herself down, sticking her sore foot under the table.

The Draegoone weapons were generally big, heavy and sharp. They were an array of steels. The Fai weapons were small, shockingly light and like nothing she had ever seen before.

Eikian and Noran joined her. They stared at the Fai swords with concern.

"Diamonds forged in steel?" Noran muttered.

"Look, they just used them as the tips." She pointed.

Eikian stared close at them. "That could pierce anything."

Osondrous poked at a Draegoone chest plate lying on the floor beside her. The sword cut right through. "This is why the Fai have a chance."

"Superior weaponry."

"The Draegoone were carrying better than this when we were there."

Noran shook his head. "The Draegoone were not going to give their best swords to soldiers who were not returning."

Osondrous sipped her tea and leaned back. An Implin entered, gave each of the Centaurs a mug of steaming tea.

"I miss them." Noran smiled sadly after the Implin, cupping the mug in his hand.

She drank her tea. "It has been a long time since you were served."

"You are treating those Draegoone and Fai better than you treat us at Rayakdool." Noran laughed.

She sneered, "You are complaining at the wrong table, Noran."

Eikian glared at her. "He was not complaining. He was stating a fact."

"Do not scold me." Her voice darkened, she stood and her chair hit the floor.

Noran raised his hands for peace and she brushed by him, headed down the hall, passed the cells. Servants walked up and down, checking them. Osondrous raised the lock on the royal Draegoone's cell door.

He had not moved.

Beside his bed a bucket of water sat cold. The door closed behind her. She knelt down, touched the Draegoone's forehead, neck and chest. The dragon ancestors were used to cold mountain air. He was damp with heat. The Draegoone was panting hard in the back of his throat.

She wrung out the rag in the bucket and sopped the cold cloth over his forehead.

The Keltch campaign had driven them early on into the Krept, over the rocky ranges of wind. The Draegoone had offered them no aid, which was a relief: Telenay had considered them a threat. After months, they had managed to wipe every last western Keltch colony out of the Krept and Kilikan, the general of the Draegoone, had met with them in peace. She remembered his size being the most staggering about the Draegoone; he rose above all of his own soldiers.

This Draegoone had many of Kilikan's features, his skin coloring, everything except his mass. This was not Kilikan.

The Keltch campaigns never drove them into the East, the Fai having annihilated their own Keltch problems centuries before. Osondrous and Telenay feared that if the entire population across the land was not destroyed, the Keltch would simply repopulate. The Vamepire, as large a problem as they were for the Draegoone, did not interfere with the destruction of the Keltch either. Instead, they stayed well away from them. It surprised the Draegoone, but she had summarized that the Keltch were probably inedible to the Vamepire and they were as glad to see them gutted as everyone else.

The Draegoone's breathing softened. Osondrous drizzled cold water down his chest, avoiding his bandages.

"Osondrous?" Eikian murmured from the door.

"Leave me alone." She did not look up and he lingered only a moment before walking away. Every time she had been near him, he had professed his suspicions of her choice to become queen. They were not suspicions for her; she was certain now that Grim had received what he had wanted from her. She was terrified that becoming queen had somehow caused the ending of the rivers. She desperately wanted to talk to Eikian about it, but her shame silenced her.

There was no wind. The snow fell without urging; it glided without purpose or might. The trees were scraggly, some bare, others scattered with tough needles. Those few evergreens were so laden with snow that even their majesty was dejected to white ghosts. Jezaline squinted in the night, could make out the snow as it fell, could feel it on her cheeks. She could hear his breathing and each of Kilikan's deliberate steps.

Kilikan turned into the trees.

He whispered, "This is one of our most sacred hills. I asked him to meet us here."

"We will not be alone?"

"No, we have too much ground to travel and too little time."

The air was breathless. Jezaline opened her eyes wide to take in all of the trees. A glimpse of a starless sky peered through the evergreen canopies. Kilikan set her down, then stepped forward to what to her eyes was a large rock or hill, covered in snow.

Kilikan bowed down to the deep snow.

Jezaline held herself, shaking in the cold. She stared.

"Is that you, Kilikan?" A voice emerged from the dark.

"Gaiden, I am sorry to have needed you this morning."

"Kilikan, I am yours as you are mine."

Two eyes began to blink and their light illuminated the pre-dawn darkness. The eyes were bigger than most men's heads. They began to focus. The black slits inside narrowed and in their light, there began to emerge a faint outline of a head, a neck, a back. The head lifted from its place in the snow and raised regally like a snake rearing back to kill. He was long-snouted and his face was delicate and slender.

She was still under his scrutiny.

Gaiden said, "Why are you carrying a Human woman around?"

Kilikan's face broke into a wry smile as though he had gotten away with a deadly crime.

"Her name is Jezaline."

The dragon laughed and the animal came into full view. His cheeks blushed like a person; the laughter that came from his gut was warm. The dragon uncurled his body and tail to stand up. He was not lizard-like, as she had imagined the dragons. Instead he was all muscle, like the dogs that Osondrous trained to kill at the castle.

His smile was full of delight. "She is beautiful," the dragon murmured.

Kilikan said, "You will give me a ride then?"

"I will give you a ride anywhere!"

Kilikan dropped their packs and stepped forward, arms wide. The dragon raised a front arm and pulled the prince against his chest. Gaiden tucked his head down and touched Kilikan on the back with his chin.

Gaiden looked up at her. "Come here, beautiful lady! There is a warm place for you between my wings that I think you may like."

She stood with her mouth open. Kilikan came back to her and the dragon stepped up beside them, grabbing the bags and setting them on his back with an agile arm.

"You wore your strap," Kilikan said, mock-accusingly, referring to a wide leather strap around the dragon's chest in front of his wings.

"It has already been a long winter."

Kilikan accused, "You were hoping I would want you to take me somewhere!"

Gaiden said, "Come along, Jezaline. You first, where the blankets are!"

She yelped when the dragon gave her a nudge from behind. She reached his shoulder and grabbed the top of the strap. Kilikan followed behind her. The dragon's back was broad and flat. Tucked under the strap was a long pouch and from it Kilikan pulled out blankets that he wrapped around her and under her. Gaiden's scales were warm.

Kilikan pressed himself behind her.

Gaiden said, "Where do we go, Prince?"

The joy that had surfaced in Kilikan's eyes dimmed. "All the way."

"Past the Vamepire is nothing but swamp, my friend."

"Nothing but one place."

"You do not intend to take her—"

"I have to take her there."

"Why?"

Kilikan said, "The prophet said we must. The southern dragons have moved out."

Gaiden snapped his mouth shut. His eyes filled with heaviness as he looked to the south and took flight.

11

It was true, Kilikan was a real dragon. She could see it all the way now,

357

down to his bones and the way they poked beneath his hide, past the massive muscle and lean meat. She saw him clearly now.

Gaiden was off on a brisk north wind that sent them sailing across the wide, blue ocean. He flew higher and higher. They were passing Vamepire territory. The dragon stayed that high all day, and so far from land that only his gaze could catch the glimpse of the shore line in the distance.

It was growing dark when he began the sweep in toward the shore and Jezaline looked close at the great cliff the rocky shore had now become. It was a mountain pass, stretching as far to the south as she could see. The sheer wall of rock faced the western ocean.

The air was warming, the sun was coming up again. She had not seen land in over a day.

Gaiden was slowly turning to the east, flapping his wings to stay balanced on the north currents. He descended beneath the clouds. The landscape of white and rock had changed. She blinked to clear her eyes of wind and sleep to see better the expanse of green.

There were no buildings, no roads or changes in the vast green.

Kilikan told her, "The swamp."

It had been written on parchment in the castle library. On old maps, the simple name of Swamp. Nothing else. No history. Seemingly nothing but an endless mass of swamp animals and plants. A place unfit for any other form of life.

As Gaiden descended, the air dramatically warmed. She took off her cape and lifted her head to feel the wind in her hair.

Kilikan laughed.

"It is so good to feel southern air!" she cried.

"And I am panting!"

Gaiden growled, "And it is only going to get worse."

She lifted her arms to feel the hot wind.

Gaiden flew on through the day; night descended. Jezaline dozed with her head against the dragon's skin.

Kilikan moved over her, to the base of Gaiden's neck. "How soon do you think we will see it?"

"It has been a long time since the dragons were here, Prince. I know we will come upon it, but I do not know how easy it will be to see."

"Go low, Gaiden, slow down. I do not want to miss it the first try."

Gaiden gasped, "We will not have to."

The two stared as they approached a relic rising from the swamp. A crumbling fortress. Before the gate of the monolith, there were two panels left of a wall that would have run around the entire fortress. Each panel seemed to be flanking what was once a road for it was the only bare place they could see, a very small patch of dirt from the air. The gate that was once wood was completely gone and in its place was a curved gap, black and empty in the side of the ruins. As Gaiden circled down, they saw that the last two panels of the stone wall were flanked by pillars.

Gaiden landed gently and Kilikan took Jezaline from the dragon's back. She woke but the dark of the night was entire and Kilikan urged her to rest. Gaiden laid out a bed for her. Kilikan tucked her down and put up a small tent over her.

The sagging trees were up past their roots in swamp water. Over the swamp, almost entirely, grew endless green algae. Its brilliant color was so vivid that it glowed up and around the trunks of all of the surrounding trees. Nothing stirred except the random croaks of frogs and the noisiness of flies and insects.

Gaiden looked close at the pillars at the ends of the wall panels. "The writings are identical on all of them."

Kilikan stepped up beside the dragon and looked into the gaping blackness where the gate should have stood.

He glanced to either side, at the pillars. "Be careful. Let us not cross until we know what it says."

"It may take time." The dragon squinted at the stone.

"Work on it."

Kilikan crawled into the little tent beside her. He lay on his back, and looked at her pretty face. He kept his panting quiet by breathing high up in the back of his throat. Eventually he fell asleep.

Gaiden laid down, taking up the last of the space on their plateau. The dragon glanced unfondly at the swamp water and wondered what beasts lurked there.

12

She woke at light that made her believe it was dawn. Jezaline slipped from the tent and looked about. The height of the trees and the growing of all things around her had totally blocked out the sun. It was nearly noon. The heat and humidity were heady but, seeing the fortress, she rubbed her arms against a chill.

She had not seen the massive place as they had flown in but, staring at it now, she felt especially small. She had never seen a structure so enormous. It was built of bricks that had been mixed of red mud that left the decapitated fortress looking as though it bled. No vines, algae or living things of any kind grew on the outside walls or the two wall panels flanking the road. The windows were cut out of the brick and they were full of emptiness.

"Jezaline." Gaiden's head rose.

She sighed. "There is hardly any room for you to lie down here."

He said, "I can sleep anywhere."

Kilikan rubbed her back before he sat up. "You manage to find anything to eat?"

The dragon grimaced. "Everything here has scales."

Kilikan and Jezaline sat cross-legged together with their pack before them. She dug in for the water jug and dried fruit. Gaiden stared down at the pillars. His tail curled around, over his front feet.

She ate very little before going to the dragon's side and touching his shoulder.

He said, "I have been unable to remember the ability to read this language."

"Remember?"

"We dragons pass on our memories through our blood. We are born with the memories of all of our ancestors."

"This place is a memory?"

He looked down at her. "Vaguely. I think this place is one of the oldest memories that we are still passing. This place has been a relic for ages. It should have crumbled to the swamp but has gone without change. We all assumed this was Grim's fortress but if this is where he has been breeding his dragons, it just does not look well-traveled."

"Do you know of his dragons?"

Gaiden grumbled, "He turned a few of us. A long time ago. He has been using some kind of power to change them ever since. They are no longer kin. I no longer consider them dragons."

"What happened to them?"

"Something that made it possible for them to fly so high that not even the rivers can touch them."

She stared at the fortress. "No plants grow on the stone."

Gaiden said, "When the dragons first came upon this place, it was in ruin and yet it has not ruined more."

"There is something wrong here," Kilikan growled.

"It should never have been left a mystery. The dragons should have taken these stones down." Gaiden made a sweeping motion with his paw.

Jezaline said, "I have never seen a place so dead."

"Do not sound so sad, Jezaline. You will not be alone." Gaiden smiled down at her. She tried to muster a smile in return. Kilikan stepped to a pillar and ran his claws over the etchings.

He looked back at Gaiden. "You cannot read a single word?"

"Only one."

"And what would that be?"

"Dragon."

"Dragon?"

"It says the word dragon again and again and again. But I guess . . . not quite dragon. Maybe 'of scales' would be more accurate."

"I just do not see what would come of harm if we cross." She stepped up to the threshold between the wall panels.

Kilikan stopped her. "There is something very wrong with this place."

She snapped, exasperated, "Then throw something!"

The two males shrugged. Gaiden reached up and tore a branch down as long as his arm. Over their heads, the dragon held the branch across the threshold, wriggled it around then tossed it over his shoulder.

She said, "Nothing happened to the branch."

"It was not a living thing. Gaiden killed it to use it." Kilikan crossed his arms over his chest.

"Then find a living thing!"

Behind Gaiden, falling down into the swamp, the branch began to sink. Deep within its leaves a small green snake, curled around a branch, was frozen in time, completely dead.

Gaiden shook his head. "This is an evil place. We all know that but I do not see how any harm could befall us by going by these pillars. It was once a wall. It once had a gate, as harmless as any other."

Jezaline nodded in agreement. "He is right, Kilikan. I will go first."

"That is not going to happen." Kilikan grabbed her arm.

She snatched free from his grasp. "Kilikan, you are both here because of me. I was the one called to this act, right? Then if this is where I am supposed to die, then this is where I die and all is well!"

She threw herself by the pillars before he could grab her. Kilikan cried out. Jezaline's feet scuffed up a little dust in the dirt. Stood with her arms out and turned back to the males. "I am fine."

Gaiden nodded. Kilikan reached for her.

"Wait!" Gaiden snapped and pulled the Draegoone back.

"Let me go first," Gaiden said. "The pillars are speaking of scaled things."

Kilikan shook his head at the dragon. "You do not need to do this."

Gaiden lowered his head to be even with the prince's face. "I will test it."

Jezaline crossed her arms over her chest, standing with an eye on the gate, not feeling comfortable putting her back to it. On the other side of the wall panels, there was flat empty dirt without growth. At their ends was the abrupt fall off of the land into swamp and all the growing things that encompassed it. It lapped up to the sides of the fortress but no trees touched the stone. The trees actually leaned away.

Gaiden raised his left paw and slowly crept it past the stone pillars. Instantly his face broke and he recoiled with a roar.

Jezaline ran to him.

The dragon grabbed his left elbow and stared down at his five-fingered paw. A deadening of his cells had begun, creeping up from the tips of his finger pads.

"Do something!" she shouted at Kilikan.

The dragon's face stripped in shock. He fell to his knees, watching the death reach his wrist; his left hand fell limp.

"Cut it off!" Gaiden cried.

Kilikan drew his sword.

Gaiden held out his paw, his grip tightening on his own elbow.

Kilikan reared back.

"Do it!" Gaiden roared.

Kilikan brought his sword down. Jezaline covered her face. The dragon's dead paw hit the ground, his blood splashed into the swamp. Gaiden panted hard. Tongue hanging out, he gasped and gasped. He put his right paw on the ground, resting.

Jezaline reached for the bleeding stub.

"No," Gaiden said. "Just a moment. It will stop bleeding. Kilikan, you need to sharpen your sword. That hurt tremendously."

Kilikan looked close at the dead paw, flat out on its knuckles, fingers spread and claws out. He poked it with a stick before flicking it into the swamp.

Jezaline held herself, stepped to the pillars and looked into the gate.

Gaiden said, "I am glad it was not you."

Kilikan sighed, "But that was not good. Not good at all."

The two males noticed her.

Kilikan stepped up behind her, touched her shoulder. She tightened the hug she held on herself.

Kilikan soothed. "Gaiden will be all right. He will be able to grow it back."

Gaiden watched his blood slow, then stop. He growled, "I am not the reason she is upset. She has to go alone."

Jezaline's face crumpled into her palm. When Kilikan touched her, she pulled away.

She whispered, "Tarrick was wrong, I will not have anyone with me for this."

Gaiden called to her, "We could fly away. I would take you anywhere, more south, to the ocean where it is always warm and the beaches are white."

She went to the dragon and looked up, into his face.

She said, "Just fly away?"

The dragon nodded. "We could just lift off."

She said, "I could feel the wind in my hair. We could go where there is no one."

Kilikan's chin was down; he was shaking his head.

"It would be easy forever," Gaiden whispered.

She stepped closer to him, touched his huge, scaled cheek. Tears fell out of the corners of her eyes.

"Gaiden, stop it," Kilikan said.

The dragon looked at him and Jezaline's hand fell from his cheek.

She said, "It will just be a little stroll in an evil fortress. All alone."

"You are sure?" Kilikan whispered.

She looked into his eyes. "I do not have to go far. I go in a little way, come back out, come back to you. I can always come back to you. Right? You will wait for me?"

"Always," he said.

The dragon and prince packed their smallest of leather bags. In it were two blankets and enough food and water for a day. She pulled her cape and high leather riding gloves on over the long sleeves of her dress. At her hip she buckled a long dagger, something given to her by Osondrous a lifetime ago.

Kilikan cracked flint over an old torch that had survived with her the whole trip from the Castle of the Wards.

"Cold oil?" Gaiden asked.

She said, "This oil was blessed by our Healing Wards and willed to burn the fire cold. It will be days that this torch is lit before it consumes any of the rag or wood."

"I am very glad you insisted on it coming with us." Kilikan handed it to her. He touched her cheek, ran his fingers down her neck until he pulled her tight.

"You can always come back to me," he said.

She felt his purr against her chest. "I know."

"You must come back to me." The Draegoone stroked down her back and her hair. He kissed her until they were both breathless and she turned away. Her torch led Jezaline past the pillars and she did not allow herself to stop before the gape of the entrance. She held out the fire and stepped in. All sounds of insects, of frogs, of any kind of life, ceased. She kept walking, not once looking back, even as the dead air of the place filled her lungs and the silence seemed to begin to hammer on her ears and even as she went deeper and all light, save for her little torch, ceased to exist.

13
Karalay

Black wings cut through the sky. The three dragons flew, stretched out like wispy clouds. They dove upon them, snatching Diggamara men from the streets and Fai from the air. But a cheer rose up in Human voices and was joined by Sicilia's Fai. Telenay rode out of the castle and into the streets, shining in Diggamara's blue armor.

Karalay gasped, "I must go help them!" She sprinted toward the staircase.

"Stop!" Sicilia held out her hand. "I will take you down there, Healer. Grim controls one of those dragons. I am sure of it! I will take them down and you will keep our soldiers strong."

Sicilia pushed her toward the window and grabbed her around the waist. Karalay's eyes opened wide and she was filled with the stench of all that she saw. Streets filled with all of the black and burning, shifting river of the dead.

Sicilia tipped them out.

Karalay bit on her scream.

The Fai controlled the fall, wings out. She never could have carried Karalay but she almost stopped them before dropping the Human on the ground. Sicilia left her in front of the castle and Karalay fell to her knees to catch her breath and feel the solid ground under her hands. The gates around the castle were vibrating. Behind the walls on every side smoke rose in billows of black and glowed in the red raw of fire, entirely concealing the sky.

Karalay ran to the gate.

"You cannot go!" The guards shook their heads in horror.

"I am your Ward! You will let me through."

They shook their heads.

She screamed, "Where are your dead and wounded?"

"We were ordered to let them lie."

Her mouth gaped. "By who?"

"The general said there was no time to tend them!"

"There is time now!" she screamed. "Let me through!"

The guard cracked open the big steel door and peered out. She pulled him aside. A wall of smoke hit her.

She stumbled into the chaos.

Diggamara men surrounded her, smeared in black ash; they stood with their swords out, shields up. They were screaming orders, commands, constantly shifting and moving. At their lead, his horse already lost, Telenay stood beside five Darkhalks. She saw him with her will through the smoke.

The men cried out when they noticed her.

"You must not be here!"

"Get away!"

"Go back to the castle!"

With her will she screamed *Telenay!*

He found her with his hands coming out of the smoke.

He pushed her back through the gate. "Karalay! What are you doing?"

"I am a Healer!"

He said, "You do not belong down here!"

"You bring me your wounded!"

He stared into her eyes. "We are all dead."

She gasped. "We are still breathing! You bring them to me, Telenay. You have your men bring them to me. I can give you living soldiers!"

He grasped the side of her face, then nodded and was gone.

High above Karalay, Sicilia was all weaponry. She covered her swords with oil and lit them on fire. She attacked the nearest dragon with a dozen Fai flying at her back. A horde of hornets, they powered through the sky. The dragon met them. Mouth open, he snatched her soldiers out of the air.

Sicilia latched onto him and pounded her swords into the animal's head.

14

Karalay pushed her hands around the face of the soldier who was brought to her. He was dead, his eyes were slashed and bleeding. She was able to bring him back and only then did she recognize his black leathers. Kackin, Jaridd's Second, opened his eyes and gasped. The Cape and Sword died when he had died. He grabbed a weapon from a corpse and rushed away and her heart wept for Jaridd.

After the last of seventy men were healed, she staggered down to her knees. The guards at the door cried out to her. But she could hear nothing; her sight was closing in. Men were screaming and running. A guard grabbed her around the waist. He threw her over his shoulder. Karalay strained to see through the smoke as the guard ran toward the castle. He dove through the door. She caught a glimpse of wings, teeth, claws and tail coming down. The guard slammed the door shut and pushed her back.

The creature hit and they were knocked to the ground with the impact.

She stumbled to the guard. "Is it alive?"

He opened the door. "Oh, no."

The dragon had fallen on the castle wall and it had crumbled beneath it. "Retreat!"

She heard the horn blowing and the Fai general screaming. "The castle wall is breached. Fall back! The castle wall is breached. Fall back!"

15

There was no sound in the chamber. No light. The sounds of war did not penetrate so deeply in the castle's basement.

The blessed water in the basin was utterly still.

The Elf's decaying flesh skimmed the water. His tattered clothes were the color of old blood. His eyes were the color of plums; when they opened, it was slowly. He lifted his hand to the edge of the basin; the water shifted. His black flesh hung from his fingers and fell to the floor.

Down the hall echoed the sound of dripping as he shifted.

He raised himself up and the water fell from him. He slipped over the edge of the basin and hit the floor. Dead bones and flesh slapped the stone. One hand went out, fingers curled under as he pulled his slippery body toward the door.

His eyes hung open, his jaw dragged on the stone. He worked his feet under him and stood with a push.

He teetered back and forth down the hall, leaving a watery trail of flesh behind.

16

"Telenay!"

He found her, grasped her hands, pushed her back toward the castle. "Shut that door!"

He protected her with his body. "Lock it behind you!"

"I will not leave you!"

He worked her backward. "You will go and protect that Crystal! Run, Karalay!"

"Grim is there?" She pointed at the sky where Sicilia rallied against the last dragon. "Your men need me!"

Telenay yelled out orders. "Fall back! Everyone behind the castle walls! Reinforce the gates! Make those bastards come through at this breach only! Set the dragon on fire!"

The Darkhalks leaped the walls to get out of the streets and back to the castle. She only saw four of them left.

Her skin burned red from the heat.

"Healer! We need you!" Soldiers called on her, dragging their wounded.

She went to them, hands out. Her tired will did not fail her. She forced their flesh to heal and they ran back to the line, shields held high to cover their faces.

The Elf army was moving over its thousands of fallen soldiers, and was coming down at them, shoulder to shoulder and back to chest.

17

He scraped along the wall, leaving pieces of shirt leather and skin behind. His black fingers dug into the rock. His feet lifted and trembled for balance.

He reached the long spiral up toward the tower. He raised his rotten foot and, with a squish, he began to climb. Far above, he could see the light

367

of the Crystal and his mouth hung open in a grin.

18

Karalay could see Sicilia high above them, sweeping and cutting. When Sicilia downed Grim, would his armies fall too?

The Elves stumbled over the dragon corpse, consumed by the flames. Oil was tossed over the dragon's hide again and again. The Elves fell under the heat.

Telenay pushed her behind him, his shield held high.

"We are losing ground!"

"Hold steady!"

The stink of burning flesh hit her. She retched hard.

"Karalay! Get in the castle!"

She healed Telenay as he pushed her. She felt the door behind her, pressed into her back.

"We are losing!"

"Get back, everyone! Get a wall behind you!"

Men were left behind. She watched them fall, trampled under the weight of marching Elves. Telenay pressed tight against her. Their sight was filled with the burning hands of corpses as they came. Five steps away. Four. Three. She squeezed her eyes shut, turned her face away.

This is it.

Telenay braced himself against her. All around her she felt the quailing of the last of the soldiers. She could find no Darkhalk. Both their wills were done. Telenay was a haggard beacon, screaming orders incessantly.

He hacked down the Elves before them, gouged a hole in the line that was instantly filled. A soldier smacked into her as he ran in panic. She hit the ground. Her nose and mouth filled with the reek. She curled up tight, squeezed her eyes shut and understood.

This was it.

What happened?

"What happened?"

Telenay screamed, "They fell!"

She looked up. Half the Elves before them hit the ground.

She heard the confused cries of the army.

"Why are they falling?"

"What is happening?"

Telenay yelled, "Attack!"

The men threw their weight against the Elves and the Elves began to stagger back.

19

Cousai paced by each window. Her heart pounded in her ears. Smoke was gathering in the tower. She coughed hard, pushed the wet tears off her cheeks. There was only one dragon left. She saw her sister, swords flying.

You kill him, Sicilia, you kill Grim and get this over with!

Among the Elves, suddenly, hundreds fell. *How could that be?*

She leaned out and stared. The Diggamaran army pushed them back from the castle.

Cousai froze.

She heard his last step. A squish of wet flesh slipping on bone.

She turned.

The Elf lunged awkwardly forward.

Cousai drew her sword. "Stop!"

The Elf tilted his head. Without moving his lips, he said, "Fai have harmed me enough. A Fai cannot stop me now."

She pointed her sword at him. "You deserved your fate for the disrespect you showed the dead."

She approached him swiftly, rallying her strength, raising her sword.

His hand flew to her neck and Cousai could not move. Her sword hit the stone. Her jaw shook in fury; she tried to speak, tried to scream. His will surrounded her. She could do nothing.

He lifted her up, stared into her gray eyes as he choked her. "No one deserved the fate your father brought on me."

The Elf slammed her to the stone. Cousai's legs crumpled and snapped like trees breaking in a wind. Her head hit the floor. Tears poured from her eyes; she could not blink.

The corpse smiled down at her, flesh falling from the bones of his face in long rivulets, then turned to the Crystal.

The light surrounded him. The Elf's milky, dead eyes filled with black as Grim came to the very surface of the Elf's body, pressed to see the Crystal, to feel the light.

Cousai felt sensation come back to her fingers. She blinked.

He fell to his knees. His hands disappeared in the light and he gazed

369

into the beauty.

Cousai eyed her sword, moved her hand and wrist closer to it. Her brow furrowed. She gritted her teeth and pushed. She clutched and reached. Her fingertips brushed the hilt. She tapped it and it jerked closer.

He stroked the Crystal with the Elf's dead fingers, pawed it like a child. "So many years . . . so many years . . ."

His attention on her evaporated. The leather hilt filled her palm. Cousai lifted the sword and dropped the blade like an ax, into the light.

20

"Telenay?" Karalay stared out from behind him, stared as hundreds more of the Elves fell to the ground, lifeless.

He gasped, "Someone must be destroying the Reapers controlling them!"

"Who?" She knelt down beside a man dragged to her.

She touched his cheek, shook her head. They took the body away.

"Someone must have found their location!"

"Are they not here?"

"No, their bodies are somewhere else."

"Where?"

"How would I know that?"

"But who would kill them?"

"Anyone who is an enemy of Grim is a friend!"

"But, Telenay—" she started.

Light erupted from the tower and blinded them. The piercing wave hit and slammed them to the ground. The Fai fell from the skies and the last dragon fell dead. The armies of the Elves hit the ground. The fire was swept out and the streets went totally dark.

21
Osondrous

Osondrous rose when a servant called for her. A Draegoone had awakened among the five that had asked for help.

He was a hunky beast, sitting up a little, trying to drink without spilling the water.

"Easy." She took the cup and helped him drink.

370

He said, "Thank you."

"What is your general's name?"

"My general is alive?"

"Yes."

"His name is Tarrick."

"Tarrick?" She frowned. "Tarrick."

"Yes, Tarrick."

She patted his arm. "What about Kilikan?"

"He is our future king. Tarrick is the youngest prince."

"More water?"

He shook his head, rolled over and passed back out.

Osondrous paused in the hall. *Where do I know that name?*

She went to Tarrick, knelt down beside his bed. His big hand moved out of the corner of her eye.

"Tarrick?" She wrung out a rag, laid it on his chest. "Tarrick?"

He grabbed her wrist, his claws curled around.

She froze. "Tarrick . . . I am helping you."

A low penetrating growl emerged from the general.

She did not move, did not breathe. "Tarrick, I—"

"I am alive!" He let loose a roar, opening his mouth in a long hard wail.

She pulled free and scrambled back against the cell wall.

Servants came running. "Osondrous!" they cried. She raised her hand at them, did not allow them to unlock the door.

The Draegoone rolled, stared around wildly. "How can this be?" He stood and screamed, slammed his fists into the wall above her head. She covered her ears as he hit the wall, time after time, his heavy panting ringing louder and louder until he was roaring with each hit of stone. Finally, he stopped, palms flat out, face dropped above her.

She looked up. "Tarrick?"

He stepped back. "Osondrous?"

He teetered, fell down to the bed.

"You are hurt, you must move slower. You know my name?"

"You know my name, you do not know me?"

She gasped, it finally coming to her, "You are the prophet, Tarrick."

He laughed darkly. "I *was* the prophet, Tarrick. I am dead now."

Osondrous spoke carefully. "Where is Jezaline?"

"You should worry on more important things." He threw himself against her, pulled her off her feet and closed his fists around her neck.

"What do you want?" Her voice choked and strained between his fingers. She beat his hands.

"I want death!"

"Then let me down and I will kill you!"

"You let me go!"

"You let her down, Draegoone, or you will fall where you stand."
Eikian held a bow in the open doorway, trained on the Draegoone's head.

Tarrick grinned. "She will be dead before I fall!"

Eikian's voice did not waver, his eyes narrowed into slits. "She is
tougher than she looks. If you are a prophet, you would know that."

Tarrick nodded. "But she is much stupider than she looks. Did you do
it, Eikian? Did you crown this stupid wench?"

Osondrous felt sick; darkness was beginning to close. *Eikian, you must
go now.*

"I am not leaving you!"

Osondrous looked Tarrick in the eyes. *Let me down. We must talk.*

"Stupid, stupid whore." Tarrick's grip softened.

She fell to her feet, grabbed her throat and gasped. "You go, Eikian, all
of you, get out of here."

"Osondrous, he will kill you!"

She gasped, "I will die when I am good and ready!"

Tarrick laughed, towering over her. Eikian swore viciously, stepped
back and shut the cell door.

She glared at the Draegoone. "Now you sit down."

Tarrick sat down. "You will let me go."

"You will talk first and stop calling me stupid unless you give me good
reason." She rubbed her sore neck.

Tarrick shook his head at her. "The Darkhalks go to Diggamara to
protect the last Crystal. You knew that from the beginning. Ironically,
somehow, a Healing Ward and a Warlord end up there, as well. You knew
that from the beginning. Did you ever consider there was a reason that city
was so prepared for war? You knew from the beginning, Reapers killed
your King, Reapers attacked you on dragons, gave you a win. Gave the
kings of Stonedowner reason to try and convince you to become queen.
You knew that too, Osondrous. They were under dark influence and you
saw it all."

"There is nothing I could have done about Diggamara. Yes, I knew from
the beginning Grim was rising again. I *would* have been stupid not to see
that. Was he rising for the last Crystal shard? Yes! It was obvious, of course
he was. The Darkhalks would not have been called to war for any less of a

cause. There is nothing I did to change any of that!"

"You became queen!"

"Yes, I became queen. What change did I make?"

"Osondrous, think about it! Grim destroyed the King, Addilade is taken and the Darkhalks are sent to protect the last Crystal. You are encouraged to become a queen."

She shook her head, stared at him, not comprehending how her becoming queen could have changed anything. But her spirit was cringing deeply and she was having trouble breathing.

The Draegoone growled low and hard. "The stupidity of Humans will kill us all. The Crystal shards weaken for one day. One day the rivers are crossable. The day a new Ward is called was the only day Grim could have taken over the last Crystal, when it was at its weakest. He attacked Diggamara, Telenay, Karalay, an army of Fai, the few Darkhalks that were left, the day you became queen. It all could have been avoided if you had just stopped to think. But, you had to save one Centaur!"

She steadied herself on the wall.

"You handed Diggamara over. They were outnumbered by thousands."

"What happened?"

"All I know is the Crystals are destroyed, probably as a last resort."

Osondrous held her hands, looked down at the bandages that covered nothing. "Jezaline? Is she all right?"

"You will never see Jezaline the Ward again."

Osondrous looked at him. "The Ward?"

"Yes."

"Will I see her again?"

"Not as you know her."

"What do you mean?"

"I mean you will not want to see her again."

Osondrous rubbed her mouth, covered her lips. "Telenay?"

"You will never see Telenay the Warlord again."

She gasped, "Why?"

"Karalay had to be saved. You will see her again."

"I do not understand!"

"Then do not understand! Let me go."

"Give me your good reason, Draegoone. You have obviously fallen from your gift. Where could you possibly desire to go?"

His face darkened. "Fai fought at Diggamara. One of them I love, one of them could still be alive. It could be her, it could be her sister. But there is a chance I could save Cousai. There is a chance! It could be her! You must let me go!"

She held up her hand. "Fai?"

"Yes."

"You love a Fai?"

"Yes."

"How—"

"I do not care what you think of me. I knew she would die in Diggamara so I flew to die here but that was taken from me as well. If it is Cousai whose heart is still beating, I may be able to save her but I must go now!"

"You are not even sure if it is her?"

"I get images—she and her sister are alike! There is one lying there with a heart that is still beating right now!"

Osondrous crossed her arms over her chest and watched the Draegoone take his head in his hands.

"Give me some time." She left.

In the hall Eikian roared, "You are mad!"

She held up her hand at him, shook her head.

"You will not even speak to me?" He stared at her back, hurt and raging.

A soldier approached her.

She shook her head. "Not now."

The soldier bowed. "I have a raven from Diggamara."

She whipped around. He held up the bird. She tenderly took it and untied the leather from around its leg. Servants, Implins and Eikian watched. Osondrous' hands shook. The raven gazed up into her eyes. The parchment read: *Osondrous, in the end there will be no one to blame except Grim.* It was signed by Karalay. She pulled the Raven to her chest and her head fell. Tears pooled in her eyes and she gasped. She pushed by Eikian and threw open Tarrick's door.

"Come with me!"

The Draegoone hurried after her. Osondrous went out into the early day air.

The skies were stark.

On the outer parapet, Osondrous touched the raven. She let the bird go and watched his flutter of wings recede until there was nothing more than a free raven gone.

"Go, Tarrick. Get out of here. I never want to hear your voice again."

The Draegoone's mouth opened and he gasped, "One thing you have done right then."

She barely nodded, too horrified to speak. *What had she done?*

He threw himself from the parapet, tattered wings unleashing in a smack of leathery wind. He was gone quickly. Osondrous doubted that the Draegoone could make the journey in his condition. He was weak, injured.

Osondrous held herself against the breeze, acknowledged no one. She got to her chamber and collapsed before the fire. She held her shaking hands, stared at the little note again. Karalay's sure and true handwriting. Had Karalay known what lay before her when she wrote it? Did Karalay know she would become queen with so little consideration? And the answer was: *Yes, of course Karalay did.*

"Forgive me," Osondrous whispered. "Karalay, forgive me."

Was Karalay even alive?

Osondrous held the note to her chest, closed her eyes. She swore she would make it up. She threw the parchment into the fire and watched it burn. She drew Mlore from her hip, laid the sword down in its place before the fire and bowed to it. Osondrous sat down on the stone floor, felt her aching muscles give to the feeling. She took off her vest and all of the wraps around her breasts and ribs. She slowly eased out of her boots.

Of all the horrific things she had said about the other Wards, she was certain now that none of them would have lacked her sense. They would have trod cautiously and done the right thing. Which was to wait and see. She even thought that she could have postponed Eli's trial if that is what it would have taken.

Grim had tried to kill her and nearly succeeded. What he did not count on was that she would be saved and it would not be Telenay standing alone, but her. And it all had worked out perfectly for Grim. Telenay would have never made such a rash decision. Not for anyone or anything.

Eikian stepped into the chamber. Curled his hooves beneath him before the fire, laid his sword down beside Mlore.

Her voice broke and there were tears of panic in her eyes. "You were right. I never should have become queen. I doomed Karalay the day I became queen. I doomed Diggamara."

Eikian stared at their touching swords.

She said, "I gave Grim his chance to take the last Crystal."

He faced her. She rose to her knees and pressed against his hard body, he on his horse belly and she on her knees. She pressed her face against the skin beneath his ear, into his hot neck. Her tongue slipped along his shoulder. She kissed him with her mouth open.

She said, "I need you."

He shushed her with his mouth, with his enormous strength. In his arms, in that moment, she was a failed queen. A failure as she had never been a failure. But Eikian held her, kissed her, moved his fingers down her body like she was not a failure but as though she were perfect. Pretty. Beautiful. A woman as she had never been a woman. He touched her as only a Warlord could. Without fear or reservation. With respect but not reverence. Laying away all of her reservations, she met him completely for the first time.

"Be mine entirely." His hot breath was on her neck.

"Yes," she said.

He stroked her gray scar and she stripped all of his swords and belts off until he was as naked. She covered his gray scar with her right hand.

She said, "Paint me."

"What?"

"Paint me. Braid my hair. Like you used to."

He agreed. Eikian brought back from his chamber the native warpaint of his people and a box of his own bones and beads for her hair.

She said, "You, too."

He swept his fingers into the black paint and started by painting her right cheek. She dipped her fingers and swept them across his left. They colored their skin down the left and right sides of their bodies until they were half and half. Her right eye peered out from the sea of black, looking bright, alive and wild. He braided her hair and she braided his tail. They plaited and tied with leathers, tied with bones and clacking red beads. He swept back the short hair on his head with the black paint.

She stood up to her mirror and stared at her real self. The girl that had stepped, painted perfectly into the Keltch wars, and had crawled out of the field a creature of war. She took a deep breath and her breasts lifted, one covered in black, the other a pink, hard eye, staring back at her.

He stood by her side and she looked at his reflection. Her heartbeat doubled and she opened her mouth to get air. He had become the beast of the field again. Her beast. The incredible muscling of his body stood before her and rippled.

She said, "You were right. I never needed him."

Eikian pulled her to him, left hip to right hip, covering their bare sides, wrapping his right arm around her as she wrapped her left around him. In the mirror they were a black beast, half male Centaur, half female Human.

Jezaline did not know if it had been hours or days. It felt like days. She had wandered from one endless hallway to another, all in the shocking, ink darkness. She felt entirely surrounded by stone, as though she was climbing slowly downwards into a grave. Her grave.

She sank to her knees. She longed for a warm bed. She longed for the big Draegoone that wanted her. The floor in the hallway was covered with hot sand. She sobbed without tears, her face breaking. Jezaline rolled her head against the wall. Across her lap the torch laid, its flame licking up beside her.

She would have given it all up then, run back to Kilikan and Gaiden and had them take her back to the black river. She would swim it if she had to. She would run back to the Warlords and beg Telenay and Osondrous to protect her.

The ache in her gaped for Waltruk and she screamed at it.

Her hands shook weakly. She trembled. The torch turned out of her fingers, flipped over, head heavy, into the sand.

She grabbed it, gasped, "No, no, no . . . no!" The sand coated the oil. The flame flickered out.

She could see nothing. Blinking did not change the depth of the blackness. Jezaline heard her heavy breathing like an echo. It filled her ears. Her heart pounded madly. She pressed against the wall.

In her exhaustion, Jezaline fell asleep.

When she awoke, it was with a jerk. She stared through the darkness, wide-eyed. She shakily got to her feet, worked her way along the wall. She knew the hallway she was stepping into. She had been past here half a dozen times. The hallway was lined with hallways, arches leading nowhere, circling back to their beginning. She turned the corner, stared down the hall. At the very end, past a dozen other hallways, she could see the definition of the sand on the floor.

She hurried toward it, gasping for breath, bypassing all the other hallways. At the end, with her feet in the light, she stared up the hall; its walls she could make out. She sprinted toward the glow. Turned down the hallway. The light grew. Down another hall, again, and again.

She stopped.

A huge garden stretched out before her, beneath the moon and the starlight. A round pool filled with clear water was flanked by statues of beautiful women, dipping into it with pots, washing their hair. Brick paths wandered between beds of green plants, ever-flowering bright orange and flame red flowers. In the moonlight, everything was silver.

She gasped, stepped into the light of the moon. Her head tipped back and she stared up at the map of stars, the blue of night sky. The wind blew by her, streaming down between the pillars and the old bricks and stones. It stroked her face. Jezaline's heart quieted; she breathed deep. She reached, rubbed the hand that warmed her shoulder. She smiled.

The wind stopped and the warmth evaporated.

She was still in the depth of the ruin and it was still deadly dark. Her wind was gone.

She stepped into the garden, went to the pool to join those women. Sat beside one of them on the edge and sighed. She could hear no living noise except her heart again. The statues were so lovely, they could never have been real women, breathing. The plants, too, were far too perfect.

She shivered, rubbed her arms. Followed the paths around, found there was only one entrance to this garden. And around it, stone benches were positioned to enjoy the sight.

One path led to a door. She stared in shock, stepped out of the moonlight and touched it. It was wooden, well made and not old. It was smooth and dark. It was the first wood she had seen in this place. There was a chain drawn across it and it was locked.

"Well, then," she murmured.

Something fell behind her. She whipped around and stared. Her heart hammered. There was a movement in the shadows. She pulled out her dagger. The tip shook.

It stood, all of darkness. A black deeper than the shadows of the garden. It slipped across the ground toward her.

"Stay back!" she cried.

"Put that away." His laughter was hot.

She gasped, "Waltruk?"

He swept her against him, pulled her chest to his.

In her ear he whispered, "Is it back?"

She fought the tears of relief that threatened to overwhelm her.

She nodded. "It is back." They were talking about the ache.

He slipped her dagger back into the sheath at her hip.

He kissed her. "You reek."

She looked away. "I suppose I do."

"Did he get to have you?"

She shrugged. "He did nothing that you could do for me."

She was so relieved to have someone with her that all thoughts of trying to escape him were evaporating. He would have followed her to the ends of the oceans and she doubted that even Gaiden and Kilikan would have a chance against this king. There was a part of her that still wondered, if she had gotten to Osondrous and Telenay, if they could have protected her. With him now, feeling the ache calling his name again, she was certain that she could not live long with it anymore without Waltruk to fill it. Between life and death, there was no other choice.

"They do not suspect anything."

"No, you are very convincing." He took her mouth in his, kissed her deeply.

She ran her fingers down the braids that wove against his scalp. "Can we just go?"

"This is important. Is this the only door you found?"

"Yes."

He dropped his pack and unrolled it. Swords and mallets lined the leather. He drew the largest mallet. She stepped back. He slammed the face of the weapon into the lock. He did it again and again. She wrapped her arms around herself, wincing. The thought never occurred to her that the lock was unreachable from the inside.

The lock fell with a tink. The chains dropped.

He opened the door.

"Waltruk, wait." She grabbed his arm.

"What?"

"I just—"

He snatched her hand and jerked her into the darkness. She stumbled and caught herself on the top few steps of an unlit staircase. He pulled his pack on, took her by the elbow. She fumbled for each step with her feet.

They spiraled down the wide staircase. Eventually the steps started coming into view for her. She recognized firelight. They stepped down into a hallway lined in a velvet rug as red as roses.

"This—" she started.

"Is not old," he said, glancing into rooms as they passed them. The rooms were big, beautifully furnished with beds and dressers. Their fireplaces crackled with flames. No doors were closed and they were all bedrooms. The hall turned into another, lined again with open rooms.

At the end of the hall was a massive wood door. They stopped at it.

"Forty-five bedrooms," he said, glancing back down the hall.

She drew her dagger.

He opened the door.

It was a long dark chamber, all black rock. Coffin-like beds lined the walls, raised up on stone and padded in white linens and silks and velvets. Upon the beds were forty-five Humans, their eyes closed, peaceful in sleep. Their hands folded over their chests. They were covered up to their fingers in red velvet blankets. A long velvet rug ran down the center of the room, raising up to the foot of each of the beds and reaching at the end, a small black door.

"Who are they?"

"You know who they are. You have to kill them all."

"What?"

"These are the Reapers of Grim."

"But these are just Humans."

"You are a Ward. You know they are not even here."

She gritted her teeth, stared down the line of them. "I cannot do this."

The people were of every age and every type: Diggamara, Stonedowner, even Willower. A lady with Jezaline's same fair hue and dark hair slept beautifully beside them.

Jezaline stared at her. "But they are only Humans."

"You feel it?"

She shook her head.

He forced her to look at him. "You feel it."

She did feel it, the emptiness of the whole place, the rooms, the Human bodies. No one was here but her and the Vamepire king. It was known that Humans could strive and will into the darkness deep enough to be able to not only rise out of their bodies, but possess others as they saw fit. It was considered malicious, and done only by the most grotesque.

"I cannot—"

"You will."

She stared at him. "Why not you?"

"You are the one that is supposed to do this."

"I am not who I was supposed to be! I cannot kill these. They . . . They—"

"You have no idea where they are right now. What evil they are doing to your species."

He took her in his arms and she felt his wings come around behind her, encasing her in his power.

He said, "You will be my queen. You will be Vamepire and live for hundreds more years by my side. I promised you that. I will give you that. But you must first finish your fate as a Human. I am certain this must be done."

"I am no warrior." Her voice was muffled into his leather shirt.

"I can help you. They will not fight. They will not cry. This will be easy."

He took her to the first bed and fitted her dagger into her hand. He squeezed her fingers around the shaft. He raised it above the Human's chest. Her eyes never left his face. He brought it down and it landed like it hit wood, dead wood. The Human's blood ran and he took her to the next.

One after another, their blood ran redder than the crimson velvet that covered them.

She wondered if she would ever know what these Reapers had been doing. If it had actually been malicious, if someone she knew was actually in danger. If she saved anyone, or anything, or only took life.

She thought of the many more years she would have in the land. Wondered if becoming Vamepire would be painful, and how much longer it would be before she could change. The Vamepire king had a plan and would not give her the extra years until that plan was finished. It involved the final blow against the Draegoone. She pushed Kilikan from her mind, certain now that she had no choice.

23

Forty-five dead bodies lay behind them. They never moved, nor let out a gasp of pain. Her dagger and her hands were bloody. She wiped them on her dress.

She sighed, "One last door."

He pecked her on the cheek. "Let us finish this."

Waltruk drew a steel mace from his pack. He opened the door and stepped in. She followed.

It was not a big room. All black, the torches on the walls burned silently. A single bed raised from the floor. And upon it, draped in silk and white velvet lay the red man from her past.

Time evaporated.

The hot, desert wind blew her hair around her face. The brilliant sun made her squint. She stumbled toward the cool waters and the shade of the palms.

And the stallion was there, nostrils wide and quivering, waiting for her. He stepped toward her and she was paralyzed to stop it. His muzzle pressed into her shoulder, her fingers slipped up beneath his mane. His coat was unblemished and smooth and she looked into his black eyes as he breathed. She could not look away. Jezaline's legs were paralyzed. She pulled back and did not move. She heard his nicker and it changed, no longer the sound of a horse.

Something else made that sound.

It could have been the throaty laugh of a man much older than her.

She gasped in panic.

The muzzle felt like a hand, it circled over her shoulder and then slipped up to surround her neck. Jezaline opened her mouth to scream and she could not. The eye of the horse grew until all she could see was vast shiny blackness of wild horse. She felt herself lowered and knew she was laid out on the ground. The smell of the stallion evaporated, her nose filled with the smell of burning. It grew so hot she could taste it in the back of her throat.

Her eyes cleared and laying between her legs, supported with his hands on her arms, was a man. His skin was the color of the stallion's coat. The definition of red. He was bare naked, hairless and his eyes were essentially black. He wasn't smiling, nor was he glaring. He looked into Jezaline's face and spoke something she never heard. She felt the rock between her legs. He shifted and she felt it against the fabric of the dress. Thin summer cotton, the only thing stopping him from penetrating her and breaking her open.

She was a virgin. She was finally able to scream.

Her stricken sound carried out from the shade of the trees and echoed across the dunes where it vanished in the heat without ever being heard by any living thing.

He attacked her, covered her scream with his wide open mouth. Her mouth filled with fire and her eyes opened wide in the realization that losing her chastity in a rape may not be the worst thing that could happen to her. She held her breath, pushing back, coughing, heaving into his mouth.

Nothing stopped the fire.

It poured down her throat.

She held her breath to stop it. But she had to breathe, had to scream; her body convulsed for air.

She gasped.

The fire filled her nose, coursed into her lungs. The boiling thing reached her heart and detonated. He uncovered her scream and it raised louder than any noise or terror she had ever made before in her life. She screamed and screamed the death howl that became no longer the noise made from a Human but that of an animal making its last noise of life. When it escaped and finally dwindled and her throat was a highway of pain, her arms were around him and her hands spread out over his solid shoulders. His face was turned into her neck and his body was as gentle as it was hard.

Jezaline gasped and the thing between her legs was as hard as rock still and it was all she knew, it was all she understood.

But she was no longer a virgin and she was many years past sixteen.

"No!" Jezaline screamed.

She slammed her open palm into his face.

The illusion evaporated. Before her the thing was standing, naked, without sex, warped beyond comparison to any Human being. Its teeth were tiny, shrunk back into its gums to tiny bleeding points. She was on the floor beneath it and her dagger was in its raised hand.

Her scream had shattered Waltruk's own illusion. As Grim brought her dagger down, Waltruk stood and swung. The blow landed and demolished the left side of Grim's face. It spun around and slammed into the stone floor with a slimy thud.

She covered her mouth.

Waltruk stared.

Grim, on its hands and knees, crawled back to its pedestal. Clamored up to the bed and lay out, gasping.

"This is Grim?" Waltruk gasped.

The creature's gray skin shone in the firelight. Grim's little, warped hands gripped each other over its chest. Its eyes were wide, empty sockets, no lashes, no lids. It was hairless and its bones were lumpy and poked out from under its skin. It had no lips. Its tongue, reaching out in little jerky movements, was black and swollen.

Grim grew still.

"Grim is not really here. I think I may have killed it." Waltruk leaned in close to the creature, trying to be certain.

"I think it is dead." He glanced back at her.

She motioned. "Kill it!"

The creature's mouth opened. She gasped.

Waltruk lifted his mace, braced his feet apart. The creature's jaw worked, his head screwed back and forth.

Grim sat up.

Waltruk reared back, swung and the head of the mace snapped Grim's head around with a crack.

Grim slammed into the bed.

She scrambled up, gasping. Waltruk picked up her dagger, laid it in her hand, closed her fingers around it. He pushed her closer and raised her hands up, over the mangled body. He forced the dagger down. She felt the give of the creature's skin, soft and rotten. The smell of a corpse erupted from it. Its blood was green and filled with white pus. It oozed out and covered the body.

She heaved backward, gagging.

Jezaline ran.

She raced past the bodies of Reapers, past the hall of bedrooms. She reached the staircase, dropped the dagger. She ran up and up, until she could see nothing. Holding her hand out to feel the door before she smacked into it.

She threw it open and fell out into the moonlight.

At the pool she dropped to her knees and drove her wet fingers into the cold water. She scrubbed and scrubbed.

She sat back on her heels and tried to catch her breath. The garden was as still as when she had first arrived.

Waltruk was standing behind her, his arms crossed.

She looked into her reflection in the pool. "Take me with you."

"You must go back to Kilikan."

"Take me with you!"

Waltruk knelt behind her. His fingers moved over her breasts and body, pulled her against his chest. He kissed her neck and hair. The smell of blood, the act of death, had left him hard and wanting. Her eyes widened in horror as what he wanted dawned in her heart. She tried to turn to look at him, to stop him. His fingers closed around her elbows, forcing her forward.

"You will be my queen. Just a little longer." His lips pressed against the back of her ear. His breath was thick and hot.

Waltruk pressed her over and stroked her dress up her back. He pulled himself out of his leathers. Her forehead on the cold stone, Jezaline squeezed her eyes shut and tried to still the retch in the back of her throat. She grasped the fountain tightly. He grabbed her thighs, pulled them apart and then adjusted himself into the slice of her. She took a deep breath and held it, bracing herself. His claws dug into her body when he thrust and forced his entire black spear inside of her, tearing what was denying any kind of desire or need. Tears pricked coldly in her eyes. He gasped with pleasure and kept thrusting long after he could have stopped.

Afterward she sat beside the pool and held herself. The dull ache was quieted at least. That was something, she told herself, attempting to ignore the deep tears he had left behind.

"I have to go." He adjusted his cloak and lifted the hood over his head.

She gaped at him. "Go?"

The night was on her face in black circles, leaving her skin bloodless and sick. He laughed at her expression and kissed her once before stretching out his wings and leaving her.

Jezaline could hear nothing but her own breath and being. She curled around herself, quivering in shock. She had never killed, not really. Her father flashed before her eyes and suddenly she could no longer remember what he looked like. As she tried, he looked more and more like Grim.

She needed to get out of the ruin.

She needed to run.

Jezaline took off her dress, scrubbed her mouth and face and neck and arms. Rubbed her skin with her cape until all she could smell was Kilikan's scent again. She did all of this in a kind of haze, the act of needing to do something and knowing what it was, was all that drove her, that kept her from collapsing into the horror.

She left the dress and the cape. She put on the one extra dress she had brought with her.

The statues remained, poised in their beauty behind her.

It was not hard to find her way back.

At the gate, almost in the same position as she had left them, Kilikan and Gaiden waited. When she appeared, they gasped and cheered and she ran to them. The sound of their breathing, the sound of the insects and birds and growing things surrounded her and the sobs took her over. Kilikan swept her up and roared. Gaiden took her into his chest and pressed his nose to her back.

Kilikan took her to the fire, removed her pack and they waited for her to speak.

She said, "It is done."

Kilikan whispered, "Grim is dead?"

"They are all dead."

He stroked her cheeks. "You astound me."

Gaiden cried, "You are remarkable!"

Jezaline cried into Kilikan's scaly neck. "They were regular people. Just people!"

Gaiden murmured, "You did what you had to."

Kilikan stroked her back. "It is all right. Tarrick knew you could do it alone, but needed to be told you would not be alone so you would go. See? You are strong."

She was exhausted and they saw it. They fed her and touched her before Kilikan lay down with her in the little tent. His fingers on her body did not ask for anything. They just wanted to touch her, to be reassured that she was with him. Not being able to tell them about Waltruk made it easy to forget he was ever there.

When she slipped over on top of his enormous bulk, she gazed into his eyes and felt like truly weeping. There had been a small part of her, a little hope, that maybe with the death of Grim, she would be made whole again.

Nothing had changed.

With Waltruk's force having filled the ache, she looked into Kilikan's face, more whole than she could ever be again.

She told him, "I believe what Tarrick said."

"I do, too."

"All of it?"

He nodded. "You were meant to be my queen."

He stroked through her dark hair with his claws.

He said, "I want you to be."

A shudder ran through her. A large piece of Jezaline wanted to tell him *No*.

She whispered, "I want to be yours."

He said, "I love you."

She pressed her mouth to his cheek. "I love you, too."

24
Karalay

"Jaridd?"

Dawn had arrived and turned the smoke from black to blue.

Karalay lifted herself slowly, feeling the castle wall cold under her hand.

"Jaridd? Where are you?"

Nothing moved. The fires were all out, leaving the bodies in an ocean of ash.

"Jaridd?" She struggled to her feet, wavered, struggled to walk over the Humans and Elves and Fai.

She saw a swath of black and rushed it. She ripped the mask off the

Darkhalk.

It was not Jaridd. She remembered four Darkhalks had returned to the castle in the last moments.

Her hands stumbled over the faces of others—dead or alive, she did not know, she did not care. Her feet struggled for purchase, stepping on legs, backs, arms, parts of people and dead things. She could not comprehend.

She found the four Darkhalks, one after the other. Tore off their masks. No Jaridd.

She felt the sob tug her down. "Jaridd, where are you?"

Karalay fumbled to the closest gate. Her exhausted fingers shook as she pulled the heavy door open. Elf bodies fell in at her. She climbed them. Her fingers gripped the charred and slipping skin. Her shaking legs kept her moving.

"Jaridd?" she cried, searching out at the street full with Elves.

She tripped, caught herself, kept moving, did not look down. The morning sun could not penetrate the smoke; it created a diffuse light that seemed to come from nowhere.

"You said we could go away together!" She knew she was screaming because her parched throat burned. She knew she was crying because the tears dripped down her cold cheeks.

Her calls echoed from building to building.

She spotted a hand covered by a black glove reaching toward the sky.

She ran. "Jaridd!"

Karalay grasped the hand, pulled it until the body fell onto its back. She ripped his mask off.

It was him.

The Darkhalk's face was white and stiff, lips blue from lying in the cold dew of morning and the mud of the dead.

She took his dead face in her hands. "Jaridd. I am here. You will live."

She closed her eyes and pushed her will into the corpse. There was no will left in her but the truth of her power was enough for this, at least.

And it was.

Karalay could not believe how cold the morning was. She looked around at the pearly smoke and it began to grow darker. The mud seemed to climb up her ankles and sink into her legs. Her head fell down. She could no longer keep her eyes open. Karalay felt the cold reach her lips and her lungs.

Her heart stopped.

Jaridd took a breath.

Telenay was the first to wake among his men.

The first thing out of his mouth before he rose was, "Karalay!" It brought him to his feet and he searched around him and could not find her.

He called out, "Karalay!"

Moans answered him. Men began to shift and move, groan and grunt. The sea of ash lifted and woke, opened white and wounded eyes. The men crawled and thrashed among the bodies of the Elves, casting them away as they got to their feet.

He yelled, "Karalay!"

The men began to look around and they began to help each other to their feet. A pitiful few left alive, but alive was alive.

He went to the open gate and hurried up the street, stiff and pained, though heeding none of his own hurts.

When Telenay found her, she was covered in blood, ash and mud. She lay face down against the wall beside Jaridd.

He reached for her and curled Karalay into his arms and lifted her out of the gore. Her hair was a wide, black wing over his arm. As he passed, the men stopped and bowed their heads. Karalay, completely covered in ash and mud, looked like a dark angel.

He took the Healer to her chamber and the hot water of her basin.

He laid her in it, washed her face and hair until he recognized her sweet face. He held her against his beating heart, his own heat. He willed into her.

"I have a woman here," he whispered. "I know you know this one. She laid her life down this morning. She gave her breath for another. I cannot let you forget. I cannot allow her to die."

He combed her hair back, stared into her dead face. Closed his eyes and entered her emptiness completely. He held out for her life all he had to offer.

26

She could smell him. Jaridd. That dark wintry smell. She opened her eyes and the room was dim. The fire was down and she could hardly make him out in the bed beside her. His chiseled nose and chin in the dark. Karalay touched his cheek and his neck, laid her hand on his chest to feel his heartbeat.

The mud had killed them both, she was sure. The very cold of the ash, the dew, the wet.

She knew he had died. She knew she had died.

"I feel your heartbeat," she said.

She could feel her own heart hammer against her chest. She pulled herself against him and buried her face in his neck. He was clean. She was clean. The bed was soft.

She kissed his neck, breathed as deep as she could.

The air smelled so sweet and warm.

The room was so bright.

When she opened her eyes, she could not believe the real light of day. It smelled like chamomile and olive oil. She turned her head to see the windows but the shutters covered the skies.

Jaridd still slept beside her.

Telenay shifted in the chair beside the bed.

"Telenay," she said, "someone tried to tell me that we were all dead."

She held out her hand and he took it.

He said, "What did you tell him, Healer?"

"I said we are breathing."

"We are breathing," he said. "Our hearts are beating."

"Tell me what happened."

"You should rest."

"Why were the armies of the Elves falling?"

"No one knows."

"We do not know at all?"

"It had to be someone strong to walk into a place where the Reapers kept themselves and then kill them all."

"If I can meet them one day and thank them, I will."

"I as well . . . It was not long until the Crystal was destroyed."

"Did Sicilia kill Grim?"

"Sicilia did not, Karalay." His amber eyes looked into her. "Sicilia was wrong. She was attacking Grim's Reapers. Grim was in the castle throughout the entire battle."

She blinked, her eyes blurry. "That cannot be. How could he have gotten by the Darkhalks and everyone? That is not possible."

"It was the Elf. Grim possessed the body. You thought life remained in the Elf. It was Grim."

Karalay covered her mouth.

"Grim was a man once. That is why you did not recognize him for what he was."

"But, the Darkhalks—"

"He fooled everyone."

She closed her eyes tight. "It was my fault then. Where is Cousai?"

"It was not your fault."

"Where is Cousai?"

"She is dead. The Crystal destroyed her when she destroyed it."

"How did—"

"From the best we can tell, Cousai would not have lived long from her injuries had the Crystal not killed her. Grim had already killed her. There is nothing left of Grim or his Reapers. The Crystal took them with it."

"Sicilia?"

"She is not reachable."

Karalay grunted and attempted to sit up. Telenay pulled her to him as the tremors of weariness shook her.

"Take me to her."

"Dind is with her, Karalay."

She laid her head on his shoulder. "Take me to her, Warlord."

Telenay laid his hand on her back. "You saved Jaridd. You deserve to stay beside him."

"I remember finding him dead. I gave him my breath, Telenay. If I am alive, how can he be alive?"

Telenay shrugged.

"Is he a Darkhalk?"

"Karalay, you only saved him. Not the Cape or the Sword."

"What of the other Darkhalks?"

"All dead except Jaridd's Second, Kackin, and most of the Diggamara army is dead. The king and his ambassadors are gone."

"The people?"

"Walking home."

"Walking?"

Telenay took her around the waist, helped her out of the bed and across to the windows. He opened the shutters so she could see.

Karalay gasped, "There was a certain part of me that did not think it would happen."

"The three realms are now one land again. We are whole."

Where the black river had once flowed, black dirt remained. Tied to docks, ships and boats lay on their sides as far as she could see. Diggamara's people were walking up the riverbed home.

"Free to wage war." She turned away.

Telenay said, "We do not know if that will happen."

"Because that is what everything does. War."

Telenay looked away. "I would have been curious to hear the words exchanged between them, before she destroyed the Crystal."

"You think Grim spoke to Cousai?"

He shrugged. "Grim waited generations of Human lives for that opportunity. He came so close, I am sure he had to have said something."

Karalay shook her head. "I do not want to know what he said."

Servants arrived in the room. They bowed, left two trays of food.

She said, "Eat with me."

He helped her to the table and then unveiled the food. Yeast bread covered in jam, dried fruit on the side, potatoes cooked in oil and breaded and baked fish.

"Oh, that looks wonderful." She drank from a tall glass of tea before trying the food. Everything melted on her tongue and she closed her eyes.

Telenay whuffed down his portion.

"You should stop and enjoy it. When was the last time you had such a wonderful meal?"

"Yesterday, and the day before . . . and the day before." He drank his tea.

"How long has it been? What day is it?"

"It is the 13th of Qalin."

She glanced at Jaridd. "Has he been accepting water or anything to drink?"

Telenay stared at her. "Karalay. He is immortal. He does not need to eat."

"I thought you said—"

"Did he eat before he asked the Sword and Cape—"

"No."

"Well, why would he now?"

"I just thought—"

"You just thought that after saving his life he would become mortal? Darkhalks can only die from wounds. Why would he choose to die of age?"

Telenay pushed his plate aside.

She chewed her bottom lip.

"What do you want?" He glared at her.

She looked down. "I had not meant for you to realize."

"Your will is exhausted. It is not difficult for me to read you."

Her will was left healing close to her spirit. She did not reach out to him with it. If she had, she would have felt that his will was gone. Telenay sat before her as regular a Human being as he had ever been. His sacrifice for her life.

When Telenay had finally felt her breathe and her heart begin to beat was when he had known that his background was not entirely Human. For though his true will of Wards was gone, his senses were still heightened, he still had some type of will and it was powerful, though not nearly as defined. He knew in that moment that his father had not been a regular Human man. But his sacrifice remained true. He had not known that he was not giving up all of his power.

She sighed. "It never was difficult for you to read me."

"What were you thinking?"

She looked into his amber eyes. "Take me to Sicilia."

He helped her stand and led her out of the room. She held his hands, leaned against his shoulder.

"When was the last time she ate?"

"She has not eaten anything since Grim attacked."

"She just refuses?"

"She is unreachable."

They reached Sicilia's chamber.

Karalay opened the door.

The shutters and windows were open and the warm sunshine and wind were breezing in from the ocean. Gulls called outside. Sicilia lay in a small slip, knees held between her fingers. Her hair fell dull and limp and her gray eyes stared. Her wings lay like dead butterflies behind her. In a chair in the corner of the room, Dind blinked at them and was sitting up from where he had fallen asleep. His face was haggard. His arm was held to his chest in tight bandages and, when he tried to rise, it was with great wincing and a limp.

Karalay held her hands out to him. "Dind."

He clutched her fingers with his one good hand.

"When I am well, I will heal you," she promised.

He nodded but did not speak. He looked upon Sicilia.

She said, "You have been vigilant for days. Let me watch her for a time."

He swallowed hard, looked at her, looked back at Sicilia, then left.

"Oh, Sicilia." Karalay stepped around the bed.

She pulled the Fai's fingers from her knees and held the cold hands. "Sicilia?"

Karalay rubbed the woman's shoulder. "Close those windows, Telenay. She feels cold."

"She has felt cold since we found her." He closed the windows.

She combed the woman's hair with her fingers. "Sicilia?"

Telenay stood back with his arms crossed.

"You can leave." She looked at him. "I am going to stay with her."

He did not hesitate. He turned and left, shutting the door behind him.

Karalay crawled into bed behind the Fai and laid her head on the pillows. The strength the Fai had to wield her swords and shields had begun to deteriorate and the already thin warrior looked gaunt and small. Her will remained a weak thing against her heart. She could feel the great walls of the Fai and knew she did not yet have the strength to press in.

The door opened. Fai entered.

When they saw her, they stopped. "We will leave."

She shook her head. "Come in."

Karalay held out her hand in greeting. She recognized Sicilia's general. He was garbed lightly in soft linens and silks in shades of green. A thick cape wrapped his shoulders, hiding his wings. He bowed his head politely and stepped around the bed to Sicilia.

The general touched Sicilia's hand.

He said, "She died in the field."

The two Fai with him nodded.

Karalay said carefully, "She is breathing, General."

He laid his hand on Sicilia's forehead, looked into her eyes. "No. She is dead. I will leave one man here to collect her body. The rest of us must flee."

"Flee?"

He looked at Karalay. "The king of the Fai is tracking down any soldiers that did not fly to their deaths. None of us believed we would survive this, so now—"

"You can hide here."

He stared at her.

"Did you think your efforts here will be forgotten by the Humans? I was here, I saw the Fai fight with great strength. You are our kin now. We will protect you as one of our own."

He glanced at the Fai with him. "We will think on that."

"Please, do."

They left and she lay down again.

Karalay said, "Sicilia, your men need you. Would you so easily abandon them now?"

27

The day began to wane, Karalay drifted in and out of sleep.

Sicilia never moved.

The servants came in and started the fire. They bowed to her.

One of the servants paused. "Would you like anything?"

"A pitcher of that cool tea, if you are not busy. And, how did the servants fare? Hracha, Acasha, Orac. Are they all right?"

They grinned. One said, "It was the command of you and the great Telenay. Servants can no longer be owned in Diggamara. We *choose* to work here as servants now. We get our fair share of food and bed."

Karalay smiled. "That is wonderful."

"We will tell Hracha, Acasha and Orac to come to you in their time."

"Thank you," Karalay sighed.

It was later, when the door opened, that Karalay was starting to feel less weak. Acasha entered with Jikrin at her side.

Karalay pulled Acasha to her and embraced the girl.

Acasha grinned. "Jikrin is taking me with him to the Castle of the Wards."

Karalay gasped. "Your mother approved that?"

"She is sad. But I want to go. Last month I did not think I would ever leave this place. Now, my whole life is without a master!"

"I am glad for you. When are you leaving?"

"Just tonight."

"Be careful. It is a long journey."

Jikrin said, "I will take care of her."

"I know you will, Centaur. Come here now."

Karalay stepped to him and Jikrin embraced her. They left soon after and Karalay frowned after them. She hoped Jikrin knew better than to let the girl look at him in such a way. It would be a shame for his life to end as a traitor after surviving so much.

Karalay reached for Sicilia. The Fai made no response.

Telenay stepped into the room. It was late and the Warlord looked tired. He pulled a chair up to the side of the bed, sat down and sighed.

"What is wrong?"

He shook his head. "Karalay, did you tell the general of the Fai we would harbor him and his soldiers?"

She sat up. "Yes."

Telenay looked into her eyes. "Do you know what the implications of such an action are?"

"Without them, Telenay—"

"I do not care what they did for the Humans. Do you realize what would happen if the Draegoone heard the Wards harbored Fai soldiers?"

She opened her mouth to argue.

Telenay stood up, paced. "Do you know what will happen if the Fai realize the Humans are helping hide traitorous Fai soldiers?"

"Telenay, I do not—" She stood and reached for him.

The Warlord stared coldly at her. "Do you know where you have put us?"

"Then tell them I was wrong! Tell the general he has to run! Tell him we will not harbor him!"

"It is too late!"

Karalay grasped her hands to her heart. "How—what happened?"

"The Fai searchers came to Diggamara and I turned them away. I told them there were none of their soldiers in this city. I had no idea we were hiding them!"

She gasped, "Telenay, I thought I was doing the right thing! It seemed so unfair. I am so sorry!"

He left her standing there, pleading with nothing.

28

Karalay struggled to the bed, her hands trembling. She got herself up beside Sicilia, lay down beside the Fai and wrapped her arms around her. Her first of few decisions made as a Ward by herself and she had failed immediately. She pushed into the Fai another time.

Finally, she was strong enough. She felt Sicilia's defenses give.

Karalay stood in a small bright red silk slip. The wind blew like a furnace and the gown pressed tight against her. Nothing grew nor lived as far as she could see. The ground was cracked in thirst, hard as a rock. It was bright as a desert but the sky was black.

Across the ground Karalay watched something blow, flipping and dipping along the ground like a leaf. It blew by her and she stared in horror. It was one of Sicilia's wings, freshly torn off her back. Something shone in the distance. She shielded her eyes and squinted into the gale-force wind.

She hurried toward it.

On the ground was a large plate of steel, engraved in symbols Karalay only recognized as Fai words. It reflected the sun blindingly and, as she approached, she felt the intense heat emanating from it.

In the center of the plate, Sicilia was sitting with her knees drawn to her chin. Her mouth was open and she was screaming. Tears of blood ran out of her eyes, down her cheeks, onto her knees and hands. Blisters were erupting across her boiled body and her skin hung in big red pieces, falling from her as she baked. Before her sat Cousai, dead and rotting, staring accusingly, pointing at Sicilia.

Karalay yelled, "That is enough!"

The wind stopped blowing.

Karalay grasped a cool, wet blanket, cast it around Sicilia's shoulders. Clouds covered the sun. Cousai disappeared.

"Torturing yourself will not help this!" Karalay sat beside her and held her shaking body.

Sicilia grew still and her body drooped.

Karalay looked at the symbols surrounding them. "What do they say?"

Sicilia pointed at each one. "Wench. Whore. Witch. Betrayer. Traitor. Bastard. Bitch!" Sicilia curled in against Karalay and sobbed. Karalay held her with all of her power. The heat completely faded. The sun went out. The distance began to disappear. Darkness closed in on them.

Karalay panicked, reached for her and the Fai was gone.

"Karalay." Telenay rubbed her shoulder.

Karalay opened her eyes, sat up. The sun was shining.

Dind stood at the back of the room, his face bent and gray.

She moved quickly out of the bed but did not go to the once Darkhalk. As she moved away, Dind went to Sicilia and pressed his face to her cheek, swept his fingers over her eyes and closed them eternally.

They left the room and Telenay murmured, "You were with her all night then."

Karalay pushed the tears from her cheeks and nodded but could not speak.

He held her protectively around the waist. "I am sorry for my anger."

Karalay shook her head. "I am the sorry one."

They walked slowly down the hall.

She asked, "When are you going back to the castle?"

"I am not going back."

They stopped outside her chamber door.

"Why?"

He shook his head.

"What happened?"

"You know I wanted to leave." His eyes shifted.

"But what of Osondrous . . . We need you." Karalay touched his chest.

"Osondrous never needed me."

"I cannot go back to her alone."

"You are strong enough."

"But why?"

He kept his eyes away. "I do not have it in me to go back."

She stared at his cold features. "Telenay, what happened to you?"

He swept her hair off her neck and kissed her collarbone with his mouth open. "We are breathing. You and me."

His breath was hot.

She shook her head. "Have you spoken to Dind?"

He frowned. "He has not spoken at all. Why?"

She looked into his eyes, shook her head. "Nothing."

They kissed softly before he left, his lips pressed to her mouth tenderly.

She turned into her chamber and was relieved to have Telenay gone. A part of her felt him very gone but she did not touch on that yet. She lacked the strength.

For a moment she looked out the window at the dry riverbed. Karalay went back to her Darkhalk and slipped into bed beside him. She could sense his presence, could sense his healing.

"When you wake, Jaridd, I will be here." Karalay kissed him and wrapped herself around him.

29

Telenay

Telenay had lost Rayue and it was a wedge in his heart. Memories of Addilade were obscure and that was probably for the best. Rayue was in that forest somewhere, fallen to a horde of death. Telenay hoped his brave horse had at least died quickly.

He could smell the field from deep within Diggamara. He could see the stars through the smoke and the endless chimneys. When Karalay finally woke, he had packed a bag. When Sicilia was finally dead and Karalay was well, he had picked up that bag and slipped unnoticed to the stables.

The horse he had ridden against the Elves was gone, too.

He walked down the line of stalls and looked into each of the horse's faces in the torchlight. It was late and the horses woke out of their sleep to see him. He stopped at the last stall and a brown mare stepped forward. She looked at him directly. He carefully touched her muzzle and let her breathe him in.

She was old but her legs were solid. She stomped her hoof at him.

He looked into her eyes. "You and me?"

She met his look. He sensed Karalay in the mare's spirit and quickly tacked her.

In the streets, he led her all the way out of the city while still on foot. He savored the quiet of the night. He savored that he did not need to run or hurry. He savored that this was the last time he would ever be in the city he had been born in. He mounted the mare and she moved forward eagerly into the night, not hesitating even as the moon set and everything was black.

When the hour was none he stopped her and they turned back to look. Neither he nor the mare could see light from life of any kind.

He grinned. She turned and ran on.

They both smelled the field.

MORE ABOUT THE AUTHOR

Tarah was born on February 24th, 1986, in Park Rapids, Minnesota. She attended public school for one year (kindergarten) before being placed in a Baptist Christian School for several years until being home schooled. She graduated early from home schooling (2001) and became the club manager at her family's golf course. When she was five years old, her family built and began operating Fair Havens Golf Course and she began work there at the age of fifteen.

In 2005, she met a man online from Oklahoma and began a long distance relationship with him. They purchased a home in Durant, Oklahoma, and renovated the entire house by themselves. She learned how to run electrical, patch a roof, drywall, plumbing and countless other manual labors. In this time, Tarah finished most of her work on *Sacrifices* and she regards those years as the most trying and darkest years of her life. Their relationship ended in August, 2010, when she finally drove home to Minnesota for the last time.

When Tarah was eleven years old, she joined The Jackpine Writers' Bloc (**www.jackpinewriters.com**) based out of her home town of Park Rapids, Minnesota. With the writers' group looking at abandonment along with their literary journal, Tarah, along with her aunt Sharon Harris, took the group over. They restarted the monthly writers' meetings and took control of the group's book, *The Talking Stick* (**www.thetalkingstick.com**). They joke yearly that they don't know if they have another book in them. But, after having been a part of publishing sixteen books with The Jackpine Writers' Bloc, it's easy to see how they will continue with their efforts. In their time, the JWB has gone from a little known writers' group to a publication with reports of books sold on the Internet from Alaska to England.

In 2005, Tarah started a web and print design business called Web Services of Park Rapids. She taught herself CSS and XHTML and enjoys writing the code and the entire design process. She also designs books and all types of print design. The business has been moderately successful for her and she continues it to this day. She will be the first to say, though, how badly she simply wishes to support herself by writing for the rest of her life. **www.parkrapidsweb.com.**

In 2010, Tarah's family sold Fair Havens Golf Course and her parents divorced. She regards that year as her landmark year of tremendous change. With her parents divorced, the golf course gone (where she had worked for nearly her entire life) and her own six year relationship over, she and her mother embraced a new life. And though there was grief in the change and loss, Tarah has never had more hope for the future:

"I can't believe where I am. Our financial troubles are still difficult. We've had to sell so much, but I can't tell you how often I look outside, see Minnesota, and am entirely filled with joy and relief: I am finally home. No matter if we have to sell everything we own to get by, I am finally where I want to be and with the people I want to be with and doing what I love. I couldn't ask for more."

In November, 2009, Tarah started her blog www.tarahlynn.com chronicling her journey of writing the Embraced By Darkness series and becoming a novelist.

Embraced by Darkness BOOK TWO Stricken **is expected for a 2012 Christmas release. You can find out more at the official Embraced by Darkness website at: www.embracedbydarkness.com.**

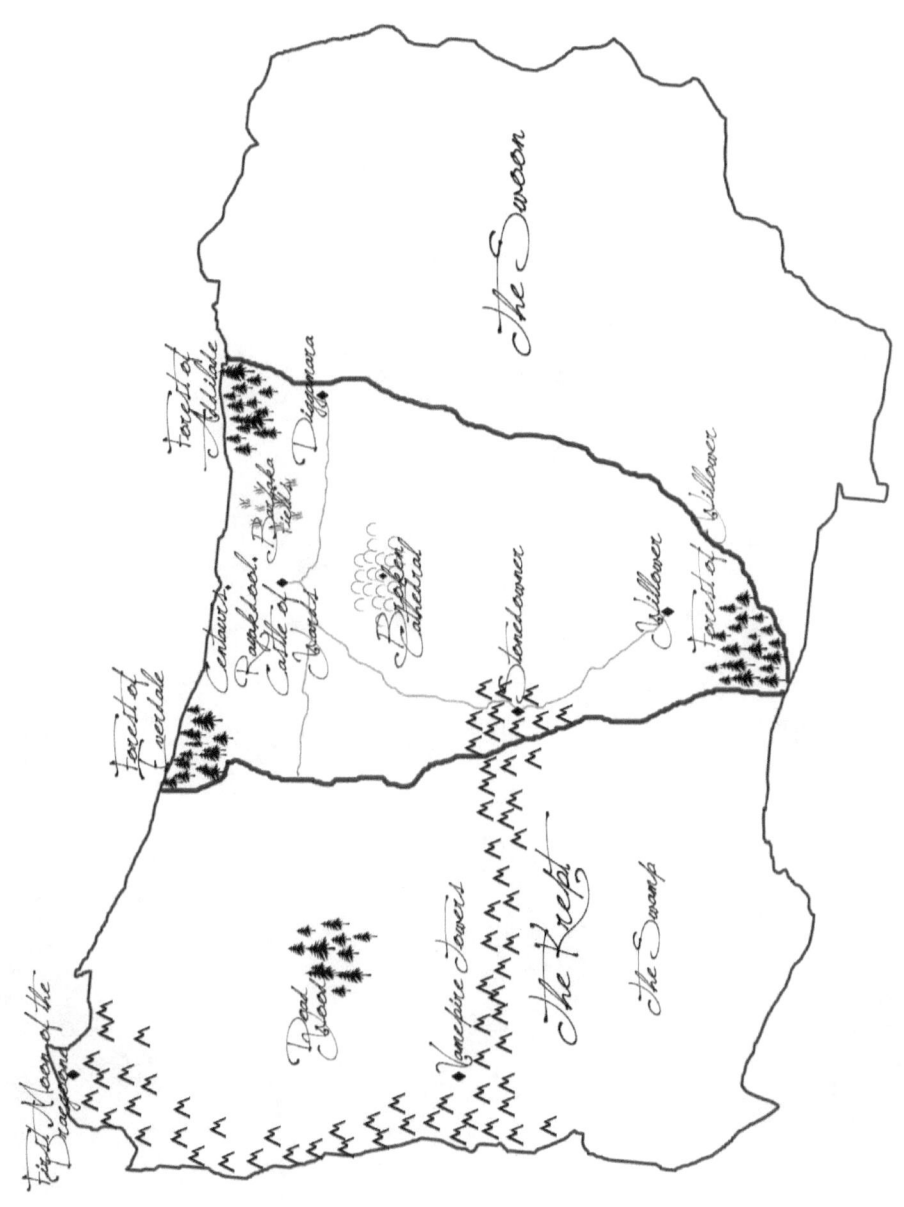